GOD BLESS US, EVERY ONE!

GOD BLESS US, EVERY ONE!

A FARCICAL FANTASY NOVEL

DAVID R. COOMBS

ARCHWAY
PUBLISHING

Archway Publishing books may be ordered through booksellers or by contacting:

Archway Publishing
1663 Liberty Drive
Bloomington, IN 47403
www.archwaypublishing.com
844-669-3957

ISBN: 978-1-6657-5892-5 (sc)
ISBN: 978-1-6657-5894-9 (hc)
ISBN: 978-1-6657-5893-2 (e)

Library of Congress Control Number: 2024907081

Print information available on the last page.

Archway Publishing rev. date: 06/07/2024

To my sister, Janice,
and my brothers, Gerald and Kevin,
all of whom I tormented egregiously
while we were growing up.

In hindsight, I must say
it was entirely worth the effort.

PREFACE

Tradition is the chain of obsolete customs that anchor us to who we are.

The last time British soldiers rode into battle wearing scarlet tunics was in 1885, yet the King's Life Guard still dress the part at Horse Guards in London today. The show of men on horseback in old-fashioned uniforms is a tradition that connects soldiers to their warrior ancestors, and this display of tradition helps the English feel more English.

Many American traditions amplify nationalism as well. Even people with the least interest in history know the story of the first Thanksgiving and what it symbolizes for the country. The Fourth of July and Veterans' Day are more than annual occasions for celebration, or remembrance and reflection—they're reminders of what it is to be American.

Then there are family traditions that strengthen our feelings of a shared past with parents, children, siblings, and so on.

One tradition we observe in our house—like many family traditions—is observed on Christmas Day. After supper, we watch the Brian Desmond Hurst movie *Scrooge*, starring Alastair Sim in the eponymous role. The film is a faithful adaptation of Charles Dickens's *A Christmas Carol*. Made in 1951, it's a black and white relic with clunky special effects and cliché motifs. Even so, Sim was a brilliant comic actor, and Hurst brought out the best in the supporting cast. No matter how many times I see it, I still smile at Scrooge's ironic humor, and tear up in the moments when he finds his compassion.

No doubt my love of the movie is in part due to my association of it with family memories, but that's what tradition is all about.

Not only have I watched *Scrooge* so often I've lost count, I've also read the novella *A Christmas Carol* four times—more than any other of Dickens's works—though I admit two of those readings were after I'd decided to use the characters in a work of my own.

Dickens is one of my favorite authors in part because I like the way he used style. Some works are best served by a transparent style like a clear glass window that allows the reader to see the story unfold without noticing the words, the meter, and the phrasing. Dickens's style is more like a stained glass window in which the text itself adds color to the images presented. A lot of the comedy found in Dickens is due to his style, and I wrote *God Bless Us, Every One!* with a similar intention in mind.

While I admire many writers who prefer transparent style and consider several works of this kind to be among the greatest written, I like to use style to highlight setting or character and foster mood. In writing *God Bless Us, Every One!*, I imagined the narrator as a supercilious twit—a naïve, smug fool who overcompensates for insecurities by flaunting the remnants of a good education. His word choices and structured sentences create a style to bring out these traits for comic effect.

Another feature I borrowed from Dickens for the writing of *God Bless Us, Every One!* is the use of names that underscore the defining traits of their owners. Dickens wasn't the first writer to do this, but he was a master of the device. You get a feel for the personalities of Pumblechook, Magwitch, Micawber, etc. from the sounds of their names. And included in that number is Scrooge whose name sounds like the creak of thumbscrews squeezing the last penny of interest out of a client.

Needless to say, I had a lot of fun coming up with fitting names for my characters: Thadeus Squidge, the slimy mobster always in search of an opportunity and an angle; Sir Axeworthy Blundt, the surgeon who looks upon patients as a necessary inconvenience; M. T. Pawkets, a claims agent who resembles a fat marmalade cat. And on and on.

And there was one other device Dickens used often that I wanted to bring over into the writing of *God Bless Us, Every One!*—the grotesque: a character with bizarre features and exaggerated behavior who exemplifies some personality type in caricatured extremes.

Miss Havisham in *Great Expectations* is an often cited example of a grotesque in Dickens. She's a woman who went mad with grief after being left at the altar in her youth. In her madness, she's lost all concern for her looks and the condition of her surroundings, and still wears the tatters of her wedding gown every day. She's the first example of insanity that Pip, the protagonist, meets in his young life, and no doubt Dickens was exploiting the common experience of every child's first disturbing encounter with someone ancient, disheveled, cranky, and irrational to make the boy more relatable. But the character of Miss Haversham also serves to satirize a common trope of the Romantic era: that of the lover whose commitment runs so deep, they're eternally wounded by the loss of their soulmate. (Think Heathcliff in Emily Brontë's *Wuthering Heights* or the narrator of Edgar Allan Poe's "The Raven".)

Many of the characters in *God Bless Us, Every One!* border on the grotesque—nearly all of them are too ridiculous to last five minutes in the real world—but some are true examples.

Eliphas Dropping is a committed disciple of capitalism, even though he can't define the term or even remember the word properly. Proud to be a self-made man and a cog in the machinery of the British Empire, he's convinced the proceeds of rat-catching have provided him an ideal existence—despite having to work in squalid conditions and accept an endless series of skin infections as a trivial occupational hazard.

The most grotesque of my grotesques is B. Philius Gazpayne, barrister. Perhaps making jokes about lawyers is a cheap shot, given the practice is ubiquitous in western culture, but as I write this, the news is filled with stories of corporations, executives, and politicians entrenched in legal battles. And it's not the sane and sober arguments and decisions that monopolize the air time; it's the razor thin bisection of legal fine hairs that captures media attention. Justice delayed is justice denied, and yet delay seems to be a defining feature of the justice system. In my opinion, the legal profession has never been more ripe for satirizing.

All of this isn't to say I imagined myself as a Dickens clone while writing *God Bless Us, Every One!*. My aim was to create a retro feel that is amusing for its similarities to Dickens and that helps establish a comic mood.

I've heard Dickens described as a moralist who shone light on the collective ethics and social conditions of his day for the purpose of inspiring change. It is possible he saw himself as influential and thought he could make a difference, or he may have reported on these elements of the Victorian world simply to provide background for setting and character. Either way, from our viewpoint in the early 21st century, we see the injustice and cruelty spawned by the imperialism, colonialism, and predatory capitalism of Victorian England in his work.

A discussion on the war of the worldviews would be beyond the scope of this introduction, but it's sufficient to say 19th century geopolitics were defined by a traditionalist social structure and early modernist economic drivers—essentially ethnocentric dominator hierarchies coupled with a winner-take-all measure of success. From my comfortable post-pluralist viewpoint, the arrogant hyper-nationalist attitudes of Victorian England seem fair game for ridicule. And since remnants of those attitudes persist in varying degrees in every country of the world today, highlighting them is more than relevant to our times.

In the same vein, the resurgence of the samurai philosophy in Japan that took hold of the country prior to World War II led it along a similar route. So, in Book 3 of this novel, I had fun caricaturing that development along with a ludicrous portrayal of naïve interpretations of religious tenets.

The primary theme of *God Bless Us, Every One!*, however, is the herd mentality and those emotion-charged trends and ideas that take center stage in mainstream thought. In the story, Tiny Tim becomes an unwitting conduit of mass mind control exploited by various characters who learn of his mystical power. Though Tiny Tim is entirely fantastical, the phenomenon is not that far from the truth.

Herd mentality has always been a feature of the human condition. It's a feature of our natural drive for cooperation, which has been a key to our survival as a species and the basis of civilization. Without it, we'd all be loners unable to get behind the grand schemes and projects that have marked progress. But unfortunately, there have always been individuals who learned to exploit the herd mentality for personal gain. With the coming of the internet and social media, this exploitation has taken a quantum leap perhaps even to the brink of our undoing.

Of course, we're all aware of targeted advertising that evokes a wide range of moral arguments. The use of algorithms to identify what will inspire an individual to buy, and when that person is most easily maneuvered into buying has many afraid the odds are stacked too heavily in favor of the marketing mavens.

But to my mind, the worst aspect of this form of mass manipulation is the way it enables authoritarian governments to fuel the chaos in the democracies. Through the use of false social media accounts and robotic propagandists, they spread stories with no basis in fact designed to stoke fear. They don't necessarily want us to adopt authoritarianism (though it is a distinct possibility we might); their aim is to sow division and hold our discord up as proof their methods are the only path to security and order—the worse we look, the better they look by comparison to their own people.

So, while my main intention in writing *God Bless Us, Every One!* was to create a funny story that would provide hours of entertainment for the reader, I hope some are inspired to consider what role public opinion has in driving us to disaster and what steps society should take to prevent us from becoming a species of two-legged lemmings in these times of artificial intelligence and social media algorithms designed to funnel us into thought silos.

At this point, I'd like to acknowledge the writers who have influenced me most in the writing of *God Bless Us, Every One!*. I've already gone into some length describing what I borrowed from Charles Dickens, but I owe a lot to humorists through the ages.

When reading this novel, those familiar with the Gilbert and Sullivan operettas will recognize phrases I stole from W. S. Gilbert's lyrics, then expanded into running gags. In writing several of the characters, I tried to imagine what P. G. Wodehouse and Saki would do to create pompous asses and feather-brained nitwits. And ever since my childhood introduction to "Jabberwocky," in Lewis Carroll's *Through the Looking-Glass*, I've been a huge fan of wordplay in all its forms from puns and portmanteau words to malapropisms and mispronunciations. Nonsense verse became something of a passion for me, notably the work of Edward Lear and Edward Gorey. Gorey was known for challenging boundaries with his material, and me— being a born iconoclast—had a huge appreciation for his cartoons, verse, and stories. Today, we'd call him edgy, and he was the first writer/illustrator I encountered who found humor in the horrific and morally outrageous.

Of course, the term edgy is a recent invention and still considered a colloquialism, but I like the double sense of sharp and cutting paralleled with pushing boundaries.

Other influences I should cite include *Monty Python's Flying Circus*, followed later by the work of John Cleese, whose TV show *Fawlty Towers* may be the best sitcom ever written; and Terry Gilliam, one of the most imaginative movie directors of English-language films. And the most recent writers whose comic work I admire include Michael Szymczyk, a master of transgressional fiction; John Waters, known for his subversive storytelling approach to satire; and Chuck Palahniuk, whose dark, transgressive humor has entered the cultural zeitgeist—I hear the phrase, "The first rule of Fight Club," used all the time to mean: "We don't talk about that."

On the subject of influences, my sources for metaphors come from everywhere. God *Bless Us, Every One!* is packed with obscure allusions meant to reinforce the asinine character of the narrator. For those who don't get the references, the lines will appear quirky, adding color and interest to the narrative that in no way affects the story. For those who do see the veiled jokes, they can enjoy the bonus of knowing I put them there for you.

The last thing I want to point out is satire should be offensive. After all, satire is the art of making someone or something look ridiculous, raising laughter in order to embarrass, humble, or discredit its targets. How can it not be offensive?

But satire isn't hateful. Trolling, name-calling, and petty spite are not satire despite the claims of those who have nothing better to offer the world.

Satire done well inspires people to look at events, norms, or institutions from different angles, primarily to entertain but perhaps also to encourage change. And though change occasionally means trashing what exists and starting over, that is far rarer than people seem to believe. Change throughout history—even revolutionary change—almost always involves tweaking established systems rather than wholesale replacement.

Satire should draw attention to the dysfunctional aspects of society and the people whose opinions and actions are at the center of that dysfunction. But it is up to society to find ways to improve. Art often points the direction; philosophy may suggest routes, but it is the body politic that must attempt solutions.

There is much about *God Bless Us, Every One!* that some will find offensive. Not only do I hold up traditionalist social structures, predatory capitalism, and hyper-nationalism for ridicule, I also poke fun at ethnic stereotyping and religious fundamentalism. In today's polarized world filled with people who see a reasoned debate as an act of violence, I feel I'm taking an enormous risk in putting this novel into the public eye. But risk is inherent in art. A writer unwilling to take risks is at best a candy man and at worst a dealer in opium. And the audience unwilling to be challenged occasionally is limiting their reading to pablum.

All said, I go back to my tenet of writing. The work must entertain, and if that's all the reader gets from it, the work is a success. If, however, the work inspires the reader to think beyond the scope of the fiction, it has achieved something great.

Simcoe, Ontario
March 2024

What does not destroy me, makes me stronger.
—Friedrich Nietzsche, in *Twilight of the Idols*

When a complex system is far from equilibrium, small islands of coherence in a sea of chaos have the capacity to shift the entire system to a higher order.
—Ilya Prigogine, Nobel laureate in chemistry, 1977

Sheep are very dim, and once they get an idea into their heads, there's no shifting it.
—*Monty Python's Flying Circus*: series 1, episode 2: "Sex and Violence"

BOOK 1

CHAPTER 1

S crooge was dead, to begin with. That is not to say he started out dead—not in the least. Scrooge started out in much the same way as all who come into this world and stay awhile for whatever purposes hold their attention beyond the basic requirements of occupying some volume of space and sustaining some mass of flesh. In other words, he had been born and grew up, kept busy with this and that, and went about the business of existence much like everyone else. He slept and he awoke. He ate and he drank. He dressed and he undressed. He spoke and he listened. In short, he did all that all who have shuffled about within this mortal coil have done since the first who donned it did so.

But the life of Scrooge has very little to do with the events of this tale, while his death is at the root of them, and so—to begin again— Scrooge was dead. As dead as a coffin nail—that being, most arguably, the deadest item of ironmongery in the blacksmith's inventory, deader even than the proverbial doornail.

It is well known that during the latter part of his life, Scrooge had undergone a sudden transformation. He had become charitable and generous of spirit with a sense of goodwill uncommon to the general population and most uncommon to his former self, having been, until then, a widely reputed most curmudgeonly miser. The rumor that had taken hold strongly enough to be taken as truth was that a dream—or nightmare, perhaps—had inspired this transformation. In this dream, Scrooge had had rather stimulating intercourse with three spirits who had shown him the error of his former ways and enticed him toward the path of goodness and humanity.

This sudden transformation of Scrooge led him to take on as his beneficiaries his clerk, Bob Cratchit, and all the family Cratchit, with especially great attention to their youngest, Tim, affectionately known as Tiny Tim.

Now it seems, prior to Scrooge adopting the family as a personal responsibility, Tiny Tim had suffered an injury to his hip that had not healed properly. The malady had been a drain on the boy's life and left him underdeveloped and frail. Nevertheless, Tiny Tim had great spirit and was known to say, "God bless us, every one!" quite cheerfully and quite often for no apparent reason.

As sad as that may seem to those poor souls who find such things sad, Scrooge found Tiny Tim's eternal optimism endearing, and the boy soon became his favorite. Once the old man had satisfied his newly acquired philanthropic sense regarding the Cratchits as a family, he focused his attention on reversing the effects that ongoing medical neglect and inadequate diet had had on their youngest member.

So every starched-collared leech within a fifty-mile radius of the Good Old City examined Tiny Tim and offered a learned opinion. The doctors often arrived en masse, resembling a gaggle of geese— or, perhaps more aptly, a badling of ducks—milling about the front door, waiting their turn to provide their often-conflicting diagnoses, prognoses, and whatever -oses of the case.

Whether surfeit of attention brought about any improvement in Tiny Tim's condition is debatable. But between the sessions of poking, prodding, palpation, and peering into orifices with arcane instruments of examination, Scrooge insisted the boy eat hearty meals—six a day, in fact—to make up for all the missed meals between infancy and the onset of puberty. And there is no doubt that did lead to a prodigious growth of Tiny Tim's person. Upon reaching the milestone of his thirteenth birthday, Tim celebrated it by crossing two growth hurdles simultaneously. On the morning of his natal day, in accordance with family tradition, his father measured his height and announced he'd reached five feet and one-eighth of an inch in stature. Then a short carriage ride to the live cattle market to avail themselves of the livestock scales indicated he weighed twenty-one stone, eight pounds, and fourteen ounces (just over three hundred pounds for our friends in the colonies).

From all this, Scrooge took great pride and considered himself a second father to Tiny Tim. He took him on holidays to various seaside resorts that were popular among those with a propensity for sunshine or for wetness. This especially pleased the boy, who took great joy in wading out into the water just deep enough that he could bob up and down in the waves like a buoy. This he would do for hours on end, laughing to his heart's content for no reason beyond pure pleasure, shouting, "Look at me, Uncle Ebenezer!" to Scrooge, or, "God bless us, every one!" to everyone else who might be present.

In the early days of their perioceanic adventuring, however, Tiny Tim's peculiar choice of recreational activity would be marred, with fair regularity, by seagulls coming to roost on the poor boy's head—with frequent squabbles between the avian squatters over what they apparently deemed to be the prime real estate. They seemed to know by some instinct that Tiny Tim was unable to shoo them away owing to the girth of his arms, which limited the height to which he could raise his hands.

It pained Scrooge terribly to see the lad unhappy, so again he came to the boy's rescue by equipping him with a vermillion cap upon which was mounted a kind of propeller or horizontal windmill that spun glitteringly in the breezes and served to frighten the unwelcome squawkers away. This did give Tiny Tim's top the appearance of a half-peeled orange, but vanity was never one of his vices.

And Tiny Tim was not the only one to derive great enjoyment from these excursions.

Scrooge acquired, for their use, a bathing machine at each of the resorts they frequented. These constructions—as the reader of sufficient age and social refinement will recall—were cabins mounted on flat wagons that would remain at the boardwalk while not in use, such that the owners, persons of quality and civilized modesty, could access them in their street clothes without having to walk upon the sand. Once inside, the owners would change into their swimming attire at their leisure without fear of lascivious eyes invading their privacy; and with this accomplished, the bathing machines would be hauled down to the water's edge, where the owners could come out and enjoy the aquatic recreation while still invisible behind the bulk of the machines themselves and at some distance from other machine owners of the opposite gender who might try a glimpse or two in the direction of what they might perceive to be more entertaining visions.

It was in the confines of these bathing machines that Scrooge found the greatest joy, for when Tiny Tim was divested of his clothing, the old man would gaze upon the full roundness of the boy and be overwhelmed with sheer ecstasy. We can only try to imagine the satisfaction Scrooge got from knowing he was the source of that wide and deep river of sound nutrition that had flowed into what was once a sickly boy and swelled him into this wondrous display of fleshly abundance.

Scrooge would bite his thin lower lip at the sight of Tiny Tim's fulsome bosom. He would bite his knuckles at the sight of the boy's chubby knees. And he would turn away and weep silently when the buttocks were bared in all their magnificent amplitude.

Indeed, even clothed the boy's derriere bore a convincing resemblance to two footballs—the variety favored by God and not those heretical deformities in use at Rugby College and in America.

But we can forgive Scrooge taking such deep pride in seeing the results of his beneficence so wondrously displayed, for his generosity to Tiny Tim was so far beyond the realm of comprehension it defies measurement.

This generosity did not end at the mouth of the cornucopia either. Scrooge continued to seek a cure for Tiny Tim's damaged hip. After an army of idiots—whose names were all suffixed with bits of alphabet signifying dubious credentials—had examined the boy, injected him with spurious concoctions, salved him with malodorous ointments, prescribed a host of ridiculous regimens, dosed him with mystically acquired extracts, chanted over him in Latin—known throughout Europe to be the only language of efficacious chanting—and arrived, more or less, at the origin of their endeavors, a team of surgeons arrived on the scene, consequently arrived at a diagnosis, and thence arrived at a figure equal to the purchase of a small resort in Switzerland that would satisfy their professional appetite for compensation and agreed to perform a restorative operation on Tiny Tim's ailing hip.

Scrooge was overjoyed, to put it mildly. He arranged everything in a frantic hurry. He arranged a hospital to host the event. He arranged accommodation for the surgical team while staying in the Good Old City. He arranged for their feeding, their drinking, and their entertainment. He even arranged for young female French and Greek language tutors to provide private lessons in the doctors' hotel rooms at a staggering hourly rate. But in his haste Scrooge forgot to arrange for payment to these several august gentlemen once their services were rendered.

And herein lies the proper beginning of our tale.

Scrooge died on the morning Tiny Tim's surgery was to take place. One would be forgiven for assuming a man of his well-advanced years would go the way of all flesh—in his sleep from unknown but natural causes. This, however, was not the case with Scrooge. His joy over knowing that Tiny Tim's torment was within hours of ending had escalated, moment by moment, through the night and, far from leaving him exhausted in the morning, had delivered him into a mania of nervous delight, leaving him overflowing with physical energies demanding expenditure. The rising sun shone through the stained-glass window at the top of his house, scattering colored swaths of light across the landing at the summit of the stairs outside Scrooge's bedroom door, and found him poised in a perfect handstand with his fingers wrapped around the bullnose of the uppermost step. Descending three flights of stairs on his hands was a feat he had tried many times in childhood, but a serialized set of unsatisfactory experiences had dampened his taste for further attempts.

Until that fateful day.

As in days long past, Scrooge's descent was accomplished much quicker than he had anticipated and with much less rewarding a result. Had he known the floors, including the stairs, had been freshly waxed, he might have reconsidered his plan—though this was unlikely, given his fantastical state of mind. His hand slipped out from under him on the first step. He fell face-first onto the top treadle, crumpled into something resembling an appendaged ball, rolled down and to one side, bounced off the wall, rolled down and to the other side, bounced off the railing, rolled down to the next landing, bounced off the far wall, and, by some law of physics yet to be described mathematically, found himself rolling dead center down the next flight of steps.

And then the next.

He came to rest on the marble floor of the first floor of his home, back down—or face up, if you prefer—with his head at the center of a widening halo of red, looking for all the world like the saint he had become, as depicted by a master artist of the Late Middle Ages. Giotto, perhaps—it matters not precisely.

The adventure of the tumble had been quite short and most exciting, but Scrooge was glad for it to be over. His boisterous energy was largely depleted, though his spirits were slow in catching up to the reality of his situation, with him having been so fully charged with the joyful anticipation of Tiny Tim's impending improvement. He had been giggling uncontrollably for the past twenty-four hours and saw no good reason to stop on account of an inconvenient discomfort. The pounding in his head did demand some verbal expression, however, and so Scrooge's last moments were spent in a kind of staccato tittering punctuated by harsh vowel sounds.

Giggle-giggle-giggle "Ow …" Giggle-giggle "Ow …" *Snort-giggle-giggle* "Ow …"

Some while later—and not far from the scene of these events—our hero, Tiny Tim, was also losing consciousness, though not from the effects of instantaneous deceleration like his benefactor but rather from the inhalation of some sweet-smelling gas provided to him by Smedley Snyffe, the anesthetist of the surgical team. Snyffe had selected this particular gas from a number of somnolent compounds at his disposal because he knew from vast experience that it not only was fairly reliable for its intended purpose but also that it served extremely well to dispose of the uncomfortable remnants of an evening spent appreciating gentlemen's whiskey.

So it was, prior to administering this miraculous ether to Tiny Tim, that this learned physician had administered several breaths to himself in preparation for what he thought would otherwise be a tedious and difficult morning.

The surgeons themselves were too engrossed in playing noughts and crosses with a grease pencil on Tiny Tim's ailing hip to notice not only that their patient had been surrendered into the gentle arms of Morpheus but also that their colleague, with his hand on the gas bottle's valve, was likewise deeply committed to the activity of slumber.

Word arrived of Scrooge's demise when Sir Axeworthy Blundt, the chief surgeon, was lining up his scalpel for the first incision.

"By all the gods!" said Sir Axeworthy upon hearing the news. "How damnably inconsiderate of the man! Bringing us all here for nine o'clock of a Wednesday morning only to tell us we're not to be paid."

"Not be paid?" said Reginald Thickstitch, Sir Axeworthy's assistant. "Not be paid? I've washed my hands and everything …! And now I'm not to be paid?"

The balance of the illustrious team was equally appalled at this outrage.

"Scandalous."

"Unconscionable."

"The devil you say."

"What is the world coming to?"

Had Tiny Tim been awake, he might have added, "God bless us, every one!" for, alas, he had little capacity for gauging the climate of a situation. But, being well and truly asleep, he did not. Instead he lay there, etherized upon the table under a sage-green sheet, in silence, looking for all the world like a rounded Dartmoor tor—minus the heather and gorse, of course.

But while Tiny Tim's silence was peaceful in the extreme, the silence of the surgeons was a meditation on embodied rage—so much so that when one finally did speak, the others leaped in shock, launching two trays of sharp instruments skyward to momentarily hazardous effect.

When the ringing clatter of steel on floor tile settled, Artemis Klamp, Thickstitch's second, began again: "I merely wanted to say that if we hurry ourselves, we can make the early train to Saint Andrews and secure ourselves a better selection of rooms than last time."

"You think of golf at a time like this?" roared Sir Axeworthy.

"The fellow's quite right," said Thickstitch. "There's clearly nothing more to be done here. I say we make the best of a bad outcome and seek for ourselves more congenial circumstances."

"Yes, yes," said Sir Axeworthy, squinting in deep consideration. He smiled broadly and said, "Capital notion, Klamp! You keep a cool head in a crisis. No dawdling, then, gentlemen. Festina velociter velociter."

And with that, the august company of Galen's apostles exited the cramped operating theater in a rush to do all that needed to be done to make the 11:42 to Scotland.

All but Snyffe.

The worthy provider of pain-free sleep was not one to make haste very quickly at the best of times, nor even just quickly at the worst of times. Indeed, he was not prone to make haste under any circumstances at all. He approached life at a somnambulant gait and retreated from it in a like manner, and there was nothing anyone could do to change that.

On that particular day, however, he was not approaching or retreating from anything at any pace—somnambulant or otherwise. He was as fast asleep as Tiny Tim, sitting beside the gas bottles with his head resting on the operating table and his hand holding down the mask that covered our hero's face. So it was that Tiny Tim continued to breathe the gentle narcotic well past the time recommended for such behavior, and because Snyffe's hand pressed only weakly on the mask, a sufficient quantity of the gas leaked out from under to keep the anesthetist unconscious as well.

The gas bottles emptied sometime that night, and Snyffe awoke the following morning, eerily groggy and greatly in need of the gentlemen's convenience. He looked about in confusion and, noticing his colleagues had left, concluded the operation was over, perfunctorily wished Tiny Tim a speedy recovery, and headed off under the propulsion of biological necessity.

Another day and night passed before the operating theater was required again, at which time Tiny Tim was discovered, still enjoying the peace of the silent infinite. As pleasant as this was for the boy, it presented something of an inconvenience for the hospital administration. A search of the building discovered Mr. and Mrs. Bob Cratchit and all the family Cratchit gathered together in a waiting room and asleep from exhaustion, having waited longer than anticipated for news of their Tiny Tim's progress. Simultaneous to the search for the clan Cratchit, a search for signs of life in Tiny Tim was also conducted, but with a far less rewarding result. The boy did not respond to tactile stimulus of any kind or magnitude, did not appear to be breathing, and failed to provide evidence of a heartbeat despite several seconds of stethoscopic observation.

And, probably not surprisingly, he went longer without saying, "God bless us, every one!" than any time in memory and continued to push the boundary of this record with every passing second of continued silence.

"Time of death: 8:07 on whatever date today's date is," said Mortimer Rigger, the coroner, with a gravity born of much practice. "Cause: self-inflicted injury."

"Self-inflicted injury, sir?" asked young Dick Scruple, his assistant, much confused as always by the mysteries of medicine.

"He agreed to the surgery, did he not?" said Dr. Rigger.

"His parents, sir. The lad's a minor."

"Have some compassion, my boy. We can hardly blame them, given the loss of their son."

"Quite so, sir," said Scruple, much embarrassed, and he appended the records accordingly. "And what proof have we that he died at 8:07?"

"What proof have we that he did not?"

"None, sir."

"Ockham's razor then, dear boy," said Dr. Rigger didactically. "Ockham's razor."

And once again Scruple stood in awe of his master's sagacious perspicacity and efficiency in slicing away the irrelevant.

But the conclusion that Tiny Tim had died was, in fact, somewhat less than accurate, for while Scrooge was indeed as dead as a coffin nail, Tiny Tim was marginally less given to that condition. Dr. Rigger can, however, be forgiven for leaping to his hasty conclusion in this case, as our hero was something of an anomaly, his condition falling outside the parameters of collective experience, and physicians are conditioned to limit their conclusions to fall within said parameters.

Tiny Tim's breathing did appear to be unapparent by all the usual standards used in gauging such things. A more protracted observation would have revealed, however, that breathing had not ceased entirely, though a single inhalation now spanned one half hour in its execution, only to be followed by an exhalation of similar duration. His heart rate, too, had slowed precipitously: from two beats a second to five an hour, with scarcely enough force to register a change in pressure.

Most compelling of all was Tiny Tim's taciturnity, for in it he mimicked death with greater verisimilitude than a Shakespearean in the role of Polonius after Act 3, scene 4, of *Hamlet*.

When Mr. and Mrs. Bob Cratchit were told of their son's demise, their reaction was not surprising at all on the part of Bob but quite surprising on the part of his wife. He—quite true to form—remained as accepting of fate as he had been in the days before Ebenezer Scrooge's enlightenment, while she—a woman of hot complaint but generally tepid conviction and ubiquitously lukewarm action—was most uncharacteristically instantaneous in charting a course for the future.

"There's nothing for it now," said the tearful Bob, "but to see to the lad's eternal comfort."

"Not bloody likely," said his enraged wife. "We'll sue! We'll sue them into bread and water, we will! We'll sue them into the gutter where they belong. They'll not make a penny from here on that three farthings don't come to us."

The unfortunate Bob reeled with shock at the sound of his wife's determinations. He did not argue at first, but upon recovery, he grew hesitant to embark on this path, having recollections of several otherwise savvy individuals being thoroughly disemboweled in court by Scrooge's barrister when they'd chosen to challenge his legal claim to even the smallest of things. Though generally sheltered in the ways of the greater world and overly optimistic in his day-to-day view, Bob could easily see that these surgeons whom Mrs. Cratchit was bent upon suing would come to court leading whole brigades of barristers equally gifted in legal knowledge and equally driven by an instinct for butchery as his late master's counsel.

"No need for that, my dear," said Bob consolingly. "We've still got the others, and you're still young. We can have another if you like."

"What? Not make them pay what's murdered our Tiny Tim?"

"But Emily, my dear," said Bob.

"Don't 'Emily, my dear,' me," said Mrs. Cratchit. "We've got here the goose what laid the golden egg if you was only to open your eyes to see it. They's done hyenas murder on our boy, they have, and them what's done it will pay."

"More like the elephant that laid the golden egg," said their now youngest son, whom they'd never thought to name but who went by Matthew for the sake of expediency and will do so more and more as our story unfolds.

"Your jocularity isn't fitting to the occasion," said Bob softly but fatherly. "Your brother has passed over and deserves your respect."

The one known as Matthew frowned in anger over his joke being so ill-received and left for a corner to console his wounded pride. Soon, though, he was amusing himself with imaginings of what he would do with the free space in the boys' room now that it was no longer required to accommodate Tiny Tim's prodigious personage.

"I'll hear no more against it, I won't," said Mrs. Cratchit. "They're proper villains, they is, and we're suing them, and that's final."

As hesitant as Bob was to embark upon the path of legal battle, he was more hesitant still to embark upon the path of matrimonial war, and so it came to pass that the parental Cratchits journeyed to the offices of Scrooge's former attorney, Mordred E. Rankin, and engaged the services of Rankin, Fowle, O'Durr, and Gazpayne: Solicitors and Barristers at Law, in general, and those of B. Philius Gazpayne, the junior partner, in particular.

Gazpayne was well-reputed to have a prodigious nose for the law. The truth to that might be debatable, but that he had a prodigious nose for any circumstances is not. Indeed, his appearance into a room could accurately be described as the arrival of an aquiline nasal appendage followed sometime later by a lawyer. This unfortunate excess of breathing apparatus was the source of many jokes that climaxed after one embarrassing slip on the part of a judge. The magistrate had meant to say solemnly, "You will provide your services pro bono," but instead solemnly said, "You will provide your services proboscis," which resulted in widespread hilarity radiating from that court on that day to all courts on every day following for some years to come.

Regardless, Gazpayne deported himself with ostentatious dignity, oblivious of the tittering that followed in his wake. His usual expression, which varied very little, resulted from his keeping his eyebrows peaked at the center of his brow, his eyes half shut at all times, his mouth turned down at the corners, and his lower lip extended as far as it might above his tense, receding chin. This singular face was perched upon a long, narrow neck that emerged from between two almost imperceptible shoulders. The remainder of the Gazpayne physiognomy was above six feet in height and fitting the general description of "spidery."

Mrs. Cratchit was well pleased with her first impression of the lawyer, for she equated height and haughtiness with success in all things. It took poor Bob, though, a second or two to shift his attention from the two hirsute nostrils that dominated his field of vision while looking up, to focus on Gazpayne's legal attributes.

"It's an open-and-shut case, I assure you," said Gazpayne, and he sniffed loudly. "Whether one is paid for services rendered or not, one does not go about gassing people into oblivion. It's simply not civilized. And, as I say that, I realize a savage would not have the means or wherewithal to gas anyone into oblivion—or into anywhere else, for the matter of that—so, civilized or not, it plainly isn't cricket. It follows, then—as clearly as *a* follows *b*—that their defense is wholly insubstantial."

"'Scuse me, sir," said Bob. "I believe you've got it backward; *a* doesn't follow *b*."

"It does in backward—as you, yourself, point out, dear fellow. But I'm glad you raise the point, though, as it indicates quite clearly you are wholly incapable of following a cogent line of thought, so I must avoid at all costs putting you on the stand. Much better to know this now, before we have reason to regret. The testimony must all fall to you, Mrs. Cratchit."

"As always," said Mrs. Cratchit in a voice betraying the depth of her long-suffering and self-sacrifice.

Gazpayne continued. "There will be costs, of course. But I shouldn't concern myself over that. At the very least, you will have enough from it all to bury poor Tiny Tim with some pomp and ceremony, and without having to stint yourself over the arrangements."

"That would be nice and all," said Mrs. Cratchit sheepishly, "but we was hoping to see a mite more than that, seeing as we suffered most 'gregious grief and suffering."

"Of course, my dear lady, of course. I did not mean to imply you, yourself, will be without proper compensation. Tiny Tim is not the only victim here. Not a bit. No," said Gazpayne before sniffing in a volume of air. "I merely state the very worst possible outcome imaginable that you might then accurately gauge your willingness to pursue the matter further. You do wish to pursue the matter further, do you not?"

"Oh, we do, we do," said Mrs. Cratchit, viciously jabbing Bob in the ribs with her elbow.

"Oh, we do, we do," said Bob through a grimace.

Gazpayne nodded and continued. "Very good, then. I understand from Mr. Rankin that you are the sole heirs to the Scrooge estate."

"That's right, Your Lordship," said Mrs. Cratchit. "The kind old gentleman did right by us, he did. Left us everything after his nephew run off to Zanzibar to become a typhoon in the lion-skin rug business, where he got hisself and his missus et by the merchandise what took unkindly to them."

"Excellent," said Gazpayne, wriggling the spidery fingers of one hand. "That simplifies matters enormously. We can deduct whatever minor costs arise in the execution of this case directly from those funds, and you need not be bothered with having to sign for every little item of minutia that arises to plague us in these times of convoluted legal flimflammeries and tomfooleries. And it will serve not only to avoid much unnecessary inconvenience to you but also to expedite proceedings that would otherwise be mired in tedious and redundant and de facto superfluous communications."

"Ooh! Don't he talk posh!" said Mrs. Cratchit. "We're bound to win with him talking posh like that."

With that, the legal titan slid an inch-thick document across his desk toward Mrs. Cratchit and, donning a rare grin, said, "Sign here," indicating the blank line located between the printed names of her husband and her with the tip of his alarmingly long finger.

"I'm not sure …" said Bob.

"Merely a formality," said Gazpayne, clearly bored with having to deal—yet once more—with the petty concerns of the limited mind. "If you will, Mrs. Cratchit. And in light of the confusion often arising from the legal status of women in these turbulent times, please sign yourself Mr. and Mrs. Robert Cratchit to indicate you are, indeed, married and not widowed at this moment in history."

"Ooh, my goodness!" said Mrs. Cratchit. "Int the law particular? 'Tis no doubt, we're glad we came to you, Your Worship, to guide us through these trying formulations."

"Indeed," said Gazpayne while she signed, and he then slid the massive missive to Bob with the words "Initial here, Mr. Cratchit, to indicate you are, in fact, present at this meeting."

Bob, having brought with him certain hesitations and prejudices regarding the legal profession in general, was not without his doubts about these proceedings. But he saw no harm in providing proof he was present when he was quite inarguably present, so he affixed his *RC* in his large, florid script next to his own name on the line indicated.

"Good then," said Gazpayne as he quickly blotted the wet ink and locked the document in a desk drawer. "We will notify you of the court date. I will see to everything from here. Go home and put it all out of your minds." To this he added most cordially, "Or you might put your minds to packing your belongings. I foresee a move to more commodious lodgings in your future."

With that, the Cratchit couple was hastily ushered out of his office, through a maze of halls, and to the street ten limestone steps down from the great brass front doors that Rankin, Fowle, O'Durr, and Gazpayne presented to the world exterior.

"A more expeditious exit I've never made, I'm sure," said Bob, adjusting his coat, which had bunched up around his waist.

"Just being efficient," said Mrs. Cratchit. But after a moment's thought, she asked, "Here! What do you think he meant by 'more commodious lodgings'?"

"A house with commodes, I'd imagine," said Bob, taking his wife's arm in his and commencing their stroll home.

"You mean indoors?"

"Quite so, my dear," said Bob confidently. "It's his way of telling us he means to make us rich, you see? It's not in the professional manner of a barrister to say things outright and plain-like, like you and I would. He has to hint at what he means and sprinkle in some Latin, all clever-like."

"Latin?"

"Oh yes," said Bob, and he plumbed the depths of his knowledge for elaboration. "I'm fairly certain 'commodious' is Latin for 'loo.' There was a Roman emperor named Commodious, if I remember my history correctly, which is 'Louis' in French, or 'Lou' for short, so you easily see the connection."

"If it's French, why do we say it, then?"

"William the Conqueror, my dear. Ten sixty-six and all that. He made us speak French because it's posh and genteel. He wouldn't have any Angry Saxon spoken in his court, so now we say 'loo' all polite-like."

This elucidation pleased Mrs. Cratchit greatly with the reassurance that their chosen lawyer was clever in the ways of his profession, her husband was clever in the ways of the world and—possibly more than either of these—she was going to acquire indoor plumbing.

CHAPTER 2

Fortunately for our hero, the arrangements for Tiny Tim's funeral were demoted from the Important/Urgent category of Mrs. Cratchit's mental list of things to do to the Unimportant/Not Urgent section, as more pressing matters pressed her concerns elsewhere. Tiny Tim rested comfortably in the hospital morgue for some time while his mother engaged her thoughts and energies in house hunting, furniture shopping, fabric selection, landscape planning, and the interviewing of servants to be hired on the day the courts awarded her her just due.

This counting of unhatched chickens—as the saying goes—was not without cost. Deposits were required for the twelve-bedroom house to be purchased; the furnishings commissioned to be fabricated; the curtains, draperies, and linens to be sewn; the statues, trees, and perennials to be installed; and the tailoring of the uniforms to be worn by the servants. Mrs. Cratchit accepted these requirements without question and wrote checks without hesitation, comfortable in the knowledge that Scrooge's estate was well beyond the limits of her imagination in a territory in which she likewise placed all sense of restraint.

When the first check was returned to her stamped "NSF" in bright red, it amused her rather than worried her, for she had no notion of what the cryptic short form meant—the writing of checks was a new concept for her, and though she had taken to the practice readily, she was an innocent in the detailed workings of the system.

She collected a number of these—all similarly decorated—before her curiosity got the better of her and she was driven to ask her husband what the bold red letters stood for.

Unlike his wife, Bob was not at all amused when he saw the checks, for having kept Scrooge's books for many years and seen many examples provided by the less reliable clients of the business, he was quite familiar with the consequences of the ominous stamp of rejection.

"It means 'Not So Fast,' my dear," he said, flinching in advance. "There's been a problem with the bank, and the money's not been paid."

"Not been paid?" said Mrs. Cratchit in a shriek. "Not been paid? With all we got from Mr. Scrooge, how can they do that? Who do they think they're dealing with?"

"I'm sure I'll have to look into it," said Bob. "Likely as not, a clerk has put the decimal in the wrong place or done his long division topsy-turvy. Easily done, I assure you. We'll get it put to right, don't you worry."

Mrs. Cratchit was not at all pleased with this answer and insisted they see to the harsh punishment of the errant clerk immediately. The two made their way to their bank—the former bank of the former Scrooge—which was a great marbled institution much prone to reverberation when accosted by the footfalls of hard-heeled shoes and words spoken much above a murmur. Mrs. Cratchit, never one to contain her anger within the confines of a whisper, set the venerable walls to ringing with the sounds of her heated protestations when an anemic teller informed her it was beyond his capacity to assist them.

Soon after the onset of the disturbance, Mr. Goldworm, the bank manager, arrived on the scene and—in an effort to quell the echoing abuse being rained down upon his employee, and to return his erstwhile solemn establishment to its former state of solemnity—invited the Cratchits into his office and closed the heavy, sound-muffling door.

"I see no problem at all," said Goldworm, after reviewing the Cratchit's massive file. "The late Mr. Scrooge's estate was disposed of quite satisfactorily and profitably in accordance with the laws of Great Britain. The houses, furnishings, and contents were all liquidated into liquidity, the securities were all secured, the real estate was all realized, and the capital all capitalized, as per the common conventions regulating these matters, and the monies—minus the fees of the various professional services—were all deposited into your account, where they now lie as ready and willing as a bride on her wedding night to provide for your satisfaction."

Goldworm grinned broadly with self-satisfaction over his choice of suggestive simile, which he generally reserved for gentlemen only but felt comfortable using with Mrs. Cratchit as he saw her as a woman of more grounded sensibilities than the wives of his titled clientele.

"How much?" asked Mrs. Cratchit.

"How much what?" asked Goldworm.

"How much is there in the account?"

"Oh, that!" said Goldworm, as if the mention of actual money were something quite odious. "Yes. Slightly more than three hundred thousand pounds. Making you one of the wealthiest women in England, Mrs. Cratchit, being married as you are to Mr. Cratchit, who is now among the wealthiest of men."

"You mean I got three hundred thousand quid to spend?"

"If you so choose. Though I remind you, wealthy people do not stay wealthy by spending their money. They stay wealthy by leaving it in my bank."

Mrs. Cratchit was seldom in the mood for taking advice, even at the best of times, and these were not the best of times in light of her reason for being there. She paid no attention to Mr. Goldworm's tangential offering of prudence and sagacity and demanded instead, "Then why in blue blazes can't I spend it?"

"Please, Mrs. Cratchit," said Goldworm, "there is no need for strong language. As far as the bank is concerned, there is no reason whatsoever you should not spend your money howsoever you see fit. You are, however, currently mired in a legal entanglement that has put upon you the requirement of temporarily signing over to the firm of Rankin, Fowle, O'Durr, and Gazpayne your power of attorney. This is quite usual, I assure you, in cases such as these, especially when it comes to the practices of your chosen barristers. You can take confidence in knowing they have nearly thirty percent of the Good Old City's private capital similarly administered through one cause or another."

"What does it mean, then? Can I spend my money or can't I?"

"You can, indeed. You only require a release from Mr. Gazpayne, and you can spend yourself into penury if you so choose."

"You mean I have to get permission from my lawyer to spend my own money?"

"No, no, not at all, Mrs. Cratchit. Mr. Gazpayne is in your employ and, therefore, obliged to do as you say within the ethical boundaries of his profession and the laws of Her Majesty's realm. He has taken control of your accounts—per your own instruction, I will remind you—for the sole purpose of seeing you do not find yourselves in incommodious circumstances. You need only inform him of your preferences, and he is then legally bound to comply with your wish, to the limits of his energies and his aforementioned obligations to higher authorities. Now, seeing you have chosen to captain your own enterprises heedless of his direction and have unwisely navigated your financial ship onto a rather treacherous heading, I suggest, Mr. and Mrs. Cratchit, you go, forthwith, to the offices of Mr. Gazpayne and get this matter resolved before your creditors descend upon you with legal actions of their own."

This unthought-of thought put poor Bob in a panic, for while he had been greatly concerned with seeing to settling Mrs. Cratchit's disgruntlement, he had failed to consider that the army of merchants and tradesmen that had been spurred to action with the receipt of her financially unsupported checks was almost certainly represented by an equal or larger army of lawyers that would be spurred to even greater action should those financially unsupported checks not be immediately propped up with monetary reinforcing commensurate with their represented value.

"Mr. Goldworm's quite right, my dear," said Bob. "Needs be we get ourselves post facto to Mr. Gazpayne's without further delay."

Once again on the streets, Mrs. Cratchit had to ask, "Here! What did he mean by 'incommodious circumstances'?"

"Without a pot to piss in, my dear."

"That's what I expected. Why is it these posh sorts are always carrying on about loos? It don't seem quite respectable, to me, when they're supposed to be all proper and such."

"Because, my dear, it's what separates the posh sorts from the not posh sorts. There's not a lord or lady in the land with slivers in their bum or chilblains on their privates. It's a matter of social pride. It sets them apart from the rest of us, as it does."

CHAPTER 3

Upon their first and earlier-described meeting, Bob had found Gazpayne's frown slightly disconcerting, but he found the lawyer's smile, upon their second meeting, profoundly shocking and disturbing. Fortunately, Mrs. Cratchit was prepared to put their purpose into words before Bob could waste any of the attorney's professionally funded time in working up the courage to formulate a sentence.

"Oh, I can't possibly do that," said Gazpayne. "The laws of the realm forbid it; the ethics of my profession restrain me from it, and the moral obligation I owe my partners cannot permit me even to consider it."

"But it's my money," said Mrs. Cratchit.

"Indeed, it is, and I would be remiss in pointing out you need to take your responsibility toward it more seriously if we are to reach any kind of success in our endeavors. I advised you to make ready your possessions for transport, not to acquire more of them. Had you acted as I had said, we would not be having this otherwise unnecessary meeting."

With that, Gazpayne noticed that the tiny hourglass on his desk was about to drop the sand grain that marked the passing of ten minutes. He dipped his quill in ink, made a short vertical line next to a previously scribed line on the sheet of paper before him, and flipped the timepiece over at the instant of that ultimate sand-grain dropping through the constriction.

"But it's my money," said Mrs. Cratchit, unaware that her repetition was only adding to the cost of the conference. "Why can't I spend it as I will?"

"You will in time, my dear lady," said Gazpayne amiably. "Only at this juncture, I am duty-bound to preserve your capital in its entirety against the unforeseen, worst-possible outcome, to ensure all parties that have been attached to your chosen action will be properly and justly accounted for in the fullness of time and the fulfillment of events now in motion."

"What parties?"

"The law firm of Rankin, Fowle, O'Durr, and Gazpayne, for one. We are incurring considerable costs in the preparation of your case—our employees do not work for free, and the fees of the bureaucratic offices with which we must deal are a nightmare in themselves. Furthermore, there are the courts. They are not made available to us gratuitously. Justice may be blind, but she is an expensive mistress, nevertheless."

"But we've got three hundred thousand nicker in the bank," said Mrs. Cratchit.

"Indeed you do. For now, at least. And it is my intention you will have somewhat more than that when our case is won, but in the meantime, you must leave it intact and where it is."

"Why all of it?"

"In short, Mr. and Mrs. Cratchit, the law proceeds on the assumption that, in matters of litigation, everyone will lose. This may, upon first hearing, sound rather Draconian or perhaps even absurd, but it has to be thus for quite logical reasons. If it were assumed everyone will win, then both parties would be free to spend themselves willy-nilly into beggary during the protracted execution of the legal action, and when that action is at last concluded, and one party has lost as must inevitably be so, then that party—having delivered itself into impecunious conditions—would be unable to meet its legally assessed obligations, meaning no one would get paid, including the courts and the lawyers. The judiciary system would collapse in on itself, and we would be reduced to savagery without an edifice of justice within which to shelter civilization. Conversely, to assume one party will win and the other will lose might seem reasonable on the surface, but for this to be an effective tenet to embrace for ensuring the financial integrity of the system, it would be necessary to decide, prior to the case being heard, which party will win and which party will lose, which I am sure you can see would defeat the whole purpose of having a trial in the first place or, indeed, at all. And so we are left with the only possible option of assuming everyone will lose, until due process can run its course and prove otherwise to ensure all are fairly treated and the solidity of the justice system and civilization itself are preserved."

Mr. and Mrs. Cratchit took some moments for their comprehension to catch up to this explanation, which Gazpayne had trotted out with the velocity of a racehorse.

Bob was next to cross the finish line, some distance behind the lawyer but a little ahead of his wife. Though he was greatly afraid of being smiled at again by Gazpayne, his desperation drove him to cry out, "But we have debts to pay."

"Yes, you do," agreed the disagreeable barrister. "And a most unfortunate unfolding of events it is, and one that is, alas, too often repeated by those new to wealth. You should have come to me sooner regarding this. I would have charged you much less then, for advising you not to act as you did, than I must charge you now for telling you that you were unwise to do so."

Upon saying this, Gazpayne penned another vertical line on the sheet before him and flipped the hourglass again, then continued. "Have you at least done as I said in getting your possessions packed and ready to be transported?"

"No, Your Worship, not yet," said Mrs. Cratchit in her misery, "being, as we were, much preoccupied with other consternations."

"Then get yourselves home and do so immediately. I will arrange for a conveyance to arrive at your place of residence tomorrow noon and relocate you to a domicile owned by this firm, where you can remain until the case is settled. I will then arrange to have your house sold and your creditors paid in full, thus extricating you from this ludicrous misadventure. Don't worry yourselves about rent. That will be agglomerated along with all the other expenditures, to be settled upon the resolution of your action against Blundt and Co." The lawyer flittered fingers over his head to indicate that the term of his patience had expired. "Along with the usual service fees, charges, and interest, of course."

"Of course," said Mrs. Cratchit, uncertain of what else to say.

"Of course," said Bob, becoming more and more certain the state of his well-being was about to decline further from its already much-deteriorated condition.

CHAPTER 4

That decline was, indeed, forthcoming, but it came rather sooner than even Bob had anticipated. Upon their arrival home, he and his wife were greeted by young Dick Scruple, whom you might recall was the coroner's assistant.

Scruple was standing before a black closed carriage, along with four gigantic men, all of whom looked as if they'd escaped from prison by eating their guards and using the splintered bones to pick the locks.

"Are you the owners of one inoperative male person, designated Timothy Cratchit?" asked Scruple.

"He's not here," said Mrs. Cratchit with knee-jerk reaction. Without thinking, she'd assumed these men were representatives of the constabulary and Tiny Tim had gotten into some mischief.

"Yes, we're his parents," said Bob. "He's passed over to the other side this past month."

"Precisely what I'm here about," said Scruple, holding out a document in one hand and a pencil in the other. "Sign here, please, and he's all yours."

"What?" said Mrs. Cratchit. "Here?"

"Yes, madam. He's overstayed his guest privileges at the morgue, and rather than burden you with additional fees for lodging, it was decided to return him to you, to do with as you see fit," said Scruple to Mrs. Cratchit. "Thank you, sir," he said to Bob, upon return of the signed receipt, and "All right boys, inside with him," to his four strong-arms.

"But we can't have him here," said Bob. "He's … It wouldn't be right."

"No, of course not," said Scruple in a respectful murmur. "Best to get him buried quickly, if you ask me."

"But our money's not at our disposal," said Bob pleadingly. "There are legal matters to exterminate. We can't afford a funeral under the present circumstances."

"Well, if you can't afford a funeral, you can't afford the storage fees either. Hospitals must be paid, or the whole medical system will collapse in on itself—and where would society be if we couldn't fix our sick and injured?"

"Yes, I see," said Bob, realizing for the first time in his life—with some dismay—that the entirety of civilization's institutions was founded on his ability to pay his bills.

The carriage was opened at the rear and a reinforced stretcher extracted, bearing the naked corpulence of Tiny Tim, who was looking quite peaceful despite the chill in the air and the attention he was gathering from passersby.

"Here," asked Mrs. Cratchit. "Why's he all shiny, then?"

"He's been waxed," said Scruple. "Cheaper than embalming, but slows the going-off process well enough. Still, I'd get him seen to more sooner than later if I were you. You can take it from me: he won't be pleasant company for long, despite all the fond memories."

The body was taken inside and set down in the living room. When the four gigantic men went to remove our hero from his conveyance, Bob had a sudden thought and said, "We're moving tomorrow. Could you leave him on the stretcher, please? It would be a great convenience to us."

"Of course," said Scruple. "I'll just add it to your bill along with all the rest. When you're done with it, the morgue will buy it back—minus depreciation, of course."

"Of course," said Bob, feeling yet another blow to his badly pummeled purse.

Scruple left with his squad of behemoths, leaving Mr. and Mrs.

Cratchit in a rather stunned and bewildered state. They knew they had to make ready for their move, but Tiny Tim—positioned as he was in the middle of the living room floor and filling the entirety of the gap between one settee on one wall and the other on the other—proved to be a significant impediment to navigation. Neither Bob nor his wife could think how they were going to get the furnishings out with their boy in. In fact, they could not think at all.

Shortly after Scruple's departure, the second of the Cratchits' daughters, Belinda, arrived home with the two unnamed Cratchit children, who went by Matthew and Lucy for the sake of convenience. Upon seeing the unclothed body of her brother on full display in the living room, Belinda recoiled with shock, turned immediately on her younger siblings, and ushered them back outside with warnings to Matthew not to let Lucy enter until she gave them permission. She then ran upstairs and acquired a bedsheet with which she returned to the living room and restored Tiny Tim to an acceptable state of modesty.

"What's the matter with you two?" said Belinda to her parents. "And what's our Tim doing here without proper clothes on?"

"He's dead, my dear," said Bob vacuously.

"That doesn't mean he can't act decent-like. Why's he here, anyway? I thought you were getting him buried and such."

"We can't see to it just yet," said Bob, ready for tears. "We have to move and sell the house."

Suddenly Belinda remembered the two younger ones waiting outside and popped out to retrieve them. She warned them of their brother's presence and bade them not to be upset over being inconvenienced by his reticence and lack of attention.

Matthew and Lucy then entered and climbed over the arm of one settee and sat cross-legged, gazing upon the mound of flesh that was their younger brother.

"He doesn't seem much bothered by it," said Matthew. "Being dead I mean."

"He's just being brave, like he always was," said Lucy, impervious to Matthew's ironic meaning. "Being dead is beastly." She was about to explain how she knew this when she suddenly burst into uproarious laughter that carried on and on with no sign of abatement.

Soon Matthew was laughing too, with an equal inability to quell the need or the display.

"Children, please," said poor Bob. "Not so disrespectful."

"Tim made a joke," said Lucy, and she continued laughing until tears rolled from her eyes and her sides ached as if she'd endured a sound kicking.

Belinda, too, took to tittering and had to leave the room to regain command of her decorum. All this set Bob greatly aback, and he leaned over to examine Tiny Tim's face closer but could discern no change in the boy's expression. "Your imagination is getting the better of you," he said, but he was quite wrong.

CHAPTER 5

To understand what had just happened, it is necessary to step back in time to the period of Tiny Tim's residency in the morgue. One can be forgiven for imagining he had passed this time uneventfully, for other than submitting to being waxed from stem to stern, he had done nothing while there that might attract the attention of an onlooker—had there been an onlooker, which there hadn't, as this particular morgue suffered in much the same way as morgues commonly do from a deficiency of spectators.

In truth, however, the profound lessening of Tiny Tim's faculties for mobility, loquacity, and perception had caused him to become rather introspective—and not in the sense of having thoughts that would remain unuttered. Indeed, in all the time Tiny Tim was reposing on his cool marble slab, he never once entertained an aching appreciation for feminine beauty well beyond his reach; never once fretted over the dressing down a teacher had given him for the failed attempt at arson when he was six; never once considered blowing up the Houses of Parliament or Buckingham Palace, nor any of the other thoughts that daily, hourly, or minutely cross the minds of all others given to introspection. No, the internal vision Tiny Tim enjoyed was the aesthetic equivalent of the bottom of a coal mine on a cloudy, moonless winter's night after those bearing lamps have all gone home. And the sound he listened to within himself was like a low, monotonous hum minus the hum. In short, his mind was as blank as blank can be, given blank to mean a complete absence of everything visual, aural, olfactory, and gustatory—which, you will note, leaves only tactile sensitivity—and, in that, our hero was limited to feeling only his emotions.

For a brief while, Tiny Tim's chief emotion was confusion, or perhaps a confused mix of emotions too muddled to allow for the identification of any one in particular. Either way, the poor boy was uncomfortable in this state, much as one might be uncomfortable in a boat out at sea without benefit of sail or oar, and left to the vagaries of fate, awash in uncertainty. In the space of a week or so, however, our hero learned to discern feeling from feeling and developed some ability in choosing how he wanted to feel for some while, in much the same way as any one of us might choose to enjoy either a work of comedy or a work of tragedy when out seeking a few hours' entertainment.

With practice—and with nothing in particular to distract his attention—Tiny Tim grew increasingly skilled in selecting the emotions he wished to enjoy. One might think, him being in possession of this gift, he would automatically choose to feel blissful, tranquil, serene, and equanimous in perpetuity, but this is not the case.

And he was not in any way unique in this. It is a common misconception that it is normal and healthy to avoid terror, rage, and grief, but nothing could be further from the truth. None of us simply endures terror, rage, and grief in reading some volume of literature because our fascination with the plot and our empathy for the characters drives us to do so despite our better judgment. No. We do so because we genuinely appreciate being terrified, enraged, and desperately forlorn when we know we have the power to switch it off as we choose. We actually crave terror, rage, and grief, but only when they are packaged prettily and in manageable portions.

So it was with Tiny Tim. When he first took command of his feelings, he did choose to feel the equivalent of running barefoot through Elysian fields in warm sunlight for some while. But this grew tiresome rather more quickly than one might expect, and he then embarked on an exploration of possibilities illuminated by the full spectrum of emotions.

As with the honing of any talent, the early attempts were clumsy and slow. Tiny Tim could raise a feeling of anger, for example, but having raised it, he was then stuck within it for some while until he found the way out and onto the next emotion. But just as one must fumble with five-finger exercises at their first foray into the mysteries of the piano, only to emerge after persistent application, capable of rendering Rachmaninoff in blurred rapidity, Tiny Tim learned to switch feeling for feeling with increasing alacrity. Soon he was composing interesting melodies of emotions, or feelings poems, or whatever name you can imagine describing a constructed series of sensations strung together for some desired effect.

And he found this highly entertaining.

What Tiny Tim did not notice was that these feelings he generated within himself were weakly spilling out such that the moods of other individuals, should they come near him as he lay on his slab in silence, would change subtly to mimic his—much as the strings of one piano will begin vibrating in accord with the strings of another piano played nearby with sufficient volume.

Of all this Tiny Tim was oblivious. The coroner's staff, as stated previously, was not similarly insensitive to this phenomenon. They all noticed there was something profoundly odd and eerie about the corpse in the corner and took to maintaining a distance from him whenever possible. Much to their chagrin, however, Tiny Tim only became more and more adept at controlling his feelings, and as his power of control grew, so grew the reach of his generated emotions. It was soon impossible for the mavens of forensic medicine to ignore the ambient mood of the morgue, which had lost all consistency. The unwavering dour but reassuring seriousness of the place had given way to wide-ranging feelings not uncommon to horror shows, carnivals, and melodramas but rare to the way stations of the recently demised.

And this they found most disturbing.

But then the great epiphanous doors of realization opened for Tiny Tim in that one morning, our hero suddenly became aware of those around him. For the first time, he could feel not only those emotions he created within himself for his own amusement but also, in much lesser amplitude, the feelings of people nearby. His immediate reaction was one of elation and ecstasy, for even the most introspective people enjoy the company of others from time to time, and Tiny Tim had been a long while out of touch with human contact.

For their part, the members of the coroner's staff found themselves basking in our hero's joy with the same pleasure one might feel upon hearing for the first time that one's long-pined-for true love reciprocated one's sense of ardor with equal passion. So, for that brief while, the morgue became a place glowing with immense jocularity, equanimity, optimism, and all things pleasing and pleasant.

As nice a change as this was for those tasked with the daily care and handling of corpses, the rest of the hospital staff quickly became unsettled by it all and decided the shift toward brighter sentiments among their previously morbid colleagues was incongruous and unprofessional. The administration launched an inventory-taking of potentially intoxicating solvents used in the morgue, which failed to turn up any discrepancies that could not more easily be explained away as evaporation into thin air than evaporation into ravenous nasal passages. So the matter was dropped after the hospital administrator called forth Dr. Rigger, the coroner, and sternly said, "It is clear to me, if your people do not stop enjoying their work immediately, morale will suffer. Get on it, man, or I'll be forced to assume a most uncomfortable attitude in relation to your department, to ensure an appropriate level of professional gloominess is restored to fullness and conveyed by all."

This warning, however, proved unnecessary, as Tiny Tim once again grew bored with being cheerful all the time and once again began experimenting with the other emotions along the spectrum. By this time, he had acquired some considerable dexterity in handling his feelings. He could create and erase a flash of anger in an instant or hold a steady note of fascination for hours. He could move through the postures of anxiety with the grace of a ballerina and the agility of a gymnast. He could blend lust and sadness, joy and envy, fear and regret, or any other combination for staggering dramatic effect. In short, he was becoming a consummate artist of pure feeling.

As entertaining as this was for our hero, it was most disruptive for the morgue. None could stand to be within its walls for long, and all secretly suspected they were going mad. Being men of science, none wanted to point the blame at Tiny Tim, though everyone could sense his presence at the center of it all. Within each man, the same debate was waged much along the following logical lines:

"I do not believe in ghosts. Ghosts are superstition. But there is something about that monstrous boy. Is he haunted? Nonsense! A corpse cannot be haunted. Everyone knows houses are haunted, gallows are haunted, dead bodies are not haunted. If there's a ghost still in the machine, the machine's not dead yet. Yes! That's it. But he is dead. Dead as a doornail. Or coffin nail perhaps. Yes, that is deader, isn't it? But I don't believe in ghosts. Not a bit of it. By Jove, I don't believe in hauntings, either. No. Nonsense, all of it. Utter nonsense. No ghost in the machine. The machine's just … Good God! What is the machine? I don't know. Nobody knows. All we know is there are no ghosts. Still, there's something about that wretched boy. Either he's haunted or I'm mad … mad to believe he's haunted. Oh, blast! I should have gone into proctology like the mater wanted."

As we all know, madness can be a pleasant and comforting thing when shared equally by friends and relations and others of one's political and religious leanings. However, for those chosen to spend their days surrounded by disused bodies—whole or dismembered, deformed by injury or the myriad fatal ailments—the prospect of insanity can be disquieting. Even difficult to bear.

And this condition of disquietude only grew worse within the morgue as Tiny Tim developed an artistic fascination for blind rage and rabid hatred. At first this outwardly manifested simply as horrible arguments between staff members, but it soon escalated to the wielding of sharp instruments—of which there were many within easy reach. But it was only when stabbings and slashings became a daily occurrence that Dr. Rigger decided enough was enough and gave the order to remove our hero to the home of those who had brought him hence and apparently forgotten him.

Of course, Dr. Rigger had no rational reason for sending Tiny Tim to the Cratchits. Like everyone else in the morgue, he could sense the boy was the source of the strange emotional manifestations; but equally so, he was afraid to say as much out loud, in the belief he was the only one who sensed it, and to announce the idea formally would risk ridicule, career, and reputation. Fortunately for him, the Department of Accounts Receivable, upon being notified Tiny Tim was to be transported home, delivered to the concerned coroner an invoice for hospital expenses that was to be conveyed along with the corpse to Mr. and Mrs. Cratchit. It was then that Rigger saw the excuse he had been craving: to wit, the boy was being returned on compassionate grounds to save his poor parents additional expense.

And so it was.

CHAPTER 6

Upon arrival at the Cratchit house and all during his carriage ride from the morgue to there, Tiny Tim had been in a state of alarm and confusion. This is understandable, given that all channels of observation leading from the external world to his internal being had been severed, leaving him incapable of seeing, hearing, tasting, smelling, or feeling anything that would indicate his geographical situation was undergoing revision. All he could sense was the proximity of some rather dull strangers (the four strong-arms), one center of nervousness (the forgettable coroner's assistant) and one melancholic, bored-with-labor creature (the carriage horse), which was not enough to tell him what was going on. He then sensed fear and anxiety mixed liberally with a growing sense of forlorn impotence, which, even in its totality, was insufficient to tell him he was in the presence of his parents.

This unabated confusion experienced by Tiny Tim was, like all his strong feelings, quite infectious, and so his arrival on the scene only served to exacerbate the complete paralysis of thought into which Mr. and Mrs. Cratchit had arrived and from which they were rescued only by the arrival of Belinda, Matthew, and Lucy.

Belinda's shock and irritation were enough to retrieve Tiny Tim's attention out of his dense miasma of mixed confusions and spark his curiosity in her direction. It was the presence of Lucy, however, next to his head that told him he was once again among family, and the joy that erupted from the center of his being equaled Vesuvius showing off to the Pompeiians.

This sudden change in mood was what Lucy found so funny, for it is the sudden shifting from one established sense of things to another unpredicted sense of things that is the essence of humor. Of course, once Lucy had started laughing, Tiny Tim was quick to pick it up internally only to radiate it externally, which was what got Matthew and then Belinda to laughing too.

Had Bob and his wife not been so embroiled in the turmoil of their problems, they would have been taken by the merriment as well, but alas, they were only marginally lifted from their torment—just enough, in fact, to allow Bob to see clearly what must be done and say, "Enough of this, for now, my dears. We must pack our few belongings, as tomorrow we must move to new lodgings and time is running short."

It was fortunate, in the short while, that Bob did not think to tell them the entirety of the story leading up to this necessity for accelerated preparation, for it would likely have gone badly for them all if he had. Had he done so, the children would then have had reason to worry about what was coming next, but ignorance is bliss—as you've likely heard said—and in their ignorance of what was about to happen, they all assumed they would be leaving on the morrow for the stately home Mrs. Cratchit had chosen and secured by way of deposit with a wholly unsubstantiated check, as has already been related.

The children, then, put to work with excited joy, which was joined in by Peter, the eldest of the Cratchit boys, and Martha, the eldest of the daughters, when they arrived home from work. The efforts of the children extended well into the night, and by the rising of the sun, their boxes and bundles of belongings were being stacked outside in readiness for the carriage due at noon. Then Bob, Peter, and Matthew put themselves to bringing out as many of the larger furnishings as they could manage while Mrs. Cratchit, Martha, Belinda, and Lucy saw to the smaller bits and pieces.

By the time the carriage arrived, the family was exhausted from their efforts. But only Bob and his wife felt any sense of concern, as the children were all still in their unfounded state of joyous anticipation.

"We's here under orders of B. Philius Gazpayne, esquire," said the wagon master officiously, "to transport one Robert Cratchit and family, along with 'abiliments and what-'ave-yers, to alternating abodes specified by the squire hisself."

"We're ready," said Bob meekly and feebly, and the loading of the wagon began.

The wagon master and his brutish assistant hefted the heavier furniture aboard but left Bob and the children to load the rest. Finally, Tiny Tim was carried out upon his stretcher by Bob, Matthew, and Peter, with the reluctant help of the hired men, and raised onto the rear of the wagon, where he was secured with rope as best the movers could manage, given that they were largely unfamiliar with the securing of corpses.

Fortunately, Tiny Tim was transmitting the excitement he picked up from his siblings, which, in turn, was picked up by the movers, and so they minded handling the dead body somewhat less than might otherwise have been the case despite it being an activity beyond the perimeter of their daily expectations.

When all was done and they were on their way, the wagon master turned to Bob and said, "It might be none of me business, sir, but I was wondering why it is you keeps a dead bloke in your house."

"He's our son," said Bob dolefully.

"Oh," said the mover, as if his curiosity was sated. "Still. Most tends to give up on keeping them about when they's dead, you know. I suppose he's got sentimental value, has he?"

"In a manner of speaking, I suppose," said Bob, feeling rather awkward. "We will see to his final rest when we get our money problems put to rights."

Martha overheard this comment. Till then, she'd been curious why they were traveling southeast, toward the docks and factories, rather than northwest, in the direction of the house her mother had chosen, but her father's statement caused her to raise her idle curiosity to a more robust concern over what was actually in the offing.

After that, except for Matthew and Lucy larking about in their seats in the rear, they traveled in silence for some while before Mrs. Cratchit asked, "Here. Why does all this look familiar, then?"

Bob raised his head from his hands to take in his surroundings. "It's where we lived before Mr. Scrooge took to looking after us," he said rather sickly.

"Here we are then," said the wagon master cheerfully, still awash, as he was, in the overflow of Tiny Tim's familial joy. "Home at last."

"We can't live here," said Mrs. Cratchit. "It's our old house! The one we give up to better ourselves."

"It's only temporary, my dear," said Bob, scarcely able to believe what was before him. "Just till we settle with the courts and the surgeons that done in our Tim."

"We can't live here," said Mrs. Cratchit again—having, as previously displayed, a propensity to repeat herself when upset.

"I can takes you wherever you wants," said the wagon master cheerily. "But B. Philius Gazpayne, esquire, is only paid to bring you here, so anywheres else I takes you will cost you out your own pocket."

"We've nowhere else to go," said the plaintive Bob, and he climbed down to inspect the painful reminder of his past. "It hasn't changed much, I must say."

Martha was well aware of what was happening the moment she recognized the street where she had grown up. Her expression was enough to tip off Belinda that their expectations of a brighter future were less than solidly founded. Peter, Matthew, and Lucy, though, sustained their misplaced optimism even up to the point when their father jumped down from the wagon to inspect the old house, which was the place of all the children's births. Indeed Matthew, in an effort to understand what he was seeing, concluded that this punctuation in their travels was merely a whim on his parents' part to take a sentimental journey for the purposes of heightening their sense of gratitude for the great fortune they were poised to enjoy, by way of contrasting it to the circumstances whence they had come, and the family would soon be on its way again to the great estate he had heard so much about.

It is easy, then, to imagine the collective disappointment of all when it became obvious to everyone this was their final destination. Tiny Tim, up to this point, had remained happy to share in the happiness of his more sanguine siblings and had not taken to heart the doubts of his two eldest sisters. The sharp shard of dismay went through him like a sword when Peter, Matthew, and Lucy, as one, realized that their foray into the future was to be a retreat into their past.

Mrs. Cratchit, as we have seen, was not willing to accept this sitting down—or standing up or lying down or in any other posture anatomically possible, for the matter of that. She allowed the wagon master's assistant to help her descend from the cart but immediately headed off in a huff back up the street they had just come down.

"Where are you going, my dear?" asked Bob.

"To see that scoundrel Gazpayne!" shouted Mrs. Cratchit over her shoulder. "I'll get this put to right, I will."

Bob was not at all certain he could stop her or even lessen the impact of her blunt will upon the situation, but he felt he had to try, nonetheless.

"Martha," he said, "see that our things get put where they belong," and he started off in pursuit of his purposeful wife.

"Here," shouted the wagon master. "Give us a help with the body afore you go. He's too bloody heavy without you."

In a tither though he was, Bob returned to help get Tiny Tim inside before heading back into the street and running full tilt to the building occupied by Rankin, Fowle, O'Durr, and Gazpayne, where he arrived in the antechamber of Gazpayne's office to find Mrs. Cratchit giving full vent to her ire upon the ear of the lawyer's clerk.

"I don't give a fig if Beelzebub hisself is with him now," said the irate woman. "I'll bloody well see him this instinct or there'll be hell to pay."

"Please, Emily, my dear," said Bob. "Let's not go making an inconvenience of ourselves. Once our case is settled, we'll have our money back …"

"You think that miserable, farthing-clutching, wrapped-scallion Gazpayne, can't put us in 'ceptable lodgings till then? He's got my—"

And, with that, the doors to the maligned attorney's office swung open to reveal a rampant nose followed by the towering figure of Gazpayne striding forth with malignant eyes and malignant bearing.

"Mr. Scribble," the lawyer commanded his clerk. "Hourglass."

The timepiece on the clerk's desk was flipped, and Bob felt a poke to his heart, for he'd come to see the lawyer's hourglass as an instrument of exsanguination.

"Fresh sheet of paper," said Gazpayne. "Title: Meeting. Today's date. My name. Your name. Robert Cratchit and wife. Two strokes to begin, as they will pay for Lord Squelch's time as well as their own while His Lordship is compelled to await my return to my office. Now then. What is the meaning of this unwarranted and unsavory disruption of my productive labors?"

"You put us back where we come from," said Mrs. Cratchit. "It weren't suitable to us when we lived there, and it ain't suitable to us now."

"I fail to see why," said Gazpayne. "It keeps the elements out with some sufficiency, does it not?"

"Yes, but …"

"And keeps your privacy in, with equal effect, does it not?"

"Mostly, I 'spects …"

"Then you should be thankful for small blessings and set yourselves to the task of making it as palatable as possible for the duration of your stay. As to my part in settling with your creditors, I have taken upon myself a personal stake that far exceeds the normal limits of caution. I am not in the habit of doing this for everyone, mind you, but fortunately for you, I was in a giddy, celebratory mood yesterday when you came to see me. My native sound judgment was thus uncharacteristically shifted toward whimsical abandon, and I lost all sense of professional distance when considering the pathetic predicament into which you have descended and from which you wish extrication. By rights, I should have forfeited all the deposits on your myriad pending purchases and held it up to you as a hard-learned lesson in fiscal prudence. But rather than see your finances pillaged in this wasteful manner, I elected to become your mortgagor and assume personal responsibility for everything. The house, the lands, the furnishings—everything you incautiously sought to acquire—is paid for in full and will be waiting in readiness for you upon satisfactory completion of our litigation."

"What's this mean?" asked Mrs. Cratchit.

"It means, my dear," said Bob, "that Mr. Gazpayne, here, has fixed our problems with the bank by lending us the money to pay for all you bought."

"Quite so, my good lady," said the lawyer. "I do not routinely extend such personal care to my clients, but your innocence of fiduciary methodology has touched my heart, as it reminds me of myself in a less tutored time of life."

Here Gazpayne stopped to flick a tear from the corner of his eye.

"When I was eleven," he said, with a slight tremor in his voice, "I craved the affection of Amelia Rayshun, the prettiest girl in school, and to win her approval, I told her I loved her. Were it not so painful a memory, I could laugh at myself now for my youthful willingness to squander my limited resources on a mere fancy." He then grew serious and commanding. "But there is no reason you cannot learn from my folly. I have spared you from considerable loss in the belief you will assume, from this date forward, a soberer course of conduct. Do you understand?"

"Of course we do, sir," said Bob in a hurry to get his wife away, but he saw Scribble flip the hourglass and put two more strokes on the page. With a sigh, the hopelessly disconsolate Cratchit slumped his shoulders and awaited what would follow.

"Good, then," said Gazpayne. "Now you need not concern yourselves over repayment. That will be settled when we win our case, along with all the other accumulated expenses to be defrayed. But, as you are here, Mr. Scribble has prepared a list of shops in which you can acquire whatever you require. These businesses are all owned by my partners and me, and we are more than comfortable forgoing all payment until matters are brought to an effective conclusion. Mr. Scribble: the list, if you please."

The clerk extracted the carefully penned document from a drawer and handed it to the couple.

"Most generous, I must say," said Bob.

"Think nothing of it," said Gazpayne. "And, having been something of an accountant yourself, Mr. Cratchit, you will understand that a simple compounding of interest on all outstanding debts is only to be expected."

"Oh, quite," said Bob with a strange sense of just having lost an organ to surgical removal.

"But our rates are more than fair," said Gazpayne. "In fact, they exceed the bounds of fairness to the full degree sanctioned by the law, and seeing that the litigation should be over soon, the impact should not be overly traumatic to your treasure."

"Thank you, sir," said Bob, and he gently attempted to pull his wife away.

The hourglass was flipped again as Scribble added two more strokes of the quill to the sheet that lay helpless before him like a victim stretched out for a whipping. In his empathy for the tortured page, poor Bob flinched with each of the strokes.

"How is it, then," said Mrs. Cratchit, "you come to own our old house?"

Gazpayne raised a palm toward heaven and replied almost reverentially, "The late Mr. Scrooge had acquired it upon your moving out, with a view to having it demolished. Fortunately for you—given recent events—he procrastinated and passed on to his divine reward before executing his intention. We, as you know, were responsible for seeing to the liquidation of the old gentleman's estate, so rather than trust it to possible undervaluing in auction, we purchased everything outright at fair market value, thereby eliminating this risk and the usual expenses that inevitably arise from less efficient means of proceeding."

"And we're most appreciative for all you've done," said Bob, pulling more insistently at his wife's arm. "Come along then, my dear. We've taken up enough of Mr. Gazpayne's valuable time. And Mr. Scribble's, too, for the matter of that."

The greatly irritated Mrs. Cratchit did not budge.

"Quite right," said Gazpayne. "Go home and make yourselves as comfortable as possible, given your circumstances. But I do encourage you to spend time in reflection over your folly and learn from your misguided ways before you regain captaincy of your fortune and pilot it onto the rocky hazards inherent in life's navigations."

Mrs. Cratchit was about to ask another question when Bob pulled, yet again, upon her arm, this time with sufficient force to topple her from her feet and against him.

"For the sake of our children, don't let him flip that hourglass again," said Bob in a whisper, and he compelled her toward the exit.

"But I wasn't finished talking," said Mrs. Cratchit upon arrival in the street.

"You can talk to the children free of charge, my dear," said Bob, taking her arm. "And to equal effect, I might add."

CHAPTER 7

The moving in was orchestrated most efficiently by Martha, who was well-seconded in these efforts by Belinda. Peter, having inherited more of his father's propensities than his mother's, was gifted with a greater capacity to obey orders than to imagine or provide them. He was strong enough of back, however, to help Matthew with the placement of the heavier furnishings, the heaviest pieces having been placed by the wagon master and his assistant.

Lucy helped as best she could under Belinda's kindly supervision, despite being in tears throughout owing to the overwhelming disappointment of finding their great expectations for their new home so greatly reversed.

And the disappointment felt by all infected Tiny Tim to the degree he became a dynamo of hopelessness, charging the atmosphere with such dark despair that those passing the house in the street felt compelled to turn back rather than approach too near the center of the gloom. This, however, crashed to an abrupt end with the return of Mr. and Mrs. Cratchit, as her simmering resentment was still hot enough to boil off the thick vapors of despondency.

Soon after the arrival of their parents, the children started bickering as Tiny Tim picked up on his mother's annoyance and, shifting his mood in that direction, began radiating waves of irritation with the same power and amplitude as the waves of despair they replaced. Within minutes of the first fight breaking out, Bob and his wife were arguing too and saying things to each other and to their offspring that would shatter the substance of any family less bound with love for one another than was the family Cratchit.

This squabbling would likely have continued unabated for days, had not a forceful knock on the door shocked them all into silence.

"Police! Open up!" came the imperious command.

Sheepishly, Bob approached the front door and opened it to an imposing wall of brass-buttoned dark blue outside.

"'Scuse me, sir," said the enormous constable. "These articles of furnishings and sundry items of a personal nature belong to you, by any chance, do they, sir?"

With that, the policeman stepped to one side and indicated the pile of belongings still remaining in the street.

"Yes, officer, they are. We only now moved here from a larger home, you see, and not everything we own now fits inside."

"Fallen on hard times, have you, sir?"

"In a manner of speaking, yes. We are temporarily inconvenienced, you might say."

"Sorry to hear it, sir. But with regard to these articles of furnishings and sundry items of a personal nature—which you have confessed to being of your possession—I must instruct you that this we have here before us is a thoroughfare of public utility, and the law prohibits the locating of items, reasonably construed as obstacles, that might bring about an impediment to the normal flow of commerce and civic enterprise within thoroughfares of public utility. I must ask you to take your belongings inside forthwith and without further delay."

"But there's no more room inside," said Bob, leaning back to look up to the blinking gray eyes.

"Then you must cart it all away."

"But we've no money. I can't afford to hire a cart."

The constable's thick eyebrows rose to disappear under his helmet. "Would it be reasonable to assume, sir, that were I to present you with the usual fine for this offense, you would be incapable of rendering payment on it?"

"Yes," said Bob. "That is the substance of the situation, as it were."

"In that case, I'm sorry, sir, to inform you I have no choice but to take you into custody until such time as the offending articles of furnishings and sundry items of a personal nature have been removed from this thoroughfare of public utility, and the amount of one pound, one shilling paid to the treasury of the city. Come along, then, sir."

Poor Bob was about to argue that the day his family could raise a guinea for his release was far, far into the unforeseeable future, but the culmination of events of the previous twenty-four hours had left him without the heart to mount an objection.

"Can I take a moment to say good-bye to my children?"

"All right then. I'm not without feelings, but—just so you're not tempted to attempt a diversionary egress out the back—I must insist upon coming inside with you while you're about it."

"Of course," said Bob, and he invited the constable in before closing the door behind him and moving around the imposing titan in blue to address his family.

"It would appear I've broken the law, my dears," said Bob to his children, "and I must go with the policeman to jail. Please, come and get me when Mr. Gazpayne wins us our money. You won't forget now, will you?"

With that, the sadness of Bob reached Tiny Tim, who amplified it well beyond containment and flooded the room with sorrow. Everyone burst into tears. Even the policeman's chin was quivering above his helmet-strap as he fought unsuccessfully to maintain a professional steeliness of deportment.

After many a lachrymose hug and kiss, Bob turned to his captor and nodded his willingness to be taken into his incarceration. The constable opened the door for Bob, and out he walked, only to be shocked into paralysis when the policeman yelled a mere foot above his ear, "Cheeky beggars! Someone's absconded with all your property, sir! And done it with an officer of the law standing right there inside your house."

With that, the big constable slapped an angry hand down on Bob's shoulder and made to propel him forward, but in that moment, a thought came to the perennially unfortunate Cratchit.

"It must be most embarrassing for you," said Bob sympathetically as he walked under the weight of the heavy hand, "to have so bold a crime committed in broad daylight with you being so close by."

"It is that," murmured the constable. "And I'll thank you to keep it to yourself when we arrives at the station."

"Oh, most certainly, officer. It was clear enough you were blameless in the matter, so no one will hear a word of it from me, I can assure you."

"That's very kind of you, sir, I must say," said the policeman. But he then sighed deeply, shook his head, and added in frustration, "Dear me. There was a time a thing like this would have been beyond believing, but today's class of criminal is a nervy lot and then some. Makes you wonder what the world's coming to, it does."

"I'm sure you've seen your share of it."

"Oh, that I have, and no mistaking."

"Yes, I thought so. And I don't mean to tell you your business or implicate anything that's not proper, but hasn't the crime for which I'm being arrested been solved to the satisfaction of the law?"

The constable stopped still, put his massive fists on his massive hips and said, "Here! What are you suggesting?"

"Oh, nothing, officer. I'm only making the observation that my offense lay in the fact of me being unable to remove my possessions from the street, but now they are gone and no longer in violation of any city orderlinesses."

"But you can hardly take credit for the crime what rendered your belongings lawful."

"Perhaps not, but all the law required from you was to see to it that the offending possessions were removed from the street, and they are now gone, so it could be said, without fear of contraception, that you have been successful in the execution of your duty."

"Hmm. I can see your point."

"So putting me in jail for the offense—I presume you can also see—would only cast doubt on your success in maintaining the law, as the need to deprive me of my freedom would only be proper if you've failed in achieving the requirements of the law. Which you haven't."

The big policeman took his chin in one hand and his elbow in the other and considered this for some while before saying, "All right then, sir. Seeing as you been a cooperative sort—which I don't see often enough in my line of work—and the offense, to which you been guilty, has been resolved to the general satisfaction of the law, I'll release you with a warning not to make further impedances of thoroughfares of public utility from here on in, and keep your belongings to yourself where they belong."

"Oh, I will, officer; I promise. And thank you."

"Off you go then," said the policeman, and he set off in search of other crimes to solve with equal skill and success.

As Bob trotted the several steps back to his house, he was overcome with joy. He could scarcely believe his great good luck in being robbed of one-third of his earthly possessions just when everything seemed to be going so badly.

Bob's unexpected return to the bosom of the Cratchit household propelled everyone to vistas of unbounded joy. In an instant, Tiny Tim felt it, too, coming upon him in swell after swell of bliss. Our hero's heart lit up like a welcoming home fire, which continued to burn for months and to sustain the wretched family through days of ever-increasing adversity.

CHAPTER 8

Following shortly after the death of Scrooge and the reading of his will, both Martha and Peter had expressed desires to leave their respective employments and become persons of leisure. This worried Bob, who—after years of keeping Scrooge's books—saw his wife's propensity to look upon their wealth as infinite and inexhaustible as evidence it was finite to the point of insufficiency. He first advised the two to bide their time awhile, just until some understanding could be gained of what the fortune was exactly. Then he persuaded them further by suggesting that once the case against the surgeons was settled, he would buy the firm that paid Peter five-and-sixpence a week and the milliners at which Martha was nearing the end of her apprenticeship. He would then see to their rapid advancement within a long-term plan of awarding them full ownership, which would bring with it both independence of means and status in society.

To this, Martha behaved wisely. Not only did she remain where she was, but she also remained silent regarding her family's altered circumstances and kept her father's plan a secret. The treatment she received at the hands of her employers and fellow workers did not change, therefore, as no one was aware of any reason to treat her any differently.

Peter, though, chose a less sagacious path to follow. He announced to one and all that Ebenezer Scrooge had left his family a massive fortune and expounded upon his father's intention to buy the firm, as soon as it could be arranged, with a view to making Peter master of it. At first, this worked to the young Cratchit's advantage. The owners saw this as a means to early and comfortable retirement, and took to doing all things possible and imaginable to enhance the appearance of the establishment's success to increase its sale value when the day arrived. They took Peter to lunches and fed him well and lightened his workload in the office in an effort to win his favor as well as glean any available intelligence regarding when an offer might be expected. Peter's workmates also took every opportunity to improve their relations with him in light of the notion they would all be raised to management when Peter took the reins and sacked everyone above the age of twenty-five.

So it came to pass, when news of the Cratchit family's move back to the old factory district gained currency, it affected Martha not at all, beyond her supervisor warning her the longer walk to work would not be accepted as an excuse for lateness.

Peter, however, was branded a liar and dismissed on grounds of untrustworthiness. Word traveled quickly that he was unsound of character and given to weaving and believing ridiculous fantasies. Soon there was not a business in the Good Old City that had not been forewarned of his blackened reputation, and all efforts on his part to find employment gained him nothing but violent ejections and deprecating rejections.

But, as has been said, the spirits of the family remained buoyant owing to Tiny Tim's ongoing emotional influence. Those who stayed at home all day stayed happy all day, and Peter and Martha quickly regained their happiness upon reentry, whatever their days outside their domicile brought them.

Lucy, especially, and Matthew, though with less certainty, could feel it was Tiny Tim who perpetrated this aura of well-being, but the rest of the Cratchits passed this idea off as nonsense. Still, Bob was quick to caution the elder members of the family to allow his youngest daughter her fanciful imaginings.

"It's her way of understanding what's too much to bear," he said. "We should be thankful our Tim's not turned green, as that would spoil it for her, I'm sure."

So, despite Lucy being at this point in time fourteen years of age and bright for her years, Mrs. Cratchit and the elder Cratchit children allowed Lucy to believe in the magic of Tiny Tim's feelings, much as all adults allow little ones to believe in wicked witches, hobgoblins, evil ogres, wise politicians, and all manner of myths created to bring comfort to undeveloped minds. For their own part, the senior members of the family believed that the glowing sense of well-being permeating their collective being was entirely due to their closeness to one another, since they had always found it reason enough to inspire optimism—even in the dark times before Scrooge's period of beneficence.

At long last, the day came for the case of Robert Cratchit, gentleman, versus Sir Axeworthy Blundt, surgeon; Reginald Thickstitch, surgeon; Artemis Klamp, surgeon; and Smedley Snyffe, physician, to be tried.

The Honorable Sir Justice Ruff-Birching entered the somber oak-lined courtroom with the funereal solemnity of a melancholic raven crossing a graveyard. He stopped before sitting to scan the contents of his court, and showing no sign of recognition for anyone there or even for where he might be, he sat.

The judge craned his head forward, fixed his eyes on Bob Cratchit—who was seated next to Gazpayne at the plaintiff's bench— and remained thus for several seconds. The features of the judge's deeply lined face seemed to defy their natural boundaries. His narrow eyes appeared not only to unite across the bridge of his great, amorphous, purple nose, but also to extend past the borders of his face. Likewise, the corners of his frown were not corners at all but canyonlike grooves that descended vertically to slice wedges in his jaw either side his wattled, lumpy chin. Bob felt himself melt and tremble and melt some more.

Ruff-Birching sat up straight, as if with surprise. He put his attention to organizing his bench. After much shuffling of paper; a perusal of documents; and the opening, closing, and setting aside of two enormous books, he looked to the bailiff and raised a gnarled finger.

The stout bailiff stepped forward and went into his long, droning recitation of date, time, place, court authority, court personnel, and summary essence of the case while the three court reporters took down his words. Nervously, Bob turned to assess the four doctors and four lawyers crowding the bench of the defense, behind which sat the congregation of secondary lawyers, law clerks, investigators, and errand runners of all sorts that constituted the population of his adversary. He looked to Gazpayne, who was seated beside him, apparently lost in a supercilious stupor or daze, with his large head and nose wavering back and forth atop his narrow neck.

Suddenly Gazpayne rose to his feet, startling Bob from his wits and nearly from his water.

"If it pleases the court …" said the barrister, but he was not permitted another syllable.

"No, it does not please the court, sir," roared Ruff-Birching. "It does not please the court one iota. And before one more drop of Her Majesty's ink is wasted on the recording of this farcical proceeding, I will tell you, Mr. Gazpayne, that the bringing of frivolous litigation into Her Majesty's courts of law is the thin end of a wedge that will be driven between the oaken planks that are the foundation of this empire, should we not do our duty to prevent it from being so—the greatest empire the world has ever known, within which we take shelter from the barbaric chaos of foreign ways, within which we enjoy greater wealth and comfort and security than has ever been possible in any time before the present, and within which we are morally obligated to feel gratitude to God for allowing us to be born British; to our queen for providing to us the fabric of civilization; and to her judiciary for protecting us from the banditry of every scoundrel that would take a shilling, undeservedly, from those among us who apply themselves selflessly to the task of building and sustaining the structure of society, which I hold dear and have sworn to preserve whole and intact. Look to that plaguy, scabrous, scurvy-clad, pox-riddled, verminous, degenerate worm seated beside you, sir, and marvel at the generosity and compassion of Her Majesty in allowing the likes of him to crawl upon the hallowed grounds of her sceptered isle, and ask yourself what moral vacuity you must have been traversing when you considered representing such a vile personage as he. Look at him! Purple with guilt and shame! [Bob's deep redness of face was actually from fear and embarrassment.] Then look to the honorable men he seeks to despoil. Bastions of learning, both ancient and modern; paragons of noble virtue; officers in the war against disease, whose sharp weapons cut to heal. In what void of virtue do you reside, Mr. Gazpayne, that you might find one shred of justification in bringing litigation against these fine British gentlemen of science and the healing arts?"

But the judge didn't give the barrister a chance to reply, not for an instant. In fact, the aged jurist continued on without a pause and with surprising stamina, in much the same vein as has been reported to now, alternately decimating every facet of Bob's character while extolling every facet of those of the doctors, and questioning Gazpayne's right to practice law while stating again and again, with exhaustive reiteration, his own sacred duty in putting an end to the fallacious assumption, within which society was then currently gripped, that the rights granted to all extended to those of no consequence.

This diatribe went on through the luncheon hour and well into the late afternoon. At length—and after the expenditure of some gallons of Her Majesty's ink (not to mention many reams of her paper)—the Honorable Sir Justice Ruff-Birching pronounced, "I am, therefore, dismissing this case, with prejudice, and placing the burden of court costs and all legal costs incurred by the defendants upon the plaintiff, and advise him to be thankful I do not fine him for making a public nuisance of himself. Furthermore, Mr. Gazpayne, I admonish you to think hard before bringing another such case before the Crown. Case closed. I'm going sailing. Court adjourned." He banged his gavel with sufficient force to split its head in half and send the two pieces down upon the two remaining court reporters seated before the bench—the third having been removed from the room about an hour earlier after passing out from exhaustion and crippling writer's cramp.

"Well," said Gazpayne bitterly once the judge had left. "That is what I get for granting the upper hand to idealism, I suppose. But all in all, it might have been worse; might it not, my dear Cratchit?"

"If you say so, sir," said Bob, still numb from the verbal battering he'd received.

"Yes, I do," said the lawyer. "But, after many a hard-fought battle, the war is over. Time to bury our dead and lick clean our wounds. We have only to settle your accounts, and we can part company in the full knowledge we have given our all in a valiant enterprise."

"If you say so, sir," said Bob, just as his family arrived at his side to commiserate and accompany him out.

"Well, at least we can move out of that hovel," said Martha as she helped her father to his feet.

"Oh, yes!" said Mrs. Cratchit, brightening greatly to the suggestion. "We can have our money back now, can't we, Mr. Gazpayne?"

"It was never outside of your possession, my dear lady, but if I am to assume you mean by that, that the firm of Rankin, Fowle, O'Durr, and Gazpayne can now relinquish the power of attorney over your financial affairs, then I can assure you that will come to fruition within the next few weeks—two months, possibly … three at the outside—once all the incurred costs have been satisfactorily covered."

"So when can we move into our new house?" asked Peter.

"What new house?" asked Gazpayne.

"The one you been holding for us," said Mrs. Cratchit, "till these legal consternations got dealt with."

"Oh, that house!" said Gazpayne, standing to his full height. "The mortgage on that house fell subject to foreclosure five months ago. The property is no longer within your possession."

"What?" said Mrs. Cratchit.

"You failed to make the payments for three consecutive months. You cannot conduct your affairs with that kind of cavalier delinquency and expect your actions to be without consequences."

"But you held that mortgage," said Bob.

"That I did. As a kindness to you, you will recall."

"And you got control of our money."

"Now, as to that, you are mistaken. I, individually and privately, do not have your power of attorney and never did. Clearly, you did not read the document before signing it. In future, I advise you never to sign anything without first seeking legal advice. Be that as it may—to correct your misconception—the firm, of which I am only the junior partner, is your designated trustee, and it takes its responsibility quite seriously. In regard to your case specifically, I was entrusted to conduct your affairs on behalf of the firm, but for me to direct funds from your accounts to my own for reasons beyond the payment of my legal services would have been a conflict of interest. My hands were tied. I had no alternative but to withhold payment and allow the mortgage to go into arrears. Fortunately for you, in the offset, my partners were willing to assume some risk on your behalf and allowed me to pay down the principle from your assets before I assumed the mortgage on the balance. The total debt you were unable to honor is, then, relatively small and should not prove excessively embarrassing for you in future financial dealings."

"I'm obliged to you for that," said Bob, having picked up more of Gazpayne's last sentence than of the preceding ones.

"Think nothing of it. Your well-being is our sole concern."

With that, the lawyer nodded his farewell and left the disheartened family to wend their way home.

"Does this mean we have to stay living where we are?" asked Matthew.

"For the time being, my dears," said Bob. "Until the accounts are all settled when we'll get what's left of Mr. Scrooge's money back and make some modest improvements on our circumstances. We just have to be patient a little while longer."

But, alas, the bubble of the paternal Cratchit's optimism was soon to suffer a quick and implosive deflation.

CHAPTER 9

The following day, Martha, the eldest of the Cratchit children—and the sole remaining avenue of income for the family—set off, as the sun was rising and a light autumn breeze blowing, to walk to work. She arrived at her usual time in her usual manner, but the manner of her sister milliners was not usual at all. Rather than the efficient pleasantness she expected upon her arrival, she was greeted with looks of hostile disdain that caused her to think she might have trodden inadvertently through horse leavings on her way through the streets, but a quick check of her shoes and skirt hem failed to validate this hypothesis.

"So you thinks you can sue your way to wealth and luxury, does you?" asked one elderly spinster.

"Like doctors don't kill people regular, like, as part of their job," said one of the apprentices.

"I never—" began Martha, but the manageress appeared from her office and all stopped to curtsey.

"Miss Cratchit! Come with me," said the matronly master of hats, and she led the way back into her tiny office, where she sidled through the narrow gap past her desk to take her imposing chair behind it.

Martha followed in terror just inside the door, closed it behind her, and stood before it, trembling, wide-eyed, and crushing the fingers of her left hand in the grip of her right.

"It has come to our attention, Miss Cratchit, that your family has made a scurrilous attempt to bring legal proceedings against some of

Britain's finest and noblest physicians. Not only does this cast serious doubt upon your character, in and of itself, but it further places me in a completely untenable position as to your continued employment here, for the reason that all the wives, daughters, sisters, and nieces of Britain's finest and noblest physicians patronize this establishment— or would if they learned of our existence—and I cannot have it known I allow one so vilely slanted toward envisioning their husbands, fathers, brothers, and uncles as targets of piracy to remain within the bosom of our fold. You are herewith dismissed. Collect your things forthwith, and leave the premises without further delay. And I suggest, should you or your kinsfolk ever be tempted to entertain piratical methods again, you should limit yourselves to the wearing of tricorn hats and eyepatches and leave the brigandage to the professionals."

Needless to say, this stunned poor Martha, first to silence and then to tears. All the way home, she wept the weeping of the unbelieving, for she could not believe this was happening to her. Furthermore, she could not help feeling that the unkindness of it all was wholly unwarranted, for she had never thought of herself as the bringer of litigation against the doctors. Indeed, she had often thought—though never said aloud—the action was more nuisance than it was worth, seeing they could be enjoying Uncle Ebenezer's fortune fully were it not for her mother's insistence on seeking her pound of flesh.

"What are you doing home, my dear?" asked Bob. "And why are you crying?"

"I've been given the sack," said Martha. "They can't have girls who sue doctors working there. It's bad for business, as doctors' wives won't shop there if they do."

"Well, never you mind. You'll find something else, and even if you don't, we'll soon get the balance of Mr. Scrooge's leavings given back to us, and you needn't work at all if you don't have a mind to."

With that, the door burst open with a bang, and in stormed Mrs. Cratchit, followed by the remainder of the Cratchit clan.

"They've all denied us further spending," she shrieked.

"What do you mean, my dear? Who's denied us?"

"Them what Gazpayne told us to buy from. The butcher, the baker, the cheesemonger—the whole bleeding lot of them. They say the owners won't allow more credit as the trial is done and over and they were only supposed to give it us till then."

"I'm sure it's just a misunderstanding," said Bob. "I'll go and see Mr. Gazpayne and get it cleared up." He rose to claim his hat on his hurried way out.

Bob had moved with enough haste to avoid anyone offering to accompany him, for despite his reassurances to his family, he was beginning to suspect things were poised for another downturn, and he wanted to preserve whatever joy remained to his wife and children for whatever moments remained to it.

"That is only to be expected," said Gazpayne, as if it were all obvious to an idiot. "We could extend credit to you while the case was before the courts, but that is no longer the case, and we must now demand cash or welcome you to shop elsewhere."

"But why?" asked Bob. "You've still got control of our money."

"Only until the required payments have been made and your various debts to us and to others have been settled. And I am compelled to say, after perusing the accounts, your good wife has no capacity for moderation whatsoever. The food, alone, your family has consumed is immodest in the extreme."

"We've only just kept ourselves fed without wasting any to speak of."

"Three meals a day?"

"Yes sir."

"Every day?"

"Yes sir."

"My point precisely. Excessive to the verge of villainy. I take it you've never heard of fasting? A few weeks of fasting each month will cleanse the soul and provide one with a refreshed outlook on life. It is highly recommended for those suffering from a wide variety of conditions."

"What kind of conditions?"

"The inability to pay for meals, among others. Once again, I find myself admonishing you for not seeking my advice on this sooner."

"But we can afford to pay. All Mr. Scrooge's money—"

"Not … all … of … it!" said Gazpayne with a long, descending, drawling emphasis. "The various accounts must be settled, and your profligacy in the accumulation of debt borders on insanity. The interest alone on what you owe our various establishments is approaching …" he came to an abrupt stop and waved a hand impatiently. "But there is no point in lecturing you further for damages done. Simply pay cash from now on, and exercise frugality."

"But I've been trying to tell you: we're without any cash. My daughter was the only one working, and she's just lost her position at the hat shop this morning."

At the mention of Martha, Gazpayne's eyes lit up in an expression Bob found most disturbing.

"That's right," said the lawyer. "You have two daughters, as I recall."

"Three," said Bob, regretting the confession as he heard himself make it.

Gazpayne squinted for a moment, then waved and said, "Yes, but the little one doesn't count. At least not yet. No. But the elder two are what ages?"

"Martha's nineteen, and Belinda's sixteen. Why?"

"I may know a way out of your immediate difficulties. A gentlewoman of my acquaintance runs a finishing school, of which this firm is part owner. I will have her call upon you and take the two young ladies into her care and training."

"But I can't afford to pay to send my daughters—"

"My dear Cratchit! I never said anything to imply you would be required to pay. No, indeed. Not even a farthing, or I wouldn't have mentioned it. How could you think such a thing when I'm only trying to help you?"

"Sorry, Mr. Gazpayne, sir."

"Quite all right. But clearly, you do not understand the workings of such fine institutions as the Toosheronde Academy of Cultural Refinement. Madame la Toosheronde accepts promising young ladies into her tutelage with a view of training them for service to the aristocracy and to gentlemen of means and exacting taste. It is these lords and gentlemen who pay Madame la Toosheronde when the young ladies are placed in satisfactory positions."

"Oh!" said Bob, amazed such an establishment could exist without his ever hearing such a thing was possible. "And they'd be looked after, would they?"

"Everything provided at no charge to you and settled with the girls when they are gainfully employed."

"Well, that's two less mouths to feed, I suppose."

"Fewer mouths, but quite so. And I failed to mention Madame la Toosheronde is in the habit of providing the families of the girls she enrolls with a small reimbursement for bringing the young ladies to her, by way of compensation for the sense of loss experienced from the separation."

"That's kind of her."

"Indeed. But I doubt that alone will be sufficient to see you through the next several months—perhaps a year—so I suggest you get yourself and your boys to work without further delay. The first of November is nigh upon us, when the rent will be due on your home."

"What? Can't you just add it to what we already owe you and settle from our accounts?"

Gazpayne's expression hardened. "I can see your wife's propensity to profligacy is contagious, but I have already covered this matter in sufficient detail and have no desire to belabor it. You will either provide the five shillings when our collector calls or you will be evicted. Consider this fair warning."

CHAPTER 10

During Bob's absence from chez Cratchit, Tiny Tim had struggled to interpret, within the limited means available to him, the feelings of his family. His sensitivity to the emotions of others was becoming more and more acute with the passage of time, and he was beginning to discern the feelings of one from the feelings of another. Furthermore, the closeness forced upon the denizens of the cramped little house far exceeded that of the morgue, where people instinctively distanced themselves from our hero. This further increased his ability to differentiate between them.

Up to the date of the abortive trial, the Cratchit clan had floated along in a kind of patient tolerance of their unsatisfactory surroundings, buoyed up by their vision of a much better future. This mood was consistent throughout from Lucy, the youngest, to Bob, the eldest, owing largely to Tiny Tim's influence. Once the joy of being returned to his kin had settled, he settled into this ongoing sense of acceptance that sustained them all quite well.

Until that fateful day.

Tiny Tim felt fully Martha's battered feelings—her sorrow and her bitterness over losing her job. He felt Mrs. Cratchit's rage over being rendered effectively destitute. He felt Peter's want for revenge. He felt Lucy's fear and Matthew's thought-filled unease. Nothing made much sense to him, for he had no way of knowing the contexts for all this.

Then Bob returned, and the Cratchit world exploded into chaos.

"What did he say?" asked Mrs. Cratchit.

"We can't have any more of it till everything's settled," said Bob. "What's worse: we got to find money for rent, or we're out on our ear."

Then Bob caught sight of Martha looking his way in fright.

"There is one ray of hope, my dears. Martha and Belinda are to go to finishing school, where they will be fed and clothed and taught domestical service and such."

"But I don't want to go to finishing school," said Belinda, stamping her foot. "I already know how to finish."

"It's only for the best, my dear," said Bob with a whimper. "You'll be well seen to, and there'll be two less to feed here. When we gets our money back, we'll settle with the lady who runs the school and have you both home with us, again, but in better circumstances than this. As it is, Peter, Matthew, and I will have to find some sort of work to keep us all from the streets."

"Why can't I go to finishing school too?" asked Peter, imagining himself in a butler's livery, taking imperious command of a bevy of pretty housemaids.

"Only girls go to finishing school," said Bob.

"Why's that, then?" asked Peter, miffed at the inequality imposed upon him.

"Boys come out already finished at birth," said Matthew, which Lucy found amusing, which amused Tiny Tim, which caused him to glow with invisible mirth, which, in turn, allowed for a scintilla of fragile hope to take possession of the wretched Cratchits.

CHAPTER 11

The following noon, a carriage arrived at the front door just as the family was sitting down to a dinner of boiled potato. Out stepped a tattooed and shaven-headed giant, much to the squeaking relief of the carriage suspension. The decorated Brobdingnagian turned to assist a plump lady down to street level. As surprising a sight as the behemoth had been to passersby, he faded into obscurity as the lady emerged, dressed as she was to approximate the color and bearing of a peacock embarked on an amorous adventure.

Madame la Toosheronde was a woman of forty-three, though all indicators common to this accumulation of birthdays were hidden beneath an arsenal of cosmetics and an impressive architecture of foundation garments. As she stepped out from her conveyance, she blinked painfully at the sudden sunlight and her long, peacock-feather eyelashes fluttered alarmingly.

The giant took one step to knock on the front door and then stepped back to stay with the carriage. The door opened. Bob jumped at the sight outside and stood agape as the lady approached. She walked with an intriguing, springlike bounce in many parts of her anatomy.

"You Bob Cratchit, are you, then, ducky?" she asked.

"I, I, I am," said Bob, coming slowly to his senses. "And you must be Madame la Toosheronde."

"Tha's right, love. Mr. Gazpayne sent me. Says you landed yourself into some misery and would be inclined to have your daughters trained up to refinements of a gentleman-pleasing persuasion."

"Yes. Come in, then, and meet them."

The haughty lady entered with a loud rustling of fabric suddenly punctuated by a ringing metallic noise like the breaking of the mainspring one hears when one has overwound one's pocket watch. She stopped abruptly and readjusted her garments, wriggled twice to test for something, and, satisfied with the result, proceeded.

Her eyes met Martha's immediately. Martha was as amazed at the lady's appearance as the rest, but her attention zoomed right to the enormous feathered hat she instantly recognized as a perfect example of a style she had been advised, during her truncated career as a milliner, never to approximate no matter what maleficent muse possessed her.

Bob made the introductions, and all responded with exemplary politeness except for Peter, who was mesmerized by the swelling bosoms of Madame la Toosheronde, which appeared to be in desperate readiness to escape past the lace perimeter of their captivity. She, however, remained unmoved by his inability to speak and turned her attention to Martha.

"Is this one of them two you wants to provide?" asked the lady.

"This is Martha, my eldest," said Bob meekly.

The woman took Martha's chin in her fingers and turned her head from side to side.

"Nothing a touch of paint can't hide. Open wide, darling."

As strange a request as this seemed to the girl, she complied, though her eyes darted from father to mother and back again for reassurance that was not to be found.

"Very nice," said the lady. "Stick out your tongue."

Again, Martha did as she was told.

"Got some attributes, she has," said Madame la Toosheronde. "Get her learning French right away, we will."

"I must say," said Mrs. Cratchit nervously, "you speak English without a trace of an accent."

"Thank you, I'm sure. Where's the other one, then?"

"Belinda?" said Bob, and his hesitant daughter stepped out from behind Peter.

"Oh, you're the pretty one, ain'cher?" said the lady with rapacious enthusiasm.

"Martha's the clever one," said Belinda, afraid her sister might be slighted by the comparison.

"That comes in handy too, I'm sure," said Madame la Toosheronde flatly, and she repeated the examination on the younger daughter she had just conducted on the elder.

"They'll do," she said. "I'll give you a pound for the pair of them."

"A pound?" said Bob in shock.

"A guinea, then, but not a farthing more," said the lady.

"We'll take it," said Mrs. Cratchit, thinking their troubles were over.

Bob had his misgivings but gave in, regardless, as his character consistently dictated he would.

Belinda burst into tears and hugged Martha, who managed a braver display.

Tiny Tim was again confused. The sorrow and trepidation of his sisters were countered by the joy and relief of his mother, while the strange, excited arousal he sensed in Peter was dampened by the doubts with which Bob, Matthew, and Lucy struggled.

Madame la Toosheronde extracted a sovereign and a shilling from her purse and handed them into the hungering fingers of Mrs. Cratchit.

"Come along then, you two," said the lady. "Let's get you to your new home."

The farewell was as tearful as that on the day of Bob's abbreviated arrest, but there was no immediate return this time to bring the family back to its joy. They all went outside to watch the girls board the carriage and the carriage disappear from sight along the cobblestone street.

Back inside, the mood was downcast, with Mrs. Cratchit being the sole holdout for an upward-facing perspective. She could see the specter of impending rent evaporate into the sunshine and the pressing threat of starvation halt indefinitely. So it was that it would not be until a later day—when the chores previously assigned to Martha and Belinda fell to her—that she would begin to miss her daughters with the same grief as the rest of her clan.

And upon her descent into sorrow, Tiny Tim, too, was condemned to grieve.

CHAPTER 12

As welcome a relief as the guinea had been to the destitute family, Bob could see that the need for additional income was still hovering above the horizon like cherry-colored clouds at dawn which sailors proverbially claim are predictive of storms. It had not escaped his attention Gazpayne had gone from promising a return of their money at the end of the trial, to promising its return in two to three months after its completion, to indicating a full year might transpire before the Cratchits would again see the glint on the silver. To that, Bob was beginning to believe—in his darker moments (which were becoming less and less rare)—that their troubles were likely to last the full twelve months at a minimum.

"Let's find ourselves some means of support," he said to Peter and Matthew with as much spirit as he could muster. "I'll look for a clerk's position, and you two see if there's something you can do in the way of light labor—sweeping up and the like, in the shops and what have you."

And so it was the three set off, the father heading uptown to where the gentlemen of finance conducted their business, and the two sons heading downtown to where the tradesmen and merchants conducted theirs.

Unfortunately for the trio, those gifted with literacy had read all about the scandalous trial in the newspapers, and those not so gifted had heard about it from the others. No one was willing to take on a Cratchit at any price, for fear of being sued for no reason, for fear of losing clientele, or for fear of both. Day after day, Bob came home empty-handed. His poor sons, however, came home empty-handed and showing signs of abuse, as their petitions for employment were being made to a less gentlemanly set of potential employers.

Still, they persisted.

Perhaps it was the Christmas spirit that saved them, or perhaps the timing was mere coincidence, but Peter and Matthew, upon arriving at the offices of Eliphaz Dropping, master rat-catcher, on December 24, found the proprietor in a state of considerable intoxication and in eager readiness to hire two assistants, as the two he had had, had had cause to leave due to a mysterious illness that left them incapacitated.

At the best of times, Mr. Dropping disported himself with a deep redness of face that was variegated with a variety of veins, warts, moles, and spots of an indeterminate and only semipermanent status, but—well into the ale as he was that Christmas Eve—his appearance presently approached the fantastical limits of dermal coloration. This brought the two boys to a halt. Fortunately for the pair, Dropping was slow to appreciate there was anyone in his presence, which gave Matthew time enough to recover his wits and explain their reason for being there, without having to explain the preceding awkward silence.

Whether or not the master rat-catcher would have hired them had he been sober enough to conduct an interview is unknown, but hire them he did, with simple instructions.

"Go to Mr. Gutblood's Butcher Shop," said Dropping. "Tell him I sent you to catch his rats, but don't say it out loud afore his customers, as it's none of their business, you see?"

"Yes sir," said Matthew, who grasped more firmly his master's meaning than did his brother.

"He's to pay you tuppence a rat," said Dropping. "Make sures you counts them right, or what's you gets wrong comes out of your earnings. Bring the rats and the money back here, and Squidge'll cart them off. He gets a ha'penny apiece, you gets a farthing apiece, and I gets the rest. See?"

"Yes sir," said Matthew, and he then led his elder—and rather more apprehensive—brother to the location of their labors.

After a slow start, in which both brothers attempted to catch, kill, and bag their quarry independently, it became clear Matthew had more of the required devil-may-care attitude and agility for the job and could make progress with greater efficiency if Peter assumed the roles of jailor and executioner, thus freeing his more athletic sibling to specialize in chase and capture of the criminal creatures.

On their first day, the duo bagged seventy-four rodents—including seven mice that Matthew convincingly claimed to be rat-midgets—which they turned in to their employer along with the coins. Matthew then counted out the earnings twice for the dubious Dropping and provided an accurate calculation of the Cratchit share.

"You're a quick one for the numbers," allowed the master ratter. "And you've a natural bent for the work, I must say. There's them what's born to catch rats and there's them what only dreams of it. You two are as much of the former as any I've had the pleasure of knowing, and in my time, I've had the pleasure of knowing quite a few. Comes here with stars in their eyes, they do, dreaming of easy wealth and the path to luxury, but they soons learns it ain't all skittles and ale."

"No sir," said Matthew. "Back tomorrow, then, are we?"

"Oh, yes, please. I know it's Christmas and all, but rats is pagans and don't take no holidays. 'Fore you go home, though, first takes them what you got round to Squidge, along with this note of the tally. I settles with him at the end of each week."

The two Cratchit boys then took the sack of dead rats and the note bearing the death toll—signed floridly "Eliphaz Dropping, M.R.C."— one street west to the dray-and-carriage business run by Thaddeus Squidge.

On the way, Matthew stepped into an alley and bade his brother join him.

"Here," said Matthew, holding out a farthing. "Mother has such trouble with small coins. It's better if I give her one-and-six and you and I keep the difference."

"But ..."

"Don't be gormless. When you were working before, you were

making five-and-six a week and giving it all to Mother. We can make twelve shillings a week catching rats for Dropping and give ten to her. She'll be happy as a lark with that, and we deserve a little, as we're the ones doing all the work."

Though the deceptive arrangement had Peter somewhat conflicted, the idea of independent wealth was too tempting to pass up, so he accepted the coin in the spirit of agreement, and the two continued on their way.

Thaddeus Squidge enjoyed the unquestioned reputation of being faithful to a policy of asking no questions. As a result, his place of business was frequented by many who were well known for wishing to remain unknown. Peter was quite shaky, then, as he followed his brother past the surly men of poorly disguised ill intent as Matthew went about identifying the one in charge.

"Mr. Squidge, sir?" asked Matthew in a murmur.

"Who's asking?" asked the smallest of the small horde.

"I was told to give him this," said Matthew, holding out the note.

The man glanced at it and motioned that they follow him into the back, where they were given over to Squidge.

"I appreciates your diss ... gretion," drawled out Squidge with a wink as he took the sack from Peter and put it out of sight. "Our little arrangement don't need be public. There's them what lives to make problems for others, there is, so you two keep quiet about what we does here, and I'll see you comes and goes without coming to no good—if you see what I means?"

"Yes sir," said Matthew with certainty.

"Good lad. Get yourselves along, then. Out the back way and along the alley to the high street."

The man who had brought them in led them out and watched them until they were once again safely within the bustling population that had no dealings with Squidge or his kind.

Matthew had taken everything in his stride while Peter had found Dropping to be a disturbing sort and Squidge wholly disagreeable. Were it not for the tiny coin in Peter's pocket, he would have been completely disinclined to go through another day like this one had been. But the dizzying idea of a farthing a day to himself to spend as he pleased was enough to eclipse his misgivings and screw his courage to the sticking-place—as another faced with a horrifying task was famously wont to do.

Matthew had predicted quite correctly Mrs. Cratchit's joy at receiving the shilling and sixpence without question. Bob was less pleased with hearing the two would have to work Christmas.

"It can't be helped, Father," said Peter authoritatively. "Rats are penguins, so holidays are a luxury we simply can't expect."

Although the logic behind this argument escaped poor Bob, he accepted it as fact, in deference to the much-needed income it justified.

And to all this, Tiny Tim was elated. The prospect of a fine Christmas dinner propelled Lucy into excitement, and it was her feelings that were always felt first and the strongest by our hero. As always, he turned this around and radiated the same back to the family, so all were happy despite their still missing Martha and Belinda.

The following day—Christmas Day—found Peter and Matthew again at the offices of Eliphaz Dropping.

"Two 'ssignments today, boys," said Dropping in a whimpering contralto—still haunted, as he was, by the ghost of spirits past. "Saint Silias's Church this morning. Minister wants them out before services starts, so you only gots till ten. See the deacon for the money, and don't let the cheeky blighter slight you. His 'rithmetic's bad and always to his favor. Come back with that lot, and then you're off to Mrs. Retch's Fancy Bakery."

Having polished their methods the previous day, the two got on rather better, bagging ninety-nine in the church basement and a further eighty-seven in the storeroom of the bakery.

The well-sugared Mrs. Retch was delighted, as it was the first time in over a decade the finding of a single rat in her larder proved to be an impossible task. She paid in full without quibbling and fed the boys cakes before sending them on their way.

Their earlier experience with the deacon was less amiable, as the spindly minder of church monies failed repeatedly to calculate the correct compensation, forcing Matthew to the extremity of laying out the long row of rodent corpses on the basement floor and insisting the pinched and pursed-lipped little man place one tuppence next to each. Still, the young ratters could see great potential in the ancient place. Had it not been for the time constraint imposed upon them, they could have harvested many, many more since—contrary to the well-worn simile—rodents do quite well on the leavings of religion.

Back at Dropping's offices, their master—quite recovered from the morning after the night before and well on his way to the night before the morning after—was most effulgent in his praise of the two boys' accomplishments.

"You'll go far in the field of rats, you will," said Dropping wistfully as he wiped a tear from his eye. "You're like the sons I wished I'd had."

He paid them their due and loaned them a wheelbarrow to take their haul to Squidge, who was equally amazed.

"A pair of terrors are you two," said the master drayman with a half-smile. "Won't be a rat within fifty mile of the Good Old City with the likes of you afoot."

Matthew had some sense of hyperbole and accepted the compliment in the light in which it was given, but poor Peter was given more to literal interpretations and worried he and his brother would success their way out of a job.

"No fear of that," said Matthew as the two made for home. "Rats are pagans, so they breed like flies. But it does give me an idea."

"It's pronounced 'penguin,'" said Peter. "Rats are penguins."

"If you like," said Matthew, handing his brother two coins. "Here: penny, ha'penny, and Happy Christmas."

"God bless us, every one!"

CHAPTER 13

Tiny Tim glowed with familial warmth to rival a potbellied stove. As long as the Cratchit clan remained committed to sharing a sense of well-being, Tiny Tim could remain committed to fueling it.

His two brothers continued bringing goodly sums of money into the home, and life grew more and more comfortable for them all. But, as is the nature of all humanity, they eventually accepted their better fortune as commonplace and then began to feel the absence of Martha and Belinda again. The family sentiment took the downward trajectory of a winged pigeon, and melancholic nostalgia gained rulership of the tiny household.

"What do you suppose our girls are doing now?" asked Bob of his wife. "Still being finished, do you think? Or would they be done now and onto domesticated service?"

"Couldn't say, I'm sure," said Mrs. Cratchit sadly. "Never having been finished meself, I wouldn't know what's to expect. They might be still learning what's 'spected, or perhaps they've assumed positions already."

"Oh, wouldn't that be grand?" said Bob. "Our Martha and our Belinda assuming positions under lords and gentlemen. After all our troubles and woes, at least we can take some comfort in that."

"Can I assume positions under lords and gentlemen?" asked Lucy.

"When you're older, my dear," said Bob paternally. "If we can only find where Madame la Toosheronde has her school."

"Can't you get it out of Gazpayne?" asked Mrs. Cratchit.

"No, my dear. He says we mustn't go there, as it would upset the girls to see us and make things difficult for them. Best they keep us out of their minds till they're established somewhere and we won't be a hindrance to them anymore."

It was with this thought that the family sentiment took that trajectory previously mentioned, whereupon Tiny Tim transformed from potbelly of warmth to beacon of sorrow.

CHAPTER 14

F ortunately for the family, Peter and Matthew were not captured in the downward emotional spiral, being, as they were, out and about in the business of ratting and outside the radius of Tiny Tim's still-limited influence.

Peter had overcome his earlier trepidations toward the work, which was good for his positive perspective on life but problematic for Matthew. Familiarity breeds contempt, as the saying goes, and no truer a saying has ever been said. As Peter became more and more accustomed to their forays into the world of rats, he became more and more vocal in his encounters with Dropping and the clients—a tendency that worried his younger brother greatly.

Matthew had, from the beginning, approached the vocation of rat catcher with what is termed "professional distance." In this, he was wise for his years, for unlike most sixteen-year-old ratters you might meet, he could see, as enjoyable an activity his career might be on its own merits, it was best to remain above this consideration and conduct himself with decorum. As any artist who has tried to make a living from his art will tell you, the argument that if one enjoys one's work, one should be willing to do it for nothing is so commonly used as an excuse to not pay, it pays not to mention how much one enjoys one's work. To this, Matthew had an instinctive insight, but he was forever having to caution his brother to keep quiet regarding the excitement, romance, and adventure of ratting lest it be seen as a reason for a renegotiation of rates.

Furthermore, Peter completely overcame his anxiety toward the men of ill repute who lingered about the stables and warehouses of Squidge's dray-and-carriage business. Indeed, Peter saw the need for discretion in their dealings with Squidge as evidence that he, himself, had been elevated to the rank of man of ill repute, even though the exact nature of that ill reputation remained unclear. So it was that he was soon conducting himself through Squidge's establishment with all the swagger a youth pushing a barrow of dead rats can swag.

For Matthew's part, this rise in Peter's estimation of himself among the community of villains gave the younger brother further cause for concern. While he may well have been the greatest slayer of rats the Good Old City had ever seen, he suspected some of Squidge's acquaintances to be in competition for the title of Greatest Slayer of Boys with Silver in Their Pockets and sincerely wished to remain unnoticed in their midst as Squidge often sagely advised.

Peter, however, could not be persuaded toward voluntary obscurity. Finally, in desperation, Matthew offered to pay the elder brother his share upon leaving Dropping's and allow him the treat of finishing early.

"No point in both of us seeing Squidge," said Matthew. "I'll deliver these, and you go on home."

"No thanks. I rather like going to Squidge's. I'll take them, and you go home."

"All right, then," said Matthew, "I've got something else that needs doing, anyway. I'll settle up with you later."

He then handed Peter the note with the day's tally and walked off in the knowledge that with no money in his pockets to speak of, Peter presented a poor target for larceny.

Peter, then, delivered the rats and returned Dropping's barrow without event, but left to his own machinations as he was, his curiosity over what Squidge did with the rodent haul got the better of him, and he went back to reconnoiter the scene before the carriage house doors.

This activity excited him greatly, for the longer he waited, hiding in expectation, the more it felt like an act of skullduggery, and skullduggery was something Peter could enjoy for its entertainment value, as readers of mystery stories can appreciate.

He was not to be kept waiting long, however, for the great doors swung open and out clopped a Clydesdale, drawing a wagon mounded high with bloodstained burlap sacks of the kind he recognized as a tool of his trade. He ducked out of sight of the driver as the great cart passed, only to come out of hiding and follow at a discreet distance.

The journey was not terribly long—just long enough to tempt Peter into abandoning his quest, but not long enough for him actually to do so. After only a few twists and turns of its route, the wagon turned into a lane leading to a great and classical ponderous stone building with the word "CREMATORIVM" chiseled above the entrance. Peter studied the letters for some moments, decided that whatever the word was, it was spelled wrongly, and returned his attention to the action that was the reason for his being there.

He trotted along the path the cart followed toward the rear of the building. As he passed the wall, he stopped once to look in a basement window, and the truth of the building's purpose became shockingly clear to him. As upsetting as this bit of intelligence was, it only refueled his curiosity to learn the secret Squidge seemed determined to keep.

He crept to the corner and peeked around.

The driver of the wagon was standing before the rear door. A pale man all in black answered it. Peter cupped his ear in his hand to hear better.

"What have we today?" asked the pale man all in black.

"Same as always. Ton of rats looking to be people," said the driver.

The two laughed, but the joke escaped Peter entirely. The pale man, all in black, called for assistants to unload the cart. When they were done, he held out his hand to the driver and said, "Everything seems to be in order. Two quid as usual, and I shall see you tomorrow."

Peter then returned to the basement window to witness furnace doors swinging open to admit sacks of rats, which were then consigned to the flames with apparent haste.

As interesting as all this was, in a grim sort of way, Peter was disappointed with the banality of it all. Squidge's demand for discretion seemed entirely out of place: why would the burning of rats need to be kept secret?

Still, his curiosity as to the final destination of the rats was well sated, so the eldest son Cratchit left the scene of his investigation and set off for home. On his way, though, this need for secrecy still niggled at him. He put more thought to it, and as he thought, the thought struck him: the pale man all in black had given the driver two pounds.

"You don't pay to do things for others," he said aloud. "You have others pay you to do things for them."

And this mystery burned a hole in poor Peter's brain all the way home. But nothing to fill that hole awaited him there.

CHAPTER 15

Upon Peter's entry into the house, the weight of nostalgic grief being felt in the Cratchit household over the absence of Martha and Belinda descended on him and nearly crushed the possibility of any other emotion rising within him. But the strangeness surrounding the selling of the rats was a question that niggled his spirit, and the desire for an answer to that question was enough to shift Tiny Tim out of the state of mourning—which was becoming tiresome for him anyway—and into a state of anticipatory frustration. Within minutes, the whole family was immersed in that feeling one gets from having something on the tip of one's tongue without having a clue as to what that something could possibly be or what it could possibly have to do with.

"We're missing something," said Bob to no one in particular after many failed attempts to bring the missing something to mind. "Though what it might be I can't say, I'm sure."

"Yes," said his wife. "But, when you thinks of it, be sure and tell us what you thinks it is, and we'll do likewise if we thinks of it first."

"Quite so, my dear. But it is troubling, isn't it? Not so much what it is as the not knowing what it is that is so terribly troubling, or so it seems to me that's what it is that is so terribly troubling, don't you see?"

"Yes, that's it, precisely," said Mrs. Cratchit as if he'd hit on the answer, but she then added sadly, "But it is terrible troubling, irregardless."

This rather puzzling bit of dialogue was the clue for Lucy to trace the source of their confusion—it was not some elusive nebulosity of an idea seeking a state of solidity in the mind, but Tiny Tim trapped in a cycle of feeling and emoting. She felt a moment of delight at this realization but then sighed, knowing another attempt to convince her family of her silent brother's power of emotional amplification would only bring yet another round of condescending smiles and disbelieving there-there-we-know-my-dears they always heaped upon her whenever she tried to broach the subject.

Rather than waste time on another pointless attempt to enlighten her clan, Lucy simply slipped quietly into the living room where Tiny Tim lay next to the window, sat beside him, and restricted herself to the thinking of happy thoughts until he felt the cord of contentment within him and began to resonate with it.

Soon, the seeking of the elusive answer to the nonquestion was abandoned, and the household was returned once more to merriment.

It was to this that Matthew came home. His long absence had gone unnoticed until then, as the family had been too deep in aimless puzzling to miss him. The mild scolding he'd expected from Bob over being late for supper went unsaid, as Bob was in no mood to scold, no matter how mildly, and Mrs. Cratchit, having not yet put a thought to preparing supper, could hardly blame him for being late for it when it was late for him.

"Where've you been?" whispered Peter when Matthew was settled.

"I'll show you tomorrow. After work."

To this, Peter nodded, then said in a boast, "I found out where Squidge takes the rats."

"Where?"

"He sells them to a creamery."

This bit of intelligence twitched in Matthew's belly since he was rather fond of clotted cream, and learning it was made from dead rats somewhat tainted its appeal. "You sure?"

"I followed him there. Or his drayman, anyways. Chap all in black answered the door, took all the sacks inside and give him two pound for the lot. I looked in the window, and there they were: burning the rats along with some dead people."

"Wait a minute. They were burning dead people?"

"That's right. Chucking them in furnaces and burning them up."

Matthew laughed, relieved to know his future relishing of clotted cream would not be diminished by considerations of its origins.

"Not creamery!" he said. "You mean crematory."

"Oh," said Peter, and he blushed lightly until Tiny Tim's joviality pushed his embarrassment aside.

Matthew reveled a moment in his triumph over error but then sighted the missing link in the logic.

"You mean Squidge pays them to burn the rats, don't you?"

"No. They pay him. I've seen it. Two quid they gave him for a ton of dead rats. It made no sense to me, neither, but I wondered if you might see how it works."

"No. It's just playing at silly sailors to my thinking. But let's ask Mr. Dropping. Maybe he knows."

And, indeed, Dropping did know.

"Well," said the master ratter sadly the following morning, "I was hoping you two'd remain innocent of all this a while longer, but seeing as you've found out, I suppose it's best you know the truth of it all."

He shook his grizzled head somberly to gather his moral strength for the unpleasant task before him. He blinked painfully several times— some of his semipermanent dermic embellishments had appeared on his eyelids, making the opening and closing of his eyes discomforting.

Finally, he sighed and said, "You see, it's like this. Rat-catching ain't 'xactly the pure and noble profession you boys has come to see it as. You's just seen the shiny exterior, as they say. What lies beneath ain't so pretty. It weren't always this way, mind you … But it is now. It's a sad fact of life, but when there's a lot of money to be made, it 'ttracts a seedy kind of person to do the making of it. It's what them clever blokes calls the 'caterpillarist system,' you see."

"Why do they call it that, then?" asked Peter.

"Not sure. But it's how business works, and it means we has to take the bad with the good. That's how it must be. And that's all there is to it."

The two nodded, but Matthew wondered where he might find a clever bloke to elucidate further on the nature of the caterpillarist system.

Dropping continued. "Now, rats is what they calls 'loo-cur-tive,' which is a fancy way of saying there's lots of money to be made in rats—as you lads knows already. That 'ttracts blokes like Squidge, you see."

The two boys nodded again, so the master ratter went on. "Now, you and me and lots like us does all right out of it. But him! Well, he's got the market cornered, he does. All the rat-catchers in the Good Old City does business with him, as we got no choice in the matter. Ain't a rat born within fifty mile what don't find its way to him sooner or later. And it didn't happen that way 'cuz he's born lucky—you can bet your mother's virtue on that! No. He made it all happen by doing nasty to them what tried to work independent-like."

"So what's all this to do with him selling the rats to the crematory?" asked Matthew.

"I was getting to that. He used to cart them out to the country and sell 'em to farmers for pig food, but word of that got out, and them what's fond of eating pork took 'ception to it. The farmers stopped buying, and Squidge had to look about for another way of disposing of them. Being a caterpillarist, as he is, he couldn't see hisself just burying them, as there's no profit in that, and what don't turn a profit ain't right by his view of how things is meant to work. Now, I don't know if it was him what approached the crematory, or was it them what came to him, but here's how they got it to work. Every minute, there's a John Doe or Jane Doe turning up somewhere in the city."

"Who are they?" asked Peter.

"People what dies with nobody knowing who they is. Blokes what falls asleep in the gentlemen's conveniences behind pubs and don't wake up. Ladies of the evening what gets in the family way, then tries to swim the river to avoid the bridge tolls. All kinds of things like that. They gets named John Doe and Jane Doe for convenience and taken to the crematory, where they's made into ashes. The crematory gets paid for each one they burns, you see?"

"Yes," said Matthew, guessing what was to follow.

"Right," said Dropping. "Now the ashes gets weighed before they's hauled away, and them what pays for the burnings knows how many pounds of person it takes to make a pound of ashes, so the bloke what runs the crematory can't claim for more Johns and Janes than he's got ashes for, you see? So here's the tricky bit, then. A hundredweight of rats renders down the same as a hundredweight of people, so it pays the crematory bloke to buy rats from Squidge and sell John Does to the city."

"Oh," said Peter, astounded by the genius of the scheme.

"Well, now you know," said Dropping. "I'm sorry rats ain't the 'olesome trade you pictured it was. But that's no reason to toss it over. You lads is doing well by it, and so am I, and we can keep on doing well by it if we treat each other square. I'm as honest as the day is long. Or at least till noon on a good day, which is as good as most. But I's always treated you two fair, and I 'ppreciates you to keep doing likewise with me."

"Of course, Mr. Dropping, sir," said Matthew. "We're most grateful to you for everything."

"Good lads. Well … Off to Smuts & Ergot's Granary with you. No end of rats there for the taking."

On their way to the wealth that awaited them, Peter asked, "How much does a rat weigh, do you think?"

"Half a pound, perhaps. On average."

"So how many for a ton, then?"

"Four-thousand," said Matthew with a glance upward to his elder brother. "But if you're thinking what I think you're thinking, you can stop thinking it. We're not doing that."

"Why not? We could get Squidge's share from Dropping and two quid more from the creamery. I mean crematory."

"And when Squidge gets wind of it, we'll be two more John Does sleeping in the kindling—three if he thinks Dropping's in on it with us, which he will. No. I've got something else figured. I'll show you when we're done."

CHAPTER 16

Cornelius Smuts and Anthony Ergot were unlikely friends but perfect partners. While Ergot was the son of a strict clergyman, brought up to conduct himself according to exacting ethical standards and capable of putting a pious, respectable face on the business, Smuts was more the kind described earlier by Dropping as a caterpillarist and better equipped to enhance the viability of the enterprise.

Unfortunately for Peter and Matthew, it was Smuts who had engaged Dropping to supply the granary with rat catchers, and so it was Smuts who greeted them at the back entrance.

"So you're the champion ratters Dropping goes on about?" said Smuts in a voice that slithered down the boys' spines.

"We're good at what we do," said Matthew anxiously.

"Well, there's plenty enough of that here, so get yourselves to it."

That alone would have been merely the unpleasant beginning of a pleasant day, but it was not alone and was, therefore, the unpleasant beginning of a quite unpleasant day, as we shall see.

To the boys' surprise, they were not the only rat catchers employed by Smuts & Ergot on that day. Six other boys—all taller than Peter and meatier than Matthew—were also engaged in the enterprise. Their leader stepped forward and leaned above the brothers Cratchit.

"You keep to your end, and we'll keep to ours," he said while pointing threateningly toward the west.

"Agreed," said Matthew, and he backed away with Peter at his side.

The two did keep to their end of the enormous granary, where they were left to themselves and their share of the rat horde. Matthew had assumed they'd been assigned the region of slimmest pickings, but they had no trouble dispatching 120 rodents before noon, which they had determined was the limit of what they could comfortably carry between them.

"If you can pay us for these, now, sir," said Matthew to Smuts, "we'll take them to Mr. Dropping and come back this afternoon for more."

"You should get yourselves a cart," said Smuts, handing Matthew a shiny sovereign. "You're not making money walking back and forth."

"Yes sir. Thank you, sir."

"He's right, you know," said Peter as they left the building for the bright sunlight. "We could make more if we had a cart."

"I know. I'm having one made special," said Matthew, but before he could go on, his eyes adjusted to the light, and he saw the six other ratters appearing before them.

"We'll 'ave those," said their leader, "and whatever Smuts give you for 'em."

Unencumbered, Matthew could have outrun the hijackers, but unwilling to shed the weight of his sixty rats, he was brought down alongside Peter, who had no chance of escape under the best of circumstances. The two were beaten soundly, followed by a rifling of their pockets, which netted their assailants two pocketknives (one from each), a collection of naughty postcards (Peter's), a two-headed coin (also Peter's) and, of course, the sovereign that was sought above all else.

And the two were left where they lay, sans money and sans rats.

They were not long in gathering enough strength to stand and stagger from the scene of their assault, but the thought of going to Dropping empty-handed was nearly as distressing as the beating had been.

"He's a good chap, under it all," said Peter. "He won't blame us for it."

And so they made their painful way back to Dropping's offices, where they told their tragic tale to the master tradesman.

"Well, it's a bad innings all way 'round, I must say," said Dropping. "First you learns the truth about Squidge and now this. I couldn't hardly blame you if you finds it all too much to bear, but the truth is you can't walk about carrying a valuable commodity like rats without some violence coming to you sooner or later. I been robbed meself, more times than I cares to think about, but here I is—one of the most successful ratters in the Good Old City. I understands if you wants to go your bitter ways, but I hopes you can put your minds to more of the good times and stays."

"We will," said Matthew with determination, though Peter was less certain.

"Good, then," said Dropping, slapping his thighs, and standing up. "Let's see to them cuts, then, shall we? I got just the thing for it. Uses it all the time, meself, to cure me what-have-yous."

Judging from Dropping's semipermanent dermic embellishments, Matthew was suspicious as to the efficacy of anything the master-ratter used to cure what-have-yous, but he submitted to the stinging dabs nevertheless, as did his brother, and the two went home early, painted liberally with the bright purple curative.

Dropping had also given them tuppence to ease the sting of the financial wounding they had taken, so they did not have to face their mother with nothing at all to justify their daily labor.

"What happened to you?" said Bob, looking shocked, upon their arrival.

"We were robbed," said Peter, who was beginning to see the nasty incident as a kind of rite of passage into the man-of-ill-repute world he imagined himself to inhabit.

Had Peter's dubiously founded jollity gained more traction, things might have gone differently, but Bob was not the only one shocked by the boys' appearance. Mrs. Cratchit and Lucy also gasped with fright at first sight of the two, and needless to say, Tiny Tim was soon radiating terror throughout the household. Mrs. Cratchit began screaming in horror. Bob tried to calm her but was himself trembling near the point of convulsion. Matthew and Peter gripped each other, each thinking he must be deformed beyond belief to elicit such a response from his mother.

Lucy, too, was awash in fear, but again, she could sense both the cause and the remedy. She pushed on Matthew and Peter and forced them to the front door.

"Go away till I can calm him down," she said. "And knock when you get back so's we can brace ourselves before you come back in."

Peter didn't understand and was frozen where he stood, but Matthew was willing to obey. With Lucy's help, he got Peter outside, where he said, "Come on. I'll show you what I've been working on."

With her brothers gone, Lucy courageously pushed her way through the waves of terror coming off Tiny Tim and forced herself to sit beside him. She stroked his brow and thought the many things she knew would restore him to his bliss.

A good hour passed before the home was again once happy. That accomplished, the heroic Lucy whispered in Tiny Tim's ear, "God bless us, every one!" and fell, exhausted, asleep.

CHAPTER 17

Meanwhile, Matthew and Peter—whose hearts were calming with every step they took away from the Cratchit residence—walked to the end of their street, to the last house, which outwardly appeared neglected but whole, while inwardly it was as decrepit a structure as a structure could be and still be called a structure without risk of the caller being called mad.

The ancient stone walls were all intact, and the shutters in place, though nailed shut. Matthew took Peter around the back, and the two scaled the wooden fence to access the space between the house and its outdoor facility. He went into the privy but immediately returned with a large key, which he inserted in the rusty lock of the back door and turned with all the squeaks and squeals of a mouse unwillingly becoming a cat's breakfast. With effort, the door was pulled open, though the smell released in doing so provided some regret for having done it.

"The floor's all rotted away," said Matthew. "Just pop your head in and have a gander."

Peter did as requested. What little lumber there was protruding from the walls did fail to meet the definition of a floor. The few shards of light that made it through the door and past Peter revealed the remains of what once had been, which was now only debris resting silently about six feet below him. He took in a short breath but let out a choking cough and pulled his head back from the maw of the abyss.

"Why d'you bring me here, then?" he asked with a grimace.

"It's ours."

"Ours?"

"Well … sort of … I rented it."

"What for?"

"We're going to grow rats here," said Matthew brightly. "All we need is a dozen live ones. Toss them in along with some rubbish, and two months from now, we're pulling twice that a day out of here."

"Why bother? We catch all we can carry as it is."

"Not always. Think of all the times we clean a place out and we've only thirty or forty to show for it. We add a few more of our own, and they'll think we've done a better job."

Peter's eyes lit up for a moment, but then he scowled and asked, "All the extra comes to us, right?"

"Course. Less the rent. But that's only fourpence a month." Matthew pulled the door shut and locked it. He then led the way a few streets over to the shop of T. Harland Quinn: Fabricator and Purveyor of Devices Fantastical.

"The item you have commissioned is not yet ready, young sir," said the wizardly looking master of the shop after he recognized Matthew beneath the purple paint, scratches, and swellings.

"I know," said Matthew. "I brought my brother by to see it."

"You two been having wars, have you?"

"No, we were robbed," said Peter. "Beaten within an inch of our lives, relieved of our riches, such as they were, and left for the crows. We gave as good as we got, but they had us outnumbered six to one, so what could we do?"

"My! That is a nasty business," said the wispy-bearded craftsman. "But you are going to be able to pay me, are you not?"

"Oh, yes," said Matthew. "They took what we had on us, but I've got your money set aside."

Peter would have questioned this last remark out loud had he heard it, but his eyes had wandered to the wonderful strangeness of his surroundings and led his mind into fascinated consideration of what lay before him, so he had been rendered dumbfounded and silent.

The sign overhanging the entrance to the shop had not informed Peter that T. Harland Quinn was a craftsman engaged in the manufacture and selling of magical apparatuses or, more accurately, conjurors' equipment. There were boxes used for sawing ladies in half. There were wardrobes used for turning ladies into white rabbits. There was even a glass case used for making ladies disappear into puffs of colored smoke. Indeed, there were all manner of contrivances designed to abuse ladies in all manner of most amusing ways.

And while there were many other items of the arts and sciences of prestidigitation—large and small, gaily colored and barely visible, elaborate and simple—designed for conjurors of all levels of skill, it was the ones displayed with the barely clad female manikins that captured Peter's imagination and set him adrift in silent speculation.

It had not been an interest in magic, though, that had brought Matthew to the shop. In actuality, few of Quinn's customers had any interest in conjuring beyond mastering a card trick or two proven effective when combined with games of chance. No. It was not for its advertised purpose that the shop was generally patronized. It was the craftsman's ability to make specialized containers—for the purpose of secreting what was wished kept secret—that provided him with the lion's share of his income. And that was Matthew's purpose in seeking Quinn's services.

"Come see this," said Matthew as he pulled Peter away from a close study of a gaudy and bejeweled scarlet corset.

They followed Quinn into the back room, where a baffling array of articles, ranging from plain to bizarre, were in various stages of construction.

"Here is where we are so far," said Quinn, drawing the boys' attention to a coffin-sized, open-topped wooden box. "All that is required for its completion is the wheels, and I have a lad out sourcing me a set as we speak. When they come in, I'll modify the axles to accommodate them and attach the steering arm. A touch of paint to cover that which is best not seen, and you're away to the races."

Matthew leaned forward to gaze at the bottom of the box but failed to find that which he sought.

"How's it work?" he had to ask.

Quinn looked to him and winked. He reached in, took hold of a cross member, gave it a quick jerk toward the rear, and lifted it up. A panel of several planks slid out of place to reveal that the entire bottom of the box was hollow to a depth of four inches beneath the floor.

"Perfect," said Matthew. "You work fast."

"Not really," said Quinn, sliding the panel back in place. "The box is a return from a chap previously engaged in the importation of items from the Far East. Items that cater to exotic tastes, one might say. Bales of silk in the top … this and that in the bottom." Quinn smiled knowingly at the two and added, "He's gone on holiday to Australia and has no further need of it."

"Australia? Golly!" said Peter excitedly at the thought of high adventure.

"Yes. Queen Victoria paid his fare in full," said Quinn, amused at Peter's obvious innocence in the realm of penology. "But if there's nothing else, gentlemen, I have work to do."

The master of concealment then ushered the two back out to the street with a promise to have the pull-cart finished within the week, on the assurance a suitable set of wheels would be found.

As they wound their way back home, Peter wondered aloud, "Do you suppose the queen would send us on holiday to Australia if we got all the rats out of the palace?"

Matthew looked sideways at his brother, never quite sure what to make of him.

He looked again toward home and said, "She might if we tried doing it without an invitation."

CHAPTER 18

L ucy's attempts to remove the purple paint from her brothers' faces proved futile.

"Let's hope it's not tattoo ink," she said as she gathered the wash things together.

"I doubt it," said Matthew. "Mr. Dropping uses it all the time, and he isn't all purple."

Of course, inwardly he knew it would be difficult to exclude, with certainty, any suggested cause to the master ratter's coloration.

Fortunately, their parents were able to accept the boys' emotional accommodation of the painful incident as proof no permanent damage had been done, and so the feelings of the household were the feelings of relief that all had turned out well enough in the end.

And Tiny Tim sustained that sense of well-being long into the next month.

During that month, Mr. Quinn completed the pull-cart to Matthew's approval, and the boys took possession of it. Thus equipped, they were able to take on additional assignments from Dropping since they could now handle much more weight and did not need to waste time walking back and forth to unload.

Matthew and Peter then put their plan into action. They selected twelve large and healthy rats (two males and ten females) whose lives they spared to stock the abyss beneath the abandoned house. They made daily stops at pubs on the way home to retrieve the kitchen wastes, helped themselves to bags of oats stacked outside stables, emptied ashcans of soiled bandages behind a surgeon's offices, and begged from a slaughterhouse what little there was that could not be made into sausage. In short, they acquired whatever they could in the way of rodent comestibles to feed their flock.

Needless to say, they needed a place to hide their cart when not in use, lest it became the property of someone else in the manner of procurement favored in their part of town. To this, Matthew put into effect some ideas he had learned in looking about the shop of the fabricator and purveyor of devices fantastical. He designed a simple system that converted a portion of the fence behind their rat house into a gate that was unidentifiable as a gate to anyone passing by on the street, and thus they were able to secure their prize possession out of sight.

When two months had passed from the date the dozen captive rats were introduced to their new home, Matthew announced to Peter it was time to assess the success of their breeding experiment. He opened the door, gave a moment for the air to exchange, then held a candle forth to illuminate the space below. What met their gaze was beautiful beyond their wildest imaginings. In the orange, pulsing glow of the candle, the bottom of the void was a writhing gray-brown carpet of rodent activity.

"They do breed like penguins!" said Peter loudly.

"Yes," said Matthew in a murmur. "But we should keep that to ourselves."

Peter took the warning to heart and hushed himself.

The following morning, they executed the first harvesting of livestock. Matthew acquired a laundry basket, into which he dropped a few shavings of cheese crust, then lowered it on a rope into the abyss, where it tilted over onto one side. Immediately, four or five rats darted inside, only to find themselves instantly elevated to the door, poured into a sack, clubbed to death, and stretched out inside the lower compartment of the cart. This procedure was repeated until sixteen of the unfortunate creatures had met their demise.

"Better leave it at that," said Matthew. "We don't want to thin out the flock too quick."

But his caution proved to be unnecessary, as the size of their investment swelled rapidly, and they were soon augmenting their wages by forty rats a day—most days.

As you may have gleaned from previous activities here reported, there were certain of Mr. Dropping's clients that provided ample supplies of rats without the need for augmentation. On the days Matthew and Peter were assigned to one of these clients, they would leave their rats alone to bolster the numbers of the herd. Clearly, to know which days this would apply required they know in advance what clients they would be servicing. To this, Matthew justified to Dropping the need to know on the grounds that time would be saved by going directly to the first client each day, thus opening the possibility of seeing an extra client each day. This, too, proved to be true, and the two were soon seeing four clients most days and averaging 360 rats per day—dead and paid for.

But this paradise was not without its serpent.

Two circumstances arose. One was simply troubling, while the other was troubling and most unpleasant.

The first problem arose as time went on, when it became apparent the bottom of the pit in which the rats frolicked was slowly rising. It was only a matter of time before the livestock—as Matthew called them—would be in a position to escape their captivity.

The second problem was in the smell. Before the house had been put to the purpose of rat farming, it was choked with dust and mold, which, as Peter could attest, was a bit overwhelming. A few months into its new raison d'être, however, the house was becoming increasingly pungent. Although Peter and Matthew could tolerate it for the short while necessary for each day's harvest, Matthew became concerned the odor, which now permeated the street on warm days, would invite investigation and possible interference from those who took exception to the practice of rodent husbandry within city limits.

At first, Matthew assumed the smell was due to the rotting of the rubbish used to feed their animals, but closer observation revealed that hardly any of the rubbish survived long enough among the hungry horde to actually rot. After much puzzling over the problem, the solution came to him while availing himself of the outdoor convenience—as solutions to weighty problems often come to everyone, though seldom as apropos as this. As he sat in meditation over the troubling complication, a flash of insight told him what lay at the bottom of it.

His joy at this realization was so great he would have hollered "eureka" had the word been known to him, but instead he saw as rapidly as possible to the necessities concomitant upon that activity to which he was engaged and ran back into the house to find his brother. This feeling of elation was immediately felt by Tiny Tim, who in turn began transmitting it throughout the family along with that subtle satisfaction one feels after a thoroughly successful emptying out of that which one has been carrying about for some while.

"I got it figured out," said Matthew to Peter. "The reason for the stink and for the floor rising is the rats don't get out to go to the loo. Their leavings are getting deeper and deeper, and that's what's making the smell."

"We can't let them use ours," said Peter warily. "They'll just run away."

"No. We'll have to get down there and dig it out."

The expression on Peter's face was ample indication of how unappealing he found this prospect.

But Matthew shrugged and said, "We have to take the bad with the good like Mr. Dropping says."

The task, however, proved even less pleasant than anticipated. It is well known, through the vehicle of a cliché simile, that a rat will run away when it has somewhere to which it can run but will stand its ground with ferocity when it does not. This proved to be quite true, for as Peter attempted to set foot on rat territory, he was immediately jumped upon and bitten through the trousers by several of the frightened creatures. He batted away as many as he could before climbing back up the rope by which he had descended, shaking this leg and then the other with each step he took up the wall.

"Ungrateful lot," he said upon rejoining his brother. "We give them food and a place to live, and they attack me for it."

"And we kill them," said Matthew in their defense.

"They don't know that, or they wouldn't get in the basket every day."

Matthew could not argue with the logic and was practical enough of mind not to try when there was a more pressing problem at hand.

He thought.

"What we need is armor," he said at last. "But I think I know what to do."

He then led the way on an expedition, looking over fence after fence in search of laundry hung out to dry. As luck would have it, they came across a set of heavy linen sheets almost immediately, and as the sun was setting, they found two pairs of trousers and two shirts of a size indicating the owner was a man of some girth. All this, I am sorry to say, they took without asking permission.

After work the following day, they set about cutting the sheets into wide strips, which they wrapped about their limbs and bodies before putting on the oversize garments. Thus fortified against tooth and claw, they descended again into the cellar and proceeded with its excavation. The armor proved sufficient to keep them from being bitten in their lower extremities, though it did not stop the creatures from climbing up their bodies to attack above their necks.

Progress was slow, and the hour they devoted to the task was not sufficient to move twenty pounds of the offending material, which constituted less than 10 percent of what Matthew estimated to be the totality of the mass.

"It's more work than I thought," said Matthew as he stripped himself of the thick padding.

"Is it worth it, do you think?" asked Peter.

"Well, once we've cleaned it once, it won't be so bad keeping it that way."

"I suppose. What are we going to do with this, then?" asked Peter, pointing to the mound of rat leavings they had extracted.

"Dump it in people's loos, I guess," said Matthew, though he had a feeling this was an inadequate and temporary solution.

When they arrived home, they were drenched in sweat, but that was not the first thing that attracted the attention of their family.

"Good heavens!" said Mrs. Cratchit. "What is that smell?" She began sniffing about the boys trepidatiously. "It's in your hair," she said with a grimace. "Come on with you. Outside."

The two followed their mother out back, where they suffered her to wash them with carbolic soap and a scrub brush, which left them raw and tingling.

Clearly, their methods needed refinement if they were to get the cellar cleared and still have skin and hair afterward. Matthew then devised they strip down before donning their linen armor to prevent their sweating into their clothes. He also had the idea of wearing masks and woolen caps to protect their heads and faces. This proved sufficient to keep the rats and the smell out of their hair, but it added to the discomfort of the ordeal.

Progress was slow.

And they began the clandestine disposal of the offensive material in the outhouses of their neighbors. This led to the widespread belief that some mysterious ailment had infected the community, and since the adults knew they were not the cause of the pestilential pong, they concluded that the carriers had to be the children who were lying out of shyness when they insisted their "doings" did not stink. Once this was agreed upon, the sale of castor oil exceeded supply in the local chemists' shops and the incidence of juvenile delinquency declined drastically for some while.

But this was not Matthew's motivation for seeking an alternate method of disposal.

"It's just not what a caterpillarist would do," he said to Peter on their way to work. "We should be selling it to someone and making all the extra work worthwhile."

"Who would want it?" asked Peter. "It stinks to high heaven."

That was just the thing Matthew needed to hear.

"Then that's where we start looking—for people who buy stinky stuff."

And so the two put a temporary halt to their excavations of the rat cellar and spent their spare time in search of those that had need of olfactorily offensive substances. This proved harder than one would imagine, for although there were many industries that produced malodorous materials as by-products of manufacture, there were far fewer that required malodorous materials for use *in* manufacture.

So it was that their efforts to sniff out a customer for their rat leavings led to serial frustration. That is until they found their way into the vicinity of Belcher's Brewery.

"What's that smell?" asked Matthew of a worker unloading sacks of barley from a wagon.

"That's your hops, innit?" said the man.

"What are hops?"

"What makes beer bitter."

"So you use hops to make beer?"

"'At's right."

"Can I see one?"

"Ask 'im," said the man nodding toward the foreman, but the foreman was less accommodating than the worker and had the two marched off the property by their collars.

"Shall we look somewhere else, then?" asked Peter as he adjusted his coat downwards into its intended place.

"No, I think we're onto something here," said Matthew. "All I need is to pinch a hop and smell it. We'll have to do a bit of burglary."

This determination led to the two returning that night under cover of darkness—as such activities are best conducted—and scaling the fence. Had not Peter been more afraid of admitting to Matthew he was afraid, he would have been too afraid to do this, for although he found modest acts of skullduggery—like following Squidge's man to the crematory or stealing bed linen from clotheslines or sneaking into outhouses to dispose of rat refuse—to be quite thrilling, he estimated trespassing on the property of a powerful company with intent to purloin was an act of elite skullduggery and beyond his capacity for duggering skulls.

They were not long in their quest, however, as Matthew's nose led him to a wagon still half-loaded with full sacks. On the side of the wagon were the words "George Luciskou—Hops Farmer—Mirrorword, Kent."

"This is it," murmured Matthew.

"That's a funny name," whispered Peter.

"Not really. All farmers are named George," said Matthew, and he extracted his new pocketknife from a pocket and proceeded to slice enough of the stitching along the side of one sack to reach in and take a handful of the contents. Then he pocketed the handful along with the knife and said, "Let's go."

All the way home, Peter was terrified of being stopped by the police and searched. In silence, he tortured his imagination to invent a plausible explanation for his brother having a pocketful of hops. This he could not do, but fortunately the need never arose, as they made it home without incident. The relief of being again within his family and still at liberty in the world at large propelled him into a joy that—as you must have expected—was magnified by Tiny Tim and felt by all.

CHAPTER 19

No doubt our dear reader has noticed that the narrative has focused on the adventures of Matthew and Peter for several chapters, with relatively few references to our hero, Tiny Tim, and the rest of the family Cratchit. This was intentional, as the activities of the rest are either unknown or of insufficient interest to merit the space of an entire chapter to report them.

In regard to Martha and Belinda, after leaving to attend the Toosheronde Academy of Cultural Refinement, their fate is lost to history, and it can only be hoped that, at this point (being sixteen months later), they have indeed been finished and are off on adventures of their own, but their role in the story is without a doubt finished, and the author will now abandon them to oblivion.

Mr. and Mrs. Cratchit, in the year following the end of the trial, sank deeper and deeper into sloth and indolence, riding the waves of emotion that flowed from Tiny Tim—those waves being waves of joy experienced by the idle rich when engaged in the activity of idling minus the minor joy of being rich.

Bob would sit for hours staring into space with a vacuous grin upon his face, only to sigh occasionally and say, "God bless us, every one!" not through his own desire to say it but through Tiny Tim's, for although our hero could not hear the words with his ears or his mind, he could still feel the serene satisfaction they inspired in his father and so was serenely satisfied himself.

Mrs. Cratchit would venture out every day to spend the money

Matthew provided to her. This was as pleasing to her as laudanum is to the opium-eater, but as with the opium-eater, the pleasure was fleeting, and had it not been for the generally calming influence of Tiny Tim, she would have likely grown bitter with the limits imposed upon her finances.

As to our hero, Tiny Tim himself, since he is the main protagonist of our story, we should provide at least one paragraph to keep the reader abreast of his contribution to the saga.

And here it is.

When Tiny Tim was lying alone in the morgue, he grew bored through the lack of interaction with others and learned to amuse himself with manipulations of his emotions in ways that affected others. When he was returned to the bosom of his family, however, he lost interest in playing with feelings in this way and settled into a life of simple emotional exchange with those near and dear to him. His skill in manipulation dwindled, as it was no longer being exercised—that is, until the time roughly coincident with Matthew returning home with a pocketful of hops.

And there you have it. Not enough there to flesh out an entire chapter, but significant nonetheless.

Of all the Cratchits who were not Matthew and Peter, the only one who really did anything of much genuine interest during this long year was Lucy. She was the only one of the family who knew for a certainty Tiny Tim was alive. To this, she lived in fear he would be buried as soon as the family finances were settled and there was money for a funeral. This fear she was careful to control lest Tiny Tim receive it and amplify it back into the rest. Nevertheless, this underlying worry inspired her to try to communicate with her silent brother in the desperate hope of getting him to demonstrate his presence and avoid succumbing to a dark and subterranean fate.

So it was that Lucy spent her days in apparent idleness, sitting on the floor next to Tiny Tim and stroking his forehead. Bob and his wife thought it sad their daughter could not accept what they perceived to be the truth, but as has been indicated, they were too given to indolence to put much effort into trying to persuade her. As long as she refrained from overt efforts to convince them of Tiny Tim's inner vivacity, they were willing to sigh and let her be.

That all came to a sudden and shocking end.

On the day after Peter and Matthew's foray into industrial espionage at Belcher's Brewery, shortly after the two boys had left for work, Gazpayne's clerk, Mr. Scribble, arrived at the door of the Cratchit home dressed in a swallowtail coat of a beautiful blue.

"I have been sent by Mr. Gazpayne, of Rankin, Fowle, O'Durr, and Gazpayne, to deliver this," said Scribble. He handed over to Bob a sealed document. "It is the relinquishment of your power of attorney. I am to witness you reading it and signing it, and to answer any questions you might have regarding it."

"Does this mean we can spend our money again?" asked Mrs. Cratchit excitedly.

"That it does, madam," said Scribble flatly. "All legal claims against you have been settled, and all expenses covered, up to and including this date. Once Mr. Gazpayne is in possession of this document with your signatures upon it, what remains in your accounts is free to be despoiled by you howsoever you may please."

Mrs. Cratchit snatched the document from Bob and, taking no time to study it, found a quill and ink and signed where Scribble indicated. Then she thrust the quill into Bob's trembling hand.

"Initial here," said Scribble.

It took but a moment for Mrs. Cratchit's excited elation to reach Tiny Tim and raise his spirits to the heavens. A moment later, all those present, including the perennially noncommittal Mr. Scribble, became engulfed in a joy that knew no equal.

Lucy, who had been upstairs getting dressed when Scribble knocked, felt this wave of emotion hit her as she came downstairs and knew something must be afoot. She entered the kitchen in time to see the legal assistant affix his signature as witness to the document.

"What's all this?" she asked happily.

"We got our money back," said Mrs. Cratchit in a cackle.

The sudden realization that her silent battle to prevent Tiny Tim's fatal funeral was at an unsuccessful end hit Lucy like lightning. She let out a scream of terror that sent pigeons scattering for blocks around. Tiny Tim's emotions about-faced with a precision as sharp as that demanded by the fiercest sergeant major and instantly double-timed everyone in the house into panicked horror.

Scribble was so distressed he immediately ran from the premises without the document and was never seen again—though it was later rumored he enlisted with an infantry unit bound for India that morning.

Within the Cratchit family, the all-pervasive fear went on unabated for over an hour before Lucy could gain control of herself and put herself to the task of calming Tiny Tim. This was especially difficult for her, as you can imagine, since her grief at the looming loss of him could not be kept entirely from her mind. But succeed she did, at last, and a much relieved Bob said, "Well we're free of it now, my dears, aren't we?"

"Please don't send our Tim away," said Lucy.

But before her parents could speak, a knock at the door drew their attention away from her desperate concerns. Bob answered it and was confronted by a familiar formation of brass buttons set against a field of blue cloth. He looked up to see the face of the policeman who had arrested and released him the previous year.

"Good day to you, sir," said the constable. "Still here, I see."

"Yes, officer. Have I done something wrong?"

"Not at all, sir," said the constable jovially. "To the best of my knowledge, you been an upstanding example of lawful conduct since our little altercation—which, I have to say, serves to restore my faith in the ability of the criminal to rehabilitate himself when the proper amount of fear puts his mind to it." Then he leaned closer and murmured, "Assuming, of course, you hasn't been engaged in other forms of conduct without me knowing of it."

"No, constable. I've not been engaged in any form of conduct at all, and if I am so in the future, I'll be sure you're the first to know of it."

"No need for that, sir. Just keep on doing nothing at all, and we'll get along fine, we will. Now, as to the reason for my calling today, I've need to enquire if you've had anything in the way of a murder take place on the premises."

"A murder?"

"Yes sir. That's when one person of a criminal nature kills another person of a less fortunate nature."

"No, officer. You're welcome to come in and look about, but no one's been murdered here, fortunate or otherwise."

The constable removed his helmet and entered. He strolled from room to room apparently quite pleased with the absence of blood and gore. Then he came to Tiny Tim, and his expression changed.

"What's all this, then?" he asked, as he tried to come to his full height but was prevented from doing so by a beam in the ceiling.

"That's our son, Tiny Tim," said Bob.

"Are you joking, sir?"

"He was smaller when we named him."

"Oh, I see. Well, I may be mistaken, but he appears to be dead."

"He is. For some eighteen months now. He was here last time you came."

"Oh, yes, I do recall, now that you mention it. I was going to ask you about it then, but with all that was happening, it slipped my mind."

"It was a busy day for both of us," said Bob with a nervous laugh.

"It was that, sir," said the policeman with a smile. "Well, your boy seems to be comporting himself properly in a legally dead manner and well within the expectations of the law, so I'll say no more about it. And, seeing as you've got no other bodies lying about, nor evidence of felonious assaults, I'll assume the murder happened elsewhere and leave you to go back about your business."

The policeman left, and calm relief filled the house once more.

The rest of the day was eerily quiet outside, which was a little disquieting for the family. What they did not know was that the entire neighborhood had evacuated following Lucy's scream. The scream itself had been chilling to the steeliest of nerves, but the subsequent tidal wave of terror sent forth from Tiny Tim had thrown the community into a frenzied panic. All had run from their homes without knowing what was happening but knowing their horror would not permit them to stay. In an effort to grasp what the great havoc could mean, they collectively ran through the list of possibilities, and finding no evidence of fire, riot, war, explosion, or religious proselytizers, they concluded there had to have been a murder at the source of the scream. Their logic was unassailable, for—barring the list of alternate terrors just provided—only a murder could inspire such horror as that which held the community in its clutches. This, then, was reported to the police, which led to the constable's investigation already described with respect to the portion of it that was conducted in the Cratchit household.

The importance of this to our tale became apparent to Lucy only the next day, after the neighbors had all returned home, when she ventured out and overheard a discussion regarding the unsolved mystery of the scream and the subsequent terror. Apparently, a strange man in a swallowtail coat of a beautiful blue was seen running at high speed through the streets right after the nerve-shattering scream filled the air. This description fit that of Mr. Scribble, which made Lucy smile to herself, for she didn't really like him much and could take some satisfaction knowing he might be inconvenienced by it all. But what made the greater impression on her, after she'd had time to consider it, was that the range of Tiny Tim's projection had now expanded manifold beyond its previous limits.

This startling realization set poor Lucy adrift in stormy thought for some while as she considered the options before her. After much soul-searching, she decided there was nothing for it but an act of self-sacrifice: she would give up her dream of going to finishing school and assuming positions under lords and gentlemen to devote her life to teaching Tiny Tim to talk.

CHAPTER 20

The next day, while Lucy was out among the neighbors, overhearing excited conversation after excited conversation about the ripper still at large and the efforts of police to hide the facts from everyone—clearly, they were incompetent and keeping the extent of the grisly carnage secret to disguise the fact—Bob and his wife were delivering the signed document to Mr. Gazpayne. Gazpayne, you can easily imagine, was curious as to the whereabouts of his clerk.

"Strangest thing, it was," said Bob, being careful not to reveal too many details. "There was a terrifying scream, and Mr. Scribble ran out like the devil himself was after him."

"A scream, you say?" asked the dubious lawyer.

"A most bloodcurdling scream," said Mrs. Cratchit. "Enough to curl your hair, it was."

"We later heard it was a murder close by," said Bob.

"And Mr. Scribble," asked Gazpayne, "egressed posthaste upon hearing this bloodcurdling, hair-curling utterance, you say?"

"As posthasty as you can imagine," said Bob.

"And then some," said Mrs. Cratchit.

Gazpayne sighed. "He always was a rather skittish sort. Never mind. It's clear he acted of his own accord, and you have not misplaced him. You won't be charged for the loss."

"Very generous, I'm sure," allowed Bob, and he allowed his wife to pull him away from further conversation—she being anxious to reach the bank and resume the spending of the remaining Scrooge fortune.

Mr. Goldworm, the bank manager, received them in his office with effulgent cordiality and, after shutting the heavy, sound-muffling door, sat to peruse the letter from Gazpayne, which was the metaphorical key to the treasure chest.

"Everything seems to be in order," said the slender banker. "The requirement of legal authorization has been lifted from your accounts, so you are free to spend."

"How much are we talking?" asked Mrs. Cratchit.

"How much what?"

"Money! How much is left in my accounts?"

"Oh, that!" said Goldworm, and he opened a file that was now nearly six inches thick. "Quite, quite. Let me see."

He flipped leaf after leaf while carrying on a muttering dialogue with himself. "Court costs were …? Oh, yes. And to Blundt's … Good heavens …! The scoundrel …! Seven pounds for …? Compounded daily …?" This continued, escalating in its intensity, for forty minutes before he extracted one page and, red-faced, short of breath, and sweating, said, "There remains £101.14s.9d."

"A hundred quid?" shrieked the disbelieving Mrs. Cratchit. "There was over three hundred thousand last year!"

"Indeed, there was," said Goldworm, nervously checking that the heavy, sound-muffling door was still closed and still muffling sound. "But you did incur some rather … hmm, shall we say, 'excoriating' … perhaps more accurately 'eviscerating' legal expenses and—as is often the case with those who avail themselves of debt financing—compounding interest that exceeds all expectations. I am most sorry, but everything appears to be in order and well within—or, at least, marginally within—the legal limits of …"

"But three hundred thousand quid?"

"I am sorry, dear lady, but I can be of no further help to you. If you question Mr. Gazpayne's handling of your affairs, I can only advise you to … Or, perhaps, you would do better to … I don't know what to tell you."

What followed would have filled several pages, but these events took place during the reign of Queen Victoria, when censorship was too robustly enforced to permit Mrs. Cratchit's choice of vocabulary to appear in print.

"We've still got a hundred pounds, my dear," said Bob, on their way home. "That's enough to rent a nicer house, and the lads are bringing in enough to feed and clothe us."

Mrs. Cratchit was too exhausted, too hoarse from shouting, and still too afraid of the possibility of imprisonment—with which Goldworm had been forced to threaten her to get her to leave quietly—to argue any further.

"At least there's that, I suppose," she said as she faded into complete despair.

CHAPTER 21

Lucy had returned from her daily errands—not to mention the overhearing of conversations—long before her parents arrived home to luxuriate in their disappointment over the loss of their fortune. Inspired by the knowledge that Tiny Tim's power of projection was increasing exponentially, she believed with all her being he could make his presence felt by everyone if only she could find a way to convince him of the importance of doing so.

So, as soon as she entered the house, she immediately put her full attention to the task of bringing Tiny Tim out of his societal exile. As always, the boy was joyful to sense her presence nearby and began glowing, purring, radiating—the proper present participle has yet to be coined that describes it accurately—with delight. As pleasant as this was for Lucy, it made it difficult for her to impress upon him the urgency of the need for him to let the world know he was still in residence within himself.

The front door opened to admit Mrs. Cratchit followed by Mr. Cratchit, who said, "As sad and sorry a place as this is, it is still a small joy to be home, isn't it, my dear?"

Mrs. Cratchit was about to give poor Bob another in a long series of lectures on his chief defect of character—that being his willingness to accept the unacceptable—but the radiant delight of her inanimate son reached her and caused the release of a sigh and the upcurling of a sad smile in its place.

"I suppose so," she said, and she put her mind to the preparation of dinner as the noon hour had passed while she was still engaged in the slandering of Messrs. Gazpayne and Goldworm, the surgeons she had failed in suing, and the Honorable Sir Justice Ruff-Birching, who had been the instrument of that failure, and she was now a mite peckish.

Lucy fought on, trying to get through to her brother. To this, it should be noted, she was becoming more and more skilled at regulating her own feelings, for it was not easy to sustain the sense of well-being necessary to keep Tiny Tim calm and attentive while also attempting to communicate that disaster was looming on the horizon of his near future in such a way as not to shock him and send a subsequent shockwave out into the world.

"Please, Tim," she imagined. "Try to let them know. If they know, they'll let me keep you, but if you don't, they'll … Just let them know, please." And on and on she went, carefully avoiding any actual thought of his descent into the yawning grave.

After dinner, Lucy, having grown exhausted from hours of attempting to get some outward sign of life to appear on Tiny Tim, went for a walk to revitalize herself, leaving her parents in a state of sated serenity.

This state of sated serenity lasted several minutes until the conversation found its way back to the unfathomable depletion of the family treasure. Now Bob was well enough practiced in the arts and sciences of being Mrs. Cratchit's husband to abstain completely from uttering the sentence "I told you so" or any linguistic construction that might convey the same or similar sense. However, Mrs. Cratchit was sufficiently practiced in the arts and sciences of being Bob's wife to know he was thinking it, regardless, and that was enough to start a hideous row.

Of course, Lucy was not there to stop her parents' anger from reaching her emotive brother and being automatically magnified beyond all hope of containment. She returned to find the family's few aging knickknacks that—up to the time of her departure—had decorated the living room had all become missiles conscripted by Mrs. Cratchit in her militant efforts to express her displeasure over her husband's wanton disrespect toward her. And from the back of the house, Lucy could hear that the tattered items of tableware and tired pots and pans populating the kitchen were being called to action in much the same martial manner.

Though Lucy had seen Mrs. Cratchit get angry from time to time before, she had never witnessed anything resembling the battle scene that greeted her upon reentry into the house. The ground floor was littered with the shattered evidence of the prolonged destruction, still in progress. And the rage coming off Tiny Tim was like a rabid dog lunging at Lucy's throat, but she knew it for what it was and fought it back.

Her first thought was to run to protect her brother from possible injury, but he was well out of the line of fire, so she ran instead to the source of the shouting in the kitchen. There she found Bob in a most uncharacteristic fury, poised ready to take advantage of his wife's having just run out of ammunition and move against her with intent to perpetrate a most vicious violence. Lucy dived into his path and screamed, "Stop!"

Bob's eyes were on fire. His right fist darted up behind his left ear in preparation to drive his daughter from his path with a backhand blow. Lucy shrieked as terror filled her small body to overflowing. Her arms flung up to protect her face as she cringed before her father. Immediately Tiny Tim felt Lucy's horror and deftly switched himself to it. With him, the whole house leaped from scorching rage to chilling fear in an instant.

Mrs. Cratchit could scarcely breathe through it. She closed her eyes and trembled. Then she opened them to see Bob readying himself to strike Lucy and, realizing her husband had gone homicidally mad, fainted dead away.

Simultaneously, Bob felt the chill race up and down his spine as Tiny Tim froze the scene with terror. He sensed his upper arm pushing into his chin and had to think why that was. A sickening horror filled him when he recalled his intention to strike his daughter—an intention frozen in the instant before it became action. Shame and sickening disgust took him in their grip and squeezed a long, plaintive moan from his soul. He burst into wailing and staggered from the room.

Lucy was the last to move. It was not until she ventured to open her eyes to see her father no longer stood before her that she was able to drop her arms and uncurl herself from her cringing anticipation of a blow. Still awash in fear, she took several deep breaths and forced herself to take command of the situation.

She looked about and saw her mother regaining consciousness as she lay on the floor and heard her father weeping woefully upstairs, but she knew her first duty was to calm Tiny Tim and restore the house to peace. She raced to his side and took a running mental leap into the land of lovely memories.

And it should be said that she was getting better and better at bringing her brother back to the serene center of the emotional spectrum. Hardly five minutes passed before he and she and the rest of the house were firmly fixed in gentle happiness once more.

Bob made a valiant effort to remain ashamed and tearful but failed. Mrs. Cratchit attempted to rekindle her ill will toward her husband but could not. And Lucy wanted to stay right where she was, basking in the warmth of her brother's love, but she forced herself away to begin cleaning up the mess that lay all around them.

With broom and coal shovel, she performed a yeoman's task of bringing the little house back to its former glory, such as it was, and soon—allowing for the conspicuous absence of plates, cups, and saucers, not to mention all the ornaments and the smaller items of furniture—no one would have known this was the scene of a fierce battle fought two hours before.

Mrs. Cratchit had watched Lucy work while seated on the floor on the spot where she had fainted and recovered, seemingly unable to motivate herself beyond the gripping fascination with what her daughter was doing. Likewise, Bob had spent this whole time lying on his bed, lost in deep contentment with life despite the this-and-that of his life that would dissuade anyone else from contentment, deep or otherwise.

Eventually, Bob came downstairs to find order fully restored and had to wonder whether the earlier events had been nothing more than a nightmare experienced during a sleep he had forgotten he'd taken. Then he noticed his wife sitting where he'd left her. He helped her up and asked, "Were we not fighting, my dear?"

"We were, I should say, but I can't remember why."

"Probably for the best, my dear. But I recall our Lucy giving me such a nasty fright. Is she all right?"

Before Mrs. Cratchit could respond, a knock at the door took Bob's attention away. It was the policeman again.

"Good day to you, sir. Sorry to bother you again, but I have to ask if you've had a spot of bother earlier today."

"Nothing serious, officer," said Bob with a twinge of nerves that always possessed him when telling a fib.

"It's just that the whole neighborhood's gone a bit mad, you see, sir, and I'm in the process of counting up the felonies, the misdemeanors, and the acts of an unnatural nature, to which I need to affix my attention."

"My missus and I had a slight raising of the voices with each other earlier, but that's all. Nothing that doesn't happen in all families from time to time."

"Indeed, sir. Can I have a quick …?

"Of course, of course," said Bob, and he stepped aside to let the constable in.

The policeman looked about as he had the day before and, just as on the day before, was quite content with all he saw. Then he came to Tiny Tim and felt his sense of peace and order swell even further.

"Good lad, that," he said. "A few years of constabulary duties gives you a sense for telling when a lad's up to no good, and I can see he's not one of that sort. Pity he's dead, though."

"Yes, constable. We would prefer he wasn't, but you can't have everything, as they say."

"Very true," said the policeman, and he took one more look about the room. "Place looking a bit sparse compared to yesterday, if I'm not mistaken, sir, isn't it?"

"My daughter's been cleaning up."

The constable looked to Lucy, who curtseyed politely and smiled shyly.

"Good girl. I must say, sir, your house is an oasis of lawfulness and orderliness in a sea of villainy and acts of an unnatural nature," said the policeman, shaking his head sadly. "We still have yet to apprehend the man in the swallowtail coat of a beautiful blue what perpetrated yesterday's mass murder. And for which we still have yet to find the bodies or the scenes of the crimes, for the matter of that. Add to all that, today, we're beset with a whole new list of felonies and misdemeanors for which we've apprehended only a few of the perpetrators and victims."

"What kinds of felonies and misdemeanors?" asked Bob.

"Much your usual sort of thing, sir," said the policeman, raising his eyebrows and widening his eyes. "Taken on an individual basis, one wouldn't think anything of it. But it's the scale of the thing which is bothersome, sir. The whole neighborhood corrupted into violence not more than three hours ago. Dead and injured still being carted away at this very moment, they are. In all my years, I've not seen anything like it. Street after street with criminal after criminal, performing acts of a criminal nature upon their fellow criminals. Gives you pause to wonder what the world's coming to, it does." But then he donned a friendly smile and said, "But you keep to yourself and yours, sir, and show a bit of caution when out of doors, and if anything of an unfortunate nature does befall you, you be sure to tell me of it, and I'll do my best to get some proper vengeance for you."

"That's very kind, I must say," said Bob, and he escorted the policeman out.

When they had all calmed from the excitement of the constabulary visit, Lucy stated, "It's Tim that's doing it."

"Doing what, my pet?" asked Bob.

"Making everyone go mad."

Bob looked to his wife, and they shared a well-worn, worried look. Lucy was now fifteen and should be long grown out of the need to have what they believed to be fantastical imaginings.

"He's dead, my dear," said Bob sadly, "and can't do anything at all more than nothing at all."

"No, he's not," said Lucy so forcefully she set her parents back on their heels. "And yes, he can. He can't talk or move about, but he feels things. And when he feels things, he makes others feel them too."

"I'm sorry," said Bob, "but there's no sense in what you're saying."

"Think about it," said Lucy. "Yesterday you were both feeling happy about getting Uncle Ebenezer's money back until I got scared. Our Tim felt that and got scared too, and then both of you and that nasty Mr. Scribble and all the neighbors got scared as well."

"That was because of the murder," said Mrs. Cratchit.

"There was no murder!" said Lucy with a stamp of her foot. "Don't you see? They're looking for a man in a swallowtail coat of a beautiful blue. That's Mr. Scribble. He didn't kill anybody. He just ran away because Tim scared the dickens out him. And you heard the bobby: they haven't found a body yet. No … body; no … murder."

"Of course there was a murder, my dear," said Bob pitifully. "Just look at all this mayhem today. Yesterday's murder was just the beginning."

"Today was because of Tim too. You two were angry about something, and Tim felt it. Then he got angry and made everything worse. You nearly wrecked the house, and all about us, everyone went mad."

"But what you say—" said Bob, but Lucy cut him short.

"All right," she said, finally losing her patience. "If you won't listen to reason, I'll show you."

With that, she knelt beside Tiny Tim and began stroking his forehead. Bob and Mrs. Cratchit watched with sad concern over their daughter's sanity. After a minute or two, Lucy spoke.

"You're beginning to feel disappointed," she said, "like the time you found out this was where we had to live."

"Yes, b, b, but …" said Bob, sinking into despair.

"And now you're feeling really happy, like the time Matthew told you he and Peter were going to catch rats."

"That's right," said Mrs. Cratchit with a giggle.

"And now you're feeling disappointed again … And happy again … And disappointed again."

Both Bob and his wife rode on this emotional scenic railway together, but it was Bob who first admitted to himself Lucy was not dallying with delusions. A painful fear gripped him but was quickly swept aside by the tide of goodwill pouring off his quiet son.

"How did you do that?" he asked at last.

"Tim feels what I feel and then makes it bigger and sends it out to everyone else. I just think things that make me feel different ways and let him feel them too. Then you feel what he feels."

Mrs. Cratchit was still doubtful, but seeing her husband ready to accept this bizarre explanation was enough to make her reconsider. Then she, too, was basking in the radiance of Tiny Tim's loving warmth.

"This is wonderful," said Bob, and he laughed. "Our Tiny Tim's not dead."

"At last!" said Lucy ecstatically. She rose to hug her father about the neck.

"Hold on a moment," said Mrs. Cratchit. "Are you saying we don't feel what we feels no more 'cuz now we just feels what our Tim feels?"

"No," said Lucy, trying to formulate an answer. "We feel what he's feeling when we're not feeling anything, but when we're feeling something else, he feels what we're feeling, and then we feel it too, only bigger."

"Oh," said Mrs. Cratchit, nodding as though she understood. "Now I see."

Bob had a thought and had to ask, "So this year gone past has been pleasant enough for the most, hasn't it? Was that all because of our Tiny Tim?"

"Mostly," said Lucy. "I've been doing my best to keep him happy 'cuz I know it makes us all happy when I do."

"You are a good one, my love," said Bob tearfully, and he took her in his arms again and hugged her to his breast. "Doing that for us when we didn't believe in what you were trying to tell us. So brave, my dear. So brave and so good."

"But there is a problem," said Lucy into the musty velvet of Bob's jacket.

Bob released her. "What's that, my dear?"

"Tim's getting stronger," whispered Lucy, afraid her brother might hear. "Before, it was only us that felt him, but now he sends his feelings a lot farther. Yesterday, he terrified the whole street into thinking there was a murder, and today he made everyone for blocks around go mad."

The seriousness of this was not lost on Bob. All at once, he was overjoyed at having his son alive and fearful for Tiny Tim's unbridled power for good or for evil.

To that, he prayed, "God bless us, every one!"

CHAPTER 22

Having considered the problem for several months in private, and having failed to come to a conclusion, Peter had to ask, "Do penguins have a heaven?"

"I don't know," said Matthew, who was well used to his brother's forays into speculation and no longer given to surprise. "Why do you ask?"

"I just think it would be nice to know the rats have someplace nice to go when we kill them. That's all."

"Then it makes sense that they do, doesn't it?"

"Yes," Peter nodded. "I suppose it does, doesn't it?"

"It does," said Matthew definitively, and he felt some satisfaction at having succeeded in extricating Peter from his perplexing metaphysical difficulty.

The two made their usual sizable haul and received their usual compliments from both Dropping and Squidge. They returned home along their usual route while engaged in their usual conversation. When they arrived at the rat house with the intention of stowing their pull-cart in its hiding place, however, conditions were not at all usual, necessitating they continue on past with their cart in tow to avoid compromising the secrecy of their clandestine operation.

Everywhere were policemen loading prisoners into black carriages with barred windows, while family members pleaded for their release.

"It's not like him to do murder; really it ain't," said one lady to a constable. "I'm sure he'll not do it again. Can't you let him go with a warning?"

"I'm sorry, ma'am, but rules is rules and we do have to take him in. Don't worry, yourself, now. He'll get a fair trial before he's hanged."

"Are you sure?"

"Oh, quite sure, ma'am."

"Well, all right, then. But please make sure he do," said the woman, and she smiled and waved to her husband as if he were going on a football weekend with his mates.

It was strange enough seeing all these arrests being made at one time, but far stranger still that everyone seemed so content with it since the circumstances concomitant upon arrests are commonly rather less convivial.

"Are you quite comfortable, sir?" asked a sergeant of a prisoner.

"Yes, thank you, guv. Comfy enough. One don't 'spect a royal coach to be hauled off to Her Majesty's pleasure, now, do he?"

"No, indeed," said the policeman, and he shared an amicable little laugh with his captive before shutting the carriage door.

As odd as it was, Peter and Matthew soon found themselves sharing in the pervasive goodwill of their surroundings—a pleasant equanimity that seemed to grow stronger and stronger the closer they got to their house.

"We can't go in now," said Matthew.

"Why not?"

"We'd have to leave the cart outside. We'll come back later when there's no one about."

"Where do you want to go?" asked Peter.

"The library."

"You mean where they keep all the books?"

"That's what I've heard."

"Whatever for?"

"I need to read about hops. Come on. I won't be long."

So the two left the tranquil scene of crimes and arrests in the vicinity of their home for the ponderous temple of learning on the other side of the river. They made their way into a park, where Matthew bought roasted chestnuts for Peter and left him to mind the pull-cart and watch the pretty girls stroll past while he went to the library to do his research.

The towering, gray Corinthian structure made Matthew feel as out of place as a snowman on the slopes of a volcano as he climbed the many, many steps to the entrance. In the spirit of the most enthusiastic thespian, he attempted to appear scholarly and academic while he strolled through the endless book-lined aisles. The wealth of words in print soon overwhelmed the poor youth, as he had no idea where to start looking. Random selections turned up *The Code of Hammurabi*, *Mathematica Principia*, and *Two Treatises on Government*, all of which might have proved fascinating to him in other circumstances, but none of which solved his problem at hand—that being: what are hops?

At length, a sense of desperation drove him to ask for assistance from a thickly bespectacled librarian slouched over a desk located at the bottom of a cloud of dust.

"Student of botany, are you?" asked the myopic minder of books.

"Yes sir, I am," said Matthew, hoping his well-worn clothes didn't belie his assertion.

"Walk this way, then," said the elderly man as he stood up—though not to full height, as years of reading and sitting had left his body resembling a question mark—and began a crouched, arthritic, limping meander that took them down two flights of stairs and through the intestinal labyrinth that was the section devoted to the biological sciences.

"Up there," said the librarian, pointing to a row of massive tomes on the top shelf of a twelve-foot rack. "There should be a ladder about here someplace. I'll wish you good luck with your studies then, young man, and thank you if you'll be so good as to point me back in the direction from which we came."

"Thank you, sir," said Matthew with a finger in the direction of what appeared to be the correct way.

The librarian left, and Matthew turned his attention to the finding of a ladder, all the while cringing at the thought of the task before him.

But find a ladder he did, and he persevered in his task according to the dictates of his character. After eleven ascents and descents carrying the cumbersome volumes down and back up, he finally found what he needed and memorized the pertinent details.

Shaking with fatigue and hunger, he left the library at sunset and found his way back to Peter. When Matthew arrived at his brother's side, Peter was in the process of negotiating a purchase from a bedraggled little man with half the usual complement of eyes and a quarter of teeth.

"Here's my brother, now," said Peter excitedly, and he explained to Matthew, "This gentleman is an international diamond merchant who's fallen on hard times and needs to sell what's left of his wares."

"They'll fetch a hundred quid, easy, they will," said the dwarfish Cyclopean. "But I's willing to let 'em go for a crown each, seeing's as my needs is pressing."

With that, he produced from a small leather bag a teardrop-shaped faceted crystal the size of an egg.

"Why's there a hole drilled through the end?" asked Matthew.

"This one I plucked from a golden idol of a craven image worshipped in Zanzibar. 'Twas one of his eyes, it was. Them 'eathens would pray to it, you see, and the idol would cry tears, and this is where them tears came out."

"What would we do with them?" asked Matthew.

"Sell 'em to a jeweler. There's plenty about."

"So why don't you?"

"Well, there's my difficulty laid out for you, innit? I got a bit of a history with the revenue blokes over duties what's wanting, you see? And that makes them what deals in diamonds leery of dealing with the likes of me direct-like. But two such lads as yourselves—being without no history and all—they wouldn't raise an eyebrow against you, would they?"

"We don't have a crown," said Matthew.

"Yes, we do," said Peter indignantly. "We've got seven shillings six. I saw Mr. Dropping count it out."

"No, we don't," said Matthew insistently. "Come on. We've got to go home."

"Well, if you don't want me diamonds," snarled the little man while producing a tiny revolver from his jacket pocket, "I'll have the money, then, won't I? And keep the glass meself."

Peter was shocked to see the gun, but Matthew just sighed with grave disappointment before emptying his pockets into the waiting hand of the thief. Satisfied with a good day's work, the one-eyed robber skipped off in a quick but awkward gait.

"Idiot," hissed Matthew to his brother.

"Me?" said Peter, lurching up insulted. "You're the one that said no to a hundred-pound diamond."

"God bless us, every one!" said Matthew to no one at all as he took hold of the handle of the cart.

CHAPTER 23

The street was much quieter when Matthew and Peter arrived home that night. Indeed, the cumulative effect of that day's murders and arrests had resulted in a considerable depopulation of the neighborhood, leaving it ghostly quiet.

The journey home had been silent, too, as the two brothers were furious—each with the other. Reflecting back on the recent robbery, each was convinced the other was a babe in the woods in the woodlands of the underworld, which had led to their losing their day's pay—for which each blamed the other—and so they were not speaking to one another.

Their anger was quelled, however, as they neared home and entered the calm serenity of Tiny Tim's influence. By the time they'd arrived at the house, they'd quite forgotten their difficulties and were greeted by their family with much greater affection than they'd anticipated.

"We're sorry we're late home," said Matthew. "We ran into a bit of a bother."

"Never mind that, for now," said Bob. "We've got some wonderful news to tell you. Our Tim's alive!"

"What?" asked Peter. "How can …?"

"I don't know how," whispered Bob. "But Lucy showed us it's true, didn't you, my love?"

Lucy then went over the events leading up to the revelation, using linguistic constructions that conveyed the same or similar sense of "I told you so" without actually using those words, but also served to explain how she had demonstrated to Bob and Mrs. Cratchit the fact of the living Tim.

For his part, Matthew had always had a healthy skepticism regarding Lucy's convictions about Tiny Tim. On the one side, his own experiences tended to lead him toward belief, plus he knew Lucy to be sounder of judgment than others he might name. But on the other side, it all seemed too fantastical, and he had to wonder whether his own feelings, and those of his sister, might be the result of wishful thinking and nothing more.

For his part, Peter had always had an unhealthy skepticism based entirely on an unwillingness to consider that anything he had not believed since birth to be true could be true. To this stance he remained entirely faithful, and so Lucy had to repeat the demonstration she had made for her parents, with several iterations of emotional gymnastics to convince her eldest brother away from his conviction that death was undebatable.

"This is wonderful," said Peter after the horn finally blew and the walls of intransigence came tumbling down. "We never have to feel bad again, no matter what happens to us."

"That's right, my dear," said Bob, patting his taller son's back. "But this comes with a great responsibility. We can't have our Tim turning everyone about us to felonies and misdemeanors and acts of an unnatural nature when they're not of a mind to be doing it of their own violation."

Lucy felt justified in assuming the role of wisest expert in the matter of Tiny Tim and said, "We have to be careful what we think when we're home. Anything that upsets one of us upsets Tim, and then everyone's feeling it too. Only worse."

"As well as everyone close to this house," said Bob.

"And Tim's getting stronger all the time," said Lucy. "It might be the whole city before long."

"Or the whole country," said Peter fantastically. "Then our Tim would be like the prime minister or—"

"Yes," said Bob. "So, you see, we need to all stay very, very calm."

"Yes, Father," said Peter and Matthew in unison.

"Good, then," said Bob with a smile. "So, what was that bit of bother you started to tell us about?"

"We were robbed again," said Peter before Matthew could stop him.

"What?" shrieked Mrs. Cratchit, and a shock ran through the house, followed by a rising wave of fury.

Lucy immediately turned to Tiny Tim and began the ritual of reining in his wild emotions. Then, just as calm was settling again, Matthew attempted a simple explanation.

"Peter got talking to this thief ..." he said.

"He wasn't a thief," said Peter, much offended and hot. "He was an international diamond merchant."

"A diamond merchant with a gun?" said Matthew, underscoring the stupidity of Peter's assertion.

"A gun?" said Mrs. Cratchit with a gasp, and anger turned to terror.

Poor Lucy was alone against her family in her efforts to think pleasant thoughts and bring an end to this escalating madness. Fortunately, she had become well-practiced in the disciplining of her mind, and with the passing of a half hour, her will triumphed, and all was peaceful again.

They sat down to a simple meal.

Supper was more cumbersome than usual as all the plates, bowls, cups, and saucers had been reduced to smithereens during Mrs. Cratchit's barrage attack upon her husband described earlier. The family had to make do with the pots and pans, which had survived their brief military service more or less intact.

"At least we have our money back," said Bob as he scooped the last of his stew from the frying pan that served as his bowl. "Tomorrow we'll go out and buy all new kitchen things that we'll have when we reach our new home."

"New home?" asked Matthew, his mind going immediately to the logistical problems of keeping his rat-breeding operation going if they moved much distance away.

"Just something a little better than this, my dears," said Bob. "There was much less left from Mr. Scrooge's estate than we'd imagined, but there's enough to put us in better circumstances if you boys can keep working for Mr. Dropping. And with the nasty business of the trial well behind us, I might find a position somewhere myself, and perhaps Lucy, too, if she's willing."

"I would like that, Father," said Lucy. "If I can trust you all to keep our Tim happy when I'm not about."

All this did little to settle Matthew's concerns, and despite the prevailing equanimity of the household, he couldn't keep his mind from the possibility of losing the lucrative adjunct to income he'd worked hard to create and was planning to expand. This niggling dissatisfaction of his manifested in an unsettling edginess that infected them all.

"Someone's not thinking happy thoughts," said Lucy at last. "Is it really too much to ask?"

Matthew realized he was the source of the problem and rose to his feet with the words "I'm sorry. I've got a small problem to solve. I'll go for a walk and come back when I've got it all sorted out."

"Don't come back till you're nice like the rest of us," said Mrs. Cratchit.

So Matthew made his way out to the street and away from Tiny Tim's influence. He wandered without destination through the alleys and avenues in the environs of his home, careful to keep his distance, lest his silent brother sense his disquietude.

To the problem at hand, he knew that wherever the Cratchit clan moved, it would make the managing of the rat cellar more awkward. And he knew that when they moved to a better neighborhood, the chances of finding an abandoned derelict within it to which he could transfer his enterprise were slim to the point of impossibility. He wandered and wandered and puzzled and puzzled and worried and worried until, at last—as is often the case with creative genius—he gave up trying to find a solution and the answer came to him immediately following his surrender.

"I've been seeing it all backward," he realized with a laugh. "It doesn't need to be close to home. It needs to be close to Dropping's."

With this epiphany came a panoply of lovely visions, each more beautiful than the previous. In his mind, he saw all the empty, ruinous warehouses within a block or two of the offices of Eliphaz Dropping, master rat-catcher, which he and Peter passed every day in their comings and goings to deliver their daily catch. And with each magnificent memory of decaying edifices, his ecstasy grew, as he could easily see this would be a vast improvement over running a clandestine operation only ten houses from his home.

His arrival back at chez Cratchit was greeted with the soft pillow of peace Lucy had grown so adept at plumping. Tiny Tim was in his heaven, and all was good with the world once again—at least that much of it as was within his emotive reach.

As happy as Matthew was with this and with his own recent triumph over pending problems, the thought came to him, nevertheless, that the lives of his family were now caught between the horns of a two-edged sword of Damocles, which had them all walking on eggshells.

He recalled his father's words of earlier that evening: "But this comes with a great responsibility"—and sensed for the first time the extent of Tiny Tim's power and the explosive danger it brought with it. He took a moment to consider his family. His father was prone to fear and worry. His mother was prone to anger and despair. And his brother was prone to not being prone to anything at all, which made him the most dangerous of the lot.

"I'll have to talk to Lucy," he muttered to himself. "Without her here to mind our Tim, we could be in for problems."

CHAPTER 24

P eter asked, "So did you learn what hops are, then?" as he and Matthew set off for work the next morning.

"They're flowers," said Matthew.

"They don't look like flowers."

"No. But that's what they are."

"So how's that going to help us get rid of the rat dumplings?"

Matthew gave his brother a sideways glance and said, "It's probably better if we get in the habit of calling it the product."

"If you like," said Peter with a smirk. "Either way, it's what you get when a rat hangs a rat."

"True," said Matthew, pretending not to notice Peter's attempt at being clever. "But what I'm thinking is this: we get hold of other flowers and mix them with the product until we get something that smells like hops. Then we sell that to the brewery."

Not being an aficionado of fermented malt beverages, Peter could consider this possibility without prejudice.

"How would you make them look like hops?" he asked.

"Hmm," said Matthew, frowning at this problem. "Like as not, the best way would be to grind the whole mix to powder and say it works better that way."

Peter nodded in thoughtful agreement but asked, "Are you sure it'll be worth the work?"

"We have to get rid of the product one way or another, so we may as well bring in a bob or two doing it. It's only what a good caterpillarist would do, after all."

"Well said, my good man," said Peter. He took pride in seeing himself as a rising man of the world and a fledgling captain of industry.

On their way to Dropping's offices that afternoon, Matthew studied the abandoned warehouses along the way with a critical eye, assessing which might offer the best combination of features to suit their needs. It had to be secluded enough for them to enter and leave without being observed, have one level below ground suitable for keeping their captive rats captive and another at ground level to allow for overnight storage of their pull-cart, and have a place to work when blending bittering agent for the brewing industry.

There were three warehouses he earmarked as possibilities, which he and Peter investigated more closely on their way home. To this, only one proved appropriate, but it was excellent in all regards. It was well away from trafficked areas, had a set of carriage doors that could be bolted and plenty of space to work, and, best of all, had a basement with a section that had once been used for storing coal, which Matthew deemed perfect for the purpose of rat shelter.

With Matthew happy at settling the problem of livestock relocation and Peter happy his brother and fellow caterpillarist was happy, they arrived home to find supper served on brand-new flatware of an intricate design artistically named Dragonfly Wings.

"It was a bit more than I was meaning to spend," said Mrs. Cratchit. "But it was reduced in price, as it's not yet come into fashion, you see. I do rather likes it though, as it don't show up them odd bits Lucy sometimes misses when she cleans them."

"Very practical, I'm sure, my dear," said Bob, who then set to devouring the heavy leg of mutton to which they had treated themselves, now that they were free to spend that which remained of their money yet to be spent.

Fully sated to a degree to which they had not been sated in many, many months, the Cratchits retired early that night to bed and slept the sleep of the fully sated. Then, without the usual growling of empty innards to waken him, Matthew failed to rise before sunrise per habit. Panic struck the moment his eyes opened to the fullness of morning light on his face. He roused Peter, and the two dressed in a frenzied dash to head off at a trot to their first client. They barreled through their day and arrived at the offices of the master rat catcher not more than a half hour later than average, to which Mr. Dropping said only, "Had a difficult day reaching your numbers, have you?"

"Bit of a late start, sir," said Matthew. "But we got three hundred forty-nine anyway."

"You two don't half take the prize," said Dropping with a yellow-toothed grin. "More on a bad day than most in a good week. If I had four daughters, I'd marry them all to the two of you and tell them each to count their blessings in having twice the man of any other girl in England."

To this, Peter thrilled at the thought of cavorting in connubial excess with a pair of bouncy maidens, while Matthew's imagination ran more toward picturing daughters Dropping might have, and despite the temporary abeyance of the semipermanent dermic embellishments known to adorn his master's visage, he decided it was best not to mix one's professional and personal lives, and seek brides elsewhere.

With Peter's head still circling about in the delights of conjugal considerations, Matthew led him off in search of a source of flowers.

Not having been born of the class that gives flowers as a gift or buys them for decoration, they did not think to look for a florist, since the existence of such a person was not within their understanding of the universe. Only after several gardeners had chased them from gardens and a policeman had escorted them out of a public park did they come across a flower girl selling posies to passersby and discover that flowers—like anything anyone wants—must be purchased.

"Mind the cart," said Matthew to his brother, and he ventured near enough the girl to hear she was charging ha'penny a bunch—a rate which he immediately saw would result in an untenable total when applied to the quantity he considered necessary for his purposes.

"We need to find out where she gets them," he said to Peter upon his return, so they bought some fish and chips and sat in their cart to eat their supper while waiting for the flower girl to leave.

And she did.

They followed.

Had not Matthew been focused on in his purpose, it would have occurred to him that two young males seen following a girl through the alleyways of the Good Old City while pulling a cart full of empty burlap sacks might draw the attention of the police, but focused he was, and occur to him it did not.

Fortunately for them, there was none of the constabulary about to notice their following of the girl, but unfortunately, there were others who recognized the two—others who took exception to their presence in the commercial district outside the hours for ratting.

The flower girl, still oblivious to being followed, turned down a street that led to the river. Peter and Matthew turned in after her but were greeted by five men who would be euphemistically described in dated works of crime fiction as persons of an unsavory demeanor.

"We seen you making deliveries to Squidge," said the ringleader. "What you on about hereabouts, then?"

"We're here to buy flowers," said Peter pleasantly enough, not yet aware the group wasn't asking out of friendly curiosity.

"Flowers?" said the man, whose face lit up in amazement.

"That's what Mr. Squidge told us to say if we were stopped by a copper," said Matthew, who'd known immediately he and his brother were looking at a sound thumping.

With that, all five men stood up straighter, and two took a step back. The ringleader braced his nerve and asked, "Do I look like a copper to you?"

"No sir," said Matthew. "But Mr. Squidge didn't tell us what to say to anyone else, except to say we shouldn't say anything to anyone."

"So what's the secret, then?"

"I'd rather keep my liver where it is," said Matthew, trying his best to sound like one of Squidge's minions. "If you get my meaning."

"Oh, it's like that, is it?" said the man, caught somewhere between his need to keep face among his colleagues and his need to keep his own liver off Squidge's dinner plate.

He took a short step toward Matthew, put his finger on Matthew's chest, and said, "You tell Mr. Squidge: in future, if he wants something done hereabouts, he's to come to me to have it done. See?"

"Yes sir. And Mr. Squidge says, if the law asks any questions, you don't know anything about us. Otherwise, it'll go bad for everyone. See?"

The ringleader's instincts told him he was in over his head and it was time to exercise the better part of valor—that being discretion, for those unfamiliar with the truism.

"All right then," he said gruffly as he moved his men aside. "Get cherself lost."

Peter and Matthew then continued their quest for the flower girl's source of flowers, but she was no longer within sight. Still, they kept going in the general direction until they were sure they were out of sight of the ruffians.

"I didn't know we were working for Mr. Squidge," said Peter.

"You never were one to pay close attention," said Matthew while searching the view up and down the wide road next to the riverbank.

At length, he asked a passerby where he might buy flowers by the cartload and was directed to where the barges docked nearby. The sun was getting low on the horizon as they reached the place where the flower mongers conducted business. The first stall still had a sparse display of red tulips.

"These look pretty," said Peter.

"We're not looking for looks," said Matthew, and he began sniffing the air. "We're looking for smells."

They strolled on for only a short while before the flower dealers started dumping their barrows into the river and leaving. It was obvious to Matthew his search would come to a fruitless end if he stood by and watched this happen, so he ran to one vendor and stopped him.

"Why are you throwing the flowers away?" he asked.

"They're all wilted, ain't they? No one'll buy 'em now. Fresh tomorrow."

"Can I have them?"

"What for?"

"I just want them."

"All right. Penny for the lot, then."

Matthew was a bit disgruntled, having to pay for what was being thrown away, but he agreed and struck the same bargain with three other vendors. Their own cart loaded high, and their load covered with the burlap sacks, they headed back to their abandoned warehouse, where they left the flowers before heading home.

"Four pence for a cart of rubbish," said Peter. "I hope you know what you're doing. What will Mr. Squidge say if you get it wrong?"

"Never mind Squidge for now," said Matthew, but his concern was more toward the strangeness unfolding in the streets when they entered their neighborhood.

People were running, trotting, darting, racing, high-tailing, and making general haste all about. A carriage clattered past at full gallop, the driver whipping the horses madly. A pack of dogs ran from an alley, leaving one behind that collapsed from exhaustion and panted out its last breaths. Matthew tried to ask a frenzied little boy what all the commotion was about but only got the answer, "Can't stop now. In a hurry."

Suddenly Peter gripped Matthew's arm in abject panic and shouted, "We're late!" and left his brother to put the cart away.

The pressing urgency drove Matthew too, but he took the time to secretly secure the wagon before running the rest of the way home in terror of missing … what?

Once inside, he found the place gleaming. The horizontal surfaces were free of dust and the vertical surfaces free of grime. The furniture had been polished to a gloss, the cutlery polished to a sparkle, the whites washed to brilliance, and the rugs beaten into submission.

In the kitchen, his mother was rolling dough for pies and had Peter chopping carrots, but supper was already on the table and growing cold. Bob came in moaning, "Please give me something to do. I can't stand not doing anything when we're all running so late."

"There's nothing for you here," said Mrs. Cratchit sharply. "Go read your book. You been meaning to finish it for donkey's years."

"Oh, yes!" said Bob with something resembling relief. "I have been putting it off, haven't I?" With that, he left.

Matthew sensed he urgently had to do something as well, but he felt his mother wouldn't tolerate another interruption, so he followed his father into the living room. There he found Lucy darning socks.

"What's going on?" he asked.

"No time to talk. I have to finish these," said Lucy.

"They've been sitting in your basket for a month."

"I know I'm late," said Lucy in a growl, "but I'm doing it now, aren't I?"

"Why do you have to do it now?"

Lucy didn't stop working but squinted a moment before saying, "I don't know. I just do, is all."

As much as Matthew felt the same inexplicable dire immediacy as everyone else, he was beginning to suspect that this sudden impulse to overcome procrastination was not due to any real need to get things done with the kind of urgency things seemed to be demanding.

"Lucy, you're not late for anything."

"Yes, I am. Leave me alone, or I won't get this done on time."

"What are you late for?"

"I don't know. It doesn't matter. Stop asking stupid questions and let me get on."

Matthew sensed he had to paddle with the current to get anywhere at all. He raised his face to the ceiling and shouted, "We're late for supper."

Bob leaped from his chair and looked at the clock over the mantle. "Oh, gracious me," he said in a tither, "so we are! Hurry everyone, hurry. Mustn't keep Mother waiting." He darted into the kitchen.

"Oh, heaven help us, it's gone cold," said poor Bob. "I am so sorry, my dear."

"As much my fault as anyone's," said Mrs. Cratchit, but she could say no more because her frenzied bolting of food prevented further conversation.

Supper was done in a trice, in deference to the infinitude of actions yet to be acted upon. But Matthew stopped Lucy from returning to her darning and said, "Tell me everything you've done today. Quick now. Don't make me late."

Without understanding Matthew's need to know, Lucy still appreciated his need for haste and so rhymed off, "First thing I woke up: I washed and waxed the floors, washed the windows, did the laundry, made my bed and yours and Peter's, cuz you two left without doing it, then started mending the socks. Now let me go, or I won't get done, and it'll be your fault."

Somehow, the milk of Lucy's list was lost on Matthew while the cream rose to the top of his mind to be skimmed off. "First thing I woke up" and "it'll be your fault" was all he needed to hear to know what was happening.

"Lucy, you're not late," he said emphatically. "It's Tim making you feel that way."

"Tim?"

"Yes. Peter and I slept in this morning, and we must have started Tim feeling late for everything."

As hard as it was for Lucy to resist the magnetic pull of holey socks and her burning drive to mend more of them, she knew she had to put a stop to this maniacal compulsion before they all dropped from exhaustion. She and Matthew raced to Tiny Tim's side and began thinking thoughts of placid ponds and setting suns and anything that came to mind that did not involve doing anything in anything of a hurry.

After a few minutes, Mrs. Cratchit came in from the kitchen covered in flour, plopped down in the plushest chair, and said, "Well, that was a day worth having, it was. I won't have to cook a thing for a week, what with all I done today. And Father mended them doors what needed mending and two more what didn't, and polished all the boots and the knives and forks and all. And Lucy cleaned the place from top to bottom and up again, all ship-shaped and Bristol fashion, she did. And now I just wants to go to bed if I can only … find the strength … to climb them … stairs." She then set herself to snoring so melodiously it would have attracted amorous water buffalo had there been any within the range of hearing—which there were, quite fortunately, not.

CHAPTER 25

Peter and Matthew arose late again the following morning, though not nearly as late as the day before and in much less of a panic. Indeed, in Peter's case, the degree to which his panic aspired would be scarcely sufficient to melt ice—if Herr Fahrenheit will permit the metaphorical application of his methodology of temperature measurement to the calibration of fear.

The whole house was still in a state of exhaustion from the previous day's unprecedented proclivity for getting things done, and Tiny Tim was still radiating the need for rest and relaxation.

"Can't we take one day to ourselves?" asked Peter, while Matthew sluggishly pulled the covers from his indolent brother's cozy bed.

"Rats are pagans," said Matthew. "They don't take off holidays."

"Still. They'll be there tomorrow."

"But not the money we can make today. We've only got today to make that."

Peter sensed there must be a flaw in this logic but decided tomorrow would be a better day to determine precisely what it was, and so arose as commanded to follow Matthew through their truncated morning rituals. They dressed as usual, as they could not go out without doing so, but did not stop to wash their faces or brush their teeth since neither of these requirements was immediately mandatory and could be put off indefinitely.

The street outside their house was peculiarly vacant. The absence of other humans was nothing new, as the two boys were always the first of their neighborhood to be at large in the world, but the deathly silence led Matthew to notice the birds were conspicuously less than ubiquitous. He looked about to see a scene as devoid of life as any metaphor that could be imagined, conveying the sense of lifelessness, could convey. There was not a single representative of the cat population, which normally numbered in the dozens, nor one dog nor one squirrel nor one of anything animate at all.

"Crikey, we've overdone it!" he said, and he turned to run back to the house.

He darted upstairs and into Lucy's room.

"You can't come in here," said his sister in a whine when he shook her.

"You've got to get up and get Tim back to normal."

"Later," said Lucy, and she pulled the covers back over her head.

"Later never comes," said Matthew as he grabbed the covers and threw them from her.

"Yes, it does," she said. "It just doesn't come now."

"That's the point. We've got our Tim feeling like later's good enough, and now he's not making now."

As difficult as this fine line of reasoning might be for the less philosophically inclined, Lucy caught the end of the thread and followed it back to the source.

"Oh, I see," she said, but she was still not motivated to do more than promise to put the matter on her list of things to do.

"Come on!" said Matthew, taking her by the arm and pulling her to her feet.

"Oh, all right," she said in a miffed moan, and followed his lead.

On their way downstairs, Matthew said, "We need everything back to normal, so just think normal thoughts until everything feels …"

"Normal?"

"Yes, exactly."

He stopped only long enough to see her settling down beside Tiny Tim and stroking the forehead of the pudgy, perennially smiling face.

Then he hurried out to find Peter sitting against the wall, where he'd left him.

"I was just coming in," said the elder brother. "But it didn't seem all that important, if you know what I mean."

"That's all right. Come on. We've got to go."

Peter huffed a sigh. "Today?"

"Yes, now."

Unable to defy Matthew's will, the procrastinating Peter took the snail by the horns and plodded lethargically toward the future.

By the time the two arrived at their rat house, things were beginning to feel more like a usual day, so they started their daily task of extracting rats for summary execution with, more or less, their usual enthusiasm.

"How're we going to move them to their new home?" asked Peter.

"We won't. We'll start a new flock there and let it breed itself up while we keep taking from here. Twenty extra a day will run them down. Whatever's left we won't worry about."

"Well, that's not very nice," said Peter between the pummeling of two victims. "We can't just leave them here to starve."

"All right, we'll put a plank down for them to climb their way out."

"You mean release them back into the wild?"

"Yes."

"All right then. That'll do," said Peter, his humanitarian concerns satisfactorily addressed. Then he brought his fist down on another tiny cranium and added, "They've been good for us. It doesn't hurt to do something good for them, even if they are penguins."

"You're a good sort, Peter Cratchit," said Matthew, and he felt his words right down to his heart.

They crammed the secret compartment of their cart full and put ten more in one of the sacks, which they buried under the rest of the sacks to obscure the evidence of jiggery-pokery.

Their first client of the day was Mrs. Retch's Fancy Bakery. Mrs. Retch was one of those rare persons who could be quite generous generally, but when it came to vermin, she would pride herself on denying them all rights to a decent living. Her standing contract with Eliphaz Dropping was such that Peter and Matthew saw her once every two months, but the number of rats they extracted—before embellishment—from her larder was usually on the light side of forty, which would have placed her among the least profitable of all their clients had they not added their own contribution to the take.

But she was always happy to see them, always happy with their work, and always fed them a breakfast of meat pies when they were done, so Peter always carried some guilt about on top of the rats for inflating the haul at her expense.

"If we stopped it now," said Matthew. "She'd suspect we're getting lazy and not doing a thorough job."

"I suppose," said Peter, and he was, as often was the case, driven to ambivalent speculation over the virtues and vices of caterpillarism.

The balance of the day bounced along brightly. The bringing with them of forty extras to enhance their efforts enabled them to finish up a little early despite their late start.

They gathered some edible rubbish from behind the local establishments and began the process of building up a food supply for the proposed expansion herd in the abandoned warehouse. To this, the ancient coal chute leading down to the future rat-cellar proved a great convenience compared to the awkward obstacles to delivery with which they contended at their first location.

Matthew then put his mind to finding the right combination of dried flower petals that, when mixed with dried rat leavings, would produce a fragrance that could pass for that of powdered hops. This proved more difficult than one might imagine.

But Matthew was nothing if not persistent. Try as he might, however, no mix of petals and the product produced anything remotely close to his olfactory goal. At length, tired and gravely disappointed, he announced it was time to leave, and the two set out for home.

As usual for that time of day, the sun was seriously considering setting. And, as usual, the well-to-do citizenry of the city, having grown tired of profitable folly, was considering an evening of profligate folly while the remainder of the population, having grown tired of making profit for the well-to-do, was considering an evening of rest. Despite Matthew's lingering frustration, everything seemed much as it always did.

Until they reached the street parallel to the one upon which they lived.

Suddenly everything seemed exactly as it always did. The two old men who commonly stumbled out to vomit in the alley next to the Dog's Cocked Leg were there vomiting in their preferred alley. Thomas Thwackum was publicly beating his children according to his propensity for sound discipline, and the sound of that discipline could be heard for some distance, as it often was. The Cherrytart sisters, Prudence and Priscilla, were giving directions to a gentleman in a stopped carriage, as they did several times a day, since gentlemen were prone to getting lost in the neighborhood and the girls were prone to giving directions.

Everything appeared as it always did. Everything was comfortingly familiar. Everything that usually happened, that happened often, or that happened with fair regularity was happening right then, in that moment, as it often did.

Matthew took a deep breath and considered this strange sensation. It was as if all moments in time had collapsed into one instantaneous now.

"But, then," he said to himself, having reached the limit of his capacity for philosophical consideration, "when else could they happen?"

Peter was out of hearing of this comment as he helped Prudence and Priscilla into the gentleman's carriage, as he always did when the opportunity arose, which was often enough, as has been intimated.

The brothers arrived home to find everything exactly as would be expected. Bob had fallen asleep, as per usual, in his chair while reading. Lucy was setting the table, as per usual, and Mrs. Cratchit was stirring a pot of something on the boil—boiling everything being her preferred method of food preparation.

"What have you for me today?" she asked.

"Five shillings, as usual, Mother," said Matthew.

"Same as always," she said, taking the coins from him.

"Same as always," he agreed. He then asked out of habit, "What kind of a day did you have?"

"Well," said Mrs. Cratchit wistfully, "if it wasn't for the strangeness of it all, it would have been much the usual sort of a day. You know what I mean? The usual kind of thing you'd usually 'spect. What I'm trying to say is: the kind of a day that's so usual, in much the kind of a usual way, as to be just like every other usual day. The sort of a day you can't tell from any other 'cuz they's all so very usual, one to another, that when you tries to recall them, nothing stands out, as they all seems just the same, one to another."

"That's normal," Matthew said.

"Yes, that's right. But what's so very odd about today was the niggling sense it was so *very* usual. I mean, you don't usually go about telling yourself a day is usual when you're in it, does you? You don't think about it at all, unless someone asks what kind of a day you're having, which makes you spend a second recalling back if there's anything unusual about it, and then when you can't think of nothing at all, you know it's just a usual sort of a day and nothing more. But today I kept having this niggling sense of how usual everything was while I was doing it, and that made me think it was unusual to think like that, which is why the day was so strange."

"I see," said Matthew, and indeed he did see, for he knew, in that instant, Tiny Tim was caught in yet another cycle of circulating and recirculating feelings for everyone to feel—although whether that cycle was vicious or virtuous was not something Matthew cared to concern himself with in the moment.

But, deciding there was no harm in having a usual sort of a day for a change, he left for the pump out back to wash the smells of hops, dried flowers, and rat leavings off his hands in preparation for supper.

CHAPTER 26

Lucy had difficulty grasping what was required of her, and Matthew lacked the sophistication of vocabulary and skills in abstract thinking to describe to her the necessity of being normal without feeling normal. When he left with Peter the next morning, she was left uncertain how to proceed.

"If I think normal," she thought, "I'll feel normal … I think. And if don't feel normal, I won't think normal. At least I don't think so."

This internal debate continued for some while, but none of that mattered, as it turned out, as a knock on the door shortly after her brothers' departure prefixed another change in the fortunes of the family Cratchit and nullified any need for Lucy to do as Matthew had requested.

"Good day to you, Miss," said the diminutive man in a swallowtail coat of a beautiful green. "Are Mr. and/or Mrs. Robert Cratchit currently *ad domum salutor* or otherwise within communicatory availability?"

Although Lucy enjoyed a natural approbation for men who spiced their speech with Latin, she suffered a greater disapprobation for men in swallowtail coats of beautiful colors, which had only recently been exacerbated by the abbreviated visit of Mr. Scribble—whom you will recall was also thus attired—in which the release of the family fortune had been revealed, to her great dismay.

"Wait here," she said, and fetched her father.

"Can I be of service?" asked Bob cordially when he arrived at the door.

"I am here at the behest of B. Philius Gazpayne, QC, of Rankin, Fowle, O'Durr, and Gazpayne: Solicitors and Barristers at Law, to deliver this invoice to you personally, Mr. Cratchit, or to your wife—which, I have been instructed, may be to your dubious preference."

"Invoice? What for?"

"Interest owing and service charges."

"But we were told everything was settled," said Bob. "All we had to do was sign, and we did."

"Indeed, you did, sir. But you will recall that the document authorizing the release of your power of attorney back to you was delivered to Mr. Gazpayne the day following the day you signed it. Without that document in his possession, Mr. Gazpayne was unable to act upon it upon the day to which the calculations of your indebtedness to the firm of Rankin, Fowle, O'Durr, and Gazpayne: Solicitors and Barristers at Law were made. The result of this tardiness, on your part, is that one additional day's interest had to be applied to the amount owing, along with the usual fee of our accountants for performing the additional calculations. That amount has been subject to further interest at the usual rate and has been calculated up to and including today's date, along with an additional hour of Mr. Gazpayne's time for having to oversee the execution of ensuing actions, within which we are currently engaged. That being two hours of my time, for the writing of this invoice (which, I am told, would have taken Mr. Scribble only an hour, but he, alas, has yet to return to work, so the job has fallen to me, and I being new to the position of clerk and legal secretary and inexperienced in these matters, required two); two hours of my time for the deliverance of this invoice and the concomitant explanation of its contents (which you are presently hearing); and the usual charge for closing. You have until three thirty this post meridiem to finalize payment, or further interest will be rendered effectual, along with the appropriate charges."

With that, the clerk handed Bob the sealed document and turned with a flourish of his beautiful green coattails to climb into his waiting carriage and leave.

Bob broke the wax seal and unfolded the sheet of parchment. His eyes ran down the column of figures previously delineated by the unnamed and now departed clerk to arrive at the final sum of £96.9s.4d.

"He's bankrupted us!" said Bob.

"Who has?" asked Mrs. Cratchit, arriving on the scene.

"Gazpayne. He's sent us another bill, and …"

Choked by despair and unable to say another word, Bob handed the odious invoice to his wife, whose eyes opened as if straining to leave the confines of their sockets.

"I'll murder him, I will!" she said.

Lucy was immediate in her response. Seeing in a flash what effect all this would have on Tiny Tim, she slipped from her parents' presence and headed directly to her brother to begin the thinking of pleasant thoughts and the feeling of pleasant feelings. This proved most fortunate, for Tiny Tim had been driven by the concussion of Mrs. Cratchit's explosive rage into a world of barbaric emotions unseen since the times of Attila or Tamerlane. And that would have propelled Mrs. Cratchit to who knows what manner of misbehavior had not Lucy snapped the swords and broken the bows of her comatose brother's army of hostile emotions.

It wasn't until Mr. and Mrs. Cratchit were nearing their bank that they realized their passions had been manipulated under their daughter's influence, but by then they had accustomed themselves to the powerlessness of their position and so entered the echoing halls of commerce without a return to violent aspirations.

"This is a nasty turn of events, I must say," said Mr. Goldworm, the bank manager, after reviewing the invoice.

"Indeed it is," muttered Bob, while the banker ran a finger down the final page of the Cratchit file.

"The withdrawal of the amount required," said Goldworm, "would leave in the account one shilling, two pence, half-penny."

"What must be, must be," said Bob, espousing fatalism to the best of his ability.

"The problem is," said the banker, "the minimum amount allowed for the maintaining of an account is five shillings."

"Then we'll have to close the account, won't we?" said Mrs. Cratchit. "Just give it all to us, and we'll keep the change."

"Unfortunately, my dear lady, there is a charge of two shillings for closing an account."

What followed would be surprising to anyone prone to the belief that people learn from their previous bad experiences and behave more appropriately when new but similar opportunities arise. On the other hand, anyone prone to the belief that people are more likely to remain unwaveringly enamored of their dysfunctional behaviors and will return to them again and again without fail despite the lessons of the past, will not be surprised at all that Mrs. Cratchit was—shortly after Mr. Goldworm uttered these last words—arrested for the assault and battery of the banker.

Past is prologue, as the bard once said.

Bob was characteristically at a loss as to how to proceed but, uncharacteristically, accepted Lucy's advice ahead of his wife's demands. Rather than spend time in trying to secure Mrs. Cratchit's release, he took two shillings from the jar in which the family's operating funds were kept and returned to the bank to close their account. Then he hightailed it immediately to Gazpayne and settled the debt finally and completely before the clock struck the end of business hours.

"I see your good lady is not with you today," said Gazpayne.

"No. She's got herself in a spot of bother with the law, and I must go to see what I can do to get her out."

"Quite. Well, if there's anything I can do …"

"Thank you, but no," said Bob with the odd sensation of fangs puncturing his neck.

"Suit yourself. Though I remind you, the law can be most unkind to those unacquainted with it."

"So I've heard."

"Quite. And, by the way, you'll be happy to learn we have decided not to demolish the houses on your street as we had planned."

"That is good news since we've now nowhere else …"

"But to make the properties worth keeping, we must raise the rents to ten shillings a month, effective immediately. In fact, now that I consider it more fully, we need to make it retroactive, effective from the beginning of the year." Gazpayne then put pencil to paper to calculate. "Five shillings a month for the first four months, plus ten shillings for May, comes to—"

"Thirty shillings," said Bob miserably.

"Not thirty-five?" asked Gazpayne, looking suspiciously through the tops of his eyes.

"Quite sure it's thirty. I am a bookkeeper by trade."

"Though not one of the highest order, I suspect. Still. For the sake of argument, we can assume it is thirty for now. If the accountants arrive at a better opinion, we will be obliged to accept their ruling."

"Oh, I agree," said Bob, confident in the belief that the mathematics of the lowly bookkeeper is the same as the mathematics of the exalted accountant.

But then Bob had never risen to the stratosphere of high finance and never attempted to breathe its rarified air.

CHAPTER 27

While Bob and Mrs. Cratchit were off exploring the nether limits of their well-being, Matthew and Peter were off faring somewhat better. Another visit to the docks, to where the flower wholesalers received and distributed their goods, yielded a fresh and more promising supply of wilting blossoms.

Without the need to spend time being evicted from gardens and parks, following flower girls at a discreet distance, and being threatened by gangs of street thugs, they were able to arrive at their destination much earlier than on their previous excursion. This was a good thing, as Matthew needed time to find species of blossoms different from the ones already tested; he suspected that doing the same thing repeatedly with the expectation of varied outcomes is in violation of some universal law or other despite its being a universally popular approach to solving problems.

"What be ye in market vur?" asked a pipe-smoking, long-whiskered little man whose accent betrayed his being from places elsewhere.

"Something that smells like hops," said Matthew.

"Oh, ah? Not a pleeezing thing, tha'. Why d'ye wa' i'?"

"To flavor ale. Hops are too expensive."

"Be they now? I be more a zider drinker, me-zelf, but—if i' be bi'er vlavor ye wants—there be no more bi'er vlower than poppies," said the gnomish-looking fellow, and he reached into his cache to break off a sad-looking blossom, which he offered to Matthew to taste.

Matthew put one petal on his tongue, but the vendor laughed. "Not the pedals, zun! The zeedpods, the zeedpods."

Matthew bit into the seedpod as instructed, and his face instantly rivaled those of gorgons for hideous distortion. Although usually quite mannerly in his dining etiquette, he could not stop himself from spitting out the offensive orb and violently wiping his mouth on his coat sleeve.

"Perfect," he said tearfully when he regained the use of his tongue. "I'll take all you've got."

The price was settled at tuppence for everything the gnarled little vendor had, with a promise to return the next day. Peter and Matthew then took their load of bitter blossoms to their warehouse, where Matthew put himself to the task of getting the proper blend—that being one that contained sufficient dried poppy to yield the appropriate taste while providing an aroma of other flowers mixed with rat droppings that did not reveal the details of its contents.

After an hour of experimentation, Matthew said, "This one doesn't exactly stink of hops, but it doesn't stink of product either."

Peter sniffed and nodded discerningly.

"How's it taste?" he asked.

"Try it and see."

"I'd rather not."

Matthew had feared this obstacle to his research but didn't argue.

"Come on then," he said, and the two left for home.

On their way, they came upon three little street urchins playing at tormenting a cat.

"Want some sherbet?" called out Matthew, and the three came running. He opened a packet of powdered hops into which they dipped their wetted fingers. They then applied said fingers to their waiting tongues before erupting with disgust.

"Ptah!" spat the one apparently in charge of the small band. "That ain't sherbet!"

"Oh, sorry," said Matthew, and he opened the second packet. "This is the sherbet."

Still grimacing from their first foray, the three repeated their ritual to identical results.

"Cha, you plonker!" said their leader, turning to spit. "'Sa same bloody thing!"

"Are you sure?" asked Matthew, anxious for scientific certainty.

"'Course I'm bloody sure," said the urchin, in a rage. "You think that's funny? You sodding, bloody …!"

With that, he aimed a kick at Matthew's shin, but swift and nimble maneuvering saved the youthful Cratchit from injury.

"Come on!" said Matthew, and he and Peter began running with their cart, bouncing over the cobblestones, in tow.

The three urchins brought their fists upon the pair but lacked the strength to inflict much pain and, having far less enthusiasm for running when chasing than when being chased, soon gave up their pursuit and resorted to raining down stones on the retreating Peter and Matthew. None of the tiny missiles did Matthew much harm, but one did open a gash on the back of poor Peter's scalp, much to Lucy's amusement, as we shall soon see.

The two found it odd to arrive home and find only Lucy and Tiny Tim in residence, but at least Lucy had Tiny Tim tranquilized away from the disturbing events of the day.

"Mother's in jail," whispered Lucy when asked, "for punching up the bank manager."

"Oh," said Matthew, as if this were a daily occurrence. "Where's Father, then?"

"Seeing about getting her out."

"Oh," said Matthew flatly, and he allowed himself a moment to reason out why this made sense—Bob's fondness for Mrs. Cratchit being the deciding factor.

"I'm still bleeding," said Peter after touching the back of his head and inspecting his sticky red fingers.

"Let me see," said Lucy, and she bade her eldest brother to sit on a kitchen chair. "How d'you do this, then?"

"Brat threw a stone at me 'cuz Matthew was having him on."

"I'm sure the brat deserved it," said Lucy, inspecting the wound.

"How do you know?" said Peter.

"He threw a rock at you, didn't he?"

Peter squinted in thought, and despite his inability to reconcile the precise pattern of cause and effect leading up to his injury, he could see the possibility—on some atemporal level—that Lucy's sense of justice was valid.

"Hmm," said Lucy. "Perhaps … Yes, perhaps I can mend this. But you'll have to be brave."

"What're you going to do?" asked Matthew.

"Sew it up, of course."

"You know how?"

"Much like darning socks, I imagine."

"Well, you've done plenty of that."

"Exactly," said Lucy with a confident smile, and she headed off to retrieve her sewing kit.

Peter, though nervous over what was about to happen, remained silent since he had grown accustomed to his brother and sister making decisions for him. Somehow he knew action was always better than indecision, and he, being natively indecisive, found life more expedient when others did the deciding—and especially more expedient when they performed the action as well.

"Brown or black?" asked Lucy when she fingered through her choices of yarn.

"You have anything to match his hair?" asked Matthew.

"I've got a bit of beige, but I was saving that in case I get a hole in my stockings."

"No one sees your stockings."

"I do."

"Brown, then," said Matthew. "He'll just have to wear a hat for a bit."

"He should be wearing a hat anyway," said Lucy while threading a needle. "You both should. Going about without one—it's indecent. Anyone would think we're poor."

"We are poor."

"I know, but we don't want others thinking it, do we?"

Lucy had to concentrate, so the household fell into deathly silence, punctuated by the occasional "ow" from Peter, who might have begun questioning the wisdom of submitting to this procedure had it not been for Tiny Tim's radiant tranquility.

"There," said Lucy after some minutes. "Pretty good for a first try, I should say."

Matthew inspected the site of the repair and, finding it less medieval in appearance than anticipated, said, "Well at least it's stopped bleeding … more or less … probably."

He then left to fetch a comb to see whether rearranging Peter's hair might avoid any speculation someone had taken a rusty ax to him. Lucy remained to admire her handiwork and to wonder whether a more rewarding career might be made in sewing up wounds than there was in sewing up socks.

As Matthew arrived from upstairs, their father arrived from the front door.

"Good evening, my dears," said Bob. "Have you told your brothers all our bad news?"

"Not all, Father," said Lucy, "as there was rather a lot of it, and I had to keep Tim quiet while I sewed up Peter's head."

Bob inspected the embroidered gash with a wince.

"A brat hit me with a stone," said Peter. "He deserved it! Lucy said so."

"Then I'm sure he must've, mustn't he?" said Bob, but he turned his attention to Matthew and asked, "Do you think you and Peter can manage thirty shillings for rent by the first of May?"

"Thirty shillings?"

"Just this once, and then it's ten a month after that."

"I suppose," said Matthew, "but there won't be much left over for anything else."

Bob's head sank with his heart. He sighed heavily and said, "Then I suppose raising ten guineas is out of the question."

"Ten guineas!" shouted the others together.

Lucy went immediately to Tiny Tim to ensure he didn't descend into fright and misery.

"That's what it will cost to get your mother home. Otherwise, it's off to Australia with her."

"And how much will that cost?" asked Peter aghast.

"Nothing," said Bob.

"Well, that makes no sense at all," said Peter with a sneer. "Holidays in Australia for free or pay ten guineas to stay here? What silly ox would go for that lark?"

Despite Lucy's efforts to keep Tiny Tim emitting soothing feelings, Bob succumbed to dejection while Matthew harbored a twitching tickle in his happiness—rather like the twitching tickle one gets in one's throat, from inopportune time to inopportune time, that draws one's attention away from the perfection of the moment. Only Peter rose to some pure satisfaction despite everything as he took the comb from Matthew and positioned himself between the hall mirror and a hand mirror to seek the exact arrangement of hair to cover his upholstered blemish.

Matthew journeyed out the back door to ruminate in the place where thoughts are commonly thought and seated himself on the seat designed for the facilitation of a biological necessity. As he mulled over this new situation, his mind meandered through a maze of considerations, as minds are prone to do when some central thread is available to follow and the mind is sufficiently disciplined—as Matthew's was—to follow it. That central thread was, of course, the need for a decision over what to do about Mrs. Cratchit. And that twitching tickle—mentioned in the previous paragraph—was his struggle to identify, within himself, a genuine desire to do anything at all.

Despite his pretending thirty shillings would be a stretch, he actually had slightly more than ten guineas saved, but that accumulated wealth represented well over a year's worth of hard work and sacrifice, with a goal of founding a financial empire. Not only would he sorely regret losing everything he'd acquired thus far, but he'd have to reveal he had the capacity to earn much more than he had led the family to believe. And, knowing his mother—as his years of acquaintance with her had made possible—he could expect her to demand a much greater share of the proceeds of rat catching than had, until then, satisfied her. That, in itself, would be difficult enough to accommodate, but seeing her squander it, as he knew she would, would be an endless torment to him. And he knew it.

Added to all this was the list of considerations of how the family might fare better with Mrs. Cratchit in absentia somewhere in Australia. Prior to her hiring Mr. Gazpayne to sue the surgeons, they had some £300,000, which had been boiled off in the crucible of justice. She squandered every spare farthing that came into her hands, being of the opinion that the measure of a person's success in life is in his or her capacity to commit waste. Matthew even recalled she'd never gotten around to naming Lucy and him until Uncle Ebenezer began inquiring as to who the "ubiquitous children" were. Even then, she often forgot Matthew was a boy and called him "Miranda" and just as often called Lucy "Gillian" until he and his sister chose to call themselves what they called themselves. This last item might seem a small thing to most, but Matthew had taken it as proof of a lack of affection on their mother's part, and it tarnished his opinion of her.

All this weighed against the possibility of Matthew wanting to spare his mother from exile.

But Matthew had something of a soft spot for his father, and he knew Bob was rather more attached to Mrs. Cratchit than he was, and even more attached to her than reason alone would allow. So reason was not enough to persuade Matthew to ignore this fact.

Then the solution to it all came to him as, once again, the atmosphere of the tiny wooden cubicle proved efficacious in inspiring innovative solutions. Matthew suddenly recalled a conversation between some of Mr. Squidge's friends.

"I didn't have the readies to square the judge," one man had said, "so Squidge squared a guard instead."

This, then, bore at least the possibility of an answer. If Squidge would be willing to accept a pound or two to arrange for Mrs. Cratchit's escape, Matthew could say it was a favor from a friend and not be forced to reveal to his family he had income beyond that already revealed. And the trauma to his treasure, though significant, would not be nearly as painful as would the total decimation of his accumulated wealth.

He returned to the house to find that Tiny Tim had overcome all household inclinations toward sadness and was engaged in tranquilizing not only its denizens but also those of the street and those of the whole neighborhood beyond.

Bob was asleep in his chair with his book on his chest and a smile on his face. Peter was asleep on the chesterfield with his face down and his injury up, and Lucy was blissfully laying out the ingredients for sandwiches on the kitchen table. The sight, not to mention the ambient feeling, pleased Matthew greatly, and another thought came to him.

"Our Tim's more use than I'd given him credit for," he murmured gleefully. "God bless us, every one! I'll have to put him to work!"

CHAPTER 28

The following afternoon, upon arrival at Thaddeus Squidge's dray-and-carriage business, Matthew and Peter headed to their usual place for unloading, but instead of the man usually assigned to the receiving of goods, they found Squidge himself waiting for them.

"Here they are, then," he said jovially enough. "The terror of the Thames with another day's take."

"Yes sir," said Matthew. "I was hoping to speak with you today."

"Was you, now? Well, that's a coincidence, ain't it, as I was hoping to have a word with you and all. I been hearing things about you two I don't much like, but being the fair sort of bloke I am, I wants to hear your side of the story before I makes up me mind what to do about it."

"What story would that be, sir?" asked Matthew.

"I heared you was engaging yourselves in some sorta … ssseeee … cretive enterprise … down by the docks, and you told some blokes you was there on account of me sending you. Now, I don't have no mind to stop you doing as you likes—so long as it don't interfere with my doings—but I do take 'ception to you using my name without me knowing about it, and me getting my fair share of what's going on what I'm supposed to be in back of. See my meaning? Now. Seeings as you did say I was in back of what you're about, I wants to know what it is and how much you're scarfing back on account of it."

"We were there to buy flowers," said Peter, having completely shed his man-of-ill-repute demeanor and struggling not to shed the tea he had drunk an hour earlier.

"That's what they said you said," said Squidge. "But that ain't what I'm buying, is it? Give us the proper goods, or I'll get someone in here who knows how to find things out."

"It's true, sir," said Matthew. "We only said you'd sent us so the men who were asking wouldn't punch us up and take our money."

Squidge squinted and pursed his lips. "What do you want with flowers, then? You two never struck me as the sort for that kind of lark."

Matthew straightened to full height and said, "I've got this idea, sir, that flowers can be used to flavor beer, and I can buy old flowers for almost nothing since they only get thrown away anyway if I don't."

"What makes you think this'll work?"

"They already use a flower called hops to flavor beer, but it's expensive. I'm sure the brewery will buy from us to save money."

Squidge nodded, respectful of Matthew's reasoning. "I likes it. It's all legit, which saves some aggro, but dishonest enough to tell me it's the right thing to do. I'm in for half plus expenses." He looked to Peter and said, "You! Go unload the rats. And [to Matthew] you come with me."

Then he led Matthew to his office, leaving Peter to the menial work, which Peter didn't mind at all, as he'd had more than enough of Squidge's company already.

Matthew told Squidge of his experiments—though he decided it was best not to mention the rat leavings, to preserve the secrecy of his proprietary blend—including the success with the three urchins who had tasted the concoction and found it identical to that of dried hops.

"They didn't know what we were after," said Matthew, "and they didn't know what they were getting, so they couldn't be lying when they said they tasted the same."

This impressed Squidge, as he was well acquainted with the fact that people, when asked questions, could be prone to agree with whatever would please the enthusiastic asker solely to get a moment's respite from the asking.

"Well," said Squidge, "it seems you're 'bout ready to work the fiddle with the brewery. For that you'll be needing me, as I got considerable 'sperience in what's called negotiations, as you might well imagine. And then there's the buying and transporting of the flowers. We'll need more quantity than you can cart about with your rat wagon, and I thinks I can get us a better price on what's needed, as that's another talent I got, if you get my meaning."

"Yes, I see," said Matthew, beginning to picture greater virtue in partnering with Squidge than he'd initially imagined. But he waited a moment before broaching the subject he had until then pushed from his mind. "There is one other thing. My mother's in prison, and I have to get her out before they ship her off to Australia."

"Fond of her, is you?" asked Squidge.

"My father is."

"Yeah, they can be like that. Not that it matters. What's she in for?"

"Thrashing a bank manager."

"Give over! Didn't know there's a law 'gainst it. Hm? Oughtn't be. Well, seeing as we's partners, two-pound-ten should buy her a key. She go by Cratchit, or she work the other side of the sheets?"

"Cratchit," said Matthew, half regretting the higher-than-expected cost of her freedom. "But she can't know I'm paying for it. Can you have your man say it's a favor to you?"

"Oh, I never does favors for no one, I don't, as them what hears of it wants in on it too. But I will say she works for me and I needs her back on account of her knowing things I can't be without. You tell her to keep quiet from 'ere on in, and I'll 'ave her out tomorrow."

"Thank you, sir."

"No worries," he replied, brushing invisible entities aside. He then pointed at Matthew. "But you might put a mind to getting her out of the city. There's them what checks records, you see, and they might notice she's not about when they comes to load the ship and all. I can arrange something in Cornwall if that suits your fancy. Fair price."

"All right," said the hesitant Cratchit, and he took his leave of the helpful Squidge. He found Peter waiting in the alley, trembling from fear for his brother's life and limb.

"Are you all right, then?" asked Peter.

"Better than that. We've got Squidge for a partner now. He'll be a big help to us."

"Really? That's a bit difficult to picture. How?"

"For one thing, he's getting Mother out of jail."

"Why's he doing that, then?"

"Favor to me. Partner to partner."

Of course, had Matthew had the benefit of further education and studied the works of Christopher Marlowe, he would likely have approached this Faustian accord with a less sanguine certainty of success, but alas, having been born a Cratchit, his schooling ended somewhere short of Elizabethan drama.

CHAPTER 29

J ail **was not** at all like Matthew had imagined. He'd walked there with Peter with pictures in mind of stone walls six-foot thick, huge oaken gates creaking on long-rusted hinges, tiny windows twenty feet overhead, and floggings and executions being performed with metronomic regularity.

What he found was quite like Mr. Squidge's dray-and-carriage business—with some noticeable modifications. Like its commercial counterpart, the jail had a series of large archways dividing its interior from its exterior. But instead of great wooden doors that swung open to allow entry and egress to carts and carriages, there were iron bars that disallowed entry or egress to anything larger than a cat. This difference aside, the similarities between the two structures led Matthew to consider that the warehousing and distribution of people was more similar to the warehousing and distribution of cheap goods than one's gentler sensibilities might prefer.

With some offense to his sense of hygiene, he made his way through the horde of poor souls gathered to visit the inmates, then arrived at the iron-barred barrier. It was darker inside, where the shadows made it difficult to make out one convict from another within the mass of miserable humanity awaiting its fate. It therefore took him some time to identify Mrs. Cratchit, who was engaged in happy conversation with three rugged and robust young men.

Against the backdrop of chatter, he had to call twice to get her attention. She excused herself to the three men and came over to the bars with an uncharacteristic sway in her walk, which did not go unnoticed by the trio.

"What do they want?" asked Matthew.

"We was just talking 'bout religion, we were."

"Religion?"

"Oh, quite. Not to bore you with the finer points, the tall one with the dimple in his chin was explaining to me that before the courts started shipping people off to Australia, they used to hang them and such. So being shipped off is in lieu of being dead, and since the marriage vows are 'till death do us part'—as they say—it only makes sense that, once we leaves England, we're all as much as dead in the eyes of God and so not beholden, no more, to them what we was beholden to before."

Matthew was not accustomed to thinking of his mother as the quarry of men's romantic quests, so it took a moment to realize the purpose to which this theological treatise on the limits of divinely binding vows was being put forward by the three. That inspired a moment of visceral aversion as he sparked to the notion that the three had intentions for her beyond simple conversation—religious or otherwise—and had to brace himself to the task of taking that knowledge in and finding for it a comfortable place in his understanding of the universe.

At first, he had trouble imagining anyone could find anything at all about his mother to hold his or her interest, despite the few remnants of youthful beauty still evident here and there. Then he scanned the other female denizens of the jail and could see—all other considerations aside—that her hair, teeth, clear skin, and general health alone put her among the elite of alluring feminine exiles.

He shuddered briefly with the sensation of an eel in his intestine, took a deep breath, and said, "I've come to tell you you're getting out tomorrow."

"How's that, then? Here! You didn't steal the money to pay the fine, did you?"

"No, of course not," said Matthew, and he leaned his face between the bars to whisper, "A friend of mine is arranging it. His name is Thaddeus Squidge, and what you have to say is you work for him. That's all. Don't say anything else. Understand?"

"No. What kind of work is it I'm supposed to be doing?"

"Mr. Squidge owns a dray-and-carriage company. Just say you work for him and nothing else. Nothing else at all. Keep quiet till you're out, and everything will be all right. Can you do that?"

Mrs. Cratchit turned to look at the three young men who were still looking at her. One waved with his fingers. She waved back and fluttered her eyelids like she was a coy fourteen, which had Matthew swallowing to keep down his dinner. Then she turned again to him and said, "I don't know. I was coming to the persuasion I weren't getting out and was gone for good. Let me think about it."

"Mother," hissed Matthew angrily. "I've gone to a lot of trouble, and Mr. Squidge is not the kind of man to muck about."

"Oh, all right, then!" said Mrs. Cratchit petulantly, and in her most plaintive, self-sacrificing voice, she added, "If that's what you really want, I suppose I can make do."

Matthew sighed in relief. "Good. Just remember: not a word to anyone. Not even the guard who lets you out."

After bidding each other good-bye, she left Matthew to return to the three amateur theologians who were quick with questions. Matthew started to worry she'd say something to rupture the entire scheme and land him and Squidge on the other side of the bars.

Together.

Within the space of seconds, he pictured himself a dozen times chained to the elder villain; and each time, the outcome was unpleasant.

Then he saw his mother talking. He was on the verge of bursting with regret over ever having embarked on this course when the three men suddenly backed away from her as if she'd said she had the plague. She stepped toward one, but he turned to push his way away from her. She stepped toward another with the same result. A hush fell upon the place, followed by a low murmur, and moments later, Mrs. Cratchit was alone at the center of a circle some ten feet in radius. She moved to a thick stone pillar, and the empty circle moved with her. At last, she sat down dejected with her back to the column.

"Good," murmured Matthew to himself. "With no one to talk to …"

With renewed confidence all would go as planned—and his father would be restored to whatever measure of happiness he enjoyed with his wife—Matthew returned to where he'd left Peter with the cart, and the two returned home for the night.

"You'll have to take Mother away from the city," said Matthew to the ebullient Bob.

"Why's that, my dear?" asked the Cratchit clan chief.

"What we're doing isn't exactly legal, and the police might come looking for her after."

"Oh, my!" said Bob in a sudden tizzy. "Oh, my! My Emily, a fugitive from justice! I'm not sure I like that very much."

"Would you rather she go to Australia with a bunch of men who don't think she's married anymore?"

"Why would they think that?"

"Something to do with Australia having a different religion. But it's too late, anyway. I've already arranged it with Mr. Squidge, and he's not the sort of man you unarrange things with. Don't worry. The deal includes getting you to Cornwall. You know, Tintagel? Where King Arthur used to live?"

"Oh, that would be nice, wouldn't it?"

"Well," said Matthew, embarrassed he may have painted too rosy a picture. "It's likely got a bit run down since he left, but you'll make it do. Lucy, Peter, and I will stay here to look after our Tim and keep on working. When we've got enough together, we'll buy someplace nice where we can all live together again."

This pleased Bob enormously—this and Lucy guiding Tiny Tim with pleasing thoughts of cozy seaside cottages.

CHAPTER 30

The empty circle surrounding the pariah Mrs. Cratchit kept pace with her as she walked to the gate when her name was called.

"I'm Mrs. Cratchit," she announced to the guard as she approached the iron bars.

"Your boss, Thaddeus Squidge, has paid your fine," said the turnkey loudly enough for all to hear as he turned the key in the lock. "You're free to go with Her Majesty's blessings and her sincere wish you don't do what you done no more, as next time it's 'angin', and there won't be no fine to pay what'll untie that knot."

Those words ended the terror in which Mrs. Cratchit had spent the night. Not that she'd feared molestation by her inmates, as the other inmates had feared for themselves. No. Her fear had been the fear that her fellow inmates feared her.

It is a strange fact of human nature that we crave the acceptance of those around us even when those around us are completely unacceptable by our usual estimations of acceptability and our usual preferences would be to not be around them at all. So it is not surprising, then, that Mrs. Cratchit was more than glad to be out and more than glad to see Bob waiting for her in the crowd of visitors to the jail.

"Who's this Mr. Squidge, then?" she asked when they reached the high street, away from listening ears.

"A business acquaintance of our Matthew's," said Bob. "And a saintly man he must be to pay to get you out as a favor to our boy."

"I don't know so much. I just mentioned his name once, and no one would have nothing to do with me. Terrified of him, they all is."

"Not surprising, my love," said Bob, pattering her hand that held his arm. "They're all villains in there, and villains are terrified of saintly men."

Mrs. Cratchit looked at her husband in profile and smiled but wondered if anyone, anywhere, villainous or not, was even the slightest bit apprehensive in his saintly presence.

Once home, Mr. and Mrs. Cratchit settled in while Lucy prepared a modest tea. The money was scant, as Matthew persisted in pretending the need to raise rent was pushing him to his financial limits, so the meal was meager at best. But it was ambrosial to the freed convict, who'd grown tired of thrice-daily porridge.

"We're going to Tintagel, where King Arthur used to live," said Bob. "Matthew's arranged everything. Can you picture it, my dear? A cottage by the sea."

Mrs. Cratchit's imagination took her to the windswept cliffs of Cornwall she'd heard described, and she recalled a pen-and-ink drawing of a tiny cottage she'd seen once on the label of a Fisherman's Blend tobacco tin. Then she looked to her husband and saw him with her in this idyllic setting. She sighed with satisfaction, but—midsigh—she recalled another image described to her only the day before. In this, three bronze-bodied Adonises walked with her along a beach in a tropical paradise.

By the end of her sigh, her anticipation of delight was depleted, but lurid fantasies of Australia loomed large over the sunny shores of what might have been.

Lucy sensed a strange stirring in the ether that was Tiny Tim's emotional aura—a longing that, though pleasing in itself despite its qualities of benigglement, disturbed her nonetheless, since she could identify the true source of the feeling from the dreamy expression on her mother's face. With that, Lucy suffered a visceral aversion, rising from parts she never mentioned to anyone. Till then, she'd never suspected her mother ever entertained longing like this—her own presence in this world and those of her siblings notwithstanding.

To quell her disquietude, Lucy put herself to the task of putting a stop to her mother's unsavory emotional uprising, but too late. Bob felt it too and put himself to clumsily fumbling for a way to convey to his wife what was on his mind without alerting Lucy to human endeavors Victorian fathers deemed best left well beyond the awareness of their impressionable adolescent daughters.

Mrs. Cratchit was experienced in the art of imagining her husband as someone other than the Bob he was in reality for the purpose of fulfilling his need to be more than the Bob he imagined himself to be when engaging in those romantic activities in which he was only marginally accomplished but preferred to believe himself a master. To this, the three young men she had befriended in jail—whom you no doubt guessed were the three Adonises in her illusory Australia—served more than adequately for the purpose when she accepted her husband's invitation to go to their bedroom to pack in preparation for their proposed journey to Cornwall.

Lucy fought to halt this rising tide of conjugal cravings and return her parents to deportment less intestinally repugnant to herself. In this she failed most miserably, since Tiny Tim found the titillation highly amusing, and his power of amplification was too much even for Lucy. Within minutes of sitting down next to her silent brother, she was quite overwhelmed with desires of her own and driven to exploit every means of dealing with this unforgiving, massing urgency her scant experience of feminine adolescence had allowed her to discover.

At length, it was too much even for that, and she left the house in search of a young Adonis of her own, though she had no real idea of what she would do with him when she found him. But alas, that never became an issue since there was not one person to be found—not man, nor boy, nor otherwise, from Greek mythology or elsewhere. The street outside their house was as devoid of people as the word "devoid" itself, and an extended search for any male primate of the genus *Homo* failed to turn up anyone until Lucy had strayed well beyond the radius of Tiny Tim's emotive influence. Then, still given to breathing heavily and sensing she was still flushed, she decided to go for a walk in the park and allow her neighborhood to return to some semblance of what she saw as proper behavior and to desires she could comfortably handle.

That was some while in coming. The reason there was no one about in the streets was that everyone for blocks around had been driven into every room, wardrobe, attic, and cubbyhole that provided some sense of privacy for the purposes of coupling, tripling, or coming together en masse in ways unknown to humankind since the time of Caligula. Indeed, had Antoine Watteau painted the scene, using the same symbolism as he did in *L'Embarquement pour Cythère*, the sky above the Good Old City would have been so packed with floating cherubs the sun would have been blocked out by the vastness of the horde of cuteness.

So it was some while before Lucy could venture home without sensing an overwhelming and frustrating need for practical masculine anatomy. When she did find it possible to enter the street leading up to her house, she was greeted with a warmth and tranquility and sense of otherworldly perfection completely unfamiliar to her. It took her some moments to realize what it meant, and when she did, she suffered a moment of shy shock—but only a moment—and then she thought, "Well! My! That's not bad at all, is it?" and took to singing softly as she went about her daily duties with the lightest heart she had ever had when going about them until then.

CHAPTER 31

Despite a rewarding career that took him out of the house on a regular basis, Matthew was enjoying his afternoon somewhat less than his housebound sister. Having to part with two pounds ten to Mr. Squidge for the release of his mother was an amputation from his body of treasure he had accepted and accommodated, but the severance from his savings of a further pound to pay for the use of a cottage in Cornwall and a further ten shillings beyond that to cover clandestine transportation to and provisioning of said cottage felt, to his youthful impatience for progress, like a crippling setback.

"To my mind," said Squidge as he accepted the money, "you was being a bit sentimental when you come to me with it. But then I was the same way with my dear old mum and dad, I was, so I ain't one to talk."

"You were?" said Matthew, immediately regretting the incredulous tone in his voice.

"Oh, I were that and a bit, I was. When it come time for me to inherit the family fortune, I paid extra to be sure they wouldn't suffer. Went the way we all has hopes to go, they did: enjoying the finer things in life one minute; entering the Pearly Gates the next. Don't get better than that, it don't. And that's why it's better not to leave it to chance. I ask you, what more can a bloke do for them what bored him?"

"Nothing comes to mind."

"No truer words been spoke. But never you mind. You'll 'ave your money back soon's we gets the brewery to buy your … Wha'cher call it?"

"Bittering agent," said Matthew bitterly.

"Right. Bittering agent. I put some feelers out, so it won't be long 'fore we knows what's what in the brewing business. When can you have some samples ready?"

"Day after tomorrow," said Matthew, marginally uplifted by a sense of rapid progress.

"That's fine, then. I'll arrange to meet with Belcher's. Always had a fancy to get me fingers into beer. Got to be some brass there, I'd imagine."

On their way home, Peter began entertaining a mild curiosity as to the unprofitable machinations in which Matthew had involved them both.

"Why do we have to send Father and Mother away?" he asked.

"Because getting Mother out of jail, the way we did, isn't legal, and the police might come looking for her."

"Oh," said Peter, nodding as if it were obvious. "Wouldn't it have been easier just to let her go on holiday to Australia?"

"It's beginning to look that way, but it's too late now. I got Mr. Squidge involved, so it's best to finish what we started and make plans from there."

"Oh," said Peter, nodding as before. "Tell me again—why is Squidge helping us?"

This line of questioning was starting to worry Matthew. He had an instinctive awareness not only of the universal law that knowledge is power, but also of its corollary: providing knowledge to an idiot is akin to arming infants with gunpowder and matches.

"Because he's our partner and partners help each other," Matthew said, hoping that would put an end to it.

"So why's he our partner, then?"

"Because we can make more money with him than we can on our own, and he can make more money with us than without us. But don't tell anyone, or we'll have rough chaps looking to replace us. If everyone thinks Squidge is doing it all by himself, no one will bother with us."

Matthew was beginning to feel genuinely nostalgic for the time when Peter's quest for deep understanding stopped at speculations over whether green beetles or blue beetles ranked higher in the aristocracy of insect society. Fortunately for him, Peter was more comfortable affecting the illusion of being a man of ill repute than attempting to assume the role in reality, and so the mention of rough chaps was enough to dissuade him from further inquiry.

Shortly after this, the two started feeling a profound tranquility and glowing contentment with life—a contentment that Peter accepted without question but which Matthew, while still enjoying it fully, sensed was not due to any natural unfolding of the flower of universal goodwill.

"Our Tim's getting stronger and stronger," he thought, but said nothing to Peter, who was heaving the heaviest sighs imaginable as he basked in the sunshine of profound satisfaction.

All along the streets leading up to their house were people walking about in a soft and gentle stupor, bumping into one another with eyes closed, smiling and laughing, rapturously appreciative of the songs of songbirds and the scents of blossoms. Cats and dogs lay asleep together while mice crawled over them and birds alighted gently on their backs and bellies. Bumblebees buzzed about, and butterflies fluttered by. All that was missing from the idyllic setting was a rainbow, but no one felt cheated by its absence.

The brothers entered their house to find their sister softly singing just as we had left her in the chapter devoted to her mother's arrival home.

"What's got our Tim like this?" asked Matthew.

"Like what?" asked Lucy with a giggle.

"Like this … happiness?"

Lucy suddenly understood and blushed quite charmingly before murmuring, "When Father brought Mother home from jail, they did *it*."

"Did what?"

"*It*."

"What's *it*?"

"You know," whispered Lucy. "*It!* What married people do."

"Oh, *that!*"

"Yes, *that.*"

"What's *that?*" asked Peter.

"You know," said Matthew, trying to be quiet. "*It!*"

"No, I don't. What's *it?*"

"What you want to do with Mary Handchester."

Peter squinted in thought and then jumped with surprise.

"Oh, *that!*"

"Shh, shh, shh. Yes, *that.*"

"You want to do *it* with Mary Handchester?" said Lucy incredulously.

"Rather!" said Peter, his eyes showing the whites all around.

"But you're not even married," said Lucy. She then recalled her own feelings of earlier that day that had driven her out in the failed search for an Adonis, and reconciled within herself—for the first time in her life and with a brief but not unpleasant shock—that the taking of matrimonial vows was not a prerequisite to feeling the desire to do *it* with a man.

"I'd marry her in a flash if we could do *it,*" said Peter.

"But she's so …" said Lucy, grimacing, unable to hide her native dislike for girls who openly enjoyed attracting boys. "And she's … How could you want to do it with someone like that?"

"I don't know. I just do," said Peter, feeling quite secure in the belief that not everything that happened everywhere to everyone needed a rational explanation.

The three stood looking from one to another for some while as the feeling of profound satisfaction radiating from Tiny Tim enveloped them and sustained them.

"So, this is what *it* feels like," said Matthew to break the long silence.

"It is rather nice," said Lucy shyly.

"Makes you want to do *it* even more, doesn't it?" said Peter with a leer.

"Don't look at me," said Lucy crossly. "I wouldn't do *it* with anyone who would do *it* with Mary Handchester, even if he wasn't my brother."

This sparked Matthew's curiosity, so he asked, "But would you do *it* with someone who wouldn't do *it* with Mary Handchester and who wasn't your brother?"

"Oh, I don't know," said Lucy in a coy, singsong voice while attempting to wrap one arm helically around the other. "I might … now that I know it's not all that bad."

"Well, that might be of some use," said Matthew as he set his mind to exploring possibilities.

"What do you mean by that?" asked Lucy, with fair certainty that whatever it was her brother was thinking, there was something unsavory about it.

"I don't know yet," said Matthew half-absently. "But it'd be nice having our Tim like this from time to time and we might … Never mind. It's just a thought."

"Well, have another one 'cuz I'm not doing *it* for that. If that's all you want *it* for, then do *it* yourself with someone else or get Mary Handchester to do *it* with Peter."

"Oh, yes, please!" said Peter.

Matthew looked to his eager brother, but the lunatic look in Peter's eyes told him the chances of getting Mary Handchester—or any other girl capable of tying shoelaces—in a room alone with Peter for the purposes of *it* were beyond the vanishing point described by Renaissance artists like Masaccio and Botticelli.

"I'll keep it in mind," said Matthew, "if we ever need to …"

"I pretty much need to all the time," said Peter, nodding with absolute certainty for a change.

"But we haven't time right now," said Matthew. "We have to get Mother and Father ready to leave tomorrow. Mr. Squidge is sending a carriage to take them to Cornwall."

"It will be different without them," said Lucy.

"It will that," said Matthew, and he suddenly realized he would be the head of their little household. He was wise well beyond his years, however, and knew great leaders do not lord their leadership over their followers, and so he merely murmured, "God bless us, every one!"

CHAPTER 32

S quidge asked, "Your old mum and dad get away all right, then, did they?"

"Yes sir," said Matthew. "And thank you, again, sir."

"'S all right, mate. I got jobs for them when they gets there, so they can earn their own keep and all."

"Father's not very good with his hands … or much else, in fact. He's never done anything except keep books for Mr. Scrooge. And Mother—"

"'At's all I needs him for. Counting infantry and making entries. Little business, I got with another bloke. Bringing quality items in from France."

"From France? Why go all the way to Cornwall with it?"

"Sharp lad, you," said Squidge, aiming a finger at Matthew like a pistol. "It do take extra time in shipping, but the port facilities is cheaper, and the warehousing costs lower by some. One thing with another, we save a bob or two and undercuts the competition. And with regard to your dear old mum, she'll be making pretty little labels for bottles. Easy enough. Light work to pass the time all pleasant-like. Don't you worry."

That was, indeed, good news to Matthew, who had assumed he would be required to pay for his parents' upkeep while they were living in hiding on the west coast.

Squidge continued. "You all ready to show Belcher's your bittering agent?"

"Yes sir," said Matthew, and so he and Peter rode with Squidge to the brewery in a shiny brougham to the door of which was affixed a coat-of-arms bearing the motto "*Et Omnia Mea*" and the name "Squidge" in somewhat fresher paint and somewhat more clumsily executed calligraphy.

Peter, seated in one of the two fold-down chairs in front, felt quite the man about town, as he had never ridden in a brougham before but had always associated the brougham as a vehicle of the upper class— which this particular brougham had indeed been prior to Squidge's acquisition of it. And riding with Thaddeus Squidge, a well-known man of ill repute—which, as we have seen, was a fraternity to which Peter aspired—made it all the more thrilling, since Peter could then picture himself as a man of ill repute about town—something of the ultimate aspiration to which to aspire, in his own estimation of aspirations.

Upon arrival, the coachman opened the door for them. Peter had to get out first, as his chair folded down to block the entrance.

"Thank you, my good man," he said to the driver, for which Matthew slapped him lightly on the back of his head, which elicited a loud "Ow!" as the gash hidden under his long hair was still far from healed.

"Just keep quiet," said Matthew.

"Good advice for the both of you," said Squidge, stepping down behind them. "I'll do all the talking. Keep your holes shut till I asks a question, and answer what I asks as simple-like as you can. In fact, you"—he indicated Peter—"go stand in a corner and keep an eye on things."

"Like I'm just there to keep the hijinks to a minimum," said Peter, quoting something he'd heard a rough fellow say once in providing his job description.

"Yeah. Something like that," said Squidge. He then put his hand on Matthew's shoulder, and they led the way in.

They were shown to a room that would have reminded them of an alchemist's laboratory had they been familiar with alchemy, which they were not, so it did not. It did, however, seem strange and mysterious. Peter felt inclined to inspect the weird glass contrivances, but the moment he raised a finger to that purpose, Matthew and Squidge had him by the arms and were pulling him to a safe distance.

"Don't touch nothing," said Squidge in a whisper, and he set his eyes to selecting a spot devoid of breakables. "Go stand over there, and don't move till I tells you to."

Peter did as instructed, assuming a pose of crossed arms and spread legs, appropriate for a man of ill repute when engaged in providing the appropriate atmosphere for the surroundings of a very important man of ill repute engaged in nefarious dealings.

Shortly thereafter, the two brewmasters entered, which provided even further amazement to Squidge and Co.

Barnabas and Barnard Budge were identical twins born into a long, long line of fermenters of malt and arrived into this world bearing so many of the identifying characteristics acquired by lovers of ale—only through years of loving ale—that had they been known to Jean-Baptiste Lamarck, they would have been cited as evidence of that theorist's chief theory of evolution. Both were quite round of body, quite red of face, and quite rife of bodily gasses. And both had been so since birth.

But had they not been born into the brewing arts, they would have been born to a manufacturer of mirrors, for they were mirror images of each other. To first glance, they appeared identical—as identical twins often do—but a longer appraisal of their performance revealed Barnabas was left-handed and spoke to the left sides (i.e., beginnings) of their sentences, while Barnard was right-handed and spoke to the right sides (i.e., endings) of their vocalized thoughts.

"Please be seated ..." began Barnabas.

"... Mr. Squidge and ...?" ended Barnard.

"This is Master Cratchit," said Squidge, "and 'at's his brother, over there, what's just here to watch and won't be saying nothing at all."

"A pleasure to meet you ..."

"... Masters Cratchit and Cratchit."

"To what purpose is …"

"… this visit, Mr. Squidge?"

Squidge took his lapels in hand and said, "Well, it's like this: I owns a dray cart business, you see, and does hauling for farmers and the like. Now. I was in the process of signing a contract with Master Cratchit's father to haul his surplus to market, when he gives me a pint of his home brew—him being a neighborly sort of bloke—and it were one of the most enlightening pints I've ever have the pleasure of shifting. So I ask after it, I did, and were told it come from a secret family recipe, but it's the hops what makes it special. Now. Mr. Cratchit don't grow hops for sale—till now—but I'm thinking Belcher's would be well served in having first go at giving his produce a try."

"Have you any …"

"… with you, today?"

Squidge turned to Matthew with eyebrows raised high and said, "Master Cratchit?"

Matthew extracted a thick bundle from his jacket pocket and handed it to Barnabas Budge, who took it in his left hand and held it out for his brother to unwrap with his right.

"It's dried and powdered," said Matthew, "to get more of the flavor out."

"Interesting," the two Budges said in unison, and put their noses to sniffing the concoction.

"The aroma is …"

"… unusual but satisfying."

"We must taste it …"

"… to know for certain."

With that, they rose from their chairs and went to a table where Barnabas placed the proprietary blend down while his brother opened two bottles of some clear liquid. Barnard handed one bottle to his brother, and together they raised the vessels to their lips and took mouthfuls into their mouths. They did not drink, however, but swilled the liquid about, going from one ballooning cheek to the other ballooning cheek, each brother mirroring the other with remarkable precision of timing. Then they leaned toward one another with a jerk that would have resulted in colliding skulls had it been any other two people, but stopped short of impact by a hair's breadth as the two spat into a waiting bucket.

"Just cleansing …"

"… the palate," they said, and Barnabas opened a drawer for Barnard to extract two white wafers of which Barnabas took one and chewed upon it while Barnard chewed upon the other.

They turned toward Matthew and Squidge like two priests performing some ancient rite, but the mobility of their faces while chewing was mystifying, both for the degree to which it appeared to exceed anatomical possibility and for the exactitude of precision of each mirroring the other. Then they swallowed as one, and their double chins rippled simultaneously with the rising and lowering of the throats they concealed. Each Budge took a teaspoon from out the same drawer, and together they tasted Matthew's concoction.

Again the mobility of their faces amazed Matthew and Squidge. But rather than swallow, they spat again in the bucket and repeated the washing of their mouths from the bottles of clear liquid. They spat again and turned to face Matthew and Squidge.

"That's not hops," they said in unison.

Matthew felt Squidge's rage rising next to him and sensed he wouldn't see home again.

"But it is …" said Barnabas.

"… interesting, nevertheless," said Barnard.

"We've brewed many a beer using …"

"… other agents than hops to make bitter."

"We once brewed up sixty hogsheads …"

"… using dried peacock brains for flavor."

"Dried peacock brains?" said Squidge.

"It was a gift to the Shah …"

"… of Persia from the prime minister."

"Image the PM's surprise …"

"… when he found out the Shah is tee-total."

The twins laughed heartily, to which Squidge joined in, and then Matthew—once his fear of Squidge's anger had melted from his flesh and dripped out the tips of his tingling fingers.

At length, the laughter subsided, and Barnabas said, "So we think we might …"

"… have a use for your blend."

"We're planning a new ale …"

"… called Ramsbottom Bitter."

"It's named after Colonel …"

"… Reginald 'Ramrod' Ramsbottom."

Squidge squinted and asked, "You mean the bloke what lost the Battle of Cleavage Rift?"

"Not his fault," the twins said together.

"A mix-up in the delivery …"

"… of supplies to his battalion."

"The unit was hauling what they thought …"

"… was a cart loaded with barrels of gunpowder."

"But what they had, much to their …"

"… dismay was barrels of Belcher's India Pale Ale."

"You can't fire a cannon …"

"… with pale ale, so …"

"… they had no choice but …"

"… to run away, leaving their cannons and …"

"… the beer behind them."

"The enemy …"

"… captured the ale and …"

"… liked it so much that …"

"… when the peace was signed at the end of the war …"

"… they started buying from us and …"

"… are now our best foreign customers."

"So, while Colonel Ramsbottom may not be …"

"… a hero to queen and country …"

"… he is a hero to Belcher's Brewery …"

"… and we honor him as such."

"Hmm," said Squidge. "Some men have greatness thrust upon them, and others just gets in its way."

"So true," said both Budges piously, and Barnabas continued with "And it is an ill wind ..."

"... that blows no one no good."

With that, there erupted a brash, rattling reverberation of flatulence from the pair that set the glass equipment nearby to tinkling.

Each pointed to the other and said, "That was you!" and laughed jovially before wincing horrifically and moving away from the *scène de crime*, as French authors say in *théâtre du crime*.

"So what, precisely ..." said Barnabas to Matthew, as the twins retook their chairs.

"... goes into your blend?"

"That would be telling secrets," said Squidge. "All's you needs to know is my lad, 'ere, can make it, and you can use it."

"Quite so," said the twins together.

"How much do you ..." said Barnabas.

"... want for it?" asked Barnard.

"How much do you think it's worth?" asked Squidge, arms crossed and head tilted back.

The two looked to each other and then to Squidge.

"Six guineas ..."

"... a ton."

Upon hearing the rate of remuneration, Matthew lit up inside. He estimated he and Peter had three hundredweights of the product accumulated in their rat cellar, which, in combination with the other ingredients, was enough to make one ton of his proprietary blend hops substitute. Half of six was three, and three guineas was more than three-fourths of that he'd had to spend in saving his mother from her exile with the three Adonises in their tropical paradise.

Squidge frowned and tried to rock back in his chair, but the geometry of the furnishing prevented it, so he leaned forward instead and said, "I'm thinking eight guineas a ton and shares in the brewery for signing a contract guaranteeing on-time delivery for the next five years."

"We can go …"

"… to seven guineas but …"

"… we would have to talk to Mr. Belcher …"

"… about the contract and the shares."

"All right, then. You arrange a meeting with Belcher, and we'll agree, right 'ere and now, to seven guineas a ton. How often you require delivery?"

"We plan on putting …"

"… two kettles to …"

"… Ramsbottom Bitter, so …"

"… one ton every six weeks."

"Done," said Squidge with a huge smile, and he rose to shake hands with the twins.

As done as Squidge was with the deal, Matthew was quite undone by it, for the one thing he hadn't anticipated was the one thing that now loomed up before him like a monstrous huge cobra poised to strike.

CHAPTER 33

Peter was compelled to say, "Well, that was disgusting," on their walk home that evening. "Spitting in their bucket right in front of us. And they didn't even say 'Pardon me' when they broke wind."

Matthew glanced sideways and thought to speak, but he then thought better of it and didn't.

"What's got you upset, then?" asked Peter.

"We haven't enough product to keep going."

"What do you mean? We got a cellar full of it! Remember? We keep it under the rats."

"Enough for the first batch and, maybe, a little more. But it took a year for the rats to make that much, and we'll need that same amount every six weeks. The rats just don't make it fast enough."

"Why didn't you tell that to Mr. Squidge before he made the deal with Belcher's?"

"You mean tell the man—who every villain in the city is afraid of—we lied to him when we said we make the hops from flowers?"

"We do make hops from flowers."

"Not entirely. That's the problem."

"Oh, right," said Peter, knitting his brow. "Still. He's a fair chap. He said so himself."

Matthew glanced sideways again. "Even so, I'd rather not run the risk of disappointing him."

"Oh. You mean him being our partner and all?"

"Something like that."

After a silent while, Peter said, "Can't you make the hops without the product?"

"No. It doesn't smell right without it. Just smells like flowers. There's nothing else for it. We have to get more rat leavings. A lot more."

"Perhaps we could scare them. I remember a time …"

"I remember that too," said Matthew, still angry over being burdened with the name "Cratchit" in the schoolyard for months after the bygone incident. "And I also remember you didn't use the loo for two days after. No. The only thing for it is for us to grow more rats."

"How many more will we need, then?"

Matthew put his head to the arithmetic before muttering, "Nine."

"Only nine? We can get them—"

"No! Not nine more. Nine times what we've already got."

"Can we do that?"

"I think so. It'll mean making some changes to the warehouse and keeping the house on our street going. But yes. I think so."

"Plus, we'll have more rats to sell to Dropping," said Peter.

"No. We're about at our limit for that," said Matthew, drifting off into speculation.

"What then?"

"We'll have to find someone else who wants to buy them. But that's a problem for better days. First things first, we have to get the numbers up—and quick."

With this in mind, the brothers set themselves to transferring eight dozen rats from the cellar of the house at the end of their street to the abandoned warehouse. To this, the rats proved to be a most inefficient cargo since the cartload of squirming, squealing burlap sacks drew dubious attention from passersby as the two passed by, resulting in several delays to answer questions for which they were wholly unprepared. Unfortunately, Matthew's muse provided him with several unconvincing explanations, which only elicited further questions, before he hit on the story that caused the crowd to give them a wide berth.

They'd been hired, he said, to transport children bitten by mad dogs to Bethlehem Hospital, and they were going the wrong way because they still had more to pick up. Armed with this fiction, they were hurried along their way by all who inquired except one lady who insisted on detaining them while relating, one by one, how she'd had to send eight of her own little ones to Bedlam—as the hospital was more popularly known—because they wouldn't be quiet while she was speaking.

Once they were into the abandoned district of abandoned warehouses, progress improved, and Matthew and Peter arrived at their destination just as the security of the sacks was being breached by the teeth of their contents.

"Quick!" said Matthew. "Down the coal chute with them before they get loose!"

But too late. Some fifteen or twenty exited, via various holes in the burlap, into the freedom of the wilds of the warehouse environs, while the boys rushed to empty the sacks into the cellar.

"We shouldn't have tried to move so many at once," said Matthew, still puffing from the exertion.

"Did feel a bit like that Noah chap, who took all those animals for a ride on his boat."

"In what way?"

"Well, I can't imagine any of his animals liked being all squeezed together in the dark any more than our rats do, even if he did tell them they were going to a better place. Think of all the complaining they must have done, being at sea all that time with nothing to do but eat and make leavings. Here! What do you suppose Noah did with all the leavings he got, then? The bottom of his boat must have been full of it by the time he was done floating about from here to there."

"He grew mushrooms," said Matthew matter-of-factly, "and started a fertilizer business."

"Really? I don't remember that part."

"They don't often read that far along."

"Just as well. Services are pretty long and dull as they are. Still, don't you wish we had all those leavings here, now, to make hops from?"

Matthew imagined an ark full of elephant, gorilla, and kangaroo dung, and smiled wistfully at the image of potential peace and prosperity on the future side of having his problem solved.

"It would be one less thing to worry about," he said, but patted his brother on the thigh as he rose. "Come on. Let's see what Lucy and Tim have done with the day."

They were still several streets from home when the smell of sweet goods began accosting their nostrils. Every kitchen window in every house was stacked with pies and tarts set to cool. Everywhere people were eating all manner of sugared fruit, candied nuts, and syrupy concoctions encased in pastry. It was as if every child's dream of every meal being nothing but pudding (dessert to our friends in the colonies) had manifested in the waking world.

Suddenly a man burst from the front door of a house pursued by a woman wielding a twig broom in battle-hammer fashion.

"But I can't be buying sugar from 'em," said the man in retreat, "when they's all out, now can I?"

"It's not like they's the only shop what sells sugar, you lazy, good-for-nothing meater!" said the woman as she landed another blow upon his back. "Find a shop that ain't out, and don't come back till you've got me five pounds of sugar and forty pounds of pastry flour."

A few houses farther along, a second man was accosting a third. "Look 'ere: All I gots is seven bob, but you can 'ave the lot for it."

"And if I shows up without it, I's done for and all. Keep your bleeding money and sod off."

"But I'm dead if I goes 'ome without no sugar."

"Better you than me, mate."

Then the one made a grab for the sack carried by the other, and a tussle ensued, which was not the only tussle to be seen transpiring.

"What's going on?" asked Peter. "Why's everyone …?"

"Don't you feel it?" said Matthew. "Our Tim's got everyone wanting sweets. Lucy must have had a fancy for … Hm. What's it matter? With Mother and Father gone, we can eat pastry all we want. Come on."

With that, they accelerated their pace and hurried home to find Lucy lost inside a ghostlike cloud of flour dust, as she frantically worked out a circle of dough under a rolling pin.

"I'm sorry," she mumbled through a mouthful. "I ate your supper, but I'm making more. Help yourselves to mincemeats while you wait."

"What is for supper?" asked Peter voraciously while loading his plate with the tiny pies from the pyramid of them at the center of the kitchen table.

"Treacle tart," said Lucy. "I thought one would do for the three of us, but I couldn't wait and … I'm making one for each of you. The mincemeats were for pudding, but … Just have what you want. Bring me one, please. Or three, so I don't have to stop working."

Peter did as requested and even went further by feeding his sister with one hand while feeding himself with his other.

Matthew knew this was all wrong, but he'd never had an entire treacle tart to himself in his entire life, and the thought of it—much empowered by Tiny Tim's ongoing influence—rendered him incapable of resisting this overwhelming, urgent need for ecstasies only to be found accompanying the consumption of massive doses of sugar.

The mountain of mincemeat tarts melted away to nothing while they waited for the treacle tarts to bake.

"You know it's our Tim that's making us want sweets like this," said Matthew.

"So what?" asked Peter. He turned to his sister. "You think they're done yet?"

"Not quite," said Lucy. "And they'll be bloody hot till they've cooled."

"Here! Language," said Matthew, having taken charge—in his own mind—of all aspects of the running of the household, including its moral upkeep.

"Mother and Father aren't here," said Lucy haughtily. "I'll swear if I want to. If you don't like it, you can bloody well make your own treacle tarts."

To this Matthew was taken abruptly aback. He had never considered the possibility Lucy had not simply assumed, as he had, he would automatically rise to supreme autocrat of the Cratchit household upon the departure of their parents. And, concomitantly, neither had he considered she would not instinctively assume the role of obedient subject to his absolute, albeit benign, dictatorship.

But Matthew was becoming less and less the boy given to hurt feelings and more and more the young man of pragmatic adaptability to the unexpected. He reasoned beyond this challenge to his rulership, put aside his instinct to defend his position of power, and considered how he might use this sudden shift in Lucy's character toward the libertine.

Clearly, Lucy was no longer the untarnished innocent of years gone by. Only the day before, she was expressing feelings and preferences about the doing of it in a manner quite unbecoming to that horde of nebulous anonymous individuals empowered to decide what is becoming. And now she was employing vulgarities of speech—perhaps not to rival the proverbial drunken sailor but certainly beyond the limits allowed to ladies of genteel taste.

To anyone shackled to the norms of propriety, the arising of such traits within his family would have been a terrifying prospect to encounter, but to Matthew—who was unshackled from norms of any sort—the arising of these traits in Lucy proved she was acquiring an independence of thought that was necessary—though not sufficient in itself—for her to be a partner in the business he and Peter ran in the shadows of their overt activities.

Being a man of few words, it took Matthew far less time to come to this conclusion than it took me to describe to you his reasoning in reaching it.

And, being a man of few words, he said, "Seeing as Mother and Father are gone away, there's something we need to talk about. Peter and I make more money than we've been giving to Mother."

"Really?" said Lucy, widening her eyes.

"Yes. I've got … No. We've got plans to build up a big business and get rich like Uncle Ebenezer did."

Peter had been concentrating hard on patiently waiting for the treacle tarts to come out of the oven but caught enough of the conversation to sense that his income from the proceeds of the business was in jeopardy of being halved to accommodate Lucy.

"Why're you telling her this?" he said.

"Because she can help us," said Matthew.

"How?"

Matthew had to think, but only for a moment. "For one thing, she can go to the warehouse and mix the flowers while we're out catching rats. That'll save us time for other things."

"How much are we going to pay her, then?"

"Same as you: two shillings a week."

"Two shillings?" said Lucy with a gasp, overcome by this sudden endowment of personal wealth.

"Oh," said Peter, greatly relieved he wouldn't suffer a loss. "Treacle tart ready yet?"

"Not quite," said Lucy flatly, and she turned to Matthew. "If you've got a bit of money aside, can I have ten-and-six, then, to pay Mr. Smallbits, the grocer?"

"Ten-and-six?" said Matthew with a grimace.

"Mother's owed him for a bit. I don't like going in there when we owe so much, but I had to today to buy treacle and oats. I didn't think he'd let me have them, but he looked at me all strange-like and said I could have as much as I like any time I like and he'd settle up with me on and on."

"What do you mean, 'all strange-like'?"

"I don't know," said Lucy, squinting to think. "Like yesterday, when Peter was talking of doing *it* with Mary Handchester. Mr. Smallbits had that same silly look on his face."

"Treacle tart read …?" said Peter, but his train of thought got derailed as fury filled his eyes. "He looked at you like *that*? Like I look at Mary Handchester?"

"Yes. Something like that."

"I'll paralyze him!" said Peter.

Matthew was hit by a wall of shock, followed by a tide of rage, but didn't take the time to consider this was the effect of Peter's feelings reaching Tiny Tim and then reflecting back after the briefest of delays. "Where is this Smallbits? I'll …" he said.

"Stop!" said Lucy. "It's all right. He's not done anything. It's Tim that's making you …" She ran to Tiny Tim's side to begin the ritual of quelling the storm at its source.

Matthew could sense through the red fog of rage what Lucy meant, but Peter was already out the front door on a quest for Smallbits and a bit of violence with the overly gregarious grocer.

"Peter, stop!" called out Matthew after him as he ran out, looked one way and then the other, spotted Peter striding away with fists raised, took up the chase, and brought his brother down with a rugby tackle.

Peter's raised fists met the cobblestones first and saved his face from really serious injury, but his nose made sufficient contact with the cold rock to commence a flow of blood that could be conservatively described as liberal.

"Bloody hell!" said Peter, spinning in a whirlpool of mixed and vicious emotions.

"Language," said Matthew without thinking.

"Mother and Father aren't here," said Peter irately. "If you don't like it, you can bloody well make your own treacle tarts."

The relative hollowness of this threat—compared to when Lucy had made it—made Matthew smirk and diverted him from his feelings of anger toward the lascivious Smallbits and his anxiety toward Peter's propensity for perpetrating feeble misdemeanors.

Peter struggled to rise, but Matthew held him down.

"It's our Tim making us mad," said Matthew in Peter's ear. "We mustn't do what he wants us to. Think happy thoughts."

This simple instruction was difficult to follow, but after a brief and useless effort to free himself, Peter calmed noticeably under the greater weight of Matthew's more muscular body. Matthew relaxed his grip and moved to help Peter up. In doing so, his face came over the back of Peter's head, and a necrotic stench accosted his nostrils.

"Whew! What have you been putting in your hair?" he asked as he rose up on his knees.

"Nothing," said Peter, as he pushed off the ground with both hands. He dabbed his upper lip with the back of his wrist and was startled at the extent of the redness made available to his observation.

"I'm bleeding," he said with some disbelief.

"Not as much as you would be had you tried thumping Mr. Smallbits. Come on. Lucy'll see to you."

"She's not going to stitch me up with yarn again, is she?"

"I doubt it. But I'll leave that up to her."

Matthew gave Peter a hand and got him to his feet. As they turned to return home, they noticed the street growing more and more alive with men and boys, who were crowding together into grumbling hordes and heading past them on their way to somewhere of their collective intent. Had it not been for Peter's need for prompt attention, Matthew would have attempted to find out what was happening, but possibly unfortunately, he did not.

Once inside, a smoky smell alarmed him, and he left his brother for the kitchen to open the oven and rescue two slightly blackened treacle tarts. The opening of the oven door released the previously trickling smoke into a rolling cloud that spread throughout the house and reached Lucy, who was still next to Tiny Tim and still valiantly battling the rage of righteous indignation inspired by Peter and amplified by our hero.

"Damn," said Lucy. "The treacle tarts!"

"It's all right, I've got them," said Matthew while rescuing the pastries. "They've caught a bit on the corners, but they're all right to eat."

"I can't do every bloody thing!" said Lucy. "I'm trying to calm down our Tim, so don't be coming on at me like every bloody thing's all my bloody fault."

"I said it's all right," said Matthew, as he set the large tarts in the window to cool.

"I mean, I wouldn't be here with Tim," said Lucy, "if Peter hadn't gone off playing the giddy ox about Mr. Smallbits and all."

"Lucy! It's all right!"

"No, it's not *all* right. Nothing's bloody well *all* right at all. Mother and Father are off hiding from the law. You and Peter are off making money you don't tell no one about, and I'm here, stuck with keeping our Tim from making everyone mad as March hares and trying to do all I did before plus all Mother did before, and all …"

"Lucy … Lucy …" said Matthew, coming to her side. But before he could say, "It's all right" again, he thought better of it and said instead, "Go see to Peter, and I'll look after Tim."

Lucy was still furious with her brother, but his pleading eyes won her over, and she did as he requested. Matthew knelt beside Tiny Tim and fought to keep his mind on recollections of the seaside excursions with Uncle Ebenezer. Lucy went to Peter and commanded him to sit. Seeing thick blood still oozing from both his nostrils, she grabbed his nose between her thumb and index finger and yanked his head back.

"Ow," he gurgled.

"Swallow or you'll drown," she said as she maintained her tight grip on the ailing facial feature.

Somehow Matthew, fresh to the task of tranquilizing Tiny Tim, had greater success than his sister, and soon the air thinned into serenity. Lucy's native compassion swelled within her breast and broke through her crust of resentment, breaking it into tinier and tinier shards that fell easily away.

"You feeling better now?" she asked Peter.

"Little bit," he mumbled in a rather goose-like voice.

She released his nose and went to get a wet cloth. When she returned, it was clear the bleeding had stopped, so she put herself to the task of cleaning his face. To this, she was gentler, and she even felt a twinge of guilt over her earlier rough handling. And she sensed this whole idiotic misadventure was evidence of Peter's fraternal protectiveness of her, which warmed her heart in ways hearts were warmed in Victorian sentimental fiction.

His task achieved, Matthew left Tiny Tim's side and came to see how Lucy was faring. Besides a shiny red glow on the tip of Peter's swelling nose, there remained no evidence of anything untoward having happened.

Satisfied with Peter's front, Matthew moved around to his back with the words, "Let's see what you've got in your hair that reeks like a sewer."

He then parted the hair his brother had carefully combed into position to hide the wound and secured invisibly with hairpins. Lucy came around to share in the spectacle as it was being unveiled. What greeted their gaze was a gray-green growth, resembling a patch of moss and lichens one might find adhering to a rock. Had it been a patch of moss and lichens growing on a rock, the two might have found it a rather pretty example of natural wonder, worthy of artistic or soulful appreciation, but as it was what it was—that being a badly festering wound to which most humans have a natural aversion—they found it less esthetically and spiritually appealing.

"Crikey!" said Matthew.

"Is it bad?" asked Peter.

"It's … not good," said Lucy. "I think you should see a doctor. If we can afford one."

A needle of irritation pricked Matthew at the thought of their savings taking yet another gouging, but family was family and Peter did have his uses.

"Tomorrow, then. After work," he said. "You want some treacle tart?"

The craving for the syrupy pastry had waned, but the boys were still hungry, and there was nothing else ready to eat, so they satisfied themselves with what was left when the black edges were knocked off. Soon, however, all three siblings were suffering the dizziness, headache, and nausea that were the living proof of the validity of their mother's warning not to fill up on sweets.

"Who'd have thought she was right about anything?" said Matthew with a moan.

"Not me," said Lucy, squeezing her temples to ease the throbbing.

Peter just threw up.

CHAPTER 34

The next day, they arrived at Dropping's offices with somewhat fewer rats than usual owing to their need to allow their livestock to breed up its numbers.

"They has their seasons too," said the sagacious Dropping, "like everything else in Creation. I've seen it all before, I has. For reasons unbeknownst to man, they starts to get scarce, and then, when no one 'spects it at all, they's back like the plague what Moses brought down on them 'gyptians—'cept that was frogs and not rats, but you gets my meaning."

"Yes sir," said Matthew. "Something to look forward to, then."

"'Tis that to be sure," said Dropping, but he noticed the red rawness lighting up the tip of Peter's nose and was compelled to ask, "I read in the papers they'd riots near where you lives yesterday. You didn't go about getting yourselves mixed up in them dust-ups, did you?"

"No sir," said Matthew. "He tripped on a cobblestone."

"That's good, then. I wouldn't want to think I had no hooligans in me employ. Things like that can come back to besmirch your unbesmirched reputation, and then some."

Matthew recalled the bellicose band of people he'd seen massing in the street the evening before but elected not to mention it. "Papers say what they were rioting about?" he asked.

"Well, 'parently the shops all run out of sugar and that's what got 'em going. Makes no sense to me. When there's nothing to be got, how does smashing windows and bashing blokes about make something to be got? It don't. A bloke's got to learn not to take life's little disappointments so much to 'eart and make do with what he do got instead of fussing hisself over what he don't."

This little summation of Dropping's moral and economic philosophy did not settle well with Matthew, having made an assumption about what had fueled the public mayhem. With difficulty, he kept his antsy anxiety from showing while he feared Peter would connect the links in the chain of cause and effect—from Lucy's initial craving for something sweet to the eventual drastic depletion of sugar stores to the subsequent smashing of windows and breaking of bones— and say out loud, for Dropping to hear, the contents of his mind.

"I agree," said Matthew. "But I just remembered: we've got to get to a doctor, as Peter has a rash that needs tending."

"Ah. Rash is it? Well, rashes goes with the work, I'm afeared to say. But we has to take the bad with the good, don't we, now?"

"Yes, we do," said Matthew, and he grabbed his brother's arm as Peter was preparing to protest the calling of his injury a rash, which—in his estimation of how the world ranked ailments—was demeaning to the masculine status of a wound acquired in conflict, even if sustained while running away.

"It's not a rash," said Peter on their way to find a physician.

"Doesn't matter."

"Does to me."

"Fine. It's not a rash."

With some inquiry and searching, they found the offices of Dr. Galenios Mugwort, located in a region of the city that had been the height of fashion in bygone days when gargoyles and mythical stone beasts ruled the imaginations of architects, but had since become a place to which the writers of romantic horror went for inspiration—the kind of place that brings Bach's Toccata and Fugue in D Minor to mind when viewing the decaying decorative elements of the buildings.

Once inside the doctor's offices, however, Matthew was willing to overlook those decaying decorative elements in light of the doctor being willing to see Peter for the sum of sixpence, which was a sum Matthew was willing to pay.

"It's quite a common enough malady," said Mugwort, "though we don't see it all that often. Never at all, in fact." Here he heaved a yawn. "One of those amusing tidbits written up in medical journals month-to-month to relieve the tedium of the everyday diseases that get so painfully repetitious." He yawned again. "But one never expects to encounter anything quite like this in practice."

"Can you fix it?" asked Matthew.

"Oh, yes, of course," said Mugwort with a chuckle and a nod. "I am a physician, after all ... Though I'm not sure, precisely, what can be done. The standard treatment, when something like this appears, is amputation." Yet another yawn escaped the learned Mugwort. "You see, normally, it's the kind of thing that appears on a foot or a hand, in which case we simply saw off the offending appendage and bandage up the remains, good as new. But I suspect that might be inappropriate in this case, given the location of the ... hmm ..."—another yawn ensued—"whatever it is."

At this point, the doctor's eyes shut as if he were immersed in deep thought.

"Yes," said Matthew. "He needs his head for seeing and hearing and such."

By way of answer, Mugwort offered something resembling a snore.

"Doctor!" shouted Matthew.

"Quite ... Quite ... Where was I ...? Oh, yes. So you see my dilemma. Life simply wouldn't be the same for him afterward if we take the radical approach."

"Yes sir. So, what will happen if you don't do anything?"

"What ...? Oh yes. Well, he'll die, most likely. Yes. Most likely." Here Mugwort resumed his pattern of yawning. "Fairly sure he will." The doctor again began nodding off.

"Doctor!" shouted Matthew.

"Yes? What?"

"Is there anything you can do for him?"

"For whom?"

"Him. My brother."

"Oh, him? Well, let me see. I suppose we could slice it out. Yes, that would be simple enough. Providing he doesn't bleed much. Which he will, of course. Scalps bleed, you know." Yet another yawn came forth. "Not sure anyone knows precisely why. But they do. Bleed, I mean. Something to do with the circulation, I'd imagine. Yes, that must be it. Still"—another yawn—"Makes it all rather messy. But yes. Cut it out and have done with it. Nothing else for it … Quite."

"That would leave a rather large hole, won't it?"

"Yes," said Mugwort, raising his eyebrows as he appraised the offensive site yet again. "I suppose it would at that. Bit of a nuisance, I must say, but then these things often are. Though I suppose we could sew in a graft. Yes, I believe that's what they're recommending these days." The doctor paused here—unsurprisingly, to let out a yawn. "Take some skin off his bottom—half from one side, half from the other—sew it in his scalp, cover up the hole. There. Good as new. He will have a bald spot, though." He yawned once again. "Not sure I'd want him going about telling people I did that to him. Perhaps he might grow his hair longer and tie it in back with a ribbon. Like one of those sailor chaps. Quite dashing an effect in a young man."

"And what about the holes left in his bottom?"

"Oh, no one will notice those. Provided, of course, he keeps his trousers on when he's out of doors," said the doctor matter-of-factly. But then he leaned toward Matthew and murmured, "He does keep his trousers on when he's out of doors and in public, doesn't he?"

"He does."

"Then there's our remedy." He again heaved a yawn. "Nothing like following a sound line of reasoning to arrive at a solid conclusion. Descartes, you know. Think it was Descartes … Yes, yes. Quite sure it was. Or was it Leibnitz?"

The doctor, once again, surrendered to slumber, and once again, Matthew rescued him from its captivity.

"How much will it cost?" asked the increasingly impatient Cratchit.

"Well, that depends on how you wish to proceed. With laudanum, I charge twelve shillings. Without … it will cost you two crown."

"What's laudanum?"

"Puts him to sleep."

"Oh, well he doesn't need that," said Matthew.

"Don't I?" asked Peter nervously.

"You want someone cutting up your head and your bottom while you're asleep?" asked Matthew with a fearful grimace.

"No!" said Peter at the nightmarish prospect.

"Well then?" said Matthew impatiently.

He wasn't particularly angry with his brother's inability to see the obvious without guidance, since he'd long ago grown accustomed to lining up the salient elements of arguments for Peter's sake. Rather, Matthew was simply growing ever more sensitive to the serial assaults on his worldly wealth that were ganging up, one upon another, of late.

"You say he'll die if we don't do this?" he asked.

"I don't want to do that," said Peter.

"Well?" said the doctor. He went on speaking between more sporadic yawns. "He may not. If he doesn't, though, that—whatever it is—will likely spread. You wouldn't want him going around looking like a moldy beetroot, would you?"

Matthew tried to imagine the effect, then said with a sigh, "I suppose not. It's awkward enough taking him out as it is. All right then. I haven't got the money with me. Can you do it tomorrow?"

"Oh yes. I'm not at all busy these days. People are either staying well or dying. Damnable nuisance, but there it is."

Arriving at the decision to go forward with the surgery did little to quell Matthew's irritability over the recent wasting away of his wallet. He didn't blame Peter for this, but on their way home, he couldn't help reviewing and regretting the rescue of their mother from transport. And he tried to imagine alternatives to spending that might enhance the family's financial recovery. Nothing came to mind, as he had already transformed the science of frugality into an art form. But ten shillings to slice out a patch of moldy flesh seemed exorbitant by any measure.

"Now that we know what to do," he said, "do you suppose our Lucy could do the mending of your head?"

"No!" said Peter aghast with horror. "She's a girl! I can't have her looking at my bare bottom."

"Oh. Right. I hadn't thought of that," said Matthew with disappointment, abandoning all hope for immediate relief.

CHAPTER 35

A short while later, Matthew's mood shifted to the better, but he knew this was not of his own doing. He could sense it was Tiny Tim, radiating feelings of beneficence under Lucy's leadership. Being of a naturally scientific bent, he took note of where he was when this feeling first came upon him and could tell his silent brother's radius of influence was growing wider over time.

Upon arrival on their street, they saw Lucy at their front door, talking with the familiar policeman who patrolled their neighborhood in the wake of problems of a criminal nature that arose from time to time.

"Crikey!" said Matthew with his head bowed to Peter. "They're looking for Mother already."

"What'll we do?"

"Just keep quiet, and I'll do the talking."

They arrived as Lucy announced their arrival.

"Good evening, Masters Cratchit," came the constabulary greeting. "I'm looking for your father, but this young lady tells me he's not about."

Matthew exaggerated the awkwardness he was feeling for better effect. "No sir," he said. "He's gone to America."

"America, you say? Why's that, then?"

"Well ... it's a bit embarrassing to say ... but a magistrate sent our mother to Australia for smacking a bank manager, which made our father quite sad, as he's rather fond of her. He said he couldn't manage staying here without her and left to start a new life."

"I see. And how is it your sister had no knowledge of this?"

"I didn't want her upset over knowing she'll never see either of them again, so I thought I'd keep it from her till she's a bit older. But now it's all out, since I can't tell lies to the police, can I?"

"No, indeed," said the policeman sternly, but with empathy he added, "Though I am sorry to be the one that caused …"

"'Scuse me," said Lucy with her face contorted grotesquely. She spun about and darted inside before exploding into laughter.

"Does she find this amusing?" said the policeman.

"No. That's the noise she makes when she's crying."

"Strange girl!"

"She is that, but we love her nonetheless."

"Well. To the matter what brought me here. I see your brother has sustained an injury to his …?" said the constable, while circling his own meaty nose with the tip of his meaty finger.

"Oh, yes. He tripped on a cobblestone and bumped it on the road. Bled something awful, but Lucy cleaned him up."

"And whereabouts did this tripping and bumping of noses occur?"

"Just over there," said Matthew, pointing to the scene of the accident. "You can probably still see the blood where it happened."

"I see. So, it's an injury of a purely happenstantial nature and not acquired during the commission of a felony, then?"

"Felony?"

"Yes," said the policeman, and he then leadingly suggested, "Like the hanging of grocers from shop signs, perhaps?"

"No. He's not been doing any of that. Just tripping and bumping his nose," said Matthew airily. He leaned closer to the constable to add, "He's a tad clumsy."

"I see. And yourself? What were you up to last evening?"

"Well, we were late home from work, like today. Our Lucy made treacle tart for supper …"

"Treacle tart for supper?"

"She was sad about our parents being away and thought it would cheer us up."

The policeman opened his mouth to speak but burst into laughter instead. Surprising as this was for Matthew and Peter, they were soon caught up in the hilarity and joined in. Passersby, too, took up the mood, and soon the whole street was alive with chuckling, chortling, guffawing, giggling, tittering, sniggering, and convulsing in all manner of fits of laughter.

"Clearly, I'm looking in all the wrong places," said the constable. He then touched his helmet in farewell and left on his merry way.

"What's so funny?" asked Peter.

"Nothing," said Matthew. "It's our Tim. Lucy's got him doing it."

They went inside to find Lucy on the living room floor, curled up in laughter and crying with the ache in her sides. To this, her brothers joined her, and it was some while before the pain of the profound pleasure was too much to bear and they were forced to regain their sobriety.

"I can't tell lies to the police, can I?" said Lucy, mimicking Matthew and starting the laughter all over again.

But the hilarity was more abbreviated in duration this time.

"So, what's happened?" asked Matthew. "The bobby said a grocer's been hanged."

"It was Mr. Smallbits," whispered Lucy, looking from side to side to ensure no non-Cratchit could hear. "A gang of men broke into his house, pulled him out of his bed, told him they wouldn't have him mucking about with their sisters, and dragged him out to string him up from his own shop sign."

That sent a chill through Matthew, as he knew—and could tell that Lucy had also guessed—it was Peter's burst of anger on the previous evening that had triggered these events through the conduit of Tiny Tim. Knowing they were responsible for the death of a grocer—albeit an allegedly lecherous one—was difficult enough to accommodate, but this specificity of intention was a new and terrifying development. Up until then, the emotions amplified by Tim had been without direction, but somehow, the identity of Smallbits as the target of rage, along with his leering eye for sisters, had gotten communicated along with the rage itself.

After lengthy consideration, Matthew revealed Dropping's news item. "We also heard there were riots over the sugar running out."

"What's that got to do with anything?" asked Lucy.

"It's not obvious? When you fancied something sweet for supper, you got our Tim sending out that fancy all about. People bought so much sugar to make pies and such, the shops all ran out, and then those who couldn't get it got shirty and smashed everything up."

"Oh," said Lucy, flushing with embarrassment.

"Well, at least we don't owe Mr. Smallbits ten-and-six anymore," said Peter.

Matthew winced for a moment, as he was not entirely without compassion for the unfortunate grocer and still had some sense of responsibility for his demise. But he knew his elder brother, though quite kindly toward those he knew personally, was sheltered by a circumscribed worldview from concerns over people outside his immediate acquaintance.

"Just as well," said Matthew. "It'll cost nearly that much to mend your head."

"You can get Peter's head mended for ten-and-six?" said Lucy, aghast at the bargain.

"Just the sore bit in back," said Matthew, wiggling a finger toward the back of his own. "Ten shillings to get that moldy bit removed."

"Oh, that," she said flatly. She then smiled and said, "Two crown for his crown, is it?"

CHAPTER 36

The next morning, Peter and Matthew took Lucy with them to the abandoned warehouse before heading off on their day's ratting. The plan was to get Lucy started on grinding the poppy seed pods and blending them with the various flower petals Matthew had formulated to make up their proprietary bittering agent. He purposely neglected to tell her rat leavings would be added to the mix prior to delivery to Belcher's on the grounds her feminine culinary sensitivities might give her pause in partaking in the project. He was equally hesitant to tell her she would be working in a building in which rats were being bred for slaughter, but they were kept in the cellar, well out of sight, and shouldn't present a problem.

"What a mess!" said Lucy with repugnance when they entered.

"Feel free to tidy up if you like," said Matthew.

"No thanks. I'll make do as is."

"Suit yourself," said Matthew, and he showed her what to do.

The boys left her to her labors and headed off to their first assignment for the day.

"I think it's better we leave our Tim alone as much as possible unless we can all be with him together," said Matthew as they walked.

"Why's that?"

"It's too hard on Lucy keeping him happy by herself. When we're together, we can remind each other not to get cross or scared or to fancy treacle tarts or anything else that will get him starting riots and hanging shopkeepers."

"Hm," said Peter. "He is a bit of a problem that way, isn't he?"

"He is that, but I think he might have his uses."

"Like what?"

"I don't know yet, but I'll think of something."

"You mean something like a caterpillarist would think of?"

"That's right."

"Well, that's good. He should start pulling his own weight. It's the proper thing to do."

"True," said Matthew. "Not that he costs all that much as it is. I mean, he doesn't even eat anything."

Peter nodded his agreement, but the mention of food opened his mind to gustatory possibilities. "You want to stop at Mrs. Retch's for a meat pie? I'll buy."

"All right then," said Matthew, and they changed course to allow for breakfast.

The two arrived at the shop of their favorite client to find a minor brouhaha coming to a displeasing conclusion.

"I can't help the price of sugar any more than you can!" shouted the otherwise calm and kindly Mrs. Retch.

"You're a grasping old shrew, you is, and I'll not be back 'ere again if you's the last bakery standing after the 'poc'lypse!" said the red-faced, cane-wagging crone as she backed her way into Peter and out the front door.

"What are you two 'ere about?" said Mrs. Retch. "It ain't been a week since …"

"We came to buy breakfast," said Matthew.

"Oh … Sorry lads," said Mrs. Retch shyly. "I'm having a bit of a bothersome day, I am, as I always do when I has to put me prices up."

"Why's that then?" asked Peter, fearing an additional farthing to cover his promise to pay.

"Cost of sugar's rising too quick to keep up. Started two days ago. By four o'clock there was gangs smashing shops, and by eight yesterday morning, every warehouse in the city was emptied. Someone's bought it all up, and now there's none to be had. Price always goes up when that happens."

"Does it?" asked Matthew, whose ears had risen upon the word "sugar."

"Oh my, yeah! And then some!" She then whispered, "'Twas lucky for me a bloke stopped by with a cartload of it and sold me all he had left. It cost me double what's usual, but at least I won't be running out anytime soon."

"A bloke with a cartload of sugar?" said Matthew, astounded someone could appear out of nowhere precisely when needed.

"That's right. The name on the wagon was Squidge. You 'eard of him?"

"No," said Matthew.

But Peter protested with "Yes we have!"

"No … We haven't," said Matthew, and he looked darts at his too-talkative brother.

Peter was petulant, peeved, and hurt but stayed silent. Matthew then asked for two meat pies—which, much to Peter's relief, had not gone up in price owing to the fact sugar was not required in their making.

"Why d'you say we don't know Mr. Squidge?" asked Peter later.

"He doesn't like us using his name, remember?"

"Oh, right," said Peter, recalling the unpleasant discussion.

"But I think I know what it is Tiny Tim can do for us."

"What's that?"

"He can make people want things we've got to sell."

"What have we got to sell?"

"What people want."

"Have we? I didn't think we had much of anything. 'Cept rats, of course."

"No, no, no," said Matthew, trying to put a patient face on his frustration. "Weren't you listening? When there wasn't any sugar to be bought, Squidge was able to charge Mrs. Retch double what she usually pays. So I'm thinking we can buy something—anything at all people buy—and then get our Tim wanting it like Lucy wanted treacle tart, wait for the shops to sell out, then sell what we have for double what we paid."

Peter scrunched up his face in deep thought and followed the logic step-by-step to its ultimate conclusion. Upon arrival, his eyes opened wide, and he smiled the smile of the enlightened mind. "And we keep doing that till we're rich!"

"Exactly."

"But won't that cause more riots?"

"Perhaps," said Matthew with a bit of a scowl. "If we're careful, we can … Wait a minute! I've got a better idea."

"What's that, then?"

"Instead of us buying things and selling them, we get Squidge to pay us to tell him what to buy."

"You think he'll do that?"

"I'm sure of it. Think about it. He can afford to buy all the sugar in the city and then sell it back for double what he paid. If I was to say to him, 'Give us five pounds, and I'll tell you what's next that people will want,' it'd be worth it to him to pay so he'd know ahead of time what to buy while the prices were still low."

"Why would he believe what you tell him?"

"I'll give him a couple of tips for free just to show him I know what I'm talking about, and then make him pay."

All this was beyond Peter's grasp, but he took confidence, knowing Matthew had mystical insight into the metaphysics of finance.

CHAPTER 37

T haddeus Squidge was waiting for Matthew and Peter at the end of their workday.

"I've made the deal with Belcher's," said Squidge. "They'll be needing the bitter in three weeks, so you'd better be ready."

"We will," said Matthew, unready to admit he'd assumed he had twice that time to prepare.

"Good, then. My man'll take you to the docks, so you can buy what flowers you needs. He'll pay for 'em and haul 'em to where you wants 'em."

This, of course, was an unexpected development, but Matthew was wisely unwilling to challenge Squidge or to suggest a postponement.

"If you'll excuse me, I need a moment with my brother," he said, and took Peter aside. "Here's the ten shillings for Dr. Mugwort. I'll be along when I'm finished with Squidge's man."

"Thanks," said Peter. "But I've been thinking more on it, and I expect I'd rather be asleep when he does it."

"Really?"

"I've heard it doesn't hurt so much that way."

"Where d'you hear that?" said Matthew, trying to cast doubt on the assertion.

"I don't know. I just did."

"Well, if you want to give him two shillings to put you to sleep, then give him two shillings."

"What? Out of my own money?" said the offended Peter.

"It's you who wants it."

"Not that much."

"Suit yourself."

So, equipped with two shiny crowns, Peter set off, Mugwortian bound, while Matthew stowed their rat wagon in the back of Squidge's stables and headed off with a drayman to purchase flowers.

"I see they've put the price of cakes and tarts up," said Matthew for casual conversation.

"Did day, now?" said the driver, demonstrably without patience for the topic.

"Of course. I knew it was coming."

"Did jer, now?"

"Yes. I heard last week there would be a shortage of sugar, and that always puts prices up. Of cakes and tarts, I mean."

As Matthew had intended, this sparked the driver's interest.

The driver eyed him with the better of his two eyes and said, "You 'eard last week that sugar'd be short this week?"

"Oh, yes. I hear all sorts of things when I'm working for different people."

"Yer don't say."

"Oh, yes," said Matthew, with that artificial assuredness often assumed by adolescents when attempting to appear more worldly and self-assured than they actually are.

"Wha'cher 'ear, then?"

"Well, last week—as I say—I heard two chaps talking, and one said, 'Sugar is getting quite low. They'll be rioting in the streets if this keeps up,' and I read in the papers yesterday that there were riots in the streets when the sugar ran out. Exactly as he said."

"Yeah," said the driver, clearly intrigued. "I 'eard 'at too. What else d'you 'ear then?"

"Well, just this morning, my brother and I were working in the back of a chocolate shop, and I heard the owner say she's worried there won't be enough cocoa to last till next month."

"Is 'at so?"

"It is. Which reminds me: I have to buy some chocolate for my sister before the price goes up."

And the conversation continued in much this same vein, with Matthew aspiring to a nonchalance of expertise and the driver showing greater and greater interest in the rising and falling of commodity prices than others of his ilk might display.

They reached their destination, bought the flowers Matthew chose—the cost of which was much lower than he'd expected once Squidge's name was mentioned—and delivered them to the derelict warehouse. Matthew opened the great doors to admit the wagon and was relieved to find Lucy was already gone, since he'd feared having to introduce her to the wagon driver, who was a man of the kind he preferred would remain outside his sister's sphere of acquaintances.

After unloading the huge cart, he returned to Squidge's with the driver, reclaimed his rat cart from its concealment and took it back to the warehouse. He checked to see what progress Lucy had made and was pleased to find she'd exhausted her supply of poppies and scented blossoms before leaving. He then dumped all the waste stems and leaves down the coal chute for the rats to eat and headed off to fetch Peter from the doctor's.

Still a goodly distance along the street from Mugwort's surgery, Matthew noticed people pausing to gaze in the direction of the doctor's offices. Several crossed the road rather than pass nearer the ponderously ornate residence. As he drew closer, the cause of this strange fascination and desire for distance became obvious, as sounds of screaming and hideous wailing were emanating from the building. After one especially chilling shriek of torment, Matthew grinned the grin of one bearing up under unpleasant circumstances and thought, "I guess Peter decided to stay awake for it, after all."

Fortunately, that was the last of the really disquieting shrieks, and Matthew had little more than a pathetic moaning and weeping to disturb the quiet of his wait in the waiting room. And, also fortunately, Peter was ready to leave only twenty minutes later, when Matthew tossed down the enormously well-thumbed copy of *Punch* magazine containing the caricatures of Napoleon Bonaparte, whom Matthew had reason to believe was no longer relevant to current affairs.

"All right?" he asked, unable to take his eyes off the huge globe of white linen bandage atop his brother.

"No, I am not all right. That bloody well hurt! I should've spent the two bob and let him put me to sleep."

"Does it hurt now?"

"Stings like blue blazes!"

"Well, if you'd been put to sleep, you'd be awake now, and it would still sting like blazes."

"Yes. So?"

"So you'd be no better off now than you would have been had you been put to sleep, but now you've still got your two shillings."

As unassailable as this logic was, it failed to quell Peter's self-pity.

"Even so, it hurts," he said with a pout.

Dr. Mugwort appeared, not yet shed of his bloodstained apron, and carrying a tiny yellow jar in his bloodied fingers.

"This will soothe the"—he yawned—"inflamed areas," he said, but he retracted it as Matthew reached for it. "Three pence, if you please."

Matthew sighed heavily and looked at his moping, pouting brother. "All right. But if you need more, you buy it yourself."

To this, Peter smiled with gratitude. Matthew paid the doctor and pocketed the jar.

"Come on, then," he said grumpily. "I have to buy Lucy some chocolate on the way home."

"What for?" said Peter. "I go through all that and she gets the chocolate?"

"Don't worry. I'm not going to let her eat it."

CHAPTER 38

The chocolatier wore spectacles of the kind that made his eyes appear treble their true size and disconnected from the plane of his face. This made it impossible for him to hide his amazement upon seeing Peter enter his shop with a massive white bandage wrapped around his head.

"My brother's just back from India," said Matthew, "and I thought we might have some chocolate to celebrate his coming home."

"Most commendable," said the chocolatier with a cordial smile. "The majority of returning soldiers celebrate with beer and get up to mischief, so I'm told. So! Milk, white, or dark?"

"Milk's white," said Peter with astonishment. "Everyone knows that."

"He's a bit confused," said Matthew. "Touch of monkey-madness, but he's nearly recovered. Which is cheapest?"

"Usually the white," said the chocolatier, indicating his displays, "as cocoa is the most expensive ingredient. But the past few days, sugar has been an awful price, so the dark is the most affordable at present."

"I'll take four ounces of dark," said Matthew, and he watched as the bespectacled man chopped, weighed, and wrapped the chocolate.

"I did hear the warehouses would run out of sugar," he said while the man worked. "And I also heard the ship that brings in the cocoa is late arriving. They're worried it might've sunk."

To this, the chocolatier looked up with his much magnified terrified eyes and asked, "Where did you hear that?"

"Down at the docks. I have to go there a lot for work, and I hear all sorts of things."

"Oh, my! First sugar and now this. I must buy extra. Thank you for telling me. Oh, my, my, my, my, my, my, my. Thank you so much. Do you like almonds?"

"Yes."

The chocolatier scooped a small scoop of chocolate orbs from a large glass container into a bag and put it and the wrapped bundle on the counter. "That'll be tuppence, please. The almonds are free, and if you ever hear anything else that might be of interest …"

"I'll be sure and tell you," said Matthew, and he gave the man two pennies.

On their way out, the chocolatier noticed Peter's painful gait and asked, "Why is he limping?"

"He was wounded by a man with a knife," said Matthew.

"Oh," said Peter, his sense of man of ill repute rising abruptly. "I was, wasn't I?"

"Brave lad," said the chocolatier, which raised Peter's spirits to the limit spirits can be raised in one whose head and bottom are simultaneously sorely throbbing.

"Here," said Matthew, opening the bag of almonds and offering it to his brother.

"Why'd he give us these, then?"

"Because I told him there won't be any cocoa soon."

"Really? You mean if I go into a tailor's shop and tell them there won't be any wool for a bit, they'd give me a new coat?"

"They might. But I wouldn't expect it. He didn't have to give me the almonds. But knowing today that cocoa is about to run out means he can buy extra before it does, and he can keep his shop open when all the others are having to close."

"How do you know all this, then?"

"Because I'm going to get our Tim to make everyone want chocolate so much there won't be an ounce left anywhere for anyone to buy."

"Why are you doing that?"

"Never mind. Here. Finish up the almonds, and don't tell Lucy about them."

With all they'd had to do, and their pace slowed in deference to Peter's stitched-up backside pulling with each flexion of his glutes, they arrived home after sunset to the aroma of roast mutton. As pleasing as this aroma was to the famished pair, Matthew had to worry Lucy was falling into the spendthrift ways of their mother.

"I bought it from Mrs. Cherrytart," said Lucy. "Her husband saw a sheep fall off a wagon on the way to the butcher's, and he brought it home. She got all she can use and sold the rest of it up and down the street cheaper than Gutblood's sausage."

Matthew had spent enough time in the company of men of ill repute—other than his brother—to know "fallen off a wagon" meant the sheep was stolen, likely during the rioting that gripped parts of the city two nights earlier. He made a mental note since this propensity to purloin, so evident among their neighbors, might be put to good use in the future. Still, he decided not to disabuse Lucy of her faith in humankind or of her belief that Fortune occasionally smiled on those who made no effort at all to elicit her goodwill.

"Chocolate is going to get expensive soon," he said instead, "so I bought some. I'll put it away for a special occasion, shall I? Where can I put it where it won't be in the way?"

"Chocolate?" gasp/moaned Lucy. "I haven't had chocolate since … Can't we have some now?"

"No. I'd rather save it for that special occasion. Like when we get paid for selling the bitter to Belcher's."

"When's that, then?"

"Three weeks."

"Three weeks? Oh, no, *please!* Can't we have just a little bit now?"

"All right, all right," said Matthew. "Give me a knife." He unwrapped the package to display the broken dark brown chunks.

"Here," he said, holding out a tiny shard.

Lucy didn't even try to take it from him but put her mouth around his fingers, captured the piece with her tongue, and then licked his digits clean of the melted residue. To this, Matthew was delighted in ways most unsuited to their familial relationship.

"Ahhhww," moaned Lucy in ecstasy, and she lingered—eyes shut—over the experience for some moments.

Matthew found her hedonistic enjoyment of the confection most entertaining but pulled himself from its consideration, rewrapped the chocolate, and took it into the kitchen. He pushed a chair up to the cupboards, climbed upon it, and stowed the package on the top shelf. As he climbed down, he recalled the little jar of ointment he'd purchased from the doctor, took it from his pocket and put it in the same cupboard on a lower shelf.

To all this, he imagined his plan was going well. The chocolate could not be retrieved without some effort, so Lucy would resist temptation long enough for the temptation—and the subsequent causative craving—to take firm hold of her and Tiny Tim and be radiated out into a world as yet unaware of its desperate, dire need for chocolate.

Of course, he had no way of knowing precisely how long it would take for the cravings to take hold, but that didn't matter all that much; two days, three, even four would be within reason to prove to Thaddeus Squidge that Matthew had access to valuable information.

Matthew carved the mutton while Lucy served up the vegetables before he and she sat to eat.

"You not having supper?" asked Lucy of Peter.

"Don't be daft! Of course I'm having supper. I prefer to stand, is all."

So the three enjoyed the best meal they'd had in a great long time, despite them all being aware of Peter's towering discomfort throughout. When they were done, Matthew rocked back on his chair in profound satisfaction and said out loud, "God bless us, every one!" to which they all laughed.

CHAPTER 39

Lucy proved herself well worth her two shillings a week not only in the labor she provided but also in the mindfulness she brought to that labor. On her second day of preparing bitter for Belcher's, she took with her various kitchen utensils she knew from her first day's experience would greatly increase her efficiency.

Over the weeks that followed, her knowledge of food preparation methodology served her well, and she completed the seventeen hundred pounds of blended leaves, petals, and seed pods required for the final mix well ahead of schedule.

But while Lucy's workdays were spent in dank and dusty conditions, she never complained again about the esthetics of her surroundings, having said all she needed to say on the subject on her first day in the warehouse. Being quite the opposite to her mother in this regard, she saw no value in repeating herself once her opinion had been made clear.

Indeed, being rather like her father in this regard, she instinctively sought ways to make the best of every situation, even when that best was only marginally better than the worst. She found the work and lack of ventilation led her to perspire rather heavily, but she also found her clothes picked up the scent of the flowers quite readily. To this, she sorted out those flowers with the prettiest fragrance, laid them out in a space she'd swept clean, stripped off her dress and petticoats and undergarments, and laid them out atop the fragrant blossoms. Then, clad only in her stockings and shoes, she worked with far greater comfort than if she'd remained fully clothed. Plus, she got a bit of a naughty thrill from being so scantily attired in a place that was not her bedroom. Furthermore, she could enjoy the pleasing aroma in her clothes all the way home once her day's work was done, and the compliments from people in the shops she stopped to shop in on her way.

Things were less pleasant for Matthew and Peter, however. As has already been described, their task of excavating rat leavings from the cellar was replete with elements to offend all five of the physical senses, as well as a few senses only speculated upon by philosophers and metaphysicians. Still, with Lucy devoted to grinding and mixing the floral portions of the proprietary blend, the young men were freed to concentrate fully on the less pleasing portion of the work and were able to empty the cellar of its foul contents in nine days.

So it was that the first shipment of the bittering agent was ready well ahead of the date required and some progress was made toward the second. To this, however, Matthew made a startling and terrifying discovery—the production of the product was far behind schedule.

Like most things that are not immediately obvious, the mistake in Matthew's calculations became painfully obvious once he realized his errant estimation was due to an incorrect fundamental assumption. He'd calculated how many rats would be required, on an ongoing basis, to provide three hundred pounds of leavings every six weeks, but he had not taken into account that the rodents would not reach that necessary number for another six weeks. Until their population peaked, production would be exponentially proportionately less.

But Matthew was a firm believer that the only time to panic over insufficient resources was when time itself had completely run out, and until that moment arrived, there were always alternatives. To that he put his full focus day and night, but to no avail. As luck would have it, however, it was Peter who trod upon the solution.

"Bloody hell!" said Peter, unintentionally announcing his discovery.

"What's …? Oh, crikey!" said Matthew, grimacing at the eye-watering stink.

Peter sat on the edge of their rat cart to remove his boot and inspect the vile muck clinging to its sole.

"That's it!" shouted Matthew in lieu of "Eureka!"

"What's it? I've stepped in dog—"

"Exactly. Dog leavings are as good as rat leavings. Smell."

Peter sniffed before he had a chance to think better of it. But rather than complain, he asked, "You mean we should keep dogs instead of rats?"

"No, they won't eat garbage. At least not just any garbage. But we don't need to keep them, as they leave their leavings everywhere. All we have to do is keep our eyes open for it."

"And not step in it."

"And not step in it. Only gather it up. I'm sure we can find twenty pounds a day if we put our minds to it. Just until we've got enough rats to make all we need."

First things first, they searched about for disused containers to contain the substitute product, but finding none, Matthew hopped a fence behind a hotel and relieved the establishment of its cuspidors set outside to be emptied and polished.

And so it was that their problem of insufficiency of product was solved and Matthew could stop worrying over disappointing Squidge—or, at least, stop worrying over what would follow *after* disappointing Squidge.

CHAPTER 40

Upon Peter's return home on the day following the day of the removal of his necrotic mossy growth, he complained the pain was not subsiding as quickly as he would have liked. This did not surprise Matthew, as he had assumed—quite correctly—Peter would have preferred the pain go away immediately, which Matthew knew would not happen.

"What about that ointment?" asked the ailing Cratchit.

"Oh, right," said Matthew, having forgotten it. "In the kitchen. Cupboard in the middle. Bottom shelf."

"I'll get it," said Lucy, who had, since the darning of Peter's scalp, promoted herself to family Florence Nightingale during her mother's absence.

"What's it look like?" shouted Lucy from the kitchen.

"Small yellow jar!" shouted Matthew back.

Lucy returned to the living room and looked at Peter's wrapped head. "Well, take off the bandage, then," she ordered.

"That's not what hurts the worst."

"What does, then?"

"My bottom," whispered Peter over his shoulder to her, and he blushed crimson.

"Then drop your trousers and let's have a look."

"No! I can't have you looking at my bottom. And the other bits."

"Don't talk daft," said Lucy, imagining what Mother would say. "I've seen them all before, you know."

"You have?" said Peter, cringing in shock.

"Course I have. You think Martha and Belinda really didn't let me take a peek when you were taking baths?"

This shocking bit of family scandal froze Peter where he stood and even caused Matthew a moment to consider, but while Matthew could find the revelation amusing, Peter was petrified to his core.

"Come on then," said Lucy. "Don't be a nitwit. I promise not to laugh."

"Here, I'll do it," said Matthew. "Just let me get a butter knife to spread the stuff."

"Lucy can do it," said Peter, and he unbuttoned his fly with the haste of one who's overdone the castor oil.

Lucy knelt behind her blushing brother and gently removed the bandages from his buttocks to expose the two stitched stripes of angry, proud flesh. After making aesthetic comparisons as to the doctor's failed attempt at symmetry, Lucy unscrewed the lid from the little jar, took a dab of the yellow cream on her finger, and applied it to the upper end of one injured area.

"Ow! Bloody hell!" said Peter as he thrust his hips forward. "Go easy!"

"I am," said Lucy.

"Crikey. It doesn't half sting," said Peter.

"Baby," said Lucy, and she smeared the second dose along the second stripe.

Peter's eyes teared up as he stoically waited for relief that did not come. Lucy continued applying the cream to her brother's twitching buttocks for some moments before Peter could take no more.

"You must be doing it wrong," said Peter. "It burns like …"

"Maybe it's supposed …" said Lucy, but she then looked at the jar, sniffed it, and giggled with embarrassment. "Oops. This is mustard."

Peter clutched his backside in both hands and began frantically hopping about and screaming, "Get it off! Get it off! Get it off!" until he tripped on his trousers, which had fallen to his ankles, and fell face-first to the floor.

Matthew burst into laughter at his brother's mad display, showing nothing of the fraternal love and compassion he felt for Peter when Peter was not in need of love or compassion, but rather more a vicious delight in what was clearly Peter's excruciating pain. Sorry to say, but so it often is with siblings.

Lucy's first reaction had been fascinated surprise over the extreme independence of movement seen in Peter's defining male characteristics as he bounced around before her prior to his tumble to the floor. Then she joined Matthew in laughter over Peter's painful distress.

But only for a moment.

Suddenly she leaped to her feet, saying, "Ow, ow, ow, ow, ow. Bloody hell!"

"What?" said Matthew.

"My bum's burning!" whispered Lucy as loudly as a whisper can be uttered and still be a whisper as she began rubbing her buttocks vigorously with both hands while hopping on the spot.

Immediately Matthew found this funny too, but before he could laugh at his sister's expense, he was on his feet, propelled there by unseen flames to his own backside.

"It's Tim again," he shouted. "Get that mustard washed off Peter!"

Lucy made the dash to the kitchen to get a cloth and then out back to the pump while Matthew retrieved the jar of proper ointment. Both moved much faster than either would have guessed possible, since both were instinctively attempting escape from the inescapable.

Peter's bottom was pointing up in all its glowing glory when Lucy returned with the icy, wet cloth which she spread out, dripping before her, and tossed down on the inflamed orbs. The sensation took Peter's breath away, but within seconds he was moaning the moans of pleasure as the sudden relief from intense agony proved to be the most pleasurable of pleasures for him, as relief often is.

With the fiery irritant thoroughly washed away, Peter relaxed into near sleep, while Lucy applied the proper ointment to his bright red buttocks. Matthew stood with his eyes closed, enjoying the diminishing of the burning—first to a prickling discomfort and then to a delightful tingling warmth. He sighed with relief and opened his eyes to see Lucy grinning broadly.

"What's so funny?" he asked.

"Nothing. It's just … Hmm, rather nice. Don't you think?"

The suggestive look in his sister's eyes when she said this led Matthew to feel feelings quite inappropriate to a brother and sister. His heart started racing, and his breath grew short. He looked intently upon her, saw her lips and cheeks reddening and her chest heaving. He stepped toward her but, in his excitement, tripped on his own feet and staggered to one side in a crazed, clumsy effort to avoid stepping on the prostrate Peter.

Recovering his balance, the realization struck him that this overwhelming illicit attraction Lucy and he had for each other was, once more, Tiny Tim's doing.

"Stop it!" said Matthew. "It's Tim again. You calm him down, and I'll put the ointment on Peter's head."

Reluctantly, Lucy abandoned her hopes for Matthew's wild affection and did as she was told. Soon all had settled back into the normalcy they had come to know as normal—though others might consider their circumstances far enough divorced from anything resembling normal ever to be called normal again. And that only shows how all things are relative.

More or less.

CHAPTER 41

Then there was the matter of the chocolate. Lucy noticed the little package poised on the edge of the upper shelf when she went to put the yellow ointment away. The thought crossed her mind to sneak a taste, but that would involve the fetching of a chair and the climbing up upon it and the unwrapping of the packet—with each step requiring absolute silence. And with Matthew only steps away in the next room, it seemed too great a risk, especially considering they had only minutes earlier recovered from wanting to do the unthinkable, and so thinking of doing something else naughty—in her current state of mind—was nearly as unthinkable as the unthinkable, though most would say sneaking chocolate pales in comparison to the unthinkable.

Instead, she closed the cupboard door and tried to put chocolate from her mind.

To no success at all.

Matthew was engaged in rewrapping Peter's head with a less turban-like approach than that preferred by Dr. Mugwort when the craving for chocolate come upon him. He sighed with satisfaction and smiled, as he knew his plan was working. Soon the irresistible want of chocolate would be widespread and overwhelming. People would be out in droves, roaming from shop to shop in search of it. Sales would soar until none remained anywhere to be had. Chocolatiers would buy enormous quantities of cocoa, word would reach Squidge, and Matthew would be elevated to the rank of prophet in the eyes of his business partner.

But, as much as Matthew wanted to get lost in dreams of the wealth soon to be flooding his way, he could not resist the want for chocolate any more than anyone else. He did fight it, however, for he knew that to give in would ruin everything. Once the craving was sated in his own household, it would cease to be felt by the neighbors, so he had to keep himself and his siblings inside the prison of aching desire for as long as possible.

He finished with Peter before inching his way around Tiny Tim to position himself at the living room window where he could watch the activity in the street. However, the street was peculiarly empty. He watched and watched but didn't see a soul.

"Perhaps they're already off buying," he speculated within himself, but couldn't work up any confidence in this thought since he didn't believe there was time enough for Tiny Tim's projections to have driven everyone off in search of chocolate. He knew while some would give in to temptation within moments of its arising, others would resist either through strength of will or laziness in light of the effort required.

So it was he decided another day of longing was in order.

The following day, he and Peter visited a few chocolate shops on their way from client to client, but the results were gravely disappointing. Not one had experienced a mad rush of sales, though most reported a better than usual evening—not nearly enough to fuel a panic. This was both frustrating and worrisome for Matthew, who had to consider the possibility that Tiny Tim's influence might be inconsistent or perhaps even waning.

His concerns were dispelled, however, shortly after their arrival at Dropping's offices.

"Here," said Dropping while nodding to Peter. "That rash you had seen to. Where abouts is it?"

"At the doctor's," said Peter, surprised something patently obvious required explanation.

"At the doctor's?"

"Well. Yeah. After he took it off, I didn't want it anymore, so I let him keep it."

"Why are you asking?" asked Matthew before the conversation could get any muddier.

"I been reading in the papers there's some mysterious ailment going about, what feels like your bum skin's burning off. All the chemists north of the river was giving out salves and creams left and right last night, but no one knows what it is. I was wondering if that's what you had."

"No," said Matthew, struggling to stifle a laugh as he imagined hordes and hordes of people hopping about with burning bottoms in search of a remedy.

On their way home, he turned to Peter and said, "By the way, when Lucy puts the ointment on you tonight, make sure she uses the proper stuff."

"You don't have to tell me!"

To this, Matthew nodded. His concern over ensuring the craving for chocolate was pure and unadulterated that evening had caused him to forget his brother already had adequate incentive to be careful without having to be reminded.

Lucy looked odd when they arrived home. Her eyes were darting from side to side, and her lips were pursed.

"Hello?" said Matthew dubiously.

She raised her eyebrows, blinked a few times, lowered them again, scowled, started turning pink in the cheeks, but said nothing.

Suddenly Matthew was riddled with guilt and embarrassment, though the reason for these feelings was far from evident since he seldom felt those things even when he had good cause to, and in that moment, he had no cause to at all.

"I'm sorry," said Peter in a moan that turned tearful, as if he were confessing to murder.

"What for?" asked Matthew.

"I don't know." He let out a couple of sobs. "I just am."

Matthew knew then that his feelings, and Peter's, were coming from Tiny Tim but were originating in Lucy.

"What have you got to say for yourself?" he demanded of her, recalling the words his father had often used with him in years gone by.

She shook her head but stayed silent and staring through fear as her cheeks flushed crimson and then beet-purple.

"The chocolate!" thought Matthew with a shock. He commanded loftily, "Open your mouth."

Lucy shook her head again, and the flood of red in her face spread farther and a vein in her forehead swelled. She looked as if she was about to faint away for lack of breath when, suddenly, she burst into tears and said, "I couldn't help it. I had to get some salt from the top shelf, saw the chocolate, and thought no one would miss a bit if I had a taste. But then I ate it all. I'm so sorry."

Though Matthew could see the evidence of her crime clearly darkening Lucy's erstwhile pearly teeth, he could not summon anger toward her. Rather, he was grief-stricken for having bullied her into this humiliating confession. He began to cry with her, took her in his arms, and hugged her. Peter, too, joined in, and the three stood hugging each other in the kitchen for the better part of an hour, crying out their guilt in painful regrets of every sin and mischief they had committed or strove to commit or thought to commit since the gift of memory had come to them upon aging out of infancy.

"That's enough," said Matthew with his last sob. "Go settle our Tim, and I'll make supper."

Still weeping—though with far less enthusiasm for it—Lucy knelt next to Tiny Tim to bring him into a more forgiving frame of mind while her brothers ham-fistedly went about preparing a meal that was nothing more than a collection of ingredients, for which the total failed to exceed the sum of its parts.

A state of forgiveness warmed their collective spirit and grew to an all-pervasive inaudible hum resonating throughout the home.

"I'm sorry I got angry with you for smearing mustard on my

bottom," said Peter to Lucy, and he glowed with the deep satisfaction of having said this.

"I'm sorry I didn't check for mustard before I did the smearing, and I'm sorry I laughed at you," said Lucy, equally radiant. She turned to face Matthew. "And I'm so sorry I ate all the chocolate."

"Not to worry, my love," said Matthew paternally. "It was all my fault," and he explained in full how he had intended Lucy to be tortured with cravings for the purpose of driving Tiny Tim to the triggering of a massive purchasing frenzy to create a cocoa shortage.

"You see," he said in conclusion, "if I can only show Mr. Squidge I know what's going to happen, he'll pay me for the information."

Lucy was not at all angered over having her weakness exploited in this fashion, even though she knew she would be if Tiny Tim were not keeping all such propensities at bay.

"Well, I don't fancy any right now," she said, craftily seizing an opportunity, "but if I don't eat anything all day tomorrow, I'll probably fancy some then. Perhaps you could buy some more on your way home?"

"I could," said Matthew thoughtfully and compassionately, but not without doubt. "But—without blaming you for having fancies you can't resist—how do I know you won't eat it before our Tim does his job?"

Peter interjected, "Oh, I see! You wanted Lucy to make Tim make the neighbors make the chocolate shops run out."

"Yes," said Matthew, quite used to his brother being several paces behind in all explanations that unfold in steps. "But right now, we're trying to find a way to have Lucy want more without her giving in again like she did today, which wasn't her fault."

"Just tie her up," said Peter, as if the answer were too obvious to anyone.

Lucy narrowed her eyes, as the prospect lacked appeal for her.

Matthew narrowed his eyes. To him, the proposal made sense but needed refinement.

"I think so," he said after some moments and turned to his sister.

"We tie you up in a chair with a plate of chocolate in front of you, and then we go to a chocolate shop and wait there until the place goes bonkers. Once it does, we run home and let you loose."

Normally, Lucy would have refused outright—her trust in her brothers not being entirely unadulterated—but she was still feeling responsible for having spoiled Matthew's first attempt at the plot that would lead to increased income. And she was in a forgiving mood—as has been explained—so she consented, on the condition she be allowed to eat her fill of chocolate upon her release even if that meant them going entirely without.

Had historians had access to the minutes of this meeting—which they could not, since there were none to be had—they would have cited it as the beginning of Matthew's career as the most gifted commodities speculator the British Empire would ever know. That date was marked as being some years later, however, when much success was already behind him.

CHAPTER 42

W hen Peter and Matthew arrived at Squidge's the next afternoon, they found all the warehouse doors shut and locked. This had never happened before, so Matthew worried their only customer for rats had met with some disaster. He knocked and waited to be acknowledged.

A tiny window opened in one of the doors, and a large, hairy, and often broken and badly healed nose poked out.

"Wha'cher want, then?" came a croaking voice from behind the nose.

"We're here to make a delivery."

"You coppers, are you?"

"You know who we are!" said Matthew. "We're Dropping's men. We're here every day."

"'At's what you say. Got any coppers with you?"

"No."

"You're not just saying that so's they don't beat you about the head with their billies, is you?"

"No. We're alone."

"Wha'cher got in 'em sacks?"

"Dead rats," said Matthew, with his frustration tickling the soles of his feet. "Like every other day we've come here."

"No coppers disguising theirselves as dead rats?"

"No. Nothing but rats. Real rats with beady black eyes and snaky pink tails."

"Well, all right then. But if I finds any coppers in 'em sacks, it won't go nicely for you."

The great oaken doors swung open, and Matthew and Peter entered. Two strongarms grabbed them, swung them up against a wall, and patted them down. Their cargo—consisting of several bags, any of which could be lifted in one hand by a man of average strength—was dumped out and clubbed thoroughly. Only then were they permitted the reloading of their cart to take it through to the back.

As Matthew tossed a dripping, bloody bag into a dray-cart, he asked the driver, "What's all this about?"

The wagon-driver said, "Six blokes turned theirselves in to the law last night and spilled to all they done. Couple of 'em's known associates of Mr. Squidge, so he's making hisself scarce for a bit and got all us dangling by the short and curlies."

"He's not left the city, has he?"

"That's more 'an you wants to know for sure, if you knows what's good for you."

Peter's curiosity was too great to ignore. "What did those chaps spill that's got Mr. Squidge so upset?"

"I'll tell you later," murmured Matthew, but the driver answered regardless.

"The usual. Bit o' burglary, bit o' leg-breaking, saying rude things in church. What don't make no sense, though, is why they turned theirselves in at all. The old Bill had nothing on 'em. Could've gone till doomsday without getting nicked, they could. Yet in they goes, all sorry-like—like they's seen ol' Nick hisself coming for 'em or something—and tells all what they done."

Of course, Matthew knew precisely what the why was behind this mass surrender of villains and confessions of same to the police. But he showed no outward sign of his internal state. His first thought was that this could pose an impediment to his progress since it was, at the very least, a nuisance for Squidge, upon whom so much of the future Cratchit fortune depended. But in a flash, the frightening, enticing, perilous truth of it all appeared before him like a girl in a cloud of pink smoke conjured up by a magician: the power to control—or even destroy—Thaddeus Squidge was within his grasp.

On the way home, Matthew purchased four more ounces of chocolate for Lucy, though this chocolatier was not moved by Matthew's warning of impending interruptions of cocoa supply and offered nothing in payment for the information. Peter saw this as an affront and created a scene for which Matthew apologized profusely and purchased an additional ounce to quiet his brother.

Next, they stopped at T. Harland Quinn, Fabricator and Purveyor of Devices Fantastical, to acquire three yards of soft rope suitable for tying up young ladies, and thus the two brothers were rendered fully equipped for the intended tormenting of their sister and so made their way home without further delay.

Lucy, meanwhile, had had second and third and fourth thoughts about the idea. Still, she knew Tiny Tim had the power to make it work and believed Matthew was making every effort possible to lift the family up into comfortable circumstances. So she allowed herself to be bound to a kitchen chair, rendering her deprived of physical articulation below the shoulders—though it was not without trepidation that she submitted.

Conversely, Peter found the process exhilarating in an odd and mischievous sort of way.

"This is more fun than I'd pictured," he said. "I rather fancy doing this with Mary Handchester."

Matthew saw the flaw in this idea and said, "I doubt the rope they'd use on you would be as comfortable as this if you did."

"I don't see why not," said Peter, but that only led to images of Mary Handchester tying him up, and his wondering how he might broach the subject with her.

Matthew left his brother to his pondering to go and fetch a roll of bandage. He returned to Lucy's side and measured out two yards or so with an air of clinical disinterest.

"You can tend to Peter later," she said, eyeing the bandage. "I want to get this over with as soon as we can."

"It's not for him," said Matthew, and he screwed his face into a sympathetic wince. "Sorry, Lucy, but I can't have you calling for help and bringing the neighbors in here. When Tim starts wanting chocolate, you won't be able to stop yourself, and all this would be too difficult to explain."

Lucy had some idea how intense her cravings were going to get and could see the need for this precaution. Still, she found the prospect of being gagged even less appealing than being bound, and though she could accept it stoically enough when Matthew began the wrapping process, what little enthusiasm she had for it flagged rapidly. Her eyes started darting nervously from Matthew to Peter and back again while the securing of her jaw shut and the covering of her lips commenced.

"That's not nice," said Matthew out loud, which surprised Lucy immensely.

A moment later, Matthew too opened his eyes in awe when he realized the nasty word he'd heard hadn't come from Lucy herself, sitting before him, but from the imaginary Lucy who lived somewhere in his mind.

"Did you just think a naughty word?" he asked.

Lucy nodded and moved her eyes quite expressively in suggestion of apology. Matthew took a moment to accommodate this new development before finishing the bandaging of her vocal apparatus. He sensed, though, that the need for expediency was upon them as this newly acquired skill of Tiny Tim to transmit words as well as emotions could complicate things enormously if it were not controlled properly.

He retrieved a plate from a cupboard and set it on the table before Lucy. Then he took the chocolate from his pocket, unwrapped it, and poured out the dozen or so irregular chunks upon the plate. He crushed one with a spoon and held the plate under Lucy's nose, fanning it with his hand to waft the seductive fragrance toward her flaring nostrils.

She moaned with such wanton desire it made her brothers' hearts race. Then she let out what sounded to be a muffled roar as she squirmed within her bindings. The want for chocolate gripped Matthew ferociously, and he knew it was time to leave.

Putting the plate down on the table, he said, "Come on," to Peter and moved toward the door.

"Can't we have one piece?" said Peter, but Matthew had him by the arm and out into the street before he could pinch a chunk.

"What's the rush?" asked Peter.

Matthew pulled him by the sleeve at a trot—an activity which proved most irritating to Peter's tender bottom.

"We've got to get outside Tim's reach before he's got us going back home and eating all Lucy's chocolate," said Matthew. "Don't get your nickers in a twist. I'll buy us some when we get to a shop."

They slowed their pace when Matthew felt the urge waning within him and was a little disappointed to note how near they still were to their home when he noticed this. His disappointment was short-lived, however, as soon the craving came upon him again, and then knew that Tiny Tim's aura of craving was spreading gradually.

The two brothers trotted a bit farther, and the enticing call diminished within them, so they slowed their pace once again. But, once again, Tiny Tim's reach expanded to embrace them, and again they had to run to get beyond it. This kept up for nearly two miles, and Matthew began to worry there might not be an end to it.

That fear proved to be unfounded. The sensation of wanting chocolate settled into little more than a mild fancy, and the two were able to turn their attention from attempting to outrun it to seeking a chocolate shop to observe the effects of their efforts.

That search led them back to the shop of the bespectacled chocolatier from whom they had made their first purchase earlier that week—the purchase Lucy had failed to resist despoiling. The magnified eyes of the chocolatier opened enormously upon seeing the pair, but it was without pleasure he recognized them.

"You're the lad that told me the ship bringing in the cocoa was late arriving," he said.

"That's right," said Matthew proudly.

"Well, I made a special trip to buy more and was told there's no truth to what you said."

"Of course they're going to say that," said Matthew with the self-assured chuckle of the expert. "They don't want news of that sort getting about or everyone would do what you did and buy extra. That would only make the problem worse, wouldn't it?"

"I suppose," said the man with the overamplified eyes.

"As a matter of fact, it seemed it was all anyone was talking about today. Word is getting about. If I were you, I'd put my prices up now, 'cuz when you run out, you won't be selling anything for a bit."

"I don't know," said the chocolatier, still unsure whether the confident young man before him was entirely to be trusted. "I've already had to put them up to cover the cost of sugar."

"Suit yourself. We just came in to buy four more ounces of dark while there's still some to be had."

"All right then," said the shopkeeper stiffly, and he set to weighing out the chocolate.

Before he'd finished, a frantic-looking man burst in and panted, "I got one-and-seven. What can I 'ave for that?"

"I'll be only one moment, sir," said the chocolatier as two girls entered and announced together, "We want chocolate!"

The chocolatier glanced at Matthew who smirked and winked back.

"One moment, if you'll all be so good," he said anxiously, and trotted to a door in the back, opened it, and shouted, "Charlotte, dear? Come down and help daddy mind the shop."

He then returned to the scales and finished weighing out Matthew's order. A pale, dark-haired girl appeared from upstairs, wearing glasses identical to her father's though proportionately smaller. She glimpsed Peter looking her way and fluttered her eyelashes, which, magnified as they were through the large lenses, looked like two frightened birds taking flight.

Matthew took the chocolate, paid for it, and retired with Peter to a corner of the shop to consume it while watching events unfold.

More people arrived, and then more still. The chocolatier left the selling to his daughter while he ambled about, surreptitiously doubling the prices on his wares. That done, he set himself to weighing out the orders while Charlotte took the money. Order after order raced out the door. It seemed every person in the city was arriving in this one little shop in want of chocolate.

In less than an hour, the shop was emptied of every box, every assortment, every crumb of chocolate from every tray, every canister, every corner of every cupboard, and the flushed and panting chocolatier—his hands trembling with fatigue—called out, "We're all sold out, I'm afraid. Please come again another time." He then looked to his daughter. "Go lock the door and put up the sign. Oh, and give that young man his tuppence back. He's more than earned it."

Charlotte took two pennies from the till and, after herding the disgruntled crowd out, smirked coyly at Peter and handed the coins to him. Matthew reached out and accepted them, but Peter was too enchanted by the girl to protest.

"Take off your glasses," he said to her, and she complied shyly. "You look prettier without them," he said.

She squinted tightly, brought her face close to his and said, "So do you."

Peter was dizzy with delight at the progress of his fledgling courtship, but Matthew tugged him away from his budding romance with the words "Come on! We've got to untie Lucy before she goes mad."

"He means our sister," said Peter to the startled Charlotte. "We left her tied to a chair."

"Come on!" said Matthew with a yank on his brother's arm.

"I'll come again," Peter called back dreamily from the street, but after hearing Peter's explanation, Charlotte was less certain her attraction for the elder Cratchit was something she wished to pursue.

Matthew noticed the craving within him for more chocolate was swelling again, and he thus knew that Tiny Tim's influence was growing even farther than before. They passed mobs of people heading out in search of satisfaction, and Matthew sensed they should have left the shop sooner to avoid the spawning of a catastrophe.

"I'll run ahead and free Lucy," he said, and left Peter half wanting to return to Charlotte and half wanting to join the crowd in their quest to quell their craving.

Matthew arrived home out of breath, but his first sight of Lucy shocked him out of all temptation to rest a moment. Her face was purple with rage, and her eyes bulged, more out of their sockets than in. He raced to untie her and undid the bow that secured her gag.

"You sodding, great …!" she hissed venomously once she was free to speak, but before she could utter another word, her hand—as if driven by an independent will—delivered the first chunk of chocolate to her mouth, effectively gagging her again.

"Mmm. Mmm. Mmm!" she moaned and growled and groaned as the breath filled and emptied from her chest.

Her eyes rolled back and closed. The purple drained from her cheeks and lips. Her head reeled atop her neck, and Matthew thought she might be dying.

She took a second piece but lingered more longingly over it than the first, letting it melt on her tongue, where she could savor the flavor in languid surrender. Color returned to her cheeks in the loveliest shade of celestial contentment, while her lips grew red and full.

Matthew's fingers were tingling with an aching need to grab up one tiny bite of the dark-brown temptation, but he kept telling himself a violation of his promise would cost him Lucy's future cooperation. He forced himself to leave the kitchen for the living room—the clawing need for more chocolate within him every step. Suddenly a wave of pure, transcendent pleasure engulfed him, and he sensed he might happily drown in it and be carried off.

On and on it went in wave after wave of contentment until Peter arrived and looked suspiciously at his brother.

"Have you been doing *it* with someone?" he asked.

"What're you blithering about?" said Matthew, barely able to raise his mind above the flowing flood of profound, ecstatic satisfaction.

"You know … *it* … What I want to do with Mary Handchester."

"Oh, *that*! No, of course not. Why would you even think …?"

"Feels like *some*one's been doing *it*."

Only then did Matthew reconnect with his reason and become once again able to fathom cause and effect behind Peter's questions. "No, it's coming from Lucy."

"Lucy's been doing *it*?" said Peter, clenching his fists. "I'll paralyze the …"

"No, no, no. It's the chocolate that's making her feel this way."

Peter lurched to full height as if spiked hard on the backside. "Chocolate makes you feel like this?"

"It makes Lucy feel like this. At least, so it would seem."

"Well, that's hardly fair! Why don't I feel like this when I eat chocolate?"

"Eat it with her next to our Tim and you will," said Matthew thoughtfully, and he put his contended mind to considering what food item would be best to next torture Lucy into ecstasy.

CHAPTER 43

Two more days passed before Squidge felt sufficiently unwanted to return to the offices of his dray-and-carriage business. He was anxious to meet with the Cratchit brothers, however, and so was waiting for them upon their arrival.

"I hears you 'ad some prior knowledge about cocoa running short," he said to Matthew.

"Not really," said Matthew in a speech he had polished and rehearsed in his mind a thousand times. "While we were going about our business, there was a chap talking with the shopkeeper and telling him to buy extra 'cuz what there was in the warehouses wouldn't last. That's all. Why? Was there a problem?"

"Not a bit of it," said Squidge with a grin. "I done all right by it, I did, what with one thing and another. I just wants to say: if you hears anything more like that—about things selling out, or there not being enough of something, or someone wanting extra of this or that—you be sure and come tell me about it as soon as you hears. You got that?"

"Of course," said Matthew enthusiastically. "And what percentage is in it for me?"

Squidge continued smiling but circled a finger in the air, and two men took hold of Matthew in hands that circumferentially grasped both his upper and lower arms, effectively circumscribing his movements as well as his confidence. Two others took control of Peter, and moments later he was dangling by his ankles with his head several feet above the floor.

"All right then," said Squidge. "Let's take a short while to consider what you just said, 'cuz I thinks you're seeing things from the wrong prospective, which makes me feel like I needs to bring you more in line with things—the way things are when you looks at them from the proper prospective, if you sees my meaning."

"No sir. I'm afraid I don't see your meaning at all."

"That's all right. Allow me to exsss … plain it to you. First. Take your brother here. Most often—likely as not—he sees things just the way they is. That's 'is usual prospective on things, don't you see? Right now, though, he's looking at things upside down. And all up in the air! Now. Perhaps he finds it exciting to look at things like that, being up above me like he is and all the rest. You find it exciting there, does you Peter?"

"Not really," panted Peter. "Actually … it's giving me a bit of a headache."

"Ah," said Squidge. "It's giving him a bit of a headache. That's because it's not a natural sort of prospective for a bloke like him. It might feel exciting at first, or it might not. But, either way, sooner or later, it gives him a bit of a headache. That's the way of things, don't cher see? But I gots to believe you can see how it puts him in some chance of getting hurt—and right serious like. You can see that, now, can't you, Matthew, me old son?"

"Yes sir," said Matthew, his feet tingling with the fear of Peter being dropped on his skull.

"Well that's good, then, 'cuz what I'm about to say requires a bit of thought, and you won't be able to follow what I says unless it's clear to you your brother is in some serious chance of getting right … serious … hurt."

"Yes sir. That's very clear to me, sir."

"Good lad. Well, it's like this: when your brother's not dangling by his ankles, he usually sees things from what I calls a practical prospective, and that's why it's easy for him to know when it is he's looking at things upside down and all up in the air. You, on the other hand, you sees things from what I calls a possible prospective, which means you don't look at things as they is; you looks at things as they might be and thinks to yourself, 'How do I get that, then?' Now, mind you, that's a good prospective to have … often enough. That's my prospective, don't cher see? I can do business with a bloke like that. But the problem you got, right now, is that your prospective is upside down and all up in the air—way up above me and all. Now. It's easy to see when your brother's got his prospective upside down, as I said—him being a practical bloke and all. I mean, here he is, all red in the face and getting hisself a right thumping headache. Ain't cher, Peter?"

"Yes, Mr. Squidge. A right thumping headache. Do you think I can come down now?"

"Soon's I'm finished talking with your brother. Now, Matthew. It's a lot harder to see when you got your prospective upside down and all up in the air, like, as you don't see things like Peter, here. So you got to be a lot more careful about keeping yourself right side up and keeping your feet on the ground. You understand what I'm saying?"

"Yes sir."

"'At's my boy," said Squidge, and he came face-to-face with Matthew, bringing with him his breath of stale ale and onions. "So. Let me tell you where the ground is—in your prospective—and then you'll always know when you gots your feet on it. I does deals with blokes like meself, blokes what wants what I got and what's got what I wants. Now, you ain't got nothing I wants, so I don't do no deals with you. But you're a clever lad, and you can do things for me. I pays blokes what does things for me, and I pays 'em fair. But I don't do deals with 'em, see? You tells me something I can use, and I'll slip you a little something for your trouble. But don't go trying to deal with me on it, or you'll get yourself a right thumping headache—a right thumping headache that goes down to your toes. You got it?"

"Yes sir."

"I'm giving you this life-altering advice free of charge. A little appreciation would not be wasted, it wouldn't."

"No sir. Thank you, sir."

"No worries," said Squidge as he turned his back on Matthew and ordered his men, "Right! Let 'em loose."

Matthew's hands were tingling from lack of blood when his captors released his arms, but his immediate concern was for Peter. He leaped forward just in time to catch his brother's shoulders in both elbows and slow the headfirst descent to the hardwood. The two Cratchits tumbled into a heap upon the floor.

"Well, that wasn't very nice," said Peter.

"Not exactly as I'd planned it," said Matthew as he helped his brother to his feet.

The two struggled their way home on shaky legs. Both were bruised from Peter's fall since Matthew had effectively assumed half the burden of injury, thus reducing his brother's share to a more manageable portion. Peter, though, still suffered the worse since the thumping headache he'd acquired during the period of his inversion was making no sign of abating, and his still raw backside was brought back to life when it made contact with terra firma.

"We'll get Lucy to put some ointment on it," said Matthew.

"I suppose. Funny how you get used to things, isn't it?"

"Like what?"

"Like Lucy rubbing ointment on my bottom. Didn't care for it at all at first, but now I rather look forward to it."

"Hm," grunted Matthew. "Now that she knows the difference between ointment and mustard."

Peter just nodded, but the thought led Matthew to recall the mass purchase of unguent concoctions triggered by Lucy's little error and considered the possibility of making soothing salves his next target commodity. Then he remembered how painful the experience had been for poor Peter, and how it had nearly brought Lucy and him to doing the unthinkable. He would have to think of something else.

But when the bruised and bothered brothers neared their home, they sensed a certain disgruntlement mixed with grief permeating the air. Soon they came upon wagons being loaded with furniture while, all about, children were crying and men and women were looking forlorn.

"What's going on?" asked Matthew of one lady.

"They've gone and put the rent up, they 'ave, and we can't pay," she said, and burst into tears.

The news gave Matthew a jolt. He'd forgotten it was the first of May—the date the onerous payment was due. With all else that was happening within the family Cratchit, he'd never taken a moment to consider their neighbors were facing the same excoriation of savings as he and his siblings.

He bade Peter hurry along the two streets to the street where they lived. They arrived at the corner and looked toward their house. All up the road were wagons being loaded as one family in three was being evicted.

The Cherrytart sisters were approaching. They smiled and said, "Hello Peter," in singsong unison.

"Everyone's being chucked out," said Matthew.

"Yeah! Innit awful?" said Prudence, in a tone more excited than grieved.

"We're all right, though," said Priscilla. "Our Da done a job, just last week, he did, so he could pay. But he's proper blazing about it. Ain't fit to be with. That's why me and Pru's going to the Dog's Cocked Leg for a pint. You want to come?"

"Yes, please," said Peter.

Without thinking, Matthew said, "I thought you wanted Lucy to rub …" but stopped when the horrified look on Peter's face told him he was about to breach the bounds of familial confidentiality regarding Peter's personal problems.

"Perhaps later," squeaked Peter, turning red with terror over the potential revelation of his secret.

"Later what?" asked Prudence.

"He needs to have the cut on his head tended," said Matthew, pointing to the bandage around his brother's brow. "But he's right. It can wait. You go on, and I'll see that Lucy's all right."

So Prudence and Priscilla took Peter arm-in-arm and arm-in-arm, and the trio headed off to the pub, while Matthew made his way the rest of the way home. As happy as he was that Peter had two pretty girls to take his mind off the day gone wrong, his pleasure changed for the worse when he arrived to find Lucy crying.

"What's the matter?" he asked.

"The rent man came today."

"I know. But there was plenty in the jar."

"No, there wasn't. I gave him the thirty shillings Father said we'd owe, but he said it was forty-three."

"Forty-three?" said Matthew.

"Yes. I only had seven-and-three more to give him, so I did. We still owe five-and-nine, so he said he'd be back tomorrow for the rest, or I'd have to do things for him if I don't want us to be chucked out."

"What kind of things?" asked Matthew, feeling the skin shrink on the back of his neck.

"I don't know. He didn't say."

But Matthew had grown worldly enough to know what kinds of things the rent man wanted without having to hear them uttered. In his mind, he knew he had more than enough money hidden away to pay the balance, but the idea of the rent man using their debt to extort unsavory favors from his sister sent him into a raging fury.

Lucy quickly sensed where Tiny Tim's feelings were going and ran to his side to bring him to a more settled state.

Matthew calmed under this influence. He knew he was being guided in this, but also knew he had to follow lest disaster be spawned in the neighborhood. So he took several deep breaths, and as he breathed, he recalled Prudence and Priscilla mentioning their father was "proper blazing about it"—it being the scathing rise in rent. But—Matthew being Matthew—he imagined this as the bud of a plot that soon blossomed into full flower in his imagination.

"All the neighbors must be quite angry over the rent, too," he said.

"I should think so," said Lucy. "There's lots who don't have much, 'cuz with all the murders and such of late, there's no one about in some families to earn any money, as those who did before are either dead or gone to prison."

Matthew looked to Tiny Tim and felt a twinge of guilt on his brother's behalf over creating this demographic anomaly that plagued the neighborhood, but he quickly put his mind back to the needs of the moment.

"It occurs to me we should invite some of them over tomorrow so we can have a chat with the rent man when he gets here."

"I don't think …" said Lucy trepidatiously.

"Of course, we'll need our Tim to keep things under control, since everyone's so angry. But never you mind. You go see to supper, and I'll go out and ask the neighbors who's in trouble and who isn't," he said, and left to organize the meeting.

Lucy was not entirely persuaded away from her doubts, but with minor reservations, she trusted Matthew to do what was best for the Cratchit clan. She set about preparing supper with what was available, which was less than she'd planned since all that day's grocery money had gone to mollifying the ravenous rent collector.

A smidgeon of guilt still lingered in Matthew's heart over the loss of several breadwinners due to Tiny Tim's bathing the neighborhood in rabid rage some two weeks earlier, so he spoke with all the families engaged in loading wagons first, wanting to catch them before they moved on. Then he knocked on the doors of those who had been able to pay the oppressive rent but who were properly blazing over it nonetheless.

He was nearly two hours informing nearly everyone within a half-mile radius the landlords had caught the rent collector falsifying the rent increase in a scheme to disguise ongoing embezzlement and had had the miscreant arrested. Furthermore, he informed them, the would-be embezzler was to be flogged the following day at the jailhouse with the landlords present to witness the punishment. Then he suggested that all grievances that had arisen from the rent collector's dishonest collections might best be resolved with the landlords at the flogging since the landlords could be surrounded while availing themselves of the entertainment.

This—as mentioned above—he said to nearly everyone. But

there were six to whom he said something quite different. These six selected representatives of the neighborhood he invited to attend the aforementioned meeting to be held at the Cratchit house. Included in this number were Mr. Cherrytart (the father of Prudence and Priscilla), his eldest son, and four other men who, coincidentally, were all above six feet in height and all ruggedly built.

Matthew returned home from the north as Peter was arriving at a trot from the south with lipstick on each cheek and panic in his eyes.

"What's the matter?" asked Matthew.

"I need one-and-four to pay the landlord at the Dog's Cocked Leg."

"Crikey! How much did you have to drink?"

"Just a half-pint that I didn't much like, but Pru and Pris had three whiskeys each, and the landlord says I owe for them as they were with me and didn't pay when they left."

"Bloody hell!"

"Language," said Peter, looking about to see if others might have heard.

"Bloody well make your own treacle tarts," muttered Matthew moodily. He then snorted a bitter laugh over it all. "All right. Here," he said, and gave Peter the coins he needed.

Matthew watched his brother race off to pay the publican and wondered whether three whiskeys for a kiss on the cheek was the usual recompense the sisters expected for their company. Then he imagined how delighted Peter must have been upon receiving their abbreviated expressions of affection.

But there was a plan in motion with much detail to attend to, and nothing would be gained by raising an issue over the girls' abuse of Peter's innocence in affairs of the heart. So Matthew reminded himself that one has to take the bad with the good, sighed, and said out loud, "God bless us, every one!" as he opened the front door to his house.

CHAPTER 44

The following day, Matthew and Peter took eighty rats from the herd they kept in the house at the end of their street, and then the younger Cratchit sent his elder brother on alone to their first assignment.

"Catch as many as you can by nine o'clock," said Matthew as they preloaded the cart with some of the day's catch. "Then add in what you need to get the tally up to forty or so. No more than that, 'cuz they won't believe you could do that much on your own. Then on to the Temple of the Mystic Centipede. If I'm not there by twelve, make the number up to fifty and move on. As soon as I've done with the rent man, I'll catch you up. Oh. And don't forget to gather up as much dog leavings as you can. Unless you want Squidge dangling us both by our ankles."

Then Matthew returned to his house, where he and Lucy prepared for their guests to arrive. The six big, burly men were shown to the cramped kitchen, where they were fed sandwiches and pickles and sausage rolls while they waited for the rent collector to arrive.

As Mr. Cherrytart passed by Tiny Tim, he said, "I did hear you keeps a dead bloke in here with you."

"That's our brother, Tim," said Matthew, stopping to pay homage to his silent sibling. "He was always afraid of the dark, so his final request was to be waxed instead of buried."

Cherrytart chuckled. "Families, eh? We makes allowances for

them what we wouldn't make for others. Still. He do look content with hisself, I must say."

"We like to think so," said Matthew leading Cherrytart to the kitchen.

"All well and good," said Cherrytart, "but—changing the subject—I don't think talking with this sodding little prat's going to do no good. He ain't the one to bring the rent back down. That's a landlord's doing, innit?"

"That's right," said Matthew to all present. "Mr. Gazpayne and his partners. We'll deal with them when the time comes."

"Who's they, then?" asked one neighbor.

"Lawyers," said another.

"They'd have to be, wouldn't they?" said a third.

"Likely," said Matthew. "But first we make our case with the collector so they know who they're up against."

The conversation around the kitchen table went from there, full of energy though devoid of substance, as Matthew and the men of the neighborhood enjoyed their snacks served to them by Lucy, whom they all agreed had grown up quite pretty and proper and not like others of their knowing—the names of whom discretion required not be mentioned since their fathers constituted half the membership of the group.

The rent collector was clearly anxious to execute his duties at chez Cratchit, as evidenced by his punctual arrival. The knock on the door came forcefully precisely at nine, and the barked announcement "Rent collector!" followed an instant later.

Matthew signaled the men in the kitchen to be silent, then turned and nodded to Lucy to answer the door. Up to that moment, he had been forcing himself to imagine only peaceful scenes available to both memory and fantasy to help Lucy keep Tiny Tim in a state of tranquility. As soon as he heard the front door open, however, he immediately brought to mind the evening before, when Lucy had said, "I'd have to do things for him, if I don't want us to be chucked out."

Thereupon, Matthew felt that same tightening of the skin on

the back of his neck and the same acidic heat rising in his chest. By the time Lucy entered the kitchen with the rent man and two strongarms—whom Lucy had failed to mention had also come with their master the day before—the blinding rage in Matthew's heart was felt by all.

Matthew and his six allies rose to their feet as one, surprising the three invaders, who were still surprised at the sudden choking fury that had just risen, for no reason, within them.

"Lucy, go upstairs," said Matthew.

Lucy was swept up in the anger as much as anyone, but she realized, too late, that Matthew had planned this all along. Part of her wanted to yell at him, and part of her wanted to order everyone out, but most of her wanted revenge on the odious little man that had tried to … she knew not what but knew it wasn't nice. So she ran to her bedroom to vent her rage on an innocent pillow.

Without words being spoken, the two opposing forces in the kitchen clashed with the savagery of berserkers. And though the clash was impeded by the cramped quarters, it was short-lived. The rent collector, being small, portly, and aging, was no match for Matthew while his two associates were outnumbered three-to-one.

While it was true Matthew had planned on seeing the rent collector thoroughly trounced, he hadn't seen that the ambient rage fueled by Tiny Tim made the sating of vengeful appetites impossible. The end came only when total exhaustion had taken its toll such that the seven angry men venting their anger felt the need to stop venting that anger on the three angry men upon whom the venting had been done.

Bent forward with his elbows on his knees, Matthew fought to get his breath back while growing concerned they'd overreached the mark by a fair stretch. The six others left standing were equally out of breath, but the three lying on the floor were past drawing breath ever again. Still panting from his exertion, Matthew pictured an untimely visit from the neighborhood constable. That would prove embarrassing and inconvenient, since the condition of the three bodies made it difficult to imagine how the cause of death might be explained away as "natural."

"We have to get them out of here," said Matthew with the first breath long enough to carry a sentence.

"Leave 'em to me," said Cherrytart. "I got a place."

Without a better plan to offer, Matthew conceded ownership of the brutalized bodies to Cherrytart and the five others, of whom Cherrytart took command. With surprising efficiency, the dispatched trio was carried out and carted away, leaving Matthew to clean up the remaining evidence of violence.

First, though, he put his mind to settling Tiny Tim back to some semblance of serenity. To this, Lucy came to help when she perceived that the deathly quiet meant hostilities had ended.

"That was a wicked thing you did," she whispered to Matthew.

"Not so much. I won't have nasty little men making you do things you don't want to. And all the neighbors can stay living where they are. How is that wicked?"

"But the neighbors can't stay. Mr. Gazpayne will get himself a new rent man, and they'll all be chucked out again."

"Hm. Well, I still haven't decided what to do about Gazpayne, but I'll think of something. And Tim can help with that, whatever it is."

Lucy was uncertain where to place her moral convictions in all this, but she had a sense her brother was being honest in saying he was protecting her and seeing to the best of the Cratchit interests, as well as those of the other families about. And she was clever enough to see that no trail of evidence could ever lead back to Tiny Tim, for being dead at the time of a crime is conceivably the most solid alibi imaginable.

CHAPTER 45

Fortunately for Matthew, cleanup in the kitchen amounted to little more than flipping a few bloodstained flagstones and mopping away the soil that clung to the undersides-turned-upper-sides. So he caught up with Peter shortly after noon, only slightly later than he'd hoped, and together they rushed through the rest of their day—a task made easier by their ability to inflate their take with those taken from their cellar. To this, having Saint Silias's Church as their last client was fortuitous, since they could add their remaining 46 homegrown rats to their catch to bring the number to 120 without anyone suspecting shenanigans of double-dealing jiggery-pokery.

"Why do you suppose the rats do so well in the church basement?" asked Peter.

"Hard to say," said Matthew, whose concerns still circled about Cherrytart's disposal of the rent collector and his cohorts.

"Well, I've been thinking about it quite a bit, and I think it's one of those miracles the priests are always going on about—bit like the loaves and the fishes."

"Could well be," said Matthew.

"So I hid a farthing under that old desk in the corner. With any luck, it'll be a pound by the time we go there again."

"Unless that deacon finds it first."

"Oh, right. I hadn't thought of him," said Peter with a shock of regret for making so risky an investment in a religious institution.

The two arrived at Dropping's offices a little earlier than usual but with 360 dead rats to show for their day's work.

"Numbers coming back up, I see," said Dropping with a smile. "You two must go at it like steam hammers when you're out there."

"We've got a system," said Matthew. "I catch and Peter kills. Neither of us would get on nearly so well working alone."

"I always knowed you to be a thinking man," said the master ratter, and he handed Matthew the signed tally to take to Squidge.

"Why'd you tell Dropping about our system?" asked Peter on their way to their warehouse.

"I don't want anyone knowing I wasn't with you all day today."

"Why's that?"

"Never mind. Just say that I was if anyone asks."

The two made quick work of blending the batch of powdered blossoms Lucy had prepared the previous day and the appropriate portion of dried and powdered product. They also spread out some thirty pounds of dog leavings to dry before setting off for home. Fatigued to the bone though they both were—not to mention Matthew's anxiety over the success or failure of Cherrytart—a strong feeling of serenity overcame the brothers and uplifted them and made pleasing the final leg of their journey when they were still several streets away from their destination.

"Our Tim can take the ache out of the worst day, can't he?" said Matthew to Peter, and Peter nodded with pride over having so gifted a brother.

Lucy had supper nearly ready when they arrived. They were about to sit down to it when a knock at the door caused Matthew to reverse his descent to his chair and ascend to answer it. It was the local policeman calling.

"Sorry to be a bother, young sir," said the massive constable, "but we're attempting to ascertain the current whereabouts of a Mr. Galahad Grindthumb."

"I don't know anyone by …"

"He is the rent collector hereabouts."

"Oh, him?" said Matthew, wide-eyed with shock. "Don't tell me he's escaped."

"Escaped, young sir? Escaped from where?"

"From jail, of course."

"And why would he be in jail?"

"Well," said Matthew, feigning a desire to appear diplomatic. "I'm only going by what everyone says, but the story has it he'd been caught stealing from our landlord, was arrested and thrown in jail, and was supposed to be flogged for it today. I would've gone to watch, but my brother and I had to go to work."

"Interesting," said the policeman, squinting thoughtfully. "So, you've got reason to believe this Grindthumb is a person of a felonious nature, currently engaged in the cowardly evasion of Her Majesty's just and lawful punishment, what he justly deserves?"

"It's not my place to decide these things, is it? But that is what I've heard. We expected him to call yesterday, as it was the first of the month, and we had his five shillings ready to pay. Our Lucy stayed in all day, so as not to miss him, but he never came to collect. And then, all about, they were talking about him being in jail. That's all I know."

"Your neighbors have been saying much the same thing—though most are not as well-spoken as you are, young sir. It's all coming clearer now. But here. Why are you bruised all about the face?"

The question startled Matthew. When beating the rent collector, he'd been so engrossed in the activity he hadn't noticed he was receiving blows himself—a strange phenomenon, no doubt, though commonly reported by those who engage in fury-driven fisticuffs.

"Oh, this?" he said, pointing to his mouth. "My brother had another nasty fall, and I jumped under him to save him. I got as bad as he did when he landed on me."

"Bit of a clumsy ox, isn't he?" asked the policeman with a knowing smirk.

"He is that." said Matthew, and he then leaned closer and whispered, "And he did spend one-and-four in the Dog's Cocked Leg last night."

"My, my. You'd best keep an eye on him, then. Many a lad's turned to trouble that way," murmured the policeman. In a louder voice, he then asked, "Your other brother and your sister still behaving themselves all right, are they?"

"To the best of my knowledge. Lucy keeps busy doing all that Mother used to do before she went away to Australia, and our Tim keeps to himself, for the most part, him being dead and all."

"I see. Well, do try and get the other one settled down for his own good."

"I will. He's just so sad all the time, what with our parents going away like they did."

"These things are sent to try us. Well, all right, then. I'll bid you good night, young sir, and when we catch this scoundrel Grindthumb, I'll be sure and let you know so you can come and watch him flogged."

"Thank you, constable. That's very kind."

The policeman continued on his quest for information leading to the location and apprehension of the escaped convict. Matthew shut the door and took a deep breath but realized in an instant he had to get to Gazpayne before the lawyer could be questioned. To add to this concern, he again took to worrying whether Cherrytart and the recently assembled fraternity of frontier justice had been successful in disposing of the three dead men.

He sat down to supper only to be raised, yet again, by yet another knock at the door. This time it was Cherrytart.

"Evening, Cratchit. The Old Bill been 'ere nosing about, 'ave they?"

Matthew related all he had said to the policeman.

"Didn't ask to come in?"

"No."

"That's good, then," said Cherrytart. "They always wants a look about when they susses something, so you knows from that you's in the clear."

"Good. Any problems getting rid of the bodies?"

"Nothing like it. Duck soup, it was. I knows this place where them devil worshippers does their magic spells and such. We just props up the bodies inside one of them penty-grams, sets 'em alight, and makes it look like one of your typical human sacrifices. Few candles here and there, goat's head on a pole, a couple of naughty postcards left lying about, and Bob's your uncle."

Despite T. Harland Quinn, fabricator and purveyor of devices fantastical, having amused Matthew with stories of occultists performing ritual sacrifice by way of explanation for devices modeled on such fantastical activities, it was not until that moment that Matthew believed these weren't merely tales told by clergymen to ensure full collection plates.

"Be that as it may," said Cherrytart, "I come to tell you I done some talking with them what lives 'ere and about, and I likes the way you handles things. Telling all them what weren't invited to deal with Grindthumb to make theirselves scarce so there'd be no witnesses about …? That's using the old kidneys, it is. And not telling us you done it—or what we was really going to do—tells me you knows which end's up. I got to tell you, Cratchit, I always thought you and your lot was all a bit soft—you talking all posh and all—but I was wrong. You got a head for making things work, you do. So me and me mates is in back of whatever you thinks up. Just give us the word and there we'll be."

"I appreciate that," said Matthew, honestly flattered.

"No worries, mate," said Cherrytart with a wink, and he held out a tiny, much-folded note. "And just to show I means it, 'ere's fifteen quid from what we got off Grindthumb."

"He was walking about with fifteen pounds in his satchel?" asked Matthew in disbelief.

"Nothing like it. Didn't 'ave hardly nothing on him other than keys and a few papers. No. We got the address for his office off a letter he had among the lot, and off we went to toss the place. Found near a 'undred seven quid in a strong box. Seven don't go into a 'undred seven, so we stopped at a pub till we had a 'undred five left and div it up all even-like. So that's your share, fair and square."

"Well, thank you very much!"

"Cheers, mate. None of us wouldn't had nothing at all if you hadn't brung us in on it."

Matthew was then ready to say good night, but a thought struck him, and he asked, "Could you meet me tomorrow at the Elephant and Castle?"

"When?"

"Two."

"I's usually up by then. Wha'cher thinking?"

"I have to talk to Gazpayne."

"Oo, you can count me in for that!" said Cherrytart. He cocked an eyebrow. "Just us, then? Me and you? No one else?"

"Just us."

So Matthew was quite late to his supper and ate it cold while Lucy tended, once again, to Peter's tender bottom. While Matthew ate, he thought of all that had transpired unexpectedly over the last several weeks—having to buy his mother's freedom and arrange his parents' escapade; the orchestration of the chocolate shortage, and the dangling of Peter at Squidge's behest; the pummeling to death of a rent collector and his henchmen; and the implicating of unknown occultists in the murder. But what he found utterly amazing was, despite the circuitous route upon which fate had taken him, he had arrived where he was better off than he'd expected.

CHAPTER 46

Mr. Cherrytart was punctual to the point of serving as the very definition of the word, uttering as he did his greeting, "Cratchit," between the two tolls of Big Ben that announced two o'clock. He allowed Matthew to lead the way to the offices of Rankin, Fowle, O'Durr, and Gazpayne: Solicitors and Barristers at Law, where they found the diminutive law clerk—whom, you will recall, delivered that last fateful invoice to Matthew's father that was to instigate an alarming cascade of events—sitting at his desk outside Gazpayne's office and wearing a swallowtail coat of a beautiful teal (owing to his having become more confident in his role, of late, though not yet confident enough to adorn himself in a beautiful blue in the fashion of his mysteriously missing predecessor, Mr. Scribble).

"We're here to see Mr. Gazpayne," said Matthew.

"And who might you be?" asked the clerk, leaning back to take in all of Cherrytart's height and breadth of shoulders.

"This is Mr. Cherrytart, and I'm Mr. Cratchit," said Matthew, elevating himself to his majority for better effect.

"I don't have you in the appointment book."

"We'll only be a moment, and it's something he'll want to know right away."

"Very well. Wait here."

The clerk disappeared through the doors, followed by his flowing coattails sustained aloft upon the draft of his rapid advance.

Shortly later, a nose appeared through the doors, followed by Gazpayne, its owner.

"What is it that you want?" asked the lawyer.

Matthew said, "We came here to tell you that all the residents of South Whitechapel paid their rent, in full, to Mr. Grindthumb before he ran off to Blackpool with that fortune teller from Glastonbury, and that it's not our fault he stole your money, so don't send anyone around to collect it again until next month. Isn't that right, Mr. Cherrytart?"

"'Tis that and all, Mr. Cratchit," said Cherrytart with a sharp nod of finality.

"My dear *Master* Cratchit," said Gazpayne in haughty self-assurance. "What are you raving about? Mr. Grindthumb hasn't stolen anything from anybody, and nor has he run off anywhere with anyone." But his haughty self-assurance flickered visibly upon his face, and he asked in a meeker tone, "Has he?"

Matthew affected an expression of incomprehensible disbelief and said, as if aghast, "The police were all up and down our street yesterday, looking for him after he escaped from jail. They said you're the one that had him arrested. How can you forget something like that?"

"I've been quite busy of late," said Gazpayne, suddenly aquiver. "It simply slipped my mind." He turned to his clerk and quietly asked, "What do you know of this?"

"I've been meaning to inform you, Mr. Gazpayne, sir, but you've been rather preoccupied," said the trembling man while shrinking down into his swallowtail coat of a beautiful teal. "It would appear Mr. Grindthumb has gone missing with more than a hundred guineas of the firm's money. The courier found his offices abandoned only this morning."

"It's not my place," said Matthew, "to tell you your business, Mr. Gazpayne"—he shook his head judgmentally—"but I have to wonder how you go about hiring people. First Mr. Scribble disappears with who knows what, and now Mr. Grindthumb with a hundred guineas … And this chap, here, doesn't seem to know his bottom from a teakettle. It's no wonder you can't win a case to save your life."

To this, Gazpayne was twisted between the counterrotating grips of rage and embarrassment and, being quite unused to having feelings of any sort, was paralyzed into silence since he knew not what to do with them now that he had them. His eyes seemed to swell as well as widen, and his frown explored new limits of depth and length. The veins in his narrow neck thickened and throbbed as his wan face darkened its way through the entire red end of the spectrum.

Suddenly a hot, rushing noise filled the room as he released a pent-up breath like a protracted sneeze. Matthew was amazed to see the hairs in the lawyer's nostrils waving frantically in the violence of the breeze thus created, but he braced himself and said, "Well, we've said all we'd come to say, so we'll be off," and, turning to Cherrytart, indicated with a nod they leave.

"You was brilliant in there, mate," said Cherrytart, chortling like a schoolboy with a naughty postcard. "But why d'you need me along?"

"Because, legally, I'm not old enough to talk to a lawyer, so if he does try to get more rent off us, we can say you were there to tell our side."

"Oh, law is it? Never had much use for it meself. Always in the way of what I had a mind to do, for the most part. Still"—he patted Matthew's shoulder—"I can see what you're about, and I appreciate your getting the boot in before he has a chance to get his wind back."

"Thank you."

"No worries, mate. You got a head on your shoulders, you has. Like I said yesterday: if you got anything going what needs a bit o' nerve or a bit o' muscle, you let me know, and I'll see to it, it gets done."

"All right then," said Matthew with a smile, and they parted company since he had to rejoin Peter to finish their workday.

Although the reason Matthew had given to Cherrytart to justify his neighbor being there in Gazpayne's office was valid, it was not the prime purpose the young Cratchit had had for making the request. In truth, he wanted Cherrytart to know what the lawyer looked like, should the need arise to have further dealings with the despicable man—dealings of a more personal-presence nature.

When he and Peter arrived at Squidge's that afternoon, Squidge asked after the progress they were making toward getting the next shipment of bittering agent ready. Matthew knew they were well ahead of schedule—thanks to Lucy's help and the unwitting contribution of many productive dogs—but merely said they'd be ready on time.

"That's good, then," said Squidge. "You get wind of anything interesting, have you?"

Matthew sensed an opportunity. "Well, the police are looking for a rent collector who ran off with a hundred guineas of his boss's money."

"A hundred guineas?"

"That's what they're saying. Story is a gypsy girl talked him into it."

"Gypsy, you say? You mean like them what lives in carriages with crystal balls and such?"

"I don't know about any carriage. All I heard was she told fortunes for money and had something to do with that peculiar religion. The one where they dance about under the full moon with nothing on."

"I can see that catching his interest. You got a name? The one what pinched the rent money, I mean, not the girl."

"Grind something. Grindstone, I think … No, that's not right. Let me think. Grindthumb! That's it. Grindthumb," said Matthew. Then, more sedately, he asked, "You're not looking to turn him in, are you?"

"Don't talk rubbish. Nothing to be had in that lark. No. I'll fine him a hundred guineas for being a burke and turn him loose for his governor to do 'im. And, as I'm a man of me word, I'll give you a crown for putting me onto him."

Of course, Matthew knew he'd never see either heads or tails of that crown, but the fiction he'd fabricated would be quick to gain currency once Squidge put the word out to look for Grindthumb in all the likely hiding places. And the part about the gypsy fortune teller with pagan proclivities provided considerable corroborative detail to an otherwise mundane and quite forgettable narrative, for—as anyone familiar with the dynamics of gossip can tell you—the gaudier the scandal, the hotter it burns and the faster it spreads.

But the talk with Squidge also served to remind Matthew he had to decide upon what commodity would be next to suffer rabid demand leading to depletion. This, he realized, would have to wait, since the onerous rent that had recently been collected in his neighborhood left most households too poor to buy much of anything, regardless of how strong their cravings might be. To this, he decided he would have to give everyone a couple of weeks to recover financially before driving them out again in search of satisfaction.

Even so, most of his time on the way home he spent wondering what should be next to run short.

After supper, Lucy asked, "Fancy some tea?"

Matthew looked into her bright blue eyes and smiled the smile of the man in control. "Yes, lovely. And you should stock up a bit, as the shops will all be empty soon."

CHAPTER 47

T he next few days passed relatively uneventfully for the family Cratchit—assuming the hearing of interesting news fails to qualify under the strict definition of "event."

Matthew heard from Cherrytart that he, Cherrytart, after leaving Matthew following the meeting with Gazpayne, had taken to mulling over what had been said at that meeting and decided further evidence of rent payments to Grindthumb would cement their claim everyone in the neighborhood was up-to-date. For that purpose, he returned to the dead rent collector's office along with his daughter, Prudence, who, being of an artistic nature was gifted with the ability of mimicking anyone's penmanship convincingly, and with the ability of altering numbers inked onto documents undetectably. She added or modified entries in Grindthumb's big, black, leather-bound journal to indicate he'd been overcharging the tenants for years. This journal Cherrytart then inserted into a secondhand satchel along with various other documents, including a love letter penned by Priscilla from one Annie Thyme to Galahad Grindthumb, which detailed various intimacies they'd shared and a reference to their fates being written by Venus in the stars. A boy was hired to take the satchel to the police and say he'd found it abandoned next to a bench at Euston Station.

"Very clever thinking, Mr. Cherrytart," said Matthew while making a mental note of his neighbor's daughters' talents without making mention of them.

Matthew heard from Eliphaz Dropping—always a dedicated

reader of newspapers—the three burned bodies, found at the center of a huge star of blood-smeared stones in a garden adjacent to the stock exchange, had led to a Good Old City–wide panic and to the arrest of all known and suspected occultists, spiritualists, and vegetarians, though all but a coven of Wiccans were released within hours. The ladies of the ancient faith were detained overnight to be interrogated by the commissioner, deputy commissioner, crown attorney, and lord chief justice, the latter of whom kindly provided the wine from his cellar.

No charges were laid, but church attendance soared and collection plates overflowed as prayers for protection from Satan and his minions were offered up—which the clergy later noted were hugely effective, as evidenced by the subsequent precipitous decline in the rate of human sacrifice.

Later, the local constable told Matthew a girl with the initials *AT* and documentation in proof of Polish nationality had boarded a ship in Liverpool bound for Montreal in the Dominion of Canada in the company of an elderly Englishman in a wheelchair.

"We're certain he's our man," said the big policeman. "It's a clever disguise, to be sure, but not clever enough. They always slips up with their choice of aliases, they do. Use the same first letters of their real name every time. And we have reason to believe this Annie Thyme is Transylvanian by birth, which sounds Polish enough to fool a customs clerk."

"Why's that?" asked Matthew.

"All them fortune tellers are," said the constable, knowingly. "Not surprising, really, when you consider the facts. What with coming from a country where they impales people instead of hanging them, all civilized-like. And their House of Lords? A few rum characters in that lot, I can assure you! Still, I hate to be the bearer of bad tidings, but this does mean the search for Grindthumb is over and we won't be flogging him after all. But you can take comfort in knowing he's jumped from the frying pan into the fire, as a month in Canada is as good as ten lashes any day, and he's put hisself there for good."

All this while, Matthew heard from a variety of sources about all manner of minor things happening in the world at large—that is to say in England, which was to Matthew, as well as nearly all who lived there, more or less all there was of the world at large.

He heard the recent rage among youthful Beau Brummels of wearing black tights to private parties had been declared indecent by an act of Parliament since the garments were obviously designed to reveal that men have legs. He heard the delivery of a box of cigars to a gunpowder factory in Somerset had resulted in the postponement of the HMS *Consternation* sailing to the Bay of Bengal. He heard a scandal involving a bishop in the north country had led to members of the Royal Society writing letters to the *Times* assuring the public that animal–human hybrids are quite impossible and any resemblance of any particular priest to a sheep, a cow, or a camel was purely an aesthetic bias on the part of the observer and not the result of any misguided doctor of divinity's attempt to make his flock more flock-like.

And—of somewhat greater interest to him—Matthew heard the coroner, the efficient Mortimer Rigger, MD, had identified the three charred corpses from the human sacrifice to be those of missing men named Aaron, Abbot, and Abednego by a process of elimination, stating that all evidence to the contrary was flimsy and extraneous.

All this and much, much more Matthew heard, but nothing of immediate value to the hungry ears of an ambitious caterpillarist.

He had to wait.

And wait he did. The task was made infinitely easier after Lucy recognized that her brother's desire for progress was infecting Tiny Tim—and everyone for miles around—and took to providing thoughts of profound satisfaction with all that was. For a little over a week, the Good Old City was a pleasant and very patient place to live.

Matthew and Peter worked an hour a day all that week, bagging bittering agent, then shared in the loading up and offloading of Squidge's wagon used to make the second delivery to Belcher's Brewery. Thaddeus Squidge then paid Matthew one shilling shy of one pound as his share of the profits from the first batch—a sum less than a third of what Matthew expected. To this, Squidge claimed his share from the sale of the powdered flowers was exactly equal to the Cratchit portion and insisted the remainder of the seven guineas had gone to pay for the purchase of raw materials and to the cost of transportation. To this, Matthew suspected his partner was telling the truth—as far as the bookkeeping went—but the yeoman's share of the disbursements was simply redirected by Squidge's accountants to Squidge through different streams.

A vision of Peter dangling by his ankles in the back of the dray-and-carriage house, however, kept Matthew from challenging the arithmetical tributaries of wealth.

Shortly thereafter, Matthew determined his neighbors had had sufficient time to recover from the evisceration of their savings due to the rise in rent. On the evening of the sixteenth, he told Lucy and Peter of his plan to drive the price of tea skyward.

"We do the same as we did with the chocolate," said Matthew. "Lucy: you'll go a day without drinking anything at all and get yourself thoroughly thirsty. Then we'll tie you up with a cup of tea in front of you."

"Why does it have to be me again?" asked his sister. "I don't even care for tea all that much. Not like Mother and Peter, anyway."

"She's right," said Matthew, turning to his brother. "It does make more sense for you to be the one."

Fortunately, Peter had little imagination to estimate the magnitude of this proposed ordeal and agreed to it without hesitation.

"Did you remember," asked Peter, "to tell Mr. Squidge England forgot to place an order with India?"

"Something along those lines," said Matthew. "But I don't expect to see a fair share from him."

"Why not?" said Peter indignantly. "He's a fair chap. He said so himself."

"Nevertheless," said Matthew. "I'm thinking we should buy all the tea we can afford and sell it back to shopkeepers when there's none about."

"That makes sense," said Lucy, but then her eyes lit up with a recollection. "Oh, you'll never guess who I saw arguing with a shopkeeper today."

"Who?"

"That nasty little man who works for Mr. Gazpayne. The one in the swallowtail coat of a beautiful green."

Matthew had to think before remembering the teal-adorned law clerk. "I would have called it a beautiful blue, myself, but I can see why you think it's a beautiful green."

"It's nothing like a beautiful blue," said Lucy, thinking her brother had failed to learn his colors properly.

"Doesn't matter," said Matthew. "What were they arguing about?"

"Well, to be honest, I didn't understand most of it. But it sounded like Mr. Gazpayne thinks he's still owed the rent Mr. Grindthumb stole."

Matthew was pleased his sister was convincingly corroborating the neighborhood legend of the runaway randy rent collector, but was equally displeased to hear Gazpayne was failing to keep his fiscal distance after having been warned to do so.

"I suppose I need to take Mr. Cherrytart with me and go and see him again."

"Shouldn't you wait till he comes here?" asked Lucy, suddenly afraid her brother might be plotting another murder. "I mean, I didn't understand all that was said, and it might have nothing to do with us at all."

"Perhaps," said Matthew. "I'll sleep on it."

Which he did. And quite unusually.

Usually Matthew could stay awake quite late of an evening, chatting with his siblings or watching Peter fail at card tricks or listening to Lucy read from some farcical novel or other, but on that particular evening, he dozed off in his father's chair while Peter and Lucy worked on their only jigsaw puzzle—that being a watercolor depiction of the Tower of London—a subject Peter found fascinating for the paradox it embodied.

Interestingly, that paradox was representative of Peter's character in that he could state as fact, "There are no such thing as ghosts," while equally accepting as fact that the Tower of London was a well-known residence of a horde of historically human ectoplasmic entities that could be witnessed walking about regularly if one were silly enough to explore the ancient castle's interior on the anniversaries of famous executions.

So it was that on that particular evening, Matthew slept while Peter droned on and on about Anne Boleyn's preference for bonnets over hats due to her having to carry her head under her arm, about Richard II forever complaining about the tardy room service, and about Edward II having gone off spicy food for practical gastrointestinal reasons too delicate to mention.

Afloat upon this line of patter, Matthew drifted about in slumber and was soon given to dreaming dreams much along the lines of Hieronymus Bosch on a lighter day, densely populated with beings fantastical to the waking self but quite in keeping with beings met by the slumbering self. He dreamed of pretty girls in flowing, diaphanous gowns; giant birds with brilliant iridescent feathers; schools of fish with glittering, shiny scales; and an elephant carrying a castle. And all these things—and he, himself—were flying quite freely above the Good Old City as if flying were as much the usual means of locomotion for pretty girls and schools of fish and elephants carrying castles, not to mention Matthew, as it is for giant birds wearing iridescent colors.

Then, in midflight toward a trio of pretty girls, he recalled an appointment to meet with Cherrytart at the Elephant and Castle and so abandoned the pursuit to veer off in the direction of the aerial pachyderm. As he approached, he noticed the castle was, in fact, the Tower of London, and circling above it was Gazpayne, followed by his clerk in the swallowtail coat of a beautiful teal and the battered body of Grindthumb trailing black smoke across the sky.

"I'm onto you, Cratchit," called out Gazpayne. "You'll not get away with it."

To that, Matthew awoke with a start.

"What is it?" asked Lucy, sounding greatly concerned.

"What's what?" asked Matthew.

"You shouted, 'No,' but no to what?"

"Oh," said Matthew, and he huffed out the lingering tingles of the shock. "Just a bad dream. I should go to bed." And with that, he climbed the Wooden Hill to the Land of Nod—as his mother used to say when ordering him upstairs to bed in his toddler years—and prepared himself for a proper slumber.

The nightmare persisted in plaguing Matthew's waking brain, however, as nightmares often do, so he could not get back to sleep for thinking of it. Though he told himself over and over the investigation into the whereabouts of the rent collector was ended to the satisfaction of all concerned, logic cannot quell that corrosive sense that the truth will out in the mind of one who has committed murder. Try as he might, he could not evade the image of ending his days abruptly at the end of a suddenly tautening rope.

Lucy noticed the tension tightening the air around her while she watched Peter put the finishing pieces in the jigsaw puzzle.

"Something's got our Tim frightened," she said. "You go to bed, and I'll settle him down."

"We shouldn't tell him ghost stories," said Peter, thinking the fear his brother was radiating was due to his telling of tales of terror with greater success than on the many previous occasions when the Tower of London puzzle provided the evening's entertainment.

"Probably for the best," said Lucy, trying not to sound too enthusiastic. "Off you go, then."

And with that, she turned to Tim, Peter turned in, and Matthew turned over and went back to sleep.

CHAPTER 48

The following morning, Matthew awoke feeling lighter, brighter, and more content with the world than he'd felt in a good long time.

He and Peter headed off in good time and, by the grace of Fortune, spied an enormous Alsatian depositing a large mound of steaming leavings outside a gentlemen's clothier. Out of respect for the dog's dignity, they waited a short distance away for it to finish and trot along before moving closer to claim their prize.

"Your turn to scoop," said Peter, but Matthew was glad to do his fair share, especially when the contribution to their collection was as large as this.

He was just working his trowel under the malodorous mass when the tailor appeared at the door and asked suspiciously, "What are you two doing?"

"Cleaning this up for you, sir," said Matthew as he dumped the lump into a pail.

"Egad, why on Earth …? Not that I'm not appreciative, mind you."

"Our uncle uses it in his tomato garden."

"Does he now? Well, I shan't be eating at his house anytime soon," said the tailor, chuckling at his own joke. He then turned to go back inside but turned again and said, "By the by. Several of my clients are members of the kennel club, and it comes to me they're having a dog show somewhere over near Saint Dunstan's today. I'm sure, if you make yourselves available to the organizers, you'll find enough of what you're after there to satisfy your uncle's most ambitious horticultural aspirations."

Being of the class to which they were born, the Cratchits had never heard of the kennel club and had no knowledge dogs were ever shown anything other than disrespect and the occasional boot, but Matthew was clever enough to arrive at the conclusion, from what the tailor had said—given the context of the conversation leading up to that point—that some form of entertainment was being put on for a canine audience and, dogs being dogs, there would be great quantities of leavings being left in the vicinity for the taking.

By the further grace of Fortune, Saint Dunstan's was a church well-known to Matthew, as, oddly enough, Matthew's religious proclivities had always leaned toward the divertissement provided by the more medieval methods of dealing with displeasing persons than might be seen as comely in one seeking spiritual uplifting. The legends surrounding Saint Dunstan—of him pinching the devil's nose with red-hot tongs and nailing horseshoes on the devil's cloven hooves—did more to enliven Matthew's imagination than stories of ancient kings comparing their girlfriends' tummies to haystacks or old men standing about before brushfires in search of ethical guidance. So, ever since Matthew was little, whenever he passed by the church of the famously punitive saint, his mind would entertain images of these acts of cruel torment from which he derived amusement.

And Fortune continued to grace the Cratchit pair in that Saint Dunstan's was not far from their next client, the Proud Hind—a public house known to ale lovers for its cellar full of excellent best bitter and to Eliphaz Dropping for its cellar equally full of rodents.

On their way toward the ancient church, they passed behind the Tower of London, which led Peter to say, "There's an amazing coincidence! Lucy and I did our puzzle just last night, and here we are, today, looking at the real thing."

"You do know we live less than a mile from here. We pass it ten times a week."

"Yes, but we don't do the puzzle nearly so often."

"You're right," said Matthew without conviction. "It is rather amazing when you look at it like that." However, the mention of William the Conqueror's monument to self-aggrandizement served to remind him (i.e., Matthew, not William the Conqueror) of his nightmare of the night before in which Gazpayne threatened to expose him as the architect of Grindthumb's demise. He studied the sky above the tower with a queasy recollection of flying fish, elephants, and lawyers.

Peter's interest was more terrestrial. "Why's there a big crowd in that field next to it?" he asked.

Matthew redirected his gaze but could make out nothing through the dense throng of people.

"Don't know, and we haven't time to find out," he said moodily, and hurried his brother along to their destination, where there were several signs to tell them they'd arrived.

"Precisely what is it you've come to collect?" asked the bulging man in the tight-maroon and-gold uniform standing before the doors leading to the dog show.

"The dog leavings," said Matthew as delicately and discreetly as he knew how. "You know. What it is dogs leave behind when they're done doing their doings."

The round, red man closed his bulging eyes impatiently but then opened them wide in realization and said, "Oh, you mean excrement!"

This word was not unknown to Matthew, though so rarely was it used in his sphere it would never enter any conversation through his lips.

"That's the word I was looking for," he said with a smirk. "Couldn't bring it to mind to save my life."

"We all have those moments," said the friendly, bulging man. "Wait here. I'll fetch Mr. Papillon, the manager."

The big, bulging man in burgundy returned with a little vulpine fellow in violet velvet whose small, dark eyes were as round as marbles; whose nose was as pointed as a pencil; and whose ears were hidden behind greased blond muttonchops and hair combed to resemble zebra swallowtail wings either side his bald white head.

"You're early," said the manager of the dog show. "We weren't expecting anyone until nearer closing."

As surprising as this was for Matthew, he didn't show it because he correctly assumed someone else had been hired to clean up after the dogs, and his and Peter's presence there constituted something of a fraud. In line with his character, he adapted quickly to the situation and said, "We like to make two trips so you won't be wading through it half the day."

The manager took on such a peculiar expression Matthew had to believe he'd said something quite out of place, but the fidgety little man signaled with a wave of a finger, spun on one heel, and led the way—finger still pointing skyward throughout the whole journey—into an enormous room filled with dogs and owners and servants of owners, all engaged in activities too bizarre by Matthew's standards to warrant questioning.

"They're brushing and combing the dogs," said Peter in disbelief.

"I know. Try not to stare," said Matthew out the side of his mouth, but it was hard not to stare, as the whole room was bursting with examples of behavior which the Cratchits would never have imagined a human being might engage in without being declared a danger to the public. Not only were strange-looking dogs being brushed and combed like children in preparation for church, but they were also being decorated with ribbons and jewels like ladies making ready for a ball.

And, furthermore, the room was bursting with evidence that breeding within too-closely related sets of offspring, for too many generations, can only lead to no aesthetic good.

But, alas, that was the way of the aristocracy at that time. Nowhere, among the dog owners, could one find an example of a bodily part that approached Polykleitos's canonical ideal proportions for that piece of anatomy. Limbs were either vastly too long or too short, noses were either enormous or nearly nonexistent, ears were either bat wings or winkle shells, chins were either whimpering in hiding or out conquering new territory, and eyes—eyes around the room seemed borrowed from every species of animal known to humankind except humankind itself.

Peter found himself studying, with aghast amazement, the features of one supercilious, squat little middle-aged woman while she supervised two lady servants in the grooming of a borzoi. The woman sensed she was being watched—a phenomenon often reported though roundly pooh-poohed by the scientific community—and turned to meet Peter's gaze. Shyly, he smiled in an attempt to ameliorate the rudeness of his bad behavior, and there appeared, on either side her face, half-hidden by her nose, a smile in return. She fluttered her eyelashes, tapped one of her servants on the elbow with her closed fan, and whispered something to the girl. Then she pointed to Peter with the fan, and the girl approached the petrified youth, who stood frozen in expectation of a severe and embarrassing lecture.

"The Countess Oleander wishes to speak with you in private," said the girl, and Peter nodded without knowing what else he could do. Failure to fulfill an aristocratic wish could get him drawn and quartered—or so he imagined in the moment.

The countess then rose, signaled Peter to follow, and walked toward the door next to the entrance with an energetic bounce to her gait as if parts of her body were propelled by springs. Peter obeyed in abject terror.

By this time, Matthew had arrived with Mr. Papillon at the other end of the large room, where he was shown several short wooden boxes about four-foot square and filled with sand. Two dogs on leashes were being allowed to relieve themselves in the sand, so no explanation was needed to tell Matthew why he was being shown these peculiar furnishings.

"They usually have greater need just before the show," said Papillon. "Stage fright, I would imagine. Say. Weren't there two of you?"

"Yes," said Matthew, and he looked over his shoulder only to be greatly disappointed to find the space that should have been occupied by Peter devoid of humanity. "He can't be far."

"He's not one to go looking for trouble, is he?"

"No, no, not at all," said Matthew, but he didn't mention that trouble made a habit of looking for Peter.

"If I see him, I'll send him in this direction," said Papillon. He started to leave but stopped and asked, "Oh, do I pay you half this morning and half later, or all when the job's done this evening."

Matthew had not yet grown accustomed to Fortune showing him such ongoing beneficence but was quick with an answer, nevertheless. "Half this morning, if that's all right with you, as the old man's likely to send two other chaps this afternoon."

"Very good then. Tell the doorman to summon me on your way out," said the little manager in violet, and he left Matthew to his work.

Luckily for Matthew, he had carried all four pails and the scoop needed for the work and not left them in the care of his delinquent brother. He was able, then, to get started sifting through the sand to expose the stinky dollops, which he found in greater and greater abundance as he passed from the boxes used by toys and lap dogs to those frequented by the Saint Bernards, the Newfoundlands, the Great Pyrenees, and the giant mastiffs.

As pleased as he was with this unexpected bounty, he could not stop feeling irked by his brother's absence. He had filled two buckets entirely and was well into filling the third when Peter appeared looking frightfully pale.

"Where the dickens have you been?" asked Matthew.

"The C-C-Countess Oleander wanted to talk to me, so I had to go," said Peter. "She didn't even give me a choice … didn't …"

Matthew suspected a lie. "What in blue blazes would a countess want to talk to you about?"

"She told me not to tell anyone," said Peter as color returned to his face but then quickly continued on well past its normal, healthy hue toward the hot end of the reds, "so I don't think I will. Not now. Not ever."

"All right then," said Matthew.

Whatever it was Peter had gotten up to, it was clear from his manner and expression he'd paid some price already and didn't need a lecture on responsibility to regret not being there to help.

"Here," said Matthew, handing his brother the scoop. "I'm nearly done. You finish."

Peter took it without protest and began his search through the sand.

"Oh, one thing the countess did say," said Peter, entering a lighter mood. "I should have had the stitches out of my bottom ages ago. It's not healthy leaving them in when I'm done healing."

"How does she …?" began Matthew, but the penny dropped, as they say, and he needed to go no further to know the answer. Instead, he smirked and asked, "So, how was it?"

"How was what?"

"You know. *It*. What you did with the countess."

Peter blanched again and said, "I can't talk about it. Not now. Not ever."

Matthew left his brother to his promise of discretion and said nothing more about Peter's introduction to erotic adventure or the strange prurient intrigues of the aristocracy.

They were soon done filling their pails and struggled to carry what was nearly a hundredweight of leavings out the way they'd come. Matthew showed the big, bulging man in burgundy the proof of their completed labors, and Papillon was fetched to pay for the work.

"There you go, my good fellow," said the manager. "One shilling six pence, and I hope we see you again. We don't often see such zeal and devotion to the task as you, young sir, have displayed."

"We hope so too, sir," said Matthew. "Don't we, Peter?"

"I can't talk about it. Not now. Not ever" was all Peter could say.

CHAPTER 49

The rest of their day was equally blessed with greater than usual good luck. The rats in their clients' places of business were in greater-than-usual abundance, and the clients themselves were all in greater-than-usual moods of generosity. And to the great delight of the brothers, when they came to inspect the progress of their herd's increasing numbers, they were met with a most unexpected surprise. But it was not that the numbers exceeded expectation—in that, the creatures were right on schedule.

"Look at that one," said Matthew. "He's huge! And there's another one. And another."

"Doesn't matter," said Peter flatly. "We still only get a farthing apiece for them."

"Yes, but they'll eat more and make more product. It won't be so long till we can stop collecting dog leavings."

"Oh, right! That will be good, won't it?"

"Bloody right, it will. Crikey! Look at that one. He's as big as a rabbit," said Matthew, pointing to one standing on his hind legs in the far corner. Then an idea struck the creative Cratchit, and he turned to his brother and said, "Big as a rabbit! Are you thinking what I'm thinking?"

"I doubt it," said Peter. "I was thinking I shouldn't have given Mary Handchester a penny to see her knickers."

Normally Matthew would gloss over divergent musings, such as this, that arose when Peter became untethered from the theme of the conversation, but this alternate path of dialogue seemed pregnant with possibility.

"You gave Mary Handchester a penny?"

"I did," said Peter glumly, "but I shouldn't have." He took in a deep breath to temper his regret. "It would have been different if she'd been in them at the time. I mean, all she did was hold them up for me to see, and they looked every bit the same as Lucy's. I see hers all the time when she's hanging out the washing. And—come to think of it—I could have just waited for Mary's mother to hang out their washing, looked over the fence, and seen them for nothing."

"But if you'd done that, you might have been looking at Mary's mother's knickers for all you knew. How much would you like that?"

A cold, paralyzing chill gripped Peter—much as it had earlier that day when the countess made her intentions known—the kind of cold, paralyzing chill that grips all men when confronted with forbidden fruit dangling from the tips of terrifyingly high branches, combined with the esthetic considerations of erotic misadventure approaching the grotesque.

When Peter failed to answer Matthew's question, Matthew returned to his original subject and said, "What I was thinking is this. If they're as big as rabbits, we can skin them and sell them as rabbits."

Peter welcomed the opportunity to stop thinking about Mary Handchester's mother's undergarments and all that they entailed and redirect his mind onto less disquieting paths.

"Sell them to who?" he asked.

"To *whom*," said Matthew before answering. "To Mrs. Retch. She can make them into meat pies. Little salt, pepper, and onion, and no one will know the difference. She's likely paying Gutblood's or Tuffgrissle's at least thruppence apiece for rabbits. We could give her a ha'penny off and she's in pocket."

Peter was conflicted over the idea of deleting rabbit pie from his list of preferred comestibles, but the potential increase in revenue shifted the balance of his internal battle toward agreement, and so agree he did.

"Tell me again," said Lucy as she pressed the proud flesh to expose a catgut suture for snipping, "how it is the countess found out you've got stitches in your bum."

Peter couldn't remember the details of any of the three versions he'd provided so far and was running out of fresh material to flesh out the thin skeletal tale he'd told over supper, so he opted for "She just knows about such things. That's why she's a countess and you're not."

Lucy had to assume Peter's logic in this was unassailable, as—quite clearly—she was not a countess, and nothing Peter had said up to this point had made any sense to her whatsoever, so it stood to reason countesses understood things common girls could not.

She tugged hard on her tweezers, which yanked hard on the severed suture, which pulled hard on Peter's poor posterior, which sent his hips thrusting forward and an *ow* echoing off all four walls.

"Will you be seeing any more of her?" asked Lucy.

"I've seen more than enough of her already, thank you."

Matthew listened, amused. He might have been envious of Peter's brief encounter with the Countess Oleander had he seen among the aristocrats at the dog show a single example of femininity that would not inspire a young man to consider seriously taking monastic orders.

Lucy felt the need to tease as she snipped another thread, and said, "So we won't be having any little Count Peters running about the place?"

Peter was much like most single men of twenty in being prone to forget the link between the doing of *it* and fatherhood within the context of all but the most academic discussions of *it*. Being reminded of this connection sent a shock down his spine, which was immediately turned around and driven upward when Lucy yanked out another suture.

The resulting *ow* was, thence, as much an expression of horror as it was of pain before trailing off in a sobbing *oh-oh*-oh-oh.

Peter saw stars. Then he imagined yeomen of the guard coming to arrest him and then standing behind him with halberds to his back as he listened to an archbishop drone on before he said, "I do," in promise of eternal faithfulness to the rotund and asymmetrical, blotchy, and lascivious little parrot, the Countess Oleander, standing next to him.

Normally Matthew would have enjoyed the novelty of watching his sister pull stitches out of his brother's bare backside, but he found instead he was growing sickly afraid of something, though the only clue as to what that something could be was a strange need to protect his manly parts from some horrific abuse. Within a flash of insight, he realized the source of this terror was Peter through the conduit of Tiny Tim. He forced himself to take a deep breath and sat next to Tim while imagining, as best he could, all things reassuring.

"That's good," said Lucy shortly after. "Peter's such a sissy. He'd have had the whole city afraid to pee if you hadn't caught Tiny Tim in time."

Peter, of course, was offended by this, but unable to think of a plausible explanation for his real fear that did not involve the violation of a promise of secrecy—a promise he felt highly motivated to keep—he allowed himself to accept the insult and settle into all things reassuring under the influence of his emotive silent brother.

Lucy finished pulling the sutures from Peter's bottom and was preparing to remove the ones from his scalp when a knock at the door roused the family Cratchit from this peaceful pastime.

Matthew answered it. It was Cherrytart, wearing a large and rather unsavory smile.

"Evening, Cratchit. Hope I ain't disturbing your grub and all, but I wanted to let you know you needn't put no mind to Gazpayne no more."

"Oh?"

"No. Last night, me and the lads done him and 'is clerk—the one in the swallowtail coat of a beautiful green what's been making a nuisance of hisself here and about."

"Done them?"

"'At's right," said Cherrytart proudly. "Tossed the two of 'em off the Tower of London, we did."

"You threw Gazpayne off the tower?" said Matthew, in disbelief, before memories of his nightmare pushed their way back through the mists of forgetfulness.

"Simple as that. We knowed he weren't about to quit on the rent, as 'is bloke was still poking about and making threats of bringing down the law hereabouts. I sussed we'd have to do something about it, though I didn't have the foggiest what. Then, last night, I comes home from the pub and sits down afore the fire, like I does, and dozes off. Out of the blue, I has this dream, see? with Gazpayne and his bloke flying about the tower like a couple of larks, saying nasty things. Then I woke up knowing just what to do. I got my Pru to write up a note saying, 'They're onto us. Meet me at the Tower of London at midnight. Come alone.' I took the note with me and fetched the lads, then onto Gazpayne's. The clerk was still there working away, but Gazpayne weren't, so we got the little git to spill on where 'is boss lives and trotted ourselves there to get 'im, too. We takes 'em both up the tower, I puts the note in the clerk's pocket, and we lets 'em both go down the quick way."

The blood that had left Matthew's face started returning with some heat, but Tiny Tim—with Lucy's help—was still radiating reassurance, so Matthew maintained his reason.

"You made it look like an accident, then?" he asked as he grew more comfortable with the concept.

"More like a couple of villains having a falling out," said Cherrytart, "with one slipping while trying to do the other in. Either way, it gives 'is partners something to think about. They won't be bothering us for a bit."

"Good. Very good, thank you," said Matthew, unable to think what else to say.

Cherrytart then nodded and turned to leave, but Matthew had a recollection and said, "Oh, by the way. I heard there's a problem with the tea crop in India."

"Yeah," said the neighbor. "What's that to do with anything, then?"

"Well, the shops will be running out shortly, and I was wondering if you might be able to get your hands on a couple hundredweight while there's still some to be had. At reasonable prices, I mean."

Cherrytart grinned broadly. "Reasonable prices it is," he said with a wink, and went his way.

Although Matthew was not terribly keen to learn he was responsible for yet two more murders, if anyone in his estimation deserved a quick descent from the tower with concomitant deceleration trauma, it was Gazpayne and his officious little clerk.

But he sensed someone watching him. He turned to meet Lucy's eyes.

She wore an expression that told him she knew everything. No doubt she had had a glimpse or two of his dream the night before and now could piece the puzzle together, in her mind, to guess all that had happened. But it didn't seem to be bothering her at all.

At last, she tilted her head pertly, smirked faintly, and said, "Told you it was a beautiful green."

CHAPTER 50

Three hundredweight of tea arrived at the Cratchit residence under cover of darkness and was stored in the unused bedroom that still, officially, belonged to Bob and his wife. Matthew informed Squidge of rumors floating about that India had suffered a drought and crops had failed to produce.

Within days, the usual musty smell within the dusty dray-and-carriage business was replaced by the heady aroma of tea, as burlap sacks and wooden crates of the dried leaves filled all the available space.

Peter was made to go without tea for a week and water for all that day before being tied and gagged just as Lucy had been, but with two family-sized teapots steaming fragrance from their spouts before him. Thus, he was made to endure an agonizing craving for the hot beverage, while his brother and sister escaped to a tea shop three miles from the Cratchit home.

"Our Tim's reach is getting longer," said Matthew as he took a sip from his fourth cup. "Peter and I didn't have to travel nearly this far when you were wanting chocolate."

"I am jolly tired, walking all this way," said Lucy. "My feet hurt, but crikey! This tea is bloody marvelous, isn't it? Can we hire a carriage to take us home, please?"

"Course. But I don't think this is going to work much longer. Whatever we do next, we won't be able to get far enough away from home not to go mad with the need for whatever it is."

"Will that be so bad?" asked Lucy. "All we really need to do is get far enough away for Tim to make things happen and then go home. What does it matter if we go a bit bonkers? We'll have all we want when we get back."

Matthew nodded his approval of his sister's sound judgment and her willingness to tolerate temporary torment for greater gain.

Just then, a man entered the tea shop and shouted from the door, "Give me the biggest flipping pot you've got!" He began weeping. "And for heaven's sake, be bloody quick about it!"

"Time for us to go," said Matthew with a smirk.

They had no trouble finding a carriage. The streets were full of them, arriving at the tea shop loaded with dozens of parched customers ready to join the mob forming at the front door. The problem was that the drivers were all in as much need of tea as the customers they carried. The carriages were abandoned upon arrival as the drivers jumped down to join the craving crowd.

Lucy looked panicked for fear of having to walk through the thick throng on legs still aching from the long trot that had brought her there.

"Don't worry, my love," murmured Matthew, and he selected a vehicle parked far enough away to be out of sight of its owner. "Get in! I'll drive."

Lucy was hesitant. But not for long. Despite her apprehensions, she could sense that even if they were arrested for stealing the carriage, Matthew would find a way of making things all right. She climbed inside while Matthew climbed up front and took his position. He lifted the whip from its holster, flicked it in the air above the horse, and they were off.

The dire thirst for more tea started to rise again within them as they made their way through the crowded streets toward home. Still, Matthew noted every policeman heading his way, and his mind mulled over believable lies to tell, but none was needed since none of the constabulary made any attempt to stop the young man, who was clearly dressed entirely unlike any driver anywhere in the Good

Old City would ever dress. Of course, every policeman was far too interested in getting himself around several cups of tea to worry about such petty things as stolen horses and carriages. After seven or eight men in brass-buttoned blue had passed him with crazed stares fixed on the direction from which he had come, Matthew gave up worrying about their impeding his progress and let his mind return to his swelling want of more tea. And his swelling want of the convenience in the Cratchit backyard.

But suddenly, when they were still half a mile from home and the crowds were at their thickest and their needs at their most desperate, the wanting of tea abruptly diminished.

"You feel that?" shouted Lucy from inside the carriage.

"Yes. Peter must have worked himself free. Not to worry. It's gone on plenty long enough."

"Can you hurry up? I need to pee."

"Can you walk now? I think we'll get on faster on foot."

Lucy was silent for some while, leading Matthew to worry. He sensed, too, that this sudden cessation of the overwhelming need for tea would cause policemen to be once again more inclined to look for crime, and this thought caused his nerves to rise.

"Lucy?" he called out anxiously.

"Just a minute," she said.

He waited in silence but scanned the road ahead for any sign of tall blue helmets emblazoned with shields.

The carriage door opened, making Matthew jump. As Lucy stepped down, he leaped from the driver's bench and landed beside her. He took her hand, and together they made their way into narrow, dark, and unused allies where they could trot unimpeded home.

They arrived to find their front door open. Despite his grave concern over this, Matthew had an overriding need to divest himself of the tea he'd consumed within the last hour. Still, not being entirely without a sense of gallantry, he turned to Lucy and said, "You use the loo, but please hurry."

"No, thank you," said Lucy with a shy grimace. "You go ahead. I can wait."

Matthew's molars were floating on used tea, so he could not stop to argue. He ran through the house and past the contented Peter seated at the kitchen table with his head lying next to two empty teapots, his hands clasping an empty cup the size of a baby's pot and the untied rope and gagging lying about him on the floor.

Matthew's relief was so intense it was excruciating for several seconds before spiraling into that profound pleasure only a small set of human experiences can provide. He luxuriated in the sensation for some while before remembering he was keeping Lucy waiting in what must have been a state of painful desperation and so packed up, buttoned up, and sallied forth a much refreshed man.

As he crossed the narrow gap from the convenience to the back door, he heard sighs and moans coming from the backyards of all his neighbors and realized his recently resolved need had been conveyed through Tiny Tim to the entire community, and all were enjoying the same satisfaction within which he was still basking.

But Peter was next to cross the divide, and Lucy only after that. Matthew could not help but think it strange she would persevere so when she had never done so in the past when needs for the convenience arose simultaneously among the siblings. Then it dawned on him— with churning disgust—why she had kept him waiting before leaving the carriage. His family pride was pummeled at the thought, and he was overcome by a strong, presumed-head-of-the-household need to lecture Lucy rising from his moral center.

But that same moral center reminded him he daily inflated his take of rats for money and sold rat and dog leavings under false pretenses to a brewery and had orchestrated the murders of five men. Chastising his sister for soiling a carriage—which he had stolen— suddenly seemed to him a tad hypocritical.

He turned his attention to Peter. "Got yourself loose, I see."

"No. It was Mr. Cherrytart," said Peter cheerily. "He'd gone completely round the bend, he had. Burst in here looking ready to kill and drank all my tea you left for me, without asking permission, and then he untied me and wanted to know where all the tea was he ..."

Matthew didn't wait for more but ran upstairs to his parents' bedroom to find the three hundred pounds in sacks gone without a trace larger than the lingering aroma.

"Damn and hell!" he said from the depths of disappointment.

He took one more look at the stacks of sacks of tea that were not there before turning to go downstairs.

"What's the matter?" asked Lucy.

"Cherrytart's taken all the tea. The whole thing's been for naught."

"Well," said Lucy sheepishly, "you did know he was a bit of a villain from the start."

Matthew's disappointment turned to rage. His eyes widened and his jaw clenched, but Lucy shouted, "Sorry! Stop that now before Tim starts ..." and ran without finishing that thought to Tiny Tim's side, where she knelt and began stroking his forehead and imagining pastoral images.

Within moments, Matthew's self-control returned, and he returned to some contentment with life. But, along with this well-being, there came a realization Tiny Tim was not entirely his servant but was—at least in part—his master.

CHAPTER 51

W hen the brothers Cratchit next met with Squidge, they were
given ten shillings for informing the master of carriages of the
precipitous tea shortage. As big a bounty as this was relative to their
usual daily income, it served only to remind Matthew of how much
he had stood to gain had his plan gone as planned—had it not been
for Cherrytart and the theft of the stolen tea.

"Why so glum, mate?" asked Squidge. "You done all right out of
it all, seeings as you done nothing for it but whisper in my ear. Lots
done a lot worse, you know. One of them China clippers got boarded
in harbor, emptied of its cargo, and set alight. Shops was robbed and
wrecked. Rioting in the streets. People run amok, they did, when they
couldn't get no tea. Who'd a sussed all'd go complete bonkers like
that? Acts of villainy everywhere, there was. One bloke even had his
carriage stole and vandalized. I know 'cuz he sold it to me right cheap,
he did, as he said he didn't think he could get the piss stink out of it."

Here, Squidge stopped to chuckle. "But I put my cleanup boys on
it, and it's as good as new. I don't get luck like that every day, I don't
mind telling you. No, not a bit of it. But, like I says, me and you done
well out of it all when lots didn't, so cheer yourself up and get yourself
lost."

Matthew made an effort to put on a better face for his business
partner and succeeded well enough. But hearing that a merchant vessel
and many shops had been destroyed only stabbed into his conscious
with a long, serrated blade. And hearing Squidge had tangentially

profited by his and his sister's crime of stealing and soiling a carriage only added to his irritation. Here he was, working so hard and causing so much mayhem to so many people and seeing almost none of the profit. It just wasn't good caterpillarism, in his estimation of how the world should work.

"All you need is to plan a little better next time," said Lucy when the little family sat around the kitchen table after supper.

"What would you have done differently, I might ask?" said the morose Matthew.

"Well," said Lucy with a little I-told-you-so glint in her eye, "I wouldn't have trusted Mr. Cherrytart, for one thing. At least not with the most important part. You should have bought the tea with the money he gave you—the money he got from the rent collector—and hidden it in our warehouse, where no one would know it was there or think to look for it."

Matthew did not like—at all—being told by his younger sister the fifteen pounds he'd acquired from Cherrytart could have been doubled or trebled in a few days, had he had the sense to avoid using known villains for honest caterpillarist ventures. Still, he had to admit she was right, and he was just about to swallow that bitter pill and do so when a knock at the door gave him reason to pause, preadmission.

It was Cherrytart.

"Evening, Cratchit," said the nefarious neighbor. "I come to 'pologize for pinching the tea like I done."

Caught between anger over having been wronged and fear over rousing a known murderer who outweighed him by half a Matthew, Matthew didn't know what to say and so said nothing.

"I couldn't stop meself," said Cherrytart. "I was just so bloody aching for a cuppa, and I knowed you had sacks of it in here, so … well, I been and sold it all, here and about, like I sussed you was planning, and I got a bit more than thirty nicker for it. Here." He held out a brown leather bag weighed heavily down with coins.

Matthew took it in two hands but took a moment to realign his indignation to delighted astonishment.

"I wants us to stay mates," said Cherrytart. "I don't know this from that with most things, but I knows a bloke what's going places when I meets him, and I knows you's one of them. And I knows what side me bread's buttered on, so ..."

"I appreciate your saying so," said Matthew, and he then opened the bag to extract a few coins before continuing. "I was going to pay you for your efforts—"

"Keep it. For the grief and aggro I give you. And your brother. Scared him proper, I did," said Cherrytart. But his expression changed, and he asked, "Oh, right. Why is it you had him tied up and gagged?"

"I'm trying to toughen him up," said Matthew as easily as if it had been the truth.

"Oh, ah?" said Cherrytart wide-eyed; then he nodded. "Yeah. Pru and Pris do say he's a bit of a Nancy. Still, family's family, as they say. Well, I do hope this makes things right between us, and remember— whatever you got going, I wants in." He then winked and left.

Matthew was elated. Not only had he made more money from the sale of the tea than he'd estimated, but he'd done so without having to apply any effort to the task; and more than any other consideration, he was saved from having to humble himself in admitting to his sister he'd been wrong—as any proud owner of a male ego can well understand.

CHAPTER 52

Work at the abandoned warehouse had to be increased dramatically. It had been within a week of the first delivery of bitter being made to Belcher's that it suddenly occurred to Matthew the flowers needed for the blend would be unobtainable during the winter months and the Cratchits would have to begin processing a much greater volume to build a reserve to carry them through to the following spring.

But this problem didn't end there. It soon became apparent the wholesalers would not be able to supply the necessary volume, so Matthew was forced to go to Thaddeus Squidge for help. Squidge then made his personal presence known among the merchants at the docks, and over the course of a few weeks, the supply of the necessary blossoms rose to meet Matthew's forecast going out several months.

Of course, this meant other kinds of flowers, destined for other purposes—nosegays and corsages for dandies and debutantes, and wreaths for the dead—became rarer and rarer in the Good Old City, and prices rose concomitantly. Squidge twigged to this, too, and engineered his way into partnerships in one-third of the city's florist shops—the one-third that continued to offer preshortage prices until the other two-thirds were trampled to death by the feet of customers who never came near them.

Matthew was led, yet again, to consider that the universe was constructed such that the more problems he encountered, the wealthier

Squidge would get. But he was committed to supplying bittering agent to Belcher's, and for now, that was all there was to it.

Meanwhile, Lucy struggled to keep up with the rising quotas, but soon the work was too much for her alone, and her brothers were too busy with their activities to provide meaningful assistance.

Regretting he had ever embarked on this venture, Matthew reluctantly explained all this to Squidge, who, perhaps not surprisingly, was not at all upset.

"Easy enough," said the master of conveyances. "We're only to find you some kids what needs a roof to keep 'em dry and walls to keep 'em outta sight."

"What do you mean?"

"Corner of your warehouse, of course."

"Who'd want to live in a filthy old warehouse?" asked Matthew, corrugating his nose at the thought of sleeping upstairs of his rat horde.

"Anyone what don't want to live in a filthy old prison," said Squidge, and he put a finger to one side of his nose to signal that question time was over. "Just don't keep nothing about worth stealing, and you'll be all right. Pay 'em what you thinks it's worth, but it all comes out your end, so don't be a burke about it. Feeding 'em's likely enough, but you do as you like."

Matthew smiled the smile you give your dentist when he says you're lucky your teeth can all be repaired and payment can be arranged over time.

Four boys arrived at the warehouse the following day along with the fresh shipment of flowers from the docks. Matthew sent Peter to buy fish and chips before showing the four what they were to do. Though it wasn't exactly the kind of activity to which twelve-year-old boys of a criminal proclivity would normally gravitate, Squidge had already had a word with them to galvanize their enthusiasm for the work. Indeed, they were trembling with anticipation to get started.

Peter arrived back with the food, so Matthew left him to provide supervision while he went to purchase blankets to make bedding.

When he returned, the boys were working hard, but Peter was nowhere to be seen.

"I'm up here," called Peter from his perch, high in the rafters.

"What are you doing up there?"

"They told me I could watch better from here, but now I can't get down."

Matthew noticed the boys exchanging giggling glances and knew his brother had yet again attempted to navigate the field of wits without a compass. With a tired sigh, Matthew set about talking his brother down—a task made all the more difficult as Peter had discovered only after reaching his lofty destination that he had a fear of heights, which meant looking down to find footing for each step caused him unmanageable terror.

"Just keep looking up and do as I say," said Matthew, and he guided Peter step-by-step to terra firma.

"That was exciting," said Peter bravely once he'd gotten his breath back.

"We can do it every day if you like."

"Not for a bit, thank you."

With the four boys settled in for the night, Matthew left them with a promise three meals would be supplied daily and a reminder the law was still looking for them—plus Mr. Squidge would be if they went missing.

"You won't be working at the warehouse anymore," said Matthew to Lucy when he and Peter arrived home.

To this, Lucy had mixed feelings. It was true, the work had become too much, but she had grown to enjoy bouncing about all day as bare as when she was born. But, of course, she couldn't say that to her brothers. Then another thought came to her with abrupt harshness.

"I suppose I won't be paid anymore, then?" she asked sadly.

"Of course you will," said Matthew. "We're in this together. But if you can cook for the boys, it'll save us having to buy food for them."

"I can do that," said Lucy, glad to maintain her income.

So it was settled.

Or so it seemed.

The next morning, Matthew and Peter set off to their warehouse with four large servings of the meat pie Lucy had prepared the night before for supper.

"Cor!" said the self-proclaimed leader of the boys. "This ain't half the best bleeding steak and kidney I ever et!"

And his comrades all agreed.

Matthew took some pride in knowing his sister's culinary endeavors could be so well appreciated, even though, from the emaciated look of the four, he might surmise a meal of beetles and worms would be the "best bleeding beetles and worms" they'd ever eaten.

Then, Matthew being Matthew, a thought came to him. Lucy could make excellent meat pies, and he had a flock of rats, some of whom were the size of rabbits. But like all brilliant ideas, this one came wrapped in a problem: the rats were in the basement of the warehouse, one floor beneath the four boys sent there by Squidge. A shock traveled from Matthew's heart to his toes as he realized it would be nearly impossible to keep the secret of the secret ingredient in the bittering agent secret from the four. If they found out three hundred pounds in every ton of bitter was rat leavings, Squidge would soon know of it, and then what?

This problem drained all hope of enjoyment from Matthew's day as he and his brother went about the business of catching and killing rats. It was a genuine catastrophe, it seemed. The need to excavate a sizeable quantity of the product for drying was growing urgent, but he could not imagine a way for Peter and him to do so without being seen by his hired help. Try as he might, he could not escape the confines of the only solution imaginable: he would have to pay the four boys enough to guarantee their silence.

But, like many a bitter pill, what comes after the swallowing of it can be rather more pleasant than that first taste—which accounts for the widespread swallowing of bitter pills. Once he had decided to go forward with this intention, Matthew started imagining himself as a true captain of industry—a corporate emperor with an aristocracy of executives beneath him and an army of employees on the ground. Of course, that aristocracy consisted of only Lucy and Peter, for the time being, but literature is rife with examples of great rulers risen from humble beginnings.

All this led Matthew to revisit his initial idea of that morning: to exploit Lucy's talent for rendering nearly inedible meat into quite delightful pies. To this, he could quickly see the Cratchit kitchen was wholly inadequate for the venture. Clearly, a shop was needed—something near to home.

At the end of their workday, Matthew sent Peter to fetch the boys' supper from Lucy while he took a meandering walk to find a suitable place for a pie shop. Perhaps ironically, he came upon the closed and boarded-up grocery store formerly owned by Mr. Smallbits (whom you may recall was lynched from a lamppost by an angry mob for supposedly untoward behavior toward the sisters of said mob). The place was rather large for a pie shop, but the location was ideal and, judging from the dates on the posters posted on the boards boarding up the big window, it had been vacant more than two months.

A moment's search led him to the name M. T. Pawkets & Associates: Claims Agents, and their pertinent information tacked to the door. He then memorized their address for the morrow.

Satisfied with his efforts, he walked the ten-minute walk home only to find Peter was yet to return from the warehouse. Imagining his brother to be stranded again in the rafters, he set off to help him down and home.

To his almost pleasant surprise, he found Peter seated not atop a broad beam forty feet up, but on a chair at the end of the table used for grinding and mixing flower parts. In one hand he held a large fan of playing cards. Two of the boys sat to his left, and two to his right, each holding a much smaller cluster of cards than Peter's. On the table sat a small stack of coins.

"Oh, hello, Matthew," said Peter. "The lads have been teaching me this new game, and I'm really quite good at it."

"Really?" said Matthew, thinking the game must be unique for Peter to have some mastery of it. "And how is it played?"

"Well," said Peter, pulling his cards close to his chest as he met Matthew's gaze. "Everyone gets five cards to start. If you have a king, queen, or knave, you can buy another card. But if you don't, you can't. So far, I'm the only one that's been able to buy cards, so I've got the biggest hand, which means I'm winning, 'cuz the one who finishes with the most cards wins unless he runs out of money before the game's over, in which case he loses and all the others divide up the pot."

"I see," said Matthew, and he attempted to look at the cards the boys held but was denied this privilege.

"So!" said Peter, looking cockily eye-to-eye with each of the other players. "Who's got some royalty?"

The four all frowned in defeat and shook their heads.

"Aha!" shouted Peter in his triumph. He tossed a farthing on the pot and took another card.

Matthew debated with himself whether to end the game then and listen to Peter moan all the way home how he had been denied an inevitable victory or to let events play out and listen to Peter moan all the way home how luck always turned against him just when everything was going well.

Oddly enough, neither came to pass. Peter continued to buy cards until the entirety of the deck—minus the cards held by the boys—was in his possession and he still had coins in his pocket.

"What happens now?" asked Peter.

The boys had not predicted this outcome and looked to one another for an answer.

"Obviously, Peter won," said Matthew with such severity of managerial sternness the boys were hesitant to challenge the assertion. "Come on, then. Collect your winnings and let's go."

As much as this was a better result than Matthew had foreseen, Peter still bent his ear with effulgent self-praise all the way home.

"All right!" said Matthew, finally losing his patience. "You won. How much did you win?"

"Seven pence. Nearly."

"And how much did you have to throw into the pot?"

"I don't know."

"Did any of the boys throw anything in?"

As niggled as Matthew was with Peter, he still felt some Socratic satisfaction in watching his brother's facial expression change as the various parts of the answer slid together in his head to arrive at the disillusioning solution.

"Not really worth the effort, was it?" Peter muttered.

"It often isn't," said Matthew knowingly, but he cheered up a little and added, "But you can't know till you try."

CHAPTER 53

Lucy protested emphatically, "I don't know anything about running a pie shop!"

"Pfft! What's there to know?" said Peter.

But if Lucy's doubts had not been enough to give Matthew pause, Peter's certainty of simplicity was plenty to tell him there must be much more to the concept than he'd considered, for he knew Peter to have an unerring knack for sensing the complexity of things in its reciprocal or inverse ratio to reality. The elder Cratchit had a history of assuming the polar opposite of what expertise held to be true and denouncing the most difficult of things as the easiest of things imaginable and the skills of the most highly accomplished people as nothing at all. In short, Peter was a consummate floccinaucinihilipilificator, but of course, Matthew would never say that out loud to his brother.

A caustic disappointment etched Matthew's innards for the next few moments. As he grew to full manhood, his tolerance for being told "no" was growing less and less, and this impediment reeked of the word "no" even though the word itself wasn't spoken.

Peter sensed that the silence that followed his comment—not to mention the judgmental glare from both his siblings—was a tacit statement he was wrong.

"Mrs. Retch does it well enough, doesn't she?" he said in indignant defensiveness. "Well? Doesn't she?"

So, in the space of three short sentences and one long pause, Peter inadvertently succeeded in plunging his brother into deep doubt and then retrieving him to full confidence.

"Of course!" said Matthew ecstatically. "I was going to sell the"—he paused for the shock of a near-slip to dissipate—"rabbits to Mrs. Retch in the first place, till I knew you can make pies just as well as she does."

"What rabbits?" asked Lucy.

"I know a chap who breeds them," said Matthew, with a short, dismissive wave. "Never mind that for now. What's important is Mrs. Retch knows how to run a pie shop. She can teach us what to do."

"Why would she do that?" asked Lucy.

Again Matthew felt the impact of an obstacle, but this time he didn't linger long in frustration. Upon consideration, he realized he'd never looked upon Mrs. Retch as a caterpillarist, but despite her apparent honesty and decency, he felt she must have at least some caterpillarist proclivities to be in business. As disillusioning as this might have been to his grandmotherly vision of the kindly lady, it still gave Matthew that feeling of elation that accompanies the solving of a problem.

"We'll pay her," he said, lifting a hand palm upward as if pulling a rabbit from a hat.

Propelled by his desire to accomplish a great deal, Matthew moved with great energy through the following day. To shorten their work hours, he and Peter took eighty rats from the cellar of the house on their street and rushed from client to client, thus freeing up the time to talk to Mrs. Retch.

They arrived at her shop sometime after three. To keep his brother quiet, Matthew bought Peter an assortment of cakes and sent him outside to guard their rat wagon while eating them. Then he made his offer to the pastry shop proprietress.

"Oh, I can't do that, my love," said Mrs. Retch. "My partners would have me for it, they would."

"Your partners?" asked Matthew.

"That's right. Fifty-one percent of the shop belongs to Rankin,

Fowle, O'Durr, and Gazpayne: Solicitors and Barristers at Law. Though I hear Mr. Gazpayne has left the firm on account of being dead. Anyway, I can't do nothing without their say-so, and I knows they won't take kindly to me working for someone else without their telling me I has to."

Matthew chilled to the sound of the all-too-familiar names but had to ask, "Why are you in partnership with them?"

"It were some years back, now, when my husband, Mr. Retch—God rest his soul, the rotten sod—got hisself into a bit of a bind with the law, you see, and I had to give them half or lose it altogether."

Fury rose in Matthew's belly. Had Mrs. Retch's partners been anyone else, he might have walked away in search of alternatives, but the taste of revenge was metallic on his tongue. He resolved on the spot to free his friend from the clutches of these parasitic malefactors.

But how?

Despite this setback, he still intended to go forward with his plan to open a pie shop from which Cratchit rabbit pies would be sold to an appreciative, albeit unsuspecting, world. So it was he stuck to the schedule he had drafted in his mind and, after finishing up with Dropping and Squidge, left Peter to see to the boys in the warehouse while he made his way to the offices of M. T. Pawkets, claims agent.

Mr. Pawkets bore a rather remarkable, though not disagreeable, resemblance to a long-haired marmalade cat. His fluffy, fine hair and sideboards were a light auburn streaked with white; his eyebrows, beard, and mustache pure white; and his eyes a clear sage green. And, as if he were aware of this resemblance and wished to enhance it, he wore a white velvet waistcoat and a white silk cravat under a swallowtail coat of a beautiful orange.

Like most men of the city, Pawkets judged Matthew on his age, which was clearly insufficient to conduct business legally, and on his appearance, which was clearly indicative of insufficient funds to conduct business seriously, and so attempted to dissuade the youthful, threadbare Cratchit from wasting his time.

"The property has proven problematic," said Pawkets. "The

family of the late Mr. Smallbits, driven to despair over the disgrace he had brought upon them, disappeared into the night, one night, along with all their belongings, following hard upon the unfortunate incident surrounding his demise. His creditors have taken possession and hired me to get from it what I can. But, I must confess, the place carries with it the repugnant reputation of its former owner—that being one of one who manipulates innocent young ladies into untenable debt for the purposes of lascivious exploitation—and so none wants even to consider it despite its clear advantages of size and location."

This gave Matthew only a moment's hesitation, as he knew Tiny Tim could easily rehabilitate the unsavory associations of the place.

"Let me see it," he said with such force it took poor Pawkets by surprise.

Still, Pawkets felt compelled to put an end to the young upstart's waste of his time. "You do realize I cannot consider less than twenty guineas for the property in question, despite its—"

"That's a fair price," said Matthew. "My brother and I came into an inheritance, and we want to do something with it to improve on what we have."

"And has your brother reached his age of majority? I'm asking as—"

"My brother turned twenty-one this past month," said Matthew, with his mind going immediately to Prudence Cherrytart and her ability to make convincing amendments to documents.

Availed of this new information, Pawkets regretted having downplayed the property earlier, made a mental promise to himself never to judge a book by its cover again, and, with an officious smile, said, "We'll take my carriage."

The shop was, indeed, large—much larger than Matthew had anticipated. He put his mind to deciding where things might go, based on his memories of Mrs. Retch's shop. From that alone, it was more than enough.

"Shall we look upstairs?" asked Pawkets.

"Upstairs?" said Matthew, who, having been narrowly concerned with the needs of his business, had forgotten the entire building was being sold.

"Yes. The family quarters."

As pleased as he was with the shop itself, the apartment on the second story flabbergasted Matthew. Though all on one floor, it offered nearly double the space of the house the Cratchits were currently renting.

"Twenty guineas, then," said Matthew.

"I know I may have …"

"Twenty guineas!" said Matthew in the manner of a man not to be toyed with.

"Yes, of course," said Pawkets, straightening his back. Nervously, the orange realtor rubbed his cheek with the back of his hand. "Um … aw … You do say your brother is twenty-one?"

"Yes, he is. We'll be at your office at nine tomorrow, with the money and proof of his age."

Matthew was relieved to find Peter at home and not providing sport for the boys at the warehouse. The two then rifled through Peter's meager possessions to disgorge his baptismal certificate from beneath his well-thumbed and weighty collection of naughty postcards and, armed with the holy document, headed out to the Cherrytart residence.

"The trick with something as old as this," said Prudence, "is to match the ink, see? See how it's faded a bit? Not precisely black no more, is it? So I mixes in a spot of old tea …"

She eyedropped a few drops from a teapot to the inkwell on the table, stirred it with the nib of her dip-pen, and drew a stroke on a scrap of paper. She blew on it to dry it and compared the result to a line on Peter's certificate. She then added a few more drops before repeating the process.

"That'll do nicely," she said. "I don't as often make numbers smaller as makes them bigger, but I'll have a go."

She then, almost magically, in a matter of seconds, changed the year of Peter's birth from 1847 to 1846. Then she went over the rest of the certificate, giving the other sixes a tiny serif on top to look more like the one she had created in the year. After ensuring the ink was dry, she offered her finished work up for inspection.

Matthew took it, held it up to his eye nearly close enough to touch his nose, and said, "Amazing!" He grinned at Peter. "Congratulations. You've come of age."

"Really?" said Peter, and he reveled in the heightened respect he felt he must now be getting from Prudence and Priscilla.

"Dog's Cocked Leg for a pint to celebrate?" asked Prudence, running a finger up Peter's lapel.

Matthew immediately recalled the last time Peter had treated the Cherrytart sisters to drinks, but the supercilious smirk on Peter's face told him his brother's recollection was less crystallized—likely because the insult had not been to his own purse.

"I've got things to do, but you go ahead," Matthew said. "Here's half a crown. Oh. And try not to think about Countess Oleander."

"Why the devil would I think about her?" asked Peter as the two girls each took one of his arms.

Matthew arrived home just as Lucy was finishing her supper.

"Sorry," she said. "I couldn't wait any longer. Where's Peter?"

"He'll be along soon."

Thirty minutes later, Peter walked through the door.

"You were right," he said, his cheeks noticeably devoid of lipstick. "I do have to stop thinking about the countess."

CHAPTER 54

"Remember," said Matthew the next morning, "you're twenty-one."

"Do you think I'm a complete idiot?" said Peter indignantly.

"Of course not. There's still a lot about you that's not done yet."

"Right," said Peter with a terse nod. "And don't forget that, my good man."

The two entered the establishment of M. T. Pawkets & Associates, Claims Agents, where Mr. Pawkets was enjoying an early-morning sherry to whet his appetite for his midmorning snack.

"You have the money?" he asked.

"Yes sir," said Matthew. "Right here. Twenty-one pounds."

"Yes, I am," said Peter proudly.

"You are what?" asked Pawkets.

"Twenty-one," said Peter. Then he thought back on what had been said and added, "Years, not pounds."

Matthew offered an expression to suggest patience was required in dealing with his brother to prevent the taxing of one's sanity.

"Fully competent, is he?" asked the claims agent.

"With a bit of minding," said Matthew.

"I'm good at most things," said Peter, speculatively and by way of enlargement, "but there's still a lot about me that's not done yet." Quite self-satisfied in this statement, he resumed smirking the smirk of the superior.

Pawkets opened his mouth in preparation to say something but thought a moment and closed it again, then opened it again, thought another moment, closed it yet again, and finally said, "That's all quite satisfactory … given the circumstances … In light of … Sign here."

Peter signed. Matthew showed Peter's baptismal certificate. Pawkets perused it and nodded. Matthew counted out twenty-one gold sovereigns and accepted the deed and the keys to the building. Pawkets shook Matthew's hand and Peter's hand.

And through it all, Peter persisted in smiling vacuously with the utmost of confidence.

Matthew led their way back to where they'd stowed their rat wagon. "Everyone makes such a fuss over being twenty-one," said Peter, "but it's really not so difficult."

"Some men have greatness thrust upon them, and others just get in its way."

"Quite so, my good man!"

They made their way through the day without much dialogue. When not thumping rats to death, Peter put his mind to differentiating the subtle nuances of experience felt by a man of twenty-one from the less well refined sensations felt by a boy of twenty years, eleven months, and thirty-one days. It was a challenging exercise, for every time he thought he'd hit on precisely the defining feeling of being twenty-one, he recalled having felt that way when he was only twenty and so had to admit that that wasn't it at all but was content to further his investigation into the signpost qualities and milestone sensations of his advancing maturity.

This worked well for Matthew, since he had his own concerns to occupy his mind. Foremost was the problem of wresting Mrs. Retch free from the clutches of Rankin, Fowle, O'Durr, and Gazpayne: Solicitors and Barristers at Law. Of course, he considered arranging to have the three remaining partners tossed from the top of the Tower of London, but he sensed that would be seen as too much of a coincidence to pass without some sort of further investigation, which would probably prove problematic.

He put lengthy consideration to the idea of some sort of scandal being discovered or manufactured—the disgrace of which would lead to the professional demise of the trio and the subsequent release of Mrs. Retch and all the other Retchs currently within the grasp of the grasping lawyers.

But that wouldn't do. Matthew had learned enough of the ways of the world to know that men like Rankin, Fowle, and O'Durr were above most of the law and that what little law they were not above they could manipulate to get out from under, and all manner of bad behavior once revealed, that would be enough to unseat a bishop, a banker, or the Lord of the Admiralty, would only prove to those empowered to empower the likes of Rankin, Fowle, and O'Durr that Rankin, Fowle, and O'Durr were fellows of the right kidney—as the saying goes—and only serve to cement their reputation more solidly among their peers.

In frustration, he reconsidered what Cherrytart had done to rid the world of Gazpayne. But he could not get past his misgivings over sending lawyers soaring through the skies above the city. Regardless of how appealing it might appear on the surface, it still seemed to Matthew an unwise habit to espouse. Then it came to him when he recalled the note Cherrytart had had forged and slid into the clerk's pocket—the one designed to cast suspicion on the two and to suggest a motive for one killing the other.

"That's it!" said Matthew out loud.

"What's it?" asked Peter, roused from reverie.

"I just need to get Rankin, Fowle, and O'Durr having at each other."

"How're you going to do that?"

"I don't know yet. But I'll think of something."

And think he did.

But to no avail.

Matthew let Peter deliver the day's take to Squidge while he headed home to get supper for the boys in the warehouse. On his way, a strange feeling came over him: a strange wanting to take off all his clothes and walk about with nothing on. At first, he assumed it was due to the unusual warmth of the day, and—there being no one about to see—he took off his jacket in deference to that. But the feeling persisted and even grew stronger.

Suddenly he felt a fright.

"What in blazes is Lucy doing?" he said aloud to the no one that was about and only then realized that the reason why there wasn't a soul about to hear was that everyone was indoors and naked.

He ran home but found the front door locked. He pounded on it.

"Just a minute," shouted Lucy from within.

Some while later, he heard the lock being turned, and the door opened to reveal his brightly blushing sister standing before him with the collar of her dress unfastened behind her neck. She was shorter than usual, too, but before he could question that, a wave of embarrassment swept over him and he was overcome with a need to get himself inside and hide from staring eyes.

He lurched forward. Lucy stepped backward in fright and reached to her throat to secure her dress in place.

"What have you been doing?" he asked.

"Nothing," said Lucy, paralyzed with shame.

Matthew was flustered, but it soon came to him what was needed.

"Go to Tim and get him calmed."

Lucy didn't move.

"What are you waiting for?" asked Matthew, struggling to settle himself down and out of the painful embarrassment engulfing him.

"Turn around," said Lucy with shy insistence. "Turn around and don't look at me."

He took a deep breath and did as requested. He heard nothing and glanced to where Lucy had been, but she was gone. Then he looked to Tiny Tim and saw her on her knees beside him. Her feet were bare, and the back of her dress was open to reveal she had nothing on beneath it.

Shock ran through him. He turned his eyes away and fought to calm the riot of emotions lurching and seething within him.

It took some time, but the huge accusing walls of embarrassment crumbled suddenly, and Matthew had to chuckle with relief. He thought to look to Lucy but stopped himself and asked, "Can I turn around yet?"

"Just a moment," said Lucy, while she struggled with the buttons behind her spine.

"What was all that about?" he asked.

"I just fancied going about with nothing on while I was by myself. Sorry, but it's something I like to do now and then."

"What about our Tim?"

"He keeps his eyes shut."

"That's not what I mean. You've got the whole neighborhood going about without clothes."

"I don't!" said Lucy mortified, and Tiny Tim sent out another shock of embarrassment.

"It's all right! It's all right!" said Matthew. "They're all indoors."

Lucy put her mind again to Tiny Tim but a short while later asked, "How do you know, then? If they're all inside, I mean."

"I felt like stripping off myself all the way home. Everyone else must have felt it too."

"Oh!" She let loose a giggle. "Sorry."

Matthew had to laugh at the thought of his neighbors all succumbing to the naughty joy of going about in the nude. Then his thoughts turned to his sister, but only for an instant, since the danger of holding on to that image was immediately apparent.

"You got the boys' supper ready?" he asked.

"It's in the kitchen."

He retrieved the meal and returned again into the street. All about, people were peeking out their front doors, quietly assessing what little was happening. The shyness of the place was palpable, as everyone had to know whether everyone else was aware of what they'd been doing behind closed doors.

"God bless us, every one!" murmured Matthew, and he shook his head in amazement over Tiny Tim's mystical power.

BOOK 2

CHAPTER 55

I n the years that followed, Matthew rose to prominence in a Great Britain, reaching her zenith of greatness. The name Cratchit was known to many but seldom spoken, as Matthew knew real power is in influence, and his influence—being entirely due to the unique power of Tiny Tim—would not stand up to scrutiny. For this reason, he contented himself first with wealth and then with power, but he avoided fame for as long as he could.

Over the years, to achieve his goals, he needed the help of Lucy more and more. But, while Lucy greatly enjoyed the better life their collaboration made possible, in her blossoming youth, she longed for a knight-in-shining-armor to sweep her off her feet and carry her away; someone with whom she could live happily ever after—or at least thrash out a thrilling honeymoon.

Through their unique connection made possible by Tiny Tim, Matthew became aware of his sister's longing and put his pragmatic mind to the problem. He'd had sufficient experience solving problems to know that if one isn't careful the solution of one problem will be the spawn of another, so he lined up the elements of this problem and considered them one by one to ensure its solution would be satisfying but seedless.

Luckily, Lucy found all the local men unappealing. This Matthew appreciated, as he could see that having a lout constantly about the house would complicate matters. But Lucy's idea of ideal matrimonial bliss pivoted on two hinges and two hinges only: her very unrealistic readings from romantic novels and her very real desire for *it*. From this, Matthew concluded her choice of a husband should be someone noble, virile, and dashing—but only in small doses and not someone who lingered around long enough to spoil the illusion or get in the way.

In most countries, the hope of finding such a man might be a mere fancy fraught with enormous difficulty, but England had built her history upon men precisely of this kind. And they were in abundance—the officers of the Royal Navy.

So, as a treat for her eighteenth birthday, Matthew took Lucy on a short vacation to Dartmouth with the intention she should select a buffoon in blue to be her beau from among the cadets at HMS *Britannia*. Of course, he didn't tell her of his intention, knowing full well nothing tarnishes the joy of a serendipitous discovery more than knowing it was planned in advance.

This almost scuttled Matthew's scheme in the offing, for on the day of the excursion, Lucy announced she had no interest in visiting the naval academy, as all things military bored her. Matthew saved the situation only by telling her the academy was on the way to where the best restaurants were and it would be a shame not to see the famous stately building, having come all this way.

For the first hour after their arrival, Matthew thought the whole idea might be meritless after all, for while Lucy was quite pretty enough to cause an erotic stir among the young cadets strolling about the grounds, there wasn't a specimen of manhood among the mix upon whom Lucy would look twice. Indeed, most were sons of the aristocracy and suffered much the same set of close-bred inherited traits as their sisters who dominated the kennel club.

But then he appeared! Tall and broad shouldered, with wavy blond hair and piercing blue eyes, descending the front steps of the academy as if he commanded all he perceived.

Matthew felt Lucy's grip tighten on his arm when the Teutonic god caught her attention.

"I say, Captain?" she called out.

The fellow looked about and, seeing Lucy waving to him, smiled and swaggered toward them on a pair of powerful sea legs the thighs of which filled his white trousers with surging muscle.

"I say, Captain," said Lucy again. "Can you settle an argument? My *brother* here says Walter Raleigh was the greatest British officer, and I say it was Francis Drake. What do you say?"

The young man's mouth opened, but nothing came out. He shook his head twice and said, "I … I … I'm n … n … not a c … c … captain … I'm a s … s … subl … l … lieu … t … t … tenant."

"Crikey," thought Matthew, thinking his one strong candidate for Lucy's love interest had just broadsided himself in a cannonade of his own consonants.

"My name's Lucy. Lucy Cratchit," said Lucy as if she hadn't noticed the sublieutenant's vocal turmoil. "And this is my brother, Matthew."

"Y … Y … Your sss … s … servant, M … M … Miss," said the struggling sailor. He then extracted a card from his side pocket and handed it to her.

Matthew read over Lucy's shoulder:

> Miles Odysseus Trippingly
> Fellow of the Royal Geographical Society

"What a charming name!" said Lucy.

Trippingly grinned with triumph, nodded, but said nothing.

"Why are you in the navy, then?" asked Matthew.

"M … m … maps. I m … m … make m … m … maps."

"Fascinating!" said Lucy, with one protracted outward breath. "I've always wanted to know how maps are made. You must tell me all about it. Are you free for tea?"

The question quite flustered poor Trippingly, since he was unaccustomed to pretty girls finding his admission of his passion serving as the inspiration for continued conversation. (Indeed, until then, his usual experience had been that the words "I m … m … make m … m … maps" had represented the defining end of countless exceedingly brief relationships.)

Matthew took hold of the reins of the conversation to bridge the awkward silence. "Yes. Wherever you want. My treat. Unless, of course, you can't …"

"I c … c … can," blurted out Trippingly.

Lucy took Trippingly's arm in hers and bade him lead the way. As they walked, she bombarded him with questions he could mercifully answer monosyllabically. And, while many shallower-souled girls might pass up a stammering cartographer in favor of someone displaying characteristics more like the cliché swashbuckler, Lucy actually found Trippingly's propensity to listen with rapt attention to her every word greatly appealing. She lost herself in his sky-blue eyes and spoke on and on and on.

And on.

Trippingly hung on every word. Within a half an hour, he'd mapped out, in his mind, every feature of her face in greater detail than Captain Cook himself would have demanded. To him (Trippingly, not Cook) she was a paradisiacal island of pure loveliness in an ocean of interminable plainness.

Matthew could not have been more pleased. Being the caterpillarist he was, however, he could not resist considering the potential opportunities of having a naval officer for a brother-in-law. What things could be brought back from far-off lands? What wants would sailors have that could be satisfied for a fee? What needs would the navy have that could be supplied?

Over the preceding couple of years, Tiny Tim's range of influence had expanded to cover a good portion of the Good Old City, so Matthew knew he could easily keep the admiralty thinking nice thoughts about Trippingly and, thus, orchestrate a profitable career for him.

But teatime came all too quickly to an end, as teatime often does when the company is enjoyable. Addresses were exchanged with promises to write.

Matthew escorted Lucy back to their hotel.

"So, what did you learn about making maps?" he asked.

"Shut up," she said with all the irritation one can feel while floating on one's anticipation of amorous perfection.

CHAPTER 56

While Matthew needed Lucy's help more and more over the years, he needed Peter's less and less. First, he hired two boys who owed their freedom to Squidge's beneficence and trained them in the refined techniques of the catching of rats—and in the refined techniques of controlling Peter while letting him believe he was in charge. These two plus Peter proved to be a productive team, just as Matthew had hoped, and so he extricated himself from the day-to-day operation of that part of his business.

By the time Matthew reached his twenty-first birthday, however, Peter had become something of an embarrassment—or, rather, more of an embarrassment than Matthew could continue to tolerate. Matthew's business holdings had grown considerably. He owned no enterprise in the legal sense but controlled the pie shop Lucy ran in cooperation with Mrs. Retch, along with taking a one-fourth share of Mrs. Retch's profits from her own bakery. He had become Eliphaz Dropping's de facto partner with a view to the master rat catcher retiring into silent partnership upon Matthew's rising to his majority. Matthew—with the help of Tiny Tim—had convinced Thaddeus Squidge to take him into his inner circle, where he impressed his fellow inner-circlers with his intelligence, intuition, and uncanny luck. He sold bittering agent to Belcher's Brewery, rat hides (as Tibetan dwarf antelope skin) to a glove maker, and rat hair (mixed with horse hair) to an upholstery shop.

In the role of unofficial partner, he expanded Dropping's business manifold by driving competitors into insolvency and then absorbing them at auction. As a key member of Squidge's inner circle, he oversaw all buying, selling, and maintenance for Squidge's stables of horses, plus he controlled under Squidge's banner one-third of the flower wholesalers and the docks where the flowers arrived daily. And independently of Dropping, Squidge, and anyone else, he earned enormous gratuities from stockbrokers and commodities traders for his perspicacious insights into, and prescience of, market movements.

As has been well displayed in his activities reported thus far, Matthew had something of a natural audacity. And as time progressed, he learned more and more about how to temper this audacity in various ways. Sometimes he would be the strongman at the head of an army of vicious berserkers, yet at other times the timid negotiator who appeared to give away far too much. But most often, he never appeared to be involved at all while things miraculously transpired as he said they would.

Peter, on the other hand, showed less and less desire to temper his manner of approach to the world, despite repeated reminders that his success in nearly everything was founded on his being his brother's brother and the brother of his brother's brother. Since his artificial rising to his majority, he'd taken to addressing everyone as "my good man" and proffering paternal advice that was universally unwanted and unasked for—habits that were universally unappealing.

He could, however, do as he was told and served well enough as a runner of errands and watcher of workers. But in reality, the only value Matthew had in keeping Peter in place was to sign legal documents and assume legal ownership of and responsibility for the Cratchit assets for the three years until Matthew reached his twenty-first birthday, when everything was signed over to him.

As the ink dried on the various legal and corporate documents, Matthew put his long-thought-out plan into action.

Eliphaz Dropping had always assumed he would simply continue living above the offices of the business that bore his name but would stop after his retirement, coming downstairs at seven every morning to manage affairs. After a celebratory supper at the Cratchit residence, however, he and his wife became enamored of the idea of moving to the Falkland Islands.

"My husband the lieutenant commander," said Lucy, "tells me it's quite beautiful. He always makes it a point to stop in when he's sailing about the Atlantic."

She went on to describe the islands in precisely the same words—but with far less expenditure of time—as Miles had used to describe the fjords of Norway, the beaches of Bermuda, the palm trees of Honduras, and the view from atop the Pyrenees, which had convinced her that, should a place exist that combined all these features, it would be paradise on earth. At great length, she spoke of rainbow-colored shimmering fish, rainbow-colored sparkling sands, rainbow-colored iridescent butterflies and sunsets the color of rainbow-colored flowers.

Lucy sighed at the thought of it. Mrs. Dropping sighed at the thought of it. Peter and Matthew sighed at the thought of it. Eliphaz took a deep breath, held it, released it, and sighed at the thought of waking up each morning without having a rat in the world to care a rat's nether parts about.

So it was that the Droppings set sail for the Falklands a fortnight later, along with three prize sheep, six stowaways disguised as sheep, and twelve paying passengers who extolled the virtues of the islands in much the same terms as Lucy had used to describe them on the night of their supper.

Peter moved into residence in the vacated Dropping apartment. Despite his initial hesitance over making the move, once Matthew arranged to have the place redecorated in the style allegedly preferred by Turkish sultans, with draperies of red satin and upholsteries of red velvet, all trimmed in gold lace, the prospect appealed to the now-independent Peter, who could easily see himself as a sheik sort of bloke from *The Arabian Nights*. He purchased long satin robes decorated with stylized sun faces and moon faces and various occult symbols, and took up smoking perique soaked in chartreuse from a hookah, but abandoned the habit when he found he cared rather less for the lingering aroma and the rampant nausea than he'd anticipated.

In the early days of Peter's living in singular bliss, Prudence and Priscilla Cherrytart came to visit him occasionally and brought friends who then visited frequently. This society grew in number, and Peter was thrilled to be the hub of a vast network of feminine companions. Soon it became usual that he seldom went out, seldom had any money, but seldom wanted for a different life than the one into which he had fallen.

Thus was completed the first part of Matthew's long-thought-out plan.

CHAPTER 57

The second portion of Matthew's long-thought-out plan involved much greater risk and required much greater skill in execution.

Squidge had long provided carriage services to the ambassadorial staffs of several minor nations that had their embassies in the Good Old City. The appeal he presented to these functionaries was in his reputation for discretion, in the willingness and ability of his drivers to become bodyguards when called upon to do so, and—perhaps oddly—in that Squidge reminded these foreigners of the rulers of the countries from which they came.

While Matthew managed the mundane aspects of running Squidge's carriages, it came to his attention the young wife of one aging military attaché from a small landlocked principality friendly to Great Britain was in the habit of instructing her driver to detour to a gentleman's club frequented by members of Parliament, where she would stop briefly to take on board a certain top-hatted influential gentleman who would share with her an hour-long ride through Hyde Park with the carriage curtains drawn.

"What's it to do with me?" said Squidge when Matthew mentioned it as the two sat sipping single malt that had lost its way on its trek down from Scotland.

"It's the oldest trick in the book," said Matthew wearily, as if his acquaintance with the book had been long, intimate, and boring. "Everything looks to the chap who's going for the rides like the lady's only drawing pictures in the margins, when what's really going on is her husband's put her up to it to get national secrets out of him."

"I still don't see what it's got to do with me."

"Well, if they ever got caught," said Matthew in a tone to suggest it didn't matter to him one way or another, "the Yard would be around here asking what your drivers know about it."

"Right," said Squidge, who had little desire to have representatives of Scotland Yard visiting for any reason. "What would you have me do, then?"

"Me? I hadn't really thought about it. Hm. Since you ask, I might suggest you set up another carriage house, just for this kind of business and under a different name."

"But they'd still know it belongs to me."

"True," said Matthew, as if this were a disappointing obstacle, but he suddenly erupted with enthusiasm. "But what if you didn't own it yourself? Say someone else was the official owner but you were a partner with a ninety percent share of the profits. Then the owner would be the one asked all the questions, while you were only an investor who didn't know anything about the day-to-day." He snapped his fingers. "And as I say this, it occurs to me you're already paying me about ten percent to manage this end of the business, so—a couple of signatures on the proper papers, and everything goes on as usual. No need for a separate company at all."

"With me out from under should anything go skew whiff."

"Exactly," said Matthew.

"Yeah, I do rather like it," said Squidge, and he thrust his jaw forward to massage it between thumb and fingers. "Had me share of sleepless nights on account of this and that already, I has—don't need no aggro if some burke in high places gets caught with his buttons undone in one of my carriages."

"No sir, you don't."

"And what's it matter if I pays you for running things or you pays yourself? Same nicker, different pocket is all."

"Exactly."

Squidge brought both hands up, interlaced his fingers and began tapping the end of his nose with his knuckles. Matthew could hear the wheels turning, as the saying goes, but shifted his attention to his fingernails, which were due for a trimming.

"In fact," said Squidge, raising the ends of his eyebrows like saber blades, "I could do this with all my businesses, then I'm outside it all no matter what."

"That does make sense," said Matthew, as if they were discussing a point of philosophy.

Squidge lunged forward in his chair. "That all you can say when I'm offering you ten percent of everything?"

"Me?" said Matthew, gasping with joy. "Mr. Squidge, this is …!" Then he sagged and said with a sigh, "No. This won't work."

"Now you look 'ere," said Squidge, spearing a twisted finger in Matthew's direction. "If you think you can squeeze me for more …"

"No, no, no," said Matthew, raising both hands before his face. "It's nothing to do with the money. Don't you see it'd look suspicious? Signing the dray-and-carriage business over to me makes sense since I've been running things awhile and everyone knows it. But if I took over everything, it would get the wrong people asking questions."

"Oh, ah?" said Squidge, squinting.

"The idea's still good, but instead of putting it all to me, divide your holdings among the dozen or so chaps you've got seeing to this and that. Then if there's a problem in any one business, nothing else is affected."

"'Cuz it's all owned by different blokes."

"Exactly," said Matthew. "No investigation goes far 'cuz nothing links anything to anything else."

Squidge rocked back on his chair and wagged the previously spearpoint finger at Matthew. "Oh, you are the crafty one, Cratchit. And you're thinking of your future. Most would've taken the lot and kept quiet till it all blew up, but you—you sees one percent of fifty years' take is better than ten percent of one, so it pays to keep things going proper." He winked. "I always got a good sense off you. And I's seldom wrong."

Four days later, Squidge called to order a meeting at his attorney's office. Matthew sat on one side of the attorney, Wordsworth Moore, and Squidge sat on the other. Opposite sat Squidge's brother-in-law, Brutus Kneebreak, who fulfilled his obligations early on in the proceedings and slept through most of the rest. Together they worked through the stack of documents authored by Moore—with Matthew's helpful advice. Squidge signed and signed and signed, and Matthew signed and signed and signed. Squidge initialed here and initialed there. Matthew initialed here, here, and here; and there, there, and there.

To the world of commerce, Squidge then appeared to be no more than an investor, fully protected from any legal responsibility for what occurred within any one of his companies by a thick wall of ink and paper. For this to work, Matthew was made legally responsible for several functions within Squidge's organization, the least of which was full ownership of the carriage company.

With all this accomplished, the sixteen other key men of Squidge's inner circle were admitted, one at a time, into the lawyer's office to sign papers making them the official proprietors of one each of the remaining sixteen businesses that were all financed by Kneebreak Investors Consortium [President and Chairman of the Board: A. Brutus Kneebreak; Vice President: Thaddeus Squidge; Treasurer: Matthew Cratchit].

Thus, Matthew consolidated his position in the grand hierarchy of a vast organization through which large sums of money flowed. One might think—knowing Matthew's lighthouse beacon through all this was the goal of being as rich as Uncle Ebenezer—he would abuse his position as treasurer to channel funds in directions other than those his share-ownership would dictate. But that was not the case. Matthew was meticulous in seeing that everything was divided up properly, down to the last farthing, and awarded to the people to whom it was legally entitled. Even when profits arrived through unconventional means that could not appear in their unvarnished form in the books (such as the sale of rat corpses to the crematory) and had to be justified in fanciful ways through one of the other businesses (such as the reporting of carriage rides provided to imaginary riders) the owner of the business, through which those profits entered the organization, would receive a gift from Mr. Squidge of an exactly appropriate value.

Matthew bode his time. He built himself a reputation of trust and trustworthiness, both with Squidge and with all the other men who managed the affairs of the great leviathan.

And he gathered around himself those he could trust to his own ends.

Mr. Cherrytart became his runner of errands and deliverer of messages. And since Cherrytart now represented an outwardly respectable enterprise, Matthew took the big man in tow to where respectable men avail themselves of the tonsorial and sartorial arts so—a haircut and some business suits later—Cherrytart was able to cut a quite respectable figure when out and about doing Matthew's bidding.

Prudence became Matthew's keeper of records; and Priscilla, his receptionist. The inseparable sisters proved invaluable in ways Matthew—being a young, healthy, and imaginative male—had imagined but not actually expected. Gentlemen entering the offices of the carriage house to hire future services, or to complain of past ones, were treated to treatment far better than they could hope to receive in any other carriage house and always left greatly satisfied in their undying loyalty to the Cratchit Carriage Company.

Furthermore, the two girls had a keen sense of when Matthew was growing overworked, frustrated, or constrained within his being, and knew precisely when to pry him from his work and offer him refreshing distractions that never failed to bring him back to his well-centered self.

And—what Matthew had not anticipated at all between the two—they had precise mental pictures of every street and every corner and every place of entertainment in the Good Old City, which made them enormously helpful to the dispatcher when planning out the most efficient routes for important clients who promised much repeat business, and the least efficient routes for visitors to the city who would be paying only once for services.

Mrs. Retch was another benefactor of Matthew's rise to power. After Matthew had freed her from her bonds of financial obligation to Rankin, Fowle, O'Durr, and Gazpayne: Solicitors and Barristers at Law, she gratefully agreed to allow Lucy to hire two of her girls to run the shop under the Cratchit residence and to work one day a week there, herself, to ensure all was being done as well as it might be. In return for that, Matthew looked after provisioning both shops with amazing economy.

But while Mrs. Retch was more than happy with her newfound freedom and added wealth, she could not believe her luck when Matthew awarded her 25 percent ownership of Cratchit Corn and Granary Products when he established the firm. Over time, several pie shops and bakeries had failed with metronomic regularity for a variety of strange and unrelated reasons. Matthew had been quick to buy out mortgages on the brink of foreclosure or scoop up the properties at auction. Some he turned to alternate purposes after removing all the valuable equipment, but most he revitalized with the help of Mrs. Retch—hence the junior partnership in the umbrella company.

All this and much more became the foundation of Matthew's formidable financial edifice.

CHAPTER 58

At this point, in all likelihood, you're wondering how it is that Matthew managed to free Mrs. Retch from the clutches of Rankin, Fowle, O'Durr, and Gazpayne: Solicitors and Barristers at Law, to make possible all that was just revealed in the penultimate and antepenultimate paragraphs of the previous chapter. It was, in fact, a long and tedious process for the most part, which would be quite unsatisfying both in the writing and in the reading, so I will distill the events down to the heavy residuum of those bearing greatest importance and allow you to deduce the lost vapors from your knowledge of Matthew's methods.

For about three months after Matthew purchased the Smallbits shop and residence, the Cratchits were engaged in remodeling the place in preparation for the opening of Lucy's pie shop. This was something of a strain, since the cost of the property itself had taken nearly all of Matthew's savings. But with some help from Cherrytart and Co. in the acquisition of materials, the work was accomplished, and all was in readiness.

Meanwhile, rumors that Messrs. Rankin, Fowle, and O'Durr were having internal disputes over something had gained greater and greater currency about the city. Though no one knew what that something might be, the contents of the bloodstained note that had been found on the clerk in the swallowtail coat of a beautiful green was revealed to the press by the police. This led to the speculation one or more of the partners was engaged in some activity not in the best interest of the others.

But what that might be, no one could guess.

Suddenly, about a week after the work on Lucy's pie shop was completed, the building housing Rankin, Fowle, O'Durr, and Gazpayne: Solicitors and Barristers at Law, exploded, killing everyone who worked there and destroying all records, files, and documents kept in its various offices.

Or nearly everyone and nearly all the records.

Upon further investigation, it was discovered the junior partner, Seamus O'Durr, was visiting relatives in Ireland when the explosion occurred, making him the sole survivor of the firm after the mysterious tragedy. It appeared everything would fall to him—everything being a collection of business interests that would render him one of the most powerful men in the Good Old City.

Two days later, however, the shattered remains of a partially burned oaken filing cabinet were found on the roof of a nearby post office building when an employee went up to feed the carrier pigeons. When the contents were sorted through, it was discovered the cabinet was the property of Seamus O'Durr, and within said contents was one journal revealing he had arranged for seven kegs of gunpowder, disguised as barrels of Ramsbottom Bitter, and seven boxes of cigars to be delivered to the basement of the building. Folded in half and inserted inside the journal was a rough draft of a letter announcing to the staff of the Records Department—which was soon determined to have been located in the basement—that the ale and cigars were given in recognition of outstanding work and should be enjoyed freely and by all.

Further study of other documents found in the cabinet disclosed that O'Durr had been a longstanding member of a secret rebel organization committed to the downfall of the British Empire and to home rule for Ireland. Not only had he arranged for the destruction of his own law firm when suspicions were being leveled against him, but he had also, years earlier, orchestrated the defeat of the British forces at the Battle of Cleavage Rift and had brought about the ruination of a gunpowder factory in Somerset, causing a delay in the deployment of HMS *Consternation* to the Bay of Bengal.

Had it not been for a bizarre twist of fate that saved the damning evidence from destruction in the flames, O'Durr would have gotten away with his heinous plot and gone on to hatch heinous plots of ever-escalating heinousness. He was hunted down, captured in a ladies' boarding house in Dublin while shaving his legs, tried for treason, and sentenced to drawing and quartering, only to have that sentence commuted to death by firing squad owing to it being easier to arrange on short notice.

There followed a crackdown on Irish organizations in the Good Old City, along with many arrests and many closures of facilities named in the documents. Not surprisingly, Thaddeus Squidge turned much of this to profit by making his services available to those inconvenienced by the sudden disappearance of those taken into custody.

And so it was Mrs. Retch recovered full ownership of her bakery.

But she was not the only one. Businesses and private individuals all over the city were freed from the powers of attorney and other legal instruments held by the now extinct firm of Rankin, Fowle, O'Durr, and Gazpayne: Solicitors and Barristers at Law. When the full measure of it was made public, the most forward-thinking members of Parliament grew concerned this sudden influx of freed capital would result in galloping inflation, but quite miraculously, all this was followed shortly after by the Great Panic of 1873, which drove the rest of the world deep into recession while bringing the British economy back into balance as God intended it to be.

Of course, Mrs. Retch was as aware of the rumors of internal strife within Rankin, Fowle, O'Durr, and Gazpayne: Solicitors and Barristers at Law as anyone else in the Good Old City but was quite stunned when Matthew advised her to withhold payment to her creditors until they were in a better position to press her for it.

"But they'll have me locked up," she said.

"I'm sure they'll threaten to," he said, "when they find out you're behind. But they won't kill the goose that lays the golden eggs. And, from what I hear, they're in such a mess, they don't know upside down from right-side up. It could be years before they get themselves sorted out. In the meantime, you can use that money for other things."

And to that, Matthew had a number of suggestions for investments that all proved profitable beyond all reason when reason is applied to the usual unfolding of events.

All this led her to wonder, after the demise of the firm, just what Matthew knew that he wasn't telling, but she was wise enough to know she didn't want to know, and was equally wise in knowing upon which side her bread was buttered, and that that butter would only get thicker the longer she listened to Matthew.

The crack of the shots fired within the walls of the Tower of London that announced the end of O'Durr was still echoing through the nearby streets when the cheer rose up throughout the whole of the Good Old City. For once, everyone agreed good had triumphed over evil, though what was good and what was evil varied from viewpoint to viewpoint.

The conservative newspapers declared that the once venerable law firm deserved what it got for lowering both its moral standards, as evidenced by the representation of members of the labor class in court, and its spiritual vigilance, apparent from its taking O'Durr into partnership when he clearly wasn't C of E.

The liberal papers stated the always reprehensible law firm deserved what it got for its longstanding policy of hamstringing progress for the sake of profit. As one reporter put it, "Why else would educated jurists be forced to deliberate over trials for months, when the lay public can see right from wrong in five minutes?"

And the socialist weekly averred that the decadent, bourgeois law firm deserved what it got for being a cog in the machine of oppression, and that the bombing would be the first of many that would ultimately bring down the capitalist system to free the workers of the world to work long, hard hours for far nobler reasons than those for which they worked long, hard hours now.

Matthew was not a habitual reader of newspapers, but he took some secret personal pride in seeing an elaborate scheme come to fruition, and so the reading of the journalistic products was something of a treat. And in a more practical vein, he wanted to be certain no one was entertaining doubts about the bizarre events—doubts that might require the tying up of as yet unseen loose ends.

He couldn't decide whether he agreed more with the conservatives or the liberals, since his mind was less geared for ideological than for pragmatic thought. And neither side seemed to say much that was worth anything at all. He did notice the socialist rag insisted on misspelling "caterpillarist," but he knew—from what everyone said about them—the writers and readers of that nonsense were all quite daft, and viewed this editorial carelessness as proof that what everyone said was correct.

CHAPTER 59

That **revenge is** more nutritious to the spirit when it resembles a plowman's lunch more closely than a steamy stew is not something Matthew would have said, but it is something he would have understood. Working as he did alongside men who were too easily propelled into all-consuming, fiery rage, he saw example after example of ill-conceived impulsive reactions leading to regrettable ends. At the very least, the acidic anger brought on by being wronged would eat away at the fellow's insides even after he'd done his worst to the one who'd garnered his ire.

All this served only to reinforce the avenging Cratchit's habits of ensuring nothing could lead back to him when he chose to take action against another, and he would remain calm throughout. And being the intelligent caterpillarist he was, he never took his revenge on anyone for revenge's sake alone; there always had to be some gain beyond mere satisfaction, or it simply wasn't time well spent.

To that—when his rare idle moments took him to remembering the slights and assaults made against him—he would consider the settling of the old scores in ways that would gain him new assets; revenge might be a dish best served up cold, but the chef must be handsomely paid for his efforts.

Once, in just such a rare idle moment, he recalled the time when six young ratters beat Peter and him outside Smuts & Ergot's Granary and stole their rats and their gold sovereign. This sparked the idea of arranging for the competitive rat catchers to lose customers and credibility, such that they would be ripe for Dropping to acquire them. Matthew didn't know for whom the six miscreants worked, but that didn't matter. He had it in mind to own the lion's share of the rat industry, so this one idea became his polestar. That he would eventually find the six and have his revenge was relegated to the realm of secondary, though pleasant, ambitions.

But find them he did.

One day, shortly after his and Lucy's return from their vacation in Dartmouth, he went with Eliphaz Dropping to finalize the takeover of Tobias Walhole's Rodent Abatement. While there, he caught a glimpse of two of the six ruffians. He recognized them, but they seemed not to remember him—being taller, broader, and better dressed. He stayed calm, remained quiet, and left with Dropping without a word or a hint of what he had in mind.

Three days later, all six woke up inside burlap sacks full of Arctic eider duck down, which they discovered—after screaming themselves hoarse to secure their release—were destined for exotic bedding manufacturers in Madras to be made into mattresses for maharajas and maharanis. All six were sick from the aftereffects of some solvent still lingering in their nostrils. All six were sick from the combined effects of the rolling sea and the stench of the bilge. All six were sick from hours of breathing duck dander. And all six, sick though they were, were put to work immediately by the captain of the ship, who didn't care whether they were there by choice or not, since most of his crew were there through no choice of their own, anyway—that being how crews came into being when the industries of the British Empire had work to be done on the high seas and no one wanting to do it.

Whether or not the six miscreants ever got back to England again was something Matthew never thought about. Revenge may be the only insatiable appetite for most people, but he was content knowing his enemies had gotten more than they'd given, and more importantly to him, they didn't know whom they'd gotten it from. Revenge can go both ways, after all.

If he was still feeling at all peckish for further vengeance on the

330 DAVID R. COOMBS

thieving ratters, he determined to satisfy this hunger by helping himself to the Smuts & Ergot Granary. Finding and punishing the six brought back memories of the surly way Cornelius Smuts had treated Peter and him. And he suspected, strongly enough to be nearly certain, Smuts had either arranged the ambush or agreed to tell the six when to attack.

One thought led to another as he and Cherrytart walked home from the docks after watching the duck down–laden ship set sail down the Thames. He was immersed in the process of growing Dropping's ratting empire, but his bakery interests were still limited to the two shops. Until then, he had relied upon subtle manipulation of demand for the various ingredients used in baking, through Tiny Tim's influence, to gain competitive advantages, but he hadn't considered owning a granary.

His still-gliding joy over sending six enemies to India soared to elation when he saw the enormous possibilities to be opened with the plundering of Smuts and Ergot. Ownership of thousands of tons of flour meant thousands of pounds of profit with even small fluctuations in price. And the costs of running the two shops would drop drastically. And why stop at two? He could use the same methods to conquer competition in the baked goods business as he used with ratters. That even made more sense, seeing as the granary would still be a massively expensive purchase even after it was driven into insolvency and the income from dozens of shops would be needed to make the huge investment.

Cherrytart never knew what Matthew was thinking but always sensed when a plan was in the plotting phase—a plan in which he would likely have an entertaining part to play. He was happy, then, to bask quietly in Matthew's radiant satisfaction as they walked in silence back to Lucy's shop. There they had their fill of meat pie, as they always did to celebrate a good day's work.

Cherrytart never asked, though he always wondered, why Matthew never chose the spicy rabbit, since the fame of its excellence had spread to all parts of the Good Old City.

CHAPTER 60

After nearly four years of successive unsuccessful attempts to align the demand for oats, barley, wheat, and rye with what appeared to be the prevailing market conditions, all the great granaries of the city were either poised precipitously on the brink of catastrophe or teetering toward it on the last legs of hope. Share values had plummeted to pennies on the pound, but none wanted to risk buying into an industry on the verge of collapse.

Matthew was not in a position to buy more than one, and being limited to only one, the one he wanted was, of course, Smuts & Ergot. But as we amply have seen, he was not one to leave his fortune to the vagaries of Fortune. If he couldn't own all five granaries outright, he would at least find ways to make all five send something his way.

Thaddeus Squidge was the first to be persuaded to the advantages of the investment. He had already profited enormously from the rapid and radical fluctuations in grain prices, which Matthew had predicted with preternatural precision, so when Wordsworth Moore, his attorney, came to see him with regard to it, the meeting was short but fruitful.

"Cratchit tells me he's gotten Smuts & Ergot," said Moore.

"He seen a doctor about it, then, has he?" asked Squidge, scratching his groin beneath the table.

"Smuts & Ergot is a granary," said Moore dryly. "He purchased it at auction for asset value."

"Oh! Well, I can see that. Seeings as he owns all them pie shops."

"Quite. But it occurs to me you've done well yourself through the rise and fall of corn. Furthermore, you own shares in Belcher's Brewery—who, I will remind you, purchase several thousands of tons of barley annually. If Kneebreak Investors Consortium were to purchase the remaining four granaries—all of which are struggling—it would have a monopoly, and the potential for profit would be beyond imagination."

"Hmm?" said Squidge and he considered the distant frontiers of his own imagination, beyond which wealth was truly hard to imagine.

"I have taken the liberty," said Moore, "of having it determined what such an acquisition would entail, and from that, I have devised a method by which you could bring it all to a sound and rather pleasing resolution."

What followed was the legal and financial equivalent of a conjuror revealing an illusion, and though fascinating for Squidge, who could envision the financial equivalent of making beautiful girls appear out of thin air, it would be quite tedious for those of us with no interest at all in seeing beautiful girls appear out of thin air or the legal and financial equivalents thereof.

For the purposes of our story, though, some changes need to be known. Kneebreak Investors Consortium changed its charter and became Kneebreak Holding Company. The entirety of the nonvoting shares were purchased by Thaddeus Squidge. Of the voting shares, 30 percent went to each of Melchior Belcher (owner of Belcher's Brewery), Wordsworth Moore, and Matthew Cratchit; 2 percent went to A. Brutus Kneebreak, and the remaining 8 percent was divided up evenly among the sixteen junior members of the board. Salaries were paid to the board members commensurate with shares owned. Net profit was dispersed in the form of dividends on nonvoting shares upon the recommendation of the treasurer and ratification by the board.

Officially, Squidge was only an investor with no say in the running of the company; unofficially, Moore echoed all he said, while Kneebreak and the sixteen subordinate members never questioned anything Moore put forward.

Besides the reserves transferred from the investment consortium, the holding company received two large injections of cash. One was from Squidge, who mortgaged everything from the suits of armor passed down through generations of someone's ancestors to his collection of petit point miniatures, to buy his nonvoting shares. The other was from Melchior Belcher to buy his seat on the board. Thus powerfully funded, Kneebreak Holding purchased all the ailing and failing granaries and set about seeing to their revitalization.

Within weeks, the problems that had beset the industry for years vanished miraculously. In the press, Melchior Belcher was lauded as the industrial maven to watch. In Parliament, Wordsworth Moore was considered for honors deemed appropriate for lawyers. In the backrooms of the commodities exchange, Matthew Cratchit was openly derided as a sorcerer but secretly paid exorbitantly for any inkling of an indication of where the winds of wealth would blow next.

As to the extent of Matthew having his revenge upon Cornelius Smuts, things could not have turned out better. Smuts, embittered by the repeated failure of his partner to outguess the whimsy of the marketplace, set sail for South Africa, where he tried his hand at farming aardvarks only to find that all extant theories as to the domestication of the species proved unsatisfactory when scaled up to commercially viable minimums of herd size. He was last seen on the veld, wandering aimlessly among the termite mounds silhouetted against the sunset—a dazed and broken man.

Anthony Ergot, conversely, declared the failure of his granary to be an act of divine will freeing him from the wrong-headed course of commerce to put him on the path of his true destiny. He returned to the rigid religious life of his childhood but then found truth— not within the orthodox faith of his father, but in the teachings of a Transylvanian mystic girl. Together, they established a spiritual retreat on an uninhabited island in the Hebrides, which attracted hundreds of lost and seeking souls. There they celebrated life in ceremonies of dance performed naked atop the windswept hills under the moon—full or otherwise, as the mood struck them. Ergot lived to an exceedingly old age, sired dozens of children by dozens of women, and died a contented man despite being a chronic sufferer of chilblains to his nether regions.

CHAPTER 61

I n March 1881, Lucy's husband, Miles Trippingly, returned from a five-month mapping mission to Madeira and was unexpectedly promoted to captain. From what Lucy was able to glean from her husband's protracted telling of the tale, the admiral in command of the mission commanded he be set ashore on the main island to establish his command post in the hotel on the estate of the principal winery. He then ordered Commander Trippingly to take the three ships of the small fleet to go off and chart the archipelago. And since Miles had managed to sail those three ships around and around the islands for weeks on end without bumping into each other or anything else, and to successfully find his way back to pick up the admiral at the end of it all, the admiral deemed him worthy of a captaincy despite the fact the Madeiras were already well-charted and the expedition achieved nothing of real merit.

To all this Miles swore Lucy to top-secrecy, just as the admiral had sworn him to top-secrecy, since the comings and goings of admirals was a matter of national security and it served no good purpose to have it known the admiralty spent its winters strategizing the defense of the Mediterranean and various sleepy tropical paradises.

Lucy's love of things military ended precisely with her being able to walk through Hyde or Regent's Park arm-in-arm with her tall, handsome husband in his dashing dress uniform when he was home; and to say, "My husband, the commander," in conversation with her friends when he wasn't, so she had no problem at all keeping the mission to Madeira top-secret.

At that period in history, however, Britannia was ruling the waves with such unchallengeable success, captains of the Royal Navy were being killed off at an alarmingly slow rate. This proved a great inconvenience to Lucy, as it meant there was no ship in need of a captain when Miles was promoted, and therefore no reason for him to go away again when she was done enjoying his return. Indeed, he was only one of several captains promoted, for one exemplary service or another, into positions of idleness, so it would be some while before Captain Trippingly would be given a command.

By this time, Lucy had the house above the pie shop all to herself when her husband was abroad. Matthew moved out shortly after assuming his position as treasurer with Kneebreak Holding Company, having purchased a block of townhouses, which he had renovated to suit the requirements of single gentlemen of trade. The largest unit—number 11—he kept for himself while renting out the odd-numbered units to men like himself and keeping the even-numbered units available for friends and associates in temporary need of discreet lodgings.

But Matthew had lunch at Lucy's at least once a week and would stay for a visit after.

"You fancy he's lost weight?" asked Matthew as he and Lucy sat next to each other beside Tiny Tim in the little room set aside for the immobilized Cratchit.

"No, I don't think so, do you? He looks as plump and happy to me as ever."

Matthew sensed his sister wasn't entirely as happy as their waxed and brazen brother. "You don't sound convinced he's all that happy."

"No, Tim's fine. It's Miles and me. I know he gets up to mischief while he's away; I feel him feeling guilty through Tim. But it doesn't seem fair to poke about with questions and such, 'cuz if I didn't have Tim to tell me, I'd never know when he's telling me fibs."

Though Matthew had some sense of what husbands at liberty

might find amusing, he was not about to burden Lucy with possibilities best left unexplored.

"Miles takes his duty as an officer seriously," he said, "so anything he does to bring dishonor on the navy would have him feeling jolly rotten. I'm sure little mistakes that you and I would forget give him no end of shame and embarrassment."

"Oh, I never thought of that. Poor lamb. It must be something awful for him, having to be perfect all the time. Oh, crumbs!"

"What now?"

"Now I feel guilty for keeping our Tim secret from Miles after he's been so honest with me. Bloody heck, it's not fair!" said Lucy. She then composed herself. "It is a bit awkward, though, isn't it? I mean, we grew up with Tim, so we love him, and we did what we had to do. But if I told Miles we had my brother bronzed, it might put him off living here, and I do like him coming home now and then."

"I've noticed," said Matthew, and he patted Lucy's knee. "Best to leave things as they are, my love. Nothing to be gained repairing a clock that tells the right time."

Lucy nodded, and they sat silently for some while. To break the silence, she said, "You did do a good job giving Tim his fresh coat of wax, though."

"Thank you."

"No worries," said Lucy. "Remember before? He didn't much like having people looking at him all queer-like when they thought he was dead. But now they think he's a statue, they're much kinder, and he notices, he does."

"I thought he might. That's why I mixed the brass filings in with the wax. I wasn't sure it would work, but it did turn out rather nice, didn't it? Gives him a pleasant sheen, I'd say."

"You don't think the jewels might be a bit much? I rather like them, but I worry they make him look a bit girlish."

"Not a bit. He looks exactly like the oriental idol in the ornamental garden outside the windows of the Merchant Marine canteen. That's where I got the idea. And why I shaved his head."

"What were you doing in there?"

"What do you think? Ratting," said Matthew, looking back with nostalgia. But he turned his attention back to Tiny Tim and said, "Wasn't half a damn sight more work than I expected, though, getting the robe on him and propping him up into position on the divan."

"Where is it you got the divan?"

"Friend of mine, Mr. Quinn. The chaps who run the Ottoman Empire Embassy wanted to trade it in on a smaller one. They used it for carrying belly dancers on stage for when the ambassador wanted entertaining. But the old ambassador died, and the new one prefers skinnier girls."

"Oh. And why's it all covered in those strange patterns?"

"That's their mystic runes. All those Middle Eastern types cover everything with their sacred writing. Brings them luck, I suppose."

"So you made our Tim into an oriental idol lying on a divan all covered in magic spells? No wonder Miles asked if we're occultists."

"You're saying Miles thinks we come in here to pray to a heathen idol?"

"Yeah, he does," said Lucy, casting her eyes across the battery of red candles that lit the room. "Come to think of it, this does look a bit like a shrine for chatting up evil spirits, doesn't it?"

"I can see that," said Matthew, trying to image what Miles might see in the flickering purple shadows cast across the brazen Tiny Tim. "Upsets him, does it? Miles, I mean."

"No, not a bit. I fancy he's more curious than worried. He told me he'd rather like getting starkers and dancing around under a full moon when it gets warmer. I think being a sailor brings out what's strange in a man, don't you?"

"Couldn't say," said Matthew, concerned his brother-in-law might be a bit of a dark horse. "Say, he isn't making unpleasant requests of you, is he?"

"What? No. Actually, I rather fancy a bit of strange now and then," said Lucy in a fanciful, drifting-away voice.

The ambient emotion slid toward the erotic. Seconds later,

Matthew realized Lucy was entertaining fond memories of strangeness with Miles, but under Tiny Tim's conductive influence, Matthew was thinking of doing the unthinkable with Lucy. Summoning up the will to resist temptation, he opened his mouth to insist they change the subject, but he didn't get the words out.

"I do love Miles," said Lucy, suddenly serious again, and she sighed. "But having him about all the time is a bit much. And," she added in a low murmur, "he never has enough of *it*. Our Tim picks up on it and … you know … then I've got all the women in the neighborhood coming in here to get some rest. It's good for business, but …"

Matthew was prone to irritation when Lucy took to complaining of having Miles around, since he believed the captain was everything his sister wanted in a man and knew—from their unique insights into each other's feelings through the channel of their brother—she was as great an aficionado of *it* as any woman alive. A little gratitude was more the order of the day, and he was about to remind her of this when she said offhandedly, "This is the first free time I've had to spend with poor Tim in days."

That reversed Matthew's attitude in an instant. It was one thing when Miles was too much of a good thing for Lucy, but quite another thing when too much of a good thing for Lucy might become an impediment to Matthew's progress toward greater wealth.

"I'll see what I can do," said Matthew.

"What can you do?" asked Lucy, as if her brother had gone around the bend.

"I don't know yet. But I have friends who have friends. It's the way things get done," said Matthew, and hearing it said out loud gave him a sense of his own power he hadn't gauged clearly before.

Then he rose to leave and, rife with self-satisfaction, said, "Oh, by the way: that pheasant terrine you gave me for lunch was quite excellent! You really outdid yourself this time."

"Oh, I forgot to tell you: we're all out of pheasant. That was rabbit."

CHAPTER 62

Matthew knew the only possibility for getting Captain Trippingly an assignment was for the navy to have a sudden need of his unique talents. It seemed unlikely map-making would ever qualify as an emergency military action, but not being a military man himself, he couldn't be certain. To make matters worse, it seemed to him all the maps of any value must have been made already. No doubt there were places yet uncharted, but if anyone had any reason to go there, they would have gone by then and made maps while they were there.

Beyond making maps, it was difficult to imagine what Miles had to offer. He was classically handsome with towering height and athletic build, and according to Lucy, he was something of a stallion in matters of intimacy. But these traits served naval officers well only in works of fiction and were not nearly so useful in the building of empire as literary audiences may have been led to believe.

There had to be something, though.

With the notable exception of the porcelain convenience—where everyone goes to solve problems—answers were prone to flash into Matthew's mind at the oddest times, in the oddest places, and for the oddest reasons. It was while he was making one of his daily visits to the mercantile exchange that the answer to the Captain Trippingly quandary came to him. He overheard two men arguing about the qualities of flour necessary for the making of sea biscuit, and he realized Miles was perfectly positioned to take command of the supply of bread and baked goods for the navy.

As always, once the idea sparked into existence, the scheme to manifest the outcome unfolded quickly and fully in Matthew's mind. He would convert one of his warehouses to the purpose. (He had purchased all the abandoned warehouses in the vicinity of that first one he and Peter had occupied to avoid the possibility of nosy neighbors, but refitted them to his various needs as those needs arose.) Then he would put Lucy and Mrs. Retch to devising recipes and hiring staff. Finally, between better pricing, better products, and Tiny Tim's tilting the scales in his favor, Matthew would win the sea biscuit contract from the Admiralty. After that, a handshake here and a handshake there, and Captain Trippingly would be traveling all about the British Isles inspecting the storehouses of Her Majesty's navy's ports and shipyards, and arranging massive shipments of goods from Cratchit Corn and Granary Products.

Perfect.

"B … B … But I don't w … w … want to b … b … buy b … b … barrels of b … b … biscuit," said Miles.

"Don't be silly," said Lucy crossly. "You need to do something. You're making yourself miserable moping about here all day with nothing to do."

"N … N … No, I'm n … n … not."

"Yes, you are. I see it every day."

"N … N … No, you d … d … don't."

"Yes, I do," said Lucy firmly, but she then softened her tone. "Don't worry, my love. I understand. I know you're a man of action and you're too brave to admit it's driving you mad not being out at sea doing battle with … with … Who are we at war with?"

"No one, just now," said Matthew.

"I m … m … make m … m … maps," said the dejected captain.

"Of course you do, darling," said Lucy, and try as she might, she could think of nothing to emphasize the grand, heroic importance of that.

"It wouldn't be permanent," said Matthew. "Just until you get a ship of your own."

Miles nodded sadly and, after a long silence, said, "T ... t ... too bad I'm n ... n ... not G ... G ... German."

"Why, on Earth?" asked the aghast Matthew, unable to believe anyone—let alone a military officer—could regret being born British.

"B ... B ... Bismarck is b ... b ... building more sh ... sh ... ships."

Matthew had heard of Bismarck, but beyond the fact of his being German, he knew nothing of the *Reichskanzler* at all. But Matthew being Matthew, he sensed there might be value in learning of the great Teuton.

And learn he did.

Within days of Miles telling him Bismarck was building ships, Matthew realized his plan to sell sea biscuit to the navy would be greatly more profitable if the navy were greatly enlarged. But every nation capable of putting a fleet to sea had taken its turn being thoroughly thrashed by the British navy at least once in the century past, and there was none interested in trying their luck again anytime soon, so there was little enthusiasm, outside the officers of the Royal Navy, to make the Royal Navy any larger than it was.

"You know anything about that German chap, Bismarck?" Matthew asked of Wordsworth Moore—the man most knowledgeable in impractical matters known to Matthew on friendly terms.

"Another upstart nuisance," said Moore with disdain. "First that Garibaldi scoundrel and now Bismarck."

"Oh, yes?"

"Yes, quite! We finish getting Europe settled nicely after all that nonsense with Napoleon, put all the borders back in their proper places, all the kings back on their proper thrones, all the proper politicians back in their proper governments, when along comes Garibaldi and puts together Italy. Why the devil would anyone want to go and do that? Like teaching kittens to waltz."

Moore sighed heavily with exasperation. Matthew nodded with sad empathy completely unfelt.

Moore continued in a tone betraying his fatalistic acceptance of the shortcomings of others. "That's the way it is with these foreigners, though. Can't see their own limitations. Always looking to better themselves. Sad, really." But his irritation rose again. "And now here's your Bismarck gone and done the same damn thing with Germany. What's more, he's even got the nerve to call it an empire! You don't just gather together a ragtag collection of duchies and principalities all speaking the same language and call it an empire!"

"No?"

"No, of course not! You have to march in and take charge. Chop off a few heads to let them know you're not simply fooling about, then you teach the local muck-a-mucks to speak English—not the high-muck-a-mucks, mind you; just the middle-muck-a-mucks—and get them seeing to the riffraff while you enjoy the gin and tonics. That's how you build an empire."

"I see."

"Still," said Moore, softening his energy once again. "Got to give Bismarck his due, I suppose. Trying to organize that lot can't be all cucumber sandwiches."

"No?"

"No. The Romans couldn't even be bothered with them. That tells you something right there."

Matthew had to assume that whatever it was that that told him right there spoke volumes to something, but that something was outside his current concerns, so he simply raised his eyebrows and nodded knowingly.

Moore continued. "But he's come rather late to the game, I'm afraid, your Bismarck. Acquiring nationhood inside Europe these days is rather like getting the sailor suit you wanted as a child for your twenty-first birthday. But he's only just realizing that now. Now that he's got what he thought he wanted, he can see that what he really wanted all along is a global empire like ours. But there's no chance of that—everything worth having's all been snatched up. Unless there's another India out there to be discovered, or another Canada, another Africa … God help us if there's another America!"

"So why's he building a navy?"

"Oh, I suppose there's still something out there not flying someone else's flag. Some scrawny hillock of forgotten land on the backside of nowhere where you could grow a few filberts or raise a few goats. Or he might try to take something off the Belgians or the Portuguese. Might even succeed if we let him."

The sun rose on Matthew's geopolitical understanding, and all was light.

"Would he try to take something from us?"

Moore chuckled. "Do be serious, old boy. We're British."

Matthew laughed too, pretending what he'd said had been meant as a joke. But he had his answer: the Royal Navy wasn't getting any bigger because no one was afraid of the Germans.

And that was something he could change.

CHAPTER 63

"**The point is,**" Matthew said over supper, "these ships cannot be sunk. Any one of them can sail about all day, sinking our old wooden ships, and keep going until he runs out of shot and powder."

"N … N … Nonsense," said Miles. "Th … Th … They w … w … wouldn't d … d … dare."

"I hope you're right," said Matthew doubtfully, with eyes wide and head tilted. "But we know Bismarck isn't building ships to defend Germany from anyone. He wants what we have—"

"Stop it, Matthew," said Lucy with a bang of her spoon on the table. "It's frightening when you talk like that."

"Well, we should be frightened. If we lose the empire, we'll all be poor again."

Though we've seen that Lucy's days of poverty had been relatively pleasant inside Tiny Tim's tranquil aura, she had grown used to having nice things and being able to make whimsical choices and telling people what to do, knowing they'd do it, so the thought of losing all of that was as frightening to her as Matthew said it should be.

One floor beneath them, resting comfortably in his quiet little den, Tiny Tim picked up Miles's irritation and Lucy's agitation.

Soon Matthew felt the first wave of anxiety. In his mind, he heard the words "Bismarck" and "ships" and "unsinkable" underscored with lines of fear, and knew he'd gotten it all right.

Within days, the Good Old City was abuzz with concerns over the rising Germany and its naval aspirations. Parliament debated the demands of the Admiralty—not whether the money should be spent, but where best to spend it first. En masse, engineering students changed their disciplines from bridge building and railway construction to shipbuilding and naval artillery. Steelworks began researching alloys suitable for seawater. Great mills sent out orders to clear fields in India for increased cotton and indigo crops necessary for uniform manufacture. The transport of criminals to Australia was ended as those captured for minor crimes were inducted into service.

And the words "navy" and "modernization" were hardly ever uttered one without the other.

As the months passed, Matthew reveled in the scale of his success. He worked longer and longer hours, keeping atop all his various duties and seeing to the preparation of his baked goods factory. For this, he had no shortage of labor. Years earlier, he'd had one of his warehouses converted to a kind of apartment building to house boys and young men in hiding, into which there was a constant flow of newcomers willing to do whatever was required to keep themselves in food and out of lockup.

When the factory was done and all the equipment installed, Matthew had Mrs. Retch set up schedules to keep the bins stocked with ingredients and oversaw the first deliveries from the granary and the markets. Lucy took charge of all the stages of processes of making and packing sea biscuit, and trained girls to supervise in her stead.

Miles wrote a letter of introduction for Matthew to take to the Admiralty. They saw him out of politeness but immediately awarded him the contract upon tasting his product and hearing his price.

But all this happened amid the ambient anxiety of a growing military threat to the empire. Matthew knew this anxiety for what it was and knew, of course, he was at its root. But that didn't make it any less disturbing for him than it was for anyone else. He was as much subject to Tiny Tim's unfailing influence as the rest of the population.

Atop of this was Matthew's commitment to his work, which had become monumental in its proportion and equally fraught with problems. In time, he found the constant worry too much to bear. But he wasn't ready to return Tiny Tim to tranquility quite yet. He wanted the anxiety to remain pervasive until construction on the ships had gone too far to risk being canceled, and that was several months away.

He fought to tolerate it all. He trained subordinates to take on the more mundane aspects of his work, delegating responsibility as best he could to lighten his load. And when it came time to get Tiny Tim stirring up demand for whatever commodity Matthew was manipulating short-term, he would relish the brief vacation from fear for all it was worth.

But it wasn't enough. Desperate to keep the anxiety going and not be shaken to bits by it, Matthew took to using laudanum in the evenings to guarantee a good night's sleep and offer some reprieve from the tension.

This worked well, at first. The soft landscapes of languorous fluidity stretched out for him nightly to explore at his leisure. One step. Two. How gentle. How numb.

His days grew more productive. After the first month of Cratchit Corn and Granary supplying baked goods to the navy, Matthew had the money to start a philanthropic organization, which he named the Ebenezer Scrooge Memorial Foundation, dedicated to the housing and rehabilitation of young offenders. This he used as an incentive to his army of boys in hiding, offering them admission to the more congenial circumstances the foundation provided to those under its care in exchange for services rendered while living in the cramped and squalid conditions of the warehouse apartments. And besides making the feeding, clothing, housing, and the management and mobilization of his army of boys in hiding much, much easier, it earned Matthew great respect in the community of influential men.

CHAPTER 64

L ord **Dudley Brightwigs** was seated behind his expansive desk, before the towering window in his office in his secluded corner of the War Office, enjoying a cup of tea while reading the latest edition of *Punch*. He was right in the middle of stifling a rather insistent laugh when a knock at the door caused him to lose control momentarily and blurt out a loud guffaw. This gross breach of decorum brought the color rising to his cheeks, but he regained his composure and shouted, "Come in!"

"Sorry to bother you, sir," said Lieutenant Smythe-Ponsonby-Jones, Lord Brightwigs's aide. "That courier chap is here again. The one that carries the post for Prussia House."

Brightwigs had to think a moment but vaguely recalled something of the fellow and said, "Yes? What the devil does he want?"

"Well, sir, he wants a cottage in Cornwall—by the sea, if possible—a pension, and an Order of Saint Dunstan—"

"Yes, yes, yes," said Brightwigs impatiently. "I know all that. What does he want *today*?"

"Oh! Quite. He's brought with him some documents from the Reichskanzler's office for us to copy before he delivers them. It's mostly the usual sort of thing, but there is one letter that might be of some interest. It's addressed to Untersekretärin Menschderschiffeimgeheimenzählt. I think it might be a coded message. I have it here, sir, if you'd care to hear it."

"Let's have it, then," said Brightwigs with a wave of two fingers.

Smythe-Ponsonby-Jones coughed to clear his throat and began. "'Mein lieber Herr Menschderschiffeimgeheimenzählt—'"

"In English, if you please, Lieutenant."

"Yes sir," said Smythe-Ponsonby-Jones, and he maintained his best German accent as he continued. "'I was so pleased to hear that you are keeping well and enjoying your time in England and that Mrs. Menschderschiffeimgeheimenzählt and all the little Menschderschiffeimgeheimenzählts are adjusting well to their new life. Thank you for the photographs of the naked ladies. We found them very interesting. We had no idea there were so many lovely ladies in England with the big bosoms and buttocks. The English are much healthier than we thought. Please send more photographs when you can. The fellows in the beer hall and I enjoy them very much. Your friend, Baron von Hundgespanntebein.'"

The color had drained from Brightwigs's face. He reached for his teacup but took his two-handled inkwell by mistake, and before Smythe-Ponsonby-Jones could alert him, he'd dyed his upper lip purple and was grimacing over the taste.

Smythe-Ponsonby-Jones diplomatically stood to attention and cast his gaze to the coving atop the far wall before saying, "Do you think it might be in code, sir."

"Of course it's in code, you blithering idiot," said the Lord as he wiped his mouth and tongue with his handkerchief. "We're talking about Germans here, man! They're no more interested in pictures of naked ladies than we are."

"No sir. Of course not, sir. Shall I have our chaps look at it then, sir?"

"No need. It's bloody obvious to anyone with half an ounce … Oh, for God's sake, look at me and tell me if I've got it all off."

The lieutenant looked to the purple-lipped Lord, bit down hard enough on his own lip to draw tears, and squeaked out, "No sir."

Brightwigs went back to scouring his mouth but continued with his explanation. "For the first thing, this von Hundgespanntebein isn't von Hundgespanntebein at all. That's a rather obvious alias used by Count Dasgeldundlachen. He's a Prussian industrialist who made his brass manufacturing the spring steel used in ladies' underthings. You know—the kind that bounce about a bit when …" Brightwigs held his spread hands palms up at chest height and undulated his fingers.

"Quite so, sir."

"Yes, well. Needless to say, there's a limit to how much steel a girl wants to haul about in her knickers, so now he's looking for any excuse he can find to expand his markets. Weaponry is the logical next step."

"If you say so, sir. May I suggest brandy, sir?"

"Brandy?"

"To get the ink off. I believe—"

"Capital notion, Smythe-Ponsonby-Jones," said Brightwigs. He tossed his handkerchief on his desk and walked to his cabinet to pour himself a glass before continuing. "They are a solid lot, by and large, the Germans. But they lack for subtlety. They couldn't code a message to save their lives that isn't as transparent as your mother's virtue. Quite obvious what they're getting at. Naked ladies are ships under construction. Bosoms and buttocks are cannon and propellers. The health of the English refers to the extent and progress of our ship construction. And, of course, the fellows in the beer-hall are the *Generalfeldmarschalls* and the admirals of their fleet."

"I see, sir. Yes sir. It is quite obvious now that you point it all out."

"Indeed. You see, Smythe-Ponsonby-Jones: the great advantage we have over the Germans is we think like them without their seeing it."

"How's that, sir?"

"They think because our lower classes are still saying 'loo' to mean 'toilet,' like William the Conqueror, we're still essentially French."

"Isn't 'toilet' a French word, sir?"

"You're missing the point, old boy. We were Anglo-Saxons long before anyone was going to the loo *or* the toilet. That's where we get our stiff upper lip. We're much more Teuton than Gaul. But we've just enough Roman in us to give us the high ground. We're born conquerors. Veni, vidi, vici, Smythe-Ponsonby-Jones; veni, vidi, vici. No more English words were ever spoken." With that, Brightwigs raised his glass as if making a toast.

"I'm fairly certain that was Caesar, sir," said the lieutenant, hesitatingly.

"Of course, it was Caesar," said Brightwigs impatiently. "But he was talking about England when he said it. Good God, man! You do have difficulty following a thread."

Brightwigs returned to his desk, looked up, and said, "Have Brigadier Haretrigger post a few secret lookouts about the shipyards. No need to overdo it. Just the obvious places." He sighed with exasperation. "And I suppose we'll have to inform the PM we've got spies mucking about taking pictures and such. No doubt he'll want to bring in Scotland Yard to keep an eye on Prussia House. I don't mind telling you, Smythe-Ponsonby-Jones, I have little patience for this wait-and-see, cloak-and-dagger nonsense. Give me back the days when a saber-rattling pissant making a speech on Monday was enough for us to dispatch a gunboat on Tuesday, and the blighter would be singing *God Save the Queen* before sitting down to breakfast on Wednesday."

"Yes sir. Quite so, sir."

"Well," said the lord, fluttering the back of a downturned hand. "Go draft something up and bring it to me. Oh, and tell that courier chap he can't have an Order of Saint Dunstan. I'm an honoree myself, and I don't fancy knowing the medal's dangling from the chest of some sniveling little pillock who'd sell his country out for a few bob and a view of the channel."

"Yes sir."

"Tell him he can have an Order of Saint Silias. That Sir What's-His-Name—that lunatic they've put in charge of explosives over at the home office—he's got one of those, and that spineless beggar's got less character than a flea biting a pantomime horse."

CHAPTER 65

With the passing of months and years, Europe descended further and further into fear of impending war.

Spies were recruited at an ever-increasing rate until—just as the plague that had swept the continent in the Middle Ages—this wave of dread anticipation claimed one-third of the population. By 1900, one could not speak to a friend at a dinner party, a stranger in a crowded shop, or even a soprano from the choir in the church custodian's utility room without the contents of one's statements being told and sold to the agencies of several countries, only to be retold and resold to yet other countries, again and again, and filed away for future reference.

The powers that were in power saw evidence in everything to prove their neighboring powers were out to take power away from them. Defenses were reinforced, then redoubled and reinforced again. And when that failed to reassure the powers in power that their positions of power were assured, they started making alliances with one another to ensure, regardless of whom they had to fight, they would win by the surrounding and outnumbering of their foe by their own and their allies' forces.

The weaker nations sought the protection of the stronger nations. The stronger nations saw the weaker nations as shields against the other stronger nations and sought to protect them for the purpose of ensuring all the shields were kept pointing in the right directions.

It all bore a frightening resemblance to those schoolyard pacts made by bullies with bullies to ensure the right to bully is never threatened by a show of courage by one being bullied.

"If so-and-so shows me a rude face, then the rest of you hold him down while I show him to a bunch of fives. And if such-and-such picks on one of you, then I'll kick him where it counts so you can treat him to a proper thrashing."

Or words to that effect. (Of course, the diplomats who draft treaties have ways of saying "show him to a bunch of fives" and "kick him where it counts" that don't sound at all loutish or indecorous.)

Thus, all Europe became a house of cards with a tenuous peace that relied upon the threat to each of overwhelming retribution by many in the event any chose to violate that peace in any small way.

While all this was happening on the continent, Britain grew ever more cautious.

Secretly, within days of Lord Brightwigs's communique to the prime minister, a lengthy list of arrests began being made throughout the United Kingdom. All the usual rabble-rousers were brought in for questioning: Irish home rule radicals, socialist pamphleteers, agnostic college students with anarchist leanings, vegetarians—all quietly detained and examined and almost all released to be clandestinely followed in hopes these little fish should lead the authorities to the really big bass with the really big mouths.

For obvious reasons, foreign language students, readers of German philosophy, and photography hobbyists were paid particular attention. As suspicions mounted, shifts in social sentiment took hold. European vacations became déclassé—though no one would chance to utter "déclassé" out loud, for all came to view any use of any foreign word as a faux pas. Sales of Hegel, Kant, and Nietzsche plummeted, while sales of Berkley, Hume, and Locke soared to fill the gap.

Camera shops all over England closed through lack of sales. One, however, in the Saint James District not far from Prussia House, seemed to be thriving through it all. This warranted a visit from

Scotland Yard that resulted in the arrest of the owner, three other men, and twelve women who were all employed there, as well as the impounding of photographic equipment and several boxes of sepia prints and naughty postcards.

And one male customer.

CHAPTER 66

Prudence and Priscilla grinned broadly as each took one of the neighborhood constable's arms and walked with him most pleasantly along the roads to Lucy's pie shop.

"I must say," said the neighborhood constable brightly, "you two have turned yourselves about most nicely since you took to working for young Mr. Cratchit."

"He's a sample to us all, he is," said Prudence.

"Hard work's a virtue, he says," said Priscilla. "And no one does it harder than our Mr. Cratchit."

"I always sensed he was an upstanding fellow."

"Oh, he's that all right," said Prudence. "All day, every day. Never disappoints, he don't."

"So why are you not at work today?"

"We are," said Priscilla. "Mr. Cratchit give us a 'signment, he has. He says we's to find you and take you to his sister's shop to meet with our Da."

"And why would he do that?"

"He says it's the proper thing to do, seeings as our Da's got something important to tell you."

"Not gotten hisself into trouble, has he?"

"Just the opposite. He'll tell you hisself."

The trio arrived at the shop. The girls bade the constable farewell and hurried back to Matthew's office. The constable watched the pair retreat into the distance before removing his helmet and entering the shop. Immediately, he saw Mr. Cherrytart beckoning him to a seat at one of the tiny tables. Lucy arrived with a pastry for each and signaled a girl to bring cups of coffee.

"What's all this, then?" asked the policeman.

"Coffee and cake," said Lucy. "Compliments of our Matthew. He says the police have a hard enough time as it is without having to pay for things on top of it."

"Very kind of him, I'm sure. I've never had coffee before," said the constable suspiciously, but he flared the nostrils of his enormous nose to take a sniff and finally took a sip. "My goodness, that is nice, isn't it?"

"We only just started offering it," said Lucy. "Matthew gets it from somewhere. South America, I think. He says we have to do something different from the tea shops."

"It is quite delightful, I must say. Still. A policeman sitting down in the middle of the day to drink coffee and eat pastry. Not the sort of thing we should make into a habit, is it?"

"No sir," said Cherrytart with a wink to Lucy and a sidelong nod to tell her to leave.

"The reason I got you 'ere, me old Bill," he said, "is 'cuz I got a bit o' skinny for you."

"Oh?"

"Yeah. You knows I gone straight since I started working for Mr. Cratchit, right?"

"I've heard as much," said the doubtful man in blue.

"Yeah, well I has. But that don't mean I don't still hear a thing or two now and again."

"Go on."

"Well," said Cherrytart, leaning forward. "It's like this, see. There's something big in the works. I don't know what it is, but the word about is someone's doing his nut trying to raise a pile of readies in a hurry to pay for a big job."

"That's most interesting, but until a crime has been committed ..."

"But that's what I'm saying, see? To raise the nicker, this bloke's gotta sell all what he's come by through this and that. You catch him trying to unload it, and you got him dead to rights for everything since Adam was a lad."

"And who is this villain?"

"That I don't know. But whoever he is, he's got them what makes their living out the second story in a bad way. There ain't a jeweler in the east end what's not tapped out buying from him, so all the rest's left holding."

"So. If I have this straight," said the constable in his rumbling bass, "this one individual of a felonious nature—alone—is currently selling articles of a stolen nature in quantities that are sufficient to strain the limits of those individuals who hide behind a reputation for honesty to engage in activities of an illicit nature—that being the purchase and resale of articles of a stolen nature."

"That's it in a nutshell. All's you got to do is keep an eye on the jewelers, the secondhand shops, what have you, for anyone what don't seem right—in and out the back door kind of thing—and you's bound to pinch him."

"And why are you telling me all this?"

"Well," said Cherrytart, scratching behind his ear. "To be honest, I weren't about to. Mind me own business, if you know what I mean. But Mr. Cratchit put me to thinking. I ain't walking the straight and narrow, all proper-like, till I stop hiding in the hedgerows every time I sees a weasel."

"Wise beyond his years, that young man. Well, I do appreciate your coming forward. And please extend my best wishes to your delightful daughters."

"I will. Another coffee?"

"Don't mind if I do. There is something about it, don't you fancy?"

"Yeah. Mr. Cratchit thinks it'll be a big thing one day. He's trying different kinds to see what people likes best. This one's flavored with flower petals."

CHAPTER 67

Disaster struck.

The price of grain—all grain—tumbled lower and lower for three weeks before hitting bottom with a dull thud. No one in the Good Old City was buying bread or baked goods or flour or meal or barley sugar or malt or anything at all that had, at any time in its history, been part of a plant in the cereal family. Prices reached lows never before seen in the records.

To make matters worse, a sudden strange illness descended upon the city, bringing with it acute and intense nausea that led to violent bouts of vomiting and severe headache. No one was immune from the illness. Needless to say, no one in this condition could stomach beer; even the mention of the beverage was enough to send most people into fits of heaving and gagging. Orders from alehouses dried up completely. And workers at Belcher's Brewery were too ill to come to work. An entire batch of Ramsbottom Bitter, having reached a critical stage in the brewing process, spoiled in the kettle and had to be destroyed.

The Directors of Kneebreak Holding Company held an emergency board meeting.

"It's a temporary situation," said Matthew, against the mood of the meeting. "When this ague that's about finishes, I'm sure prices will return to normal soon enough."

"Not soon enough for me," said Melchior Belcher. "It's all right for you, Cratchit. You're still waist-deep in rats. The rest of us aren't so blessed. I need capital quickly to get my brewery running again."

"I understand," said Matthew, "but there's nothing we can do till prices rise again."

"I say we vote ourselves a rise in salary," said Belcher. "At least we can keep ourselves afloat until this situation's over."

"How much of a rise?" asked Wordsworth Moore.

"Two hundred percent," said Belcher. "I haven't the foggiest what you chaps all need to get by, but that's what I need to keep my brewery going."

"That's impossible!" said Matthew.

"I don't think so," said Belcher. "Unless you've been lying to us."

Matthew looked skeptically first at Belcher and then at Moore. He opened the company ledger and began jotting down notes in pencil.

After some while, he raised his eyebrows in surprise and said, "You're a lot closer than I would have guessed. Two hundred would put the company in the red, but not so badly as I thought."

"What is the number, then?" asked Moore.

"One hundred eighty four percent," said Matthew, wielding his pencil like a baton. "But that would empty the reserves with nothing left to pay a dividend."

"Then so be it," said Belcher. "We're not bound to pay a dividend. For the health of the company—"

"I won't agree," said Matthew.

"My dear fellow," said Moore. "If Mr. Belcher doesn't get the rise, the brewery is in jeopardy, and if it goes, so does a good portion of Kneebreak's future profits. I say we accept the rise to do what we must and suspend the dividend for six months."

"I can't—" said Matthew, but Moore cut him off.

"Look! I understand your loyalty to Squidge—I even applaud it— but he's not without resources. He can last it out, while Mr. Belcher, here, cannot. And he's not the only one. You know as well as I there are others of our interests that will be in trouble soon if things don't turn about. On top of all that, to be quite honest, I think the work we

360 DAVID R. COOMBS

all do for the company is inadequately compensated and always has been. I say we take a rise now to get us through this and reconsider our position when things have recovered."

Matthew shook his head.

"Put it to a vote," said Belcher.

The vote was taken. Matthew and Brutus Kneebreak voted nay, and one minor shareholder abstained in his sleep, while the rest voted yea, so the motion carried.

Under the discussion that followed, Wordsworth Moore agreed to purchase 10 percent of Belcher's Brewery; the junior members agreed to purchase a further 2 percent between them, and after some persuasion, Matthew agreed to buy 5 percent.

Melchior Belcher was greatly pleased. Between the money he got from his rise in salary and the sale of Belcher's stock to the other board members, he had enough to save his brewery from years of financial struggle.

Matthew calmed away from his disgruntlement and conceded—in the end—it might all be for the best.

"It's all a bit hard to swallow," he said. "Things have always gone so well."

"You're still young, yet, my dear fellow," said Wordsworth Moore, reassuringly. "This is your first downturn. Take my word for it: there'll be others."

"Everyone's suffering," said Belcher. "Not just us. I'd not be surprised to see one or two of the other breweries having to close down."

"Hmm …" said Matthew, corrugating his brow as if this bit of news was news to him. "If one does—hypothetically—and I were to buy it at auction, would you partner with me, Melchior? Let's say fifty percent of my brewery in trade for twenty-five percent of yours?"

Moore burst into laughter and the others joined in.

"That's the Matthew Cratchit I know!" he said, and slapped Matthew on the back.

CHAPTER 68

P eter was as pale as a full moon in winter. This was not the first time he'd ridden upon waves of beer until they'd crashed upon the rocks of regret, leaving him feeling dry and shattered. But he'd never suffered the aftereffects for more than the morning after, so spending a full month in bed while unable to keep down anything more than water after a single night of drinking was something he couldn't take lying down.

"You're getting too old for this kind of thing," Matthew reassured him.

"I'm only thirty," said Peter, attempting to reposition the cold, wet towel around his head so it would stay in place.

"Actually, you're twenty-nine. But the point is you're not the sort for drink and never were. It was bound to catch up to you."

"Nothing's caught up to me. I'm still a long way out in front of everything," said Peter, easing back to lie full-length on the chesterfield. "Over the horizon, in fact."

"Good to hear it. Care to go for a pint, then?"

Peter launched himself to his feet and raced to the bedroom—wet towel unspiraling from his head as he went—to claim his bucket. He heaved agonizingly for five minutes, to no avail. Try as his innards might, there was nothing to force up.

Matthew smiled sadly to see his brother suffer so. "Just two more days," he said to himself, but nausea hit him like a shovel to the guts. Feverishly, with trembling hands, he extracted a tiny cobalt-blue bottle from his jacket pocket, opened it, and put it to his lips. The taste of mint was enough to settle him a little. He put the tiny bottle away and took from another pocket his flask of laudanum. From that, he took a healthy mouthful, held it in place while he inhaled to get the vapors flowing, felt the first soothing effects, and then swallowed.

"I'm leaving you more of the medicine," he shouted to Peter as he rose to leave.

"Don't bother. It's not helping," came the feeble reply from the bedroom.

"It's not a lot of good, I'll admit, but the chemist says you'll feel worse if you don't take it till the hangover's run its course."

"All right, then," said Peter between dry heaves. "As if it could be worse than this."

"Oh, I got a telegram from Lucy. She's coming home next week."

Peter appeared—jaundiced and drooping—through the door and staggered his way back to his chair.

"She done visiting Miles in Scotland, then?" he asked.

"Seems so."

"Not surprising. He's a nice chap and all, but I mean really! I can't imagine Lucy just sitting about chatting with him for a full month."

"Neither can Lucy."

"Humph!" chortled Peter pathetically. "I'll say! I mean why'd she pick him, anyway?"

"He suits her."

"Oh, don't talk wet! What's he got that I haven't got?"

"Well, for one thing, he's not her brother."

Peter's face danced about in confusion for a moment. "Other than that, I mean."

"You want me to start at the toes and work up, or the other way around?"

Peter squinted in doubt. "Can't say as I've ever seen his toes. He does have them, I suppose. Must have. They wouldn't let him in the navy without them. Or would they? Oh! Hang on. I've been meaning to tell you. Remember Mary Handchester?"

"Vaguely."

"I heard the other day she's working in a camera shop over in Saint James."

"Really," said Matthew, as flatly as he could manage.

"Yes. Got me thinking I should take up photography when I'm feeling better. I always was a bit of an artist, you know. I just never did anything with it 'cuz I can't draw worth buttons. So I should be quite good at taking pictures with a camera, don't you think?"

The effects of the laudanum were reaching Matthew. He knew he had to get home before sleep overtook him.

"I should imagine," he said as he rose. "Must dash. Keep taking the medicine. I'll wager you're up and about before Lucy gets home."

"I am starting to miss my townhouse. This place is a bit too married for a gay blade such as myself. Lucky I've been puking a blue river, as it's put me off the ladies for now."

"Yes, well, someone had to be here to mind our Tim."

Matthew was barely keeping his eyes open as he descended the stairs and left through the deserted pie shop on his way out to his waiting carriage.

"Your brother still poorly, is he?" asked his driver.

"He's on the mend."

"Cheers to that. I don't mind telling you I don't much fancy coming down here no more. Something about the place gives me a right nasty headache."

CHAPTER 69

"**I need your help,** bad, Cratchit," said Squidge as he stood in the pouring rain at the front door of Number 11, Albatross Mews—Matthew's townhouse.

"Come inside where we can talk," said Matthew with great concern.

Squidge entered, removed his coat and hat, shook the water from them, and hung them on the ornate brass coat stand next to the ornate brass mirror in the entrance hall richly decorated in ornate brass this, that, and everything.

"Brutus told me what you done for me. Or tried to," he said as he stood in awe of the enormous airy painting of three lithe girls in diaphanous dresses that dominated the high hall.

Matthew led the way to his study while Squidge continued. "Them other burkes needs a thorough walloping, but 'at's another story. You done your best for me, and I 'ppreciates it. But it's like this, see? When it got voted that I don't get nothing for a bit, I had to pay me mortgage out of hand."

"Hm," said Matthew as he led the way. "Wordsworth said you would."

Squidge was taken aback by the fantastical sparkling furnishings of Matthew's study. Everything glittered in the gilded style of Louis XIV except the paintings in the style of Watteau. Nothing matched the patently practical manner of the plainly explicit Cratchit.

"Whisky?" asked Matthew.

"Cheers," said Squidge, bringing his mind back to his problems.

"So you had to pay your mortgage out of savings?" said Matthew as he poured the fine old Scotch.

"Yeah, well, I don't keep that much in readies lying about, do I?"

"I wouldn't."

"No. So I gives me bloke a bar of gold and sends him along with me driver to the jewelers to flog it—just as I always done when I needs a bundle, quick-like. But when he gets there, there's a couple of coppers what says he has to show it them."

"Why?" said Matthew with a disbelieving jerk of his head. "There's no law against selling gold to a jeweler."

"No, there ain't. But there is one against selling stolen property, and the bar I happened to give him got numbers and such stamped in it saying it belongs to the Royal Mint. Me bloke's been nicked along with me gold."

"Will he talk?" asked Matthew, as he handed Squidge his drink.

"Already has, the sodding rotter. My driver saw him being carted off, then got hisself back quick as he could and fetched me from the shop. But when we got to my place, there was coppers everywhere, going through everything."

"What are you going to do?"

"What can I do?" said Squidge, and he downed his drink. "Make myself scarce till Moore can square things for me."

"How are you for money?"

"Near skinned. And all I got worth selling is in me house."

"Let me see what I can do," said Matthew. He stepped over to a painting of a lovely girl in a dress of a beautiful blue, took hold of it by the frame on the right, and pulled it from the wall like a door opening on its hinges. From a hook on the exposed wall, he retrieved a ring of enormous keys and used one to open the cabinet behind the desk. Inside was a strongbox hidden behind books. He opened the strongbox, extracted an empty leather bag, and filled it with coins. Then he closed and locked everything before returning to Squidge and offering him the bag.

"That's everything I've got right now. Send word where you are, and I'll see you're looked after."

"I knew I could count on you, Cratchit. I won't forget you for this."

"Think nothing of it," said Matthew, and he sipped his whisky. "I haven't forgotten a single thing you've done for me."

CHAPTER 70

T hree days later, Chief Superintendent Sir Percival Prye of Scotland Yard fumbled his pipe into a wild trajectory that ended in his lap.

"Dash it all!" he said, brushing burning tobacco embers from his trousers front. Then he said, "Come in," in answer to the knock on the door that had startled him into fumbling his pipe.

"Progress on the Squidge case, gov'nor," said the sergeant of detectives upon entry.

"Remind me again," said Prye as he swept his naughty postcards into the upper drawer of his desk and closed it. "Which is the Squidge case?"

"It was Squidge's man we apprehended with a gold ingot bearing the identifying marks of the Royal Mint."

"Ah, yes. And what have we learned?"

"Well, sir," said the sergeant of detectives, taking out his notebook and flipping to the appropriate page. "Acting upon information provided by the man what was apprehended entering the jewelers, we proceeded to the Squidge residence and made a thorough search of the place, whereupon we discovered several more bars of gold along with other stolen items. Furthermore, when the search was extended to include the grounds, a lead roof was found rolled up in a garden shed. A small quantity of the lead had been trimmed off, but the overall measurements fit the description of that what disappeared from atop Saint Silias's Church a month ago. Likely as not, it were stolen somewhere afore that, but what with the long stretch of lovely weather we had, it only got missed when a heavy downpour treated the entire congregation to a second baptism."

Prye looked up from loading his pipe through the tops of his eyes and said, "We don't indulge in humor at the expense of the victims, sergeant of detectives."

"No sir. But them was the clergyman's words, not mine. Bit of a dry wit, he is."

"Clearly one of these modernist types—turn the other cheek and all that rot. Nevertheless, carry on."

The policeman flipped his page, scanned his notes, and said, "We also found several molds of the type used to make lead soldiers."

"You're saying he stole the roof off a church to indulge a hobby making model soldiers? What? Did he intend to reconstruct the entire military history of the empire?"

"We did think it a bit odd, sir, but with time pressing, we didn't look no further into it right then. With evidence connecting Squidge to a dozen robberies—the Royal Mint being the one bearing the most significance for the Yard—we put his name on the wanted list and circulated his description. He was then apprehended last night in Effingham."

"Quick work, I must say!"

"Not precisely, sir. Bit of the old good luck, as it were. Squidge made to pay for a hotel room with a sovereign but flipped the coin all smart-like to the desk clerk, like the showy tosser he is. The clerk didn't like the ring of the coin but sussed Squidge wasn't a bloke to mess about, so he waited for him to go up to his room, then bent the coin in his teeth—which was easy enough, being made out of lead like it was."

"Gold plated?"

"Only enough to give it color. The clerk rabbited round to the local nick and brought back one of theirs. The constable went through the door, but Squidge went out the window into the alley, only to do hisself a right nasty injury when he landed on a lady of the evening while she was in the act of plying her trade."

"Good heavens! Was the girl badly hurt?"

"No sir. Bit of a glancing blow, you might say. Though the gentleman she was seeing to won't be seeking her services further, nor anyone else's neither, having suffered a debilitating bite in the course of the action."

"Ee *gad!*" said the chief superintendent with a grimace. He then tightened his lips around the stem of his pipe to light it.

"Yes sir. The lady was stunned a bit, but quick to recover. Thinking Squidge was one of them rippers looking to do her in, she took out a couple of hat pins and went at him like two steam hammers, stabbing him multiple times, resulting in the aforementioned right nasty injury. By the time the constable arrived on the scene, she had Squidge backed in a corner, looking like he'd gone ten rounds with a pair of porcupines."

"Serves the blighter right!"

"Yes sir," said the sergeant of detectives, sniffing the air. "I must say, gov'nor, this new blend of yours is right pleasing. The last lot rather stung the eyes."

"Quite. There's half a hundredweight sitting in evidence—confiscated from some bounder attempting to bring it in without paying duty. When will they learn there's no profit in crime?"

"Boggles the mind they keep trying."

"Indeed. Help yourself to a few pouches. I can't possibly smoke it all before it dries out."

"No sir. Thank you, sir."

"Don't mention it," said Prye, waving smoke from his field of vision. "Just remember to adjust the records accordingly, or we'll have the auditor general accusing us of all manner of impropriety."

He then turned in his swivel chair to raise his feet up on his desk, drew on his pipe; blew a billowing, voluminous, satisfying cloud ceilingward; and said, "But back to the case."

The sergeant of detectives read on. "Upon identifying Squidge as a felon wanted by Scotland Yard, the Effingham Constabulary contacted us and brought him into our custody this morning. After intense interrogation, Squidge copped to being in back of the mint job but says he didn't know the coins were counterfeit, claiming to have got them given him by one Matthew Cratchit of Number 11, Albatross Mews. We proceeded to said address and questioned Cratchit at length. I must say he were most cooperative, sir, though most perplexed over the accusations. Without our asking, he invited us in to look about the place and sat chatting with me over tea while the constables searched top to bottom."

Prye puffed himself into an obscuring cloud of tobacco smoke and asked from within it, "You believe the chap to be reliable, do you?"

"That I do, gov'nor. No doubt in my mind we caught him off guard when we showed, but he never batted an eye over nothing all the while we was there. But that's not all, sir."

"No?"

"No, sir. Squidge give us a detailed description of Cratchit's domicile so we'd know where to look and for what. When we got there, though, nothing matched what the tosser said. He'd told us the place was all gilt furniture in the style of them dead French kings, with huge paintings of right smashing corkers in flimsy attire all over the house. Far be it from that, Cratchit's furnishings is rather plain, it is, and all in dark wood. What you might call puritanical. And as to paintings, he had only the one—a portrait of Queen Victoria over the fireplace. On the rest of the walls, he had maps."

"Maps?" said Prye from within a sphere of fragrant fumes. "What kind of maps?"

"Naval maps, sir. His brother-in-law's a cartographer with Her Majesty's fleet—or was till they put him in charge of logistical support."

"His brother-in-law is an officer in the Royal Navy?"

"That's right, gov'nor. And right proud he is of him, too."

Prye waved away his thick helmet of smoke and said, "Clearly, this Squidge is a raving lunatic who's conjured up a fantastical vision of a puppet master that has him under some mystical spell and is the author of all his villainy. Now that the queen has taken all his pieces, he wants to castle and cringe in the corner squares by inserting Cratchit as his puppeteer."

"Not sure I follow, sir," said the sergeant of detectives, lifting one side of his face.

"Chess, sergeant of detectives, chess. You must learn to play— sharpens the mind for staying one step ahead of your opponent."

"Yes sir. Does this mean we're the queen?"

"Of course," said Prye with pride, though he then grew doubtful over the implication. "Or rather Victoria is, and we, by extension. We are the instruments of her will to keep order, after all."

"Ah. Now I got it. And the other bit? About Squidge inventing fantastical visions of Cratchit doing a Punch and Judy show—that what them psychology types is saying makes for a criminal mind?"

"It is. Or something along those lines. Don't believe a word of it, myself, but we'll go with it for the time being, since I think we can call this case closed."

"There is one other thing, sir."

"What's that?"

"Upon learning Squidge was in possession of counterfeit coins, we made a closer examination of them molds used to make toy soldiers and found they'd been modified to make sovereigns and half sovereigns in rather large quantities."

"So!" said the chief superintendent superiorly. "In the game of Squidge versus the Yard, Yard takes knight … Check … Mate." With that, he puffed himself into oblivion.

CHAPTER 71

"The strength of Her Majesty's realm and empire is founded on the ineluctable and inviolable knowledge that Her Majesty's coinage is sound and unadulterated. No more reprehensible act, no viler deed, can be committed than the undermining of the eternal faith in the pound sterling. No greater perversity can be imagined. No more loathsome, abhorrent …"

Thus began the booming tirade of The Honorable Sir Justice Ruff-Birching from his chair behind the bench as he prefixed Squidge's sentencing. The trial had been short; Wordsworth Moore hadn't finished his opening sentence of defense before Ruff-Birching gave him the worst dressing down of his career. The sentencing itself, however, lasted well into the supper hour before the words "… and may God have mercy on your soul" signified the end of the speech, the end of the trial, and the end of Thaddeus Squidge.

Three months hence, after three missed payments, the mortgage on the Squidge estate went into foreclosure and the property came into the ownership of the Ebenezer Scrooge Memorial Foundation, which had purchased the mortgage as one of its first investments.

In early February of the following year, the Ebenezer Scrooge Memorial Foundation held a fundraising auction. All the furnishings and adornments of Squidge's home were sold off, including the suits of armor passed down through generations of someone's ancestors, the collection of petit point miniatures, the exquisite Louis XIV furnishings and the much-praised paintings in the style of Watteau, of which the enormous airy painting of three lithe girls in diaphanous dresses and the one of the lovely girl in the dress of a beautiful blue fetched the highest prices.

The great mansion itself was converted into a boarding house for young men mending their broken lives and building futures for themselves, modeled after the example of the venerated Matthew Cratchit.

And thus was settled the second part of Matthew's long-thought-out plan.

CHAPTER 72

With foreign spies everywhere to be followed, the resources of Scotland Yard were stretched to their limits. Never in history had the arts and sciences of skullduggery been in such demand for the cause of queen and country.

Everywhere in the Good Old City, gentlemen in tweed could be seen following pretty girls, leaning on pillars in railway stations watching pretty girls, or sitting in taverns paying close attention to pretty girls. The masters and students of skullduggery in those days knew quite well in secret (only to be revealed to the lay public later through the avenue of the spy novel) that enemy spies gravitate toward pretty girls—often to their ultimate downfall—so the following of, watching of, and paying close attention to pretty girls will inevitably turn up a spy or two.

The theory was first put forth in 1841 by Sylvester Pierrepoint-Peering, Professor of Skullduggery at Cambridge, in his treatise *Exploitation of Character Defects in the Enemy Espionage Agent*. In it, Pierrepoint-Peering points out that enemy spies are chosen for their extreme self-confidence and willingness to take risks as well as their amoral perception of those they meet—all necessary qualities to do naughty things as needed, without concern for the dire circumstances that might result from their actions. The candidates are then trained, says Pierrepoint-Peering, in the arts of deception, pretense, and the winning of confidence. Put all this together, along with the natural propensity of the male of the species to seek romantic adventure free of commitment and consequences, and we have the makings of a cad. To catch a spy, then, one need only follow the trail of deflowered women left in his wake.

All science aside, however, the method was not foolproof. In its unrefined form—the only form available to those who know no better—it required an army of highly trained professionals to spend days upon days in the field with little to show for their efforts beyond a mountain of reports. While the bureaucracy viewed the mountain of reports as a success in itself, the War Office was disappointed with the shortness of the list of verifiable spies it was at last given. And, what proved to be even more problematic, Parliament was embarrassed with the shocking length of the list of lords and MPs who had fallen under suspicion of espionage.

So it was that Chief Superintendent Sir Percival Prye found himself short-staffed when he took possession of Thaddeus Squidge's journals after the dust cast off the tautening hangman's rope had settled beneath the dangling twitching toes of the felon.

Needless to say, these journals were not the streamlined versions kept by Squidge's accountants, which were models of efficiency, but a fuller, more detailed set of documents that provided much more interesting reading for policemen seeking an understanding of bookkeeping.

"He was a clever one, that Squidge," said Prye, shaking his head in grudging admiration. "But not … clever … enough. His believing we wouldn't think to look beneath his underpants shows he had a lot to learn about the investigation of crime."

"Quite so, gov'nor," said the sergeant of detectives. "If he'd had any inkling where we go poking about for evidence in the lockup …"

"Ho, ho!" said Prye. "I'm sure that came as something of a rude surprise."

"Indeed, sir. But it's all for nowt now, innit? Whatever else he's done; he's done doing it now."

"No doubt. Still, I'd like us to close the books on a few more crimes, if we can," said Prye, and he let out a sigh of exhaustion.

"With all this difficulty we're having, making any headway with this spy nonsense, the commissioners have become quite insistent we put in a greater effort to improve our showing with the rest of it. As if we haven't got better things to do."

"A policeman's lot is not an 'appy one, sir."

"Quite so, sergeant of detectives, quite so. Be that as it may, I've combed through these Squidge journals with a fine-toothed …"

"Comb, sir?"

"Indeed. He may not have known how to hide evidence, but he was at least clever enough not to write down anything incriminating. All I've managed to cull from this lot is a list of addresses to investigate. Mostly local establishments, but there is one place in Cornwall. In consideration of staff shortages, owing to our having so many men busy following baronets into ladies' conveniences, I'll head down there myself to see what that's all about." He waved away a cloud of smoke. "A little fresh air will do me good."

So it was that the various businesses that had at one time belonged to Squidge all came under clandestine investigation, which led to several puzzling discoveries but few arrests. One might use the word "fortunate" to describe the vague and inconclusive quality of the puzzling discoveries, the minor status of all the crimes leading to the arrests, or the fact that Kneebreak Holdings was separated from suspicion by the wall of ink and paper Wordsworth Moore had erected, but the truth is "fortunate" would be wholly inaccurate for these purposes, as it was the foresight of Matthew that made for the vagueness surrounding the discoveries, the absence of evidence that would have inflated the status of the misdemeanors, and the insulating properties of the wall of ink and paper. Leaving things to the vagaries of Fortune was not something Matthew often did.

When Sir Percival arrived in Cornwall, however, he was elated to find something his superiors would consider something of real merit—something from which Matthew had never thought to insulate himself, since Squidge had kept the operation separate from his businesses in the Good Old City and did not include it under the umbrella of agreements that kept him at arm's length from Kneebreak Holdings. But while all things related to the operation were made to appear legitimate and legal, things were neither legal nor legitimate, and—to complicate matters further—they had a direct bearing on Matthew.

Chief Superintendent Prye stopped only a moment to take in the breathtaking view of the English Channel from atop the hillside, upon which sat the long row of attached, thatched-roof cottages. The air was so clean and cool it hurt his lungs—grown accustomed to soot and fog—to breathe it.

"I could get to like this," he said aloud. "If only they had more crime down here, it would be paradise on Earth."

With a sense of paradise lost, he turned to knock on the first door of the five. No one answered. He went to the next. And the next. At the fifth, when he knocked, he heard a faint "Help" in response, but no one came to the door. He knocked again, and again he heard the faint "Help," followed by another "Help," followed by "For God's sake, bloody help us" in a different, perhaps feminine, but definitely demanding voice.

He tried the door, only to find it was locked. He raced to a window and tried there, only to find the shutters barred on the inside.

"Help us," came the cries from within.

"I'll be there shortly," shouted Prye, and he put his mind to the methods of burglary he'd never imagined himself using.

First he tried whittling his way through a shutter with his pocketknife, but the tiny blade was not up to the task. Then he tried smashing his way in with a large rock, but the oak shutters showed no sign of giving. After some looking about for anything else that might prove tool-worthy, he noticed that the tall grass on the slope was yellowed and dry, and the method he was seeking came to him in a flash. He gathered up handfuls of the kindling and stuffed it under the shutters and between the cracks. Then he lit it with a match from his tobacco pouch. Soon the oak was burning furiously. Prye tried the rock again. Still nothing. He waited some moments and tried once more. Success. The rock shattered the flaming wood to splinters, and what remained of the shutters swung open.

He picked up the rock once more and used it to break the panes of glass before cutting away enough of the lead framework to fold it out of the way. Then he climbed through and shouted, "Where are you?"

"Down here!" came his answer.

He raced down the steps to the cellar, where he found Mr. and Mrs. Cratchit chained to chairs and looking quite forlorn.

"I'm Chief Superintendent Sir Percival Prye of Scotland Yard. How can I be of service?"

"How in blue blazes do you think you can?" said Mrs. Cratchit, who, though considerably aged and reduced in size through want of meals, was as short of patience as ever. "Untie us!"

"The keys are on that hook," said Bob, indicating Prye look over his shoulder.

No sooner had Prye released Mrs. Cratchit than she strained to stand upon creaking and cramped joints, then sniffed the air and said, "Smoke."

"I had to burn my way in," said the chief superintendent as he freed the teary-eyed and trembling Bob.

"I think it's more than that," said the fearful Mrs. Cratchit.

"How did you come to be here?" asked Prye.

"Smugglers," said Bob.

"Smugglers?"

"Indeed, sir. We came here for the purpose of settling down and starting a new life, but when we arrived, we ..."

"Never mind all that!" shouted Mrs. Cratchit from the stairs. "The roof's on fire!"

The three made their way up and out of the building to safety and far enough away that the shower of sparks from the first explosion didn't reach them.

"That would be the cognac," said Bob.

Another explosion followed. And another and another. On and

on the whooshing explosions continued, sending flames chasing flows and flows of spark-filled black smoke skyward.

"Cognac?" asked the chief superintendent.

"123 barrels," said Bob, "If I may be precise."

"The devil you say!" said the chief superintendent as he clutched his brow in disbelief.

CHAPTER 73

Matthew thought the office was rather more cramped than that which he would have guessed a high-ranking policeman would occupy, but he kept his views to himself.

"No doubt you're wondering why I've brought you here," said Chief Superintendent Prye. "I must admit, I'm in a bit of a quandary myself as to how I should proceed."

"I'm at your service, Sir Percival," said Matthew, who was making a conscious effort to use more gentlemanly modes of expression.

"I'm happy to hear that. In this line of work, we get far more resistance than assistance."

"I don't doubt it for a moment."

"Yes. Well. Here's my dilemma. You are an important man with important and influential friends. Your company provides an essential service to Her Majesty's navy, and you are the founder of a charitable organization that has been mentioned in Parliament and perhaps even the palace. You are highly respected in a time when the nation needs highly respectable men for the purpose of looking upon as sterling examples of what can be achieved through hard work, honest living, and love of queen and empire. The problem is: you've been … a very … naughty … boy."

Matthew twisted inside but showed nothing in expression or gesture. Instead, he asked, "And what is it I'm supposed to have done?"

"Ho, ho! There's no 'supposed to' about it. You arranged for the escape of your mother from transport to Australia and for the hiding of her as a fugitive from justice."

Matthew often saw denial as the shovel for the escape tunnel, but he sensed in this instance it would be the shovel of self-burial. "Yes sir," he said. "It was a long time ago. My family was in a bad way, but—"

"I quite understand. But motives for wrongdoing are not license for it. If they were, assassination of Liberal MPs would become a national pastime. No. I cannot let this matter go without some better resolution than simply: in the spirit of compassion, we must be understanding. That won't do at all, not at all. But I'm at something of a loss as to how I should proceed. Your reputation alone gives me great pause to see a scandal raised, but your father's role in smashing a major criminal organization complicates matters enormously."

"My father …?" said Matthew, but disbelief stymied the further utterance of words.

"Quite. He was instrumental in our apprehending a gang of French smugglers in the act of unloading a boat filled with contraband. We seized thirty barrels of cognac, thirty more of red wine and ten of white, sixty crates of perfume, humidors of quite ghastly Turkish cigars, and several dozen boxes of ladies' unmentionables of German manufacture in the most disturbingly unmentionable designs."

"My father?"

"Oh yes! And that was just what was on the boat. We would have had gotten a lot more where the villains had it all hidden, but someone—not certain who—quite accidentally burned the place down."

"So, with my father being such a help, you think you might find it in your heart not to charge me?"

"What?" said Prye, struggling for a moment to make sense of the question. "Ha!" he said in sudden understanding. "Good heavens, man! How on earth could you ever think that? No, no, no. No one's thinking of charging you with anything. Not a bit of it. Perish the thought!"

The chief superintendent's chuckling brought on a fit of coughing, and he coughed for some while before regaining himself. To avoid a return to this respiratory distress, he took out his black clay pipe—which Matthew would have described as cliché for a detective had he had the word "cliché" in his vocabulary—and began loading it.

Prye continued. "You needn't worry yourself in the least over that. Good Lord, man! Short of saying rude words in church or sending love letters to members of the Royal Family, a chap in your position can do pretty much as he pleases. This is Great Britain, after all. The seat of civilization. We don't go about arresting lords and gentlemen for breaking the law. Not here. No, not a bit of it. That's what Magna Carta was all about, don't you know? Wealthy men claiming the same rights to break the law with the same impunity as the upper class. It's the foundation of our culture and economic system. Life as we know it would collapse in on itself if it weren't for that. No, no. Put all thoughts of prosecution completely from your mind!"

Matthew was beginning to wish he'd paid more attention in history class as a child, that he wouldn't be so naive in moments like this.

"So what's the problem, then?" he asked.

"Ah! Of course. Bit of a sticky wicket, but here it is. When it comes out in trial that your parents were held captive by the smugglers and forced into doing their bidding, it might be asked how it was they came to be captured in the first place—your parents, I mean, not the smugglers. That could lead to the embarrassing revelations of your mother's flight from justice and your felonious contribution to it. In short … scandal."

Prye stopped to light his pipe and disappeared, momentarily, in a sphere of smoke.

"But you said I could do as I please," said Matthew.

"Well, yes, you can. Of course you can," said Prye, as he waved a hand to clear a path of clear vision through the cloud. "But we can't have people knowing about it. Don't you see? It's all about keeping up appearances. We know no one's perfect, but it's imperative we maintain the illusion those in charge are. The might of Great Britain depends on it. The empire depends on it. Fifty-million half-naked savages aren't about to do as they're told unless they believe the one that's doing the telling is invincible. To do that, we must have everyone believing men like you and I—gentlemen of wealth and position—are incapable of breaking the law. Above scrutiny. The social order is founded upon it. Justice need not be done so long as it is seen to be done."

"I see."

The chief superintendent puffed again and was again lost in a rippling ball of pleasing aromatic smoke.

Matthew began to feel uncomfortable with matters hanging in this state of irresolution. It was clear to him all that was required was to have his mother and father lie about their reasons for traveling to Cornwall a decade earlier, but despite Prye's assurances he could do as he pleased, he was hesitant to suggest what appeared so obvious to him to a policeman of elevated rank.

A harsh knock at the door portended a harsh end to his uncertainty.

"Come in," called out the chief superintendent.

The door opened, and in walked Peter—hands cuffed before him—followed by Prye's sergeant of detectives.

Peter's eyes lit up.

"Matthew!" he said.

"Shut yourself up and sit down!" said the sergeant of detectives and turned to Prye to say, "I got something you need to know."

Peter took the chair next to Matthew while the sergeant went behind Prye's desk, upon which he placed a notebook, opened it, and began murmuring to the chief superintendent.

"They caught me trying to buy a camera," whispered Peter. "What've they got you for?"

Not surprisingly, this surprised Matthew. Before he could think how to reply, however, he saw the expression on Chief Superintendent Prye's face turn hard and cold. Time passed as the sergeant of detectives murmured on. Finally, the policeman stood to his full height, backed up to the bookcase behind Prye's desk, and crossed his arms in a most judgmental and accusative posture.

Sir Percival pointed his pipe stem at Matthew and said bitterly, "It would seem I've overestimated your moral character, Mr. Cratchit."

"Well, thank you," said Peter, thinking this was an admission of error and his release was imminent.

"Not you," said Prye. "Your brother, here. I thought this was a simple enough case, as I'm sure you meant it to appear, but the truth will always out. And a very damning … truth … it is."

"What's my brother done?" asked Matthew, thinking the answer must lie there.

"Only your bidding, sir! Only your bidding, I would hazard a guess," said the chief superintendent.

"But I haven't told him to do anything."

Prye glowered. "Let's stop playing silly sausages, shall we? It's all far too neat for it to be anything but a carefully … planned … plot." He paused to study Matthew's reaction, saw none, and continued. "We find your father keeping books for a gang of smugglers and your mother printing their counterfeit tax labels. Those, in themselves, would be indictable offenses carrying heavy sentences, but they tell us they were forced into it, and we believed them. Now we find your brother here, frequenting the same photography shop that supplied naughty postcards to those same smugglers, to be sent to France and sold to British schoolboys on holiday."

"Those cards are made in England?" asked the aghast Peter.

"As you well know."

"I do not! Did not! I wouldn't have paid tuppence apiece for them if I'd known that."

"Shut up," said Matthew out the side of his mouth.

"Furthermore," said Prye, "this same camera shop has long been suspected—"

The sergeant of detectives leaned forward and whispered something before standing again.

"Has been recently implicated," said Prye, "in various espionage efforts on the part of the German Empire. We have observed, on many previous occasions, one Menschderschiffeimgeheimenzählt, an

Untersekretärin of Prussia House, whom the War Office has identified as a spy, making visits to the shop disguised as a clergyman. It's obvious now he was in collusion with the smugglers to get information out of England. And we must believe that a good deal of that intelligence was being supplied by you, Mr. Cratchit"—here he indicated Matthew— "through the surreptitious actions of you, Mr. Cratchit," and here he indicated Peter.

"Thank you," said Peter, beaming, as he took any sentence addressed to him with the word "intelligence" in it to be a compliment.

"Shut up," said Matthew under his breath.

"Of course," said Prye, "we can have no doubt as to where that intelligence came from, can we? Your brother-in-law is Captain Miles Trippingly, the assistant director of stores for the Royal Navy—a position you, yourself, Mr. Cratchit, were instrumental in him acquiring. Very clever. Very clever, indeed. But not … clever … enough."

The chief superintendent rose and came out from behind his desk to tower over Matthew before continuing. "You sell sea biscuit to the navy at prices from which no company could make a profit, yet you grow wealthier and wealthier. How is that? Clearly, the Germans pay well for information about the state of Her Majesty's military inventories. And then there's the business of this Mr. Cratchit," he nodded toward Peter "and the Countess Oleander."

All the color except the green of his bulging eyes drained from Peter's face at the mentioning of the name. Again he imagined standing next to the countess before the altar with yeomen of the guard holding halberds to his back.

Prye continued tauntingly. "Didn't think we knew about her, did you? The War Office has had us keeping an eye on her for years. She's been a lifelong friend of Count Dasgeldundlachen. Visits him regularly at his castle in Prussia. In their childhood, their parents had arranged for their marriage, which allegedly never happened. We have reason to believe the marriage did take place, but the count wishes to keep it secret for his own … despicable … ends."

The chief superintendent returned to his chair behind his desk.

"It's the oldest trick in the book. Send the wife out, pretending she's looking for love in all the wrong places, where she can gather information from every unsuspecting, gormless fool who loses his wits over a wink from a pretty face."

Peter had been following along at a considerable distance, but the words "pretty face" in reference to the Countess Oleander severed all hope of him catching up.

Prye continued. "Yes, we saw you making contact with the countess. I only regret we didn't have the wherewithal to look into it further at the time. You posing as canine excrement extractors—or whatever those poor devils call themselves—that raised a flag, to be sure. But really, gentlemen! You must think we're a cabal of doddering idiots to imagine we'd believe anyone would go to that much effort to steal four pails of dog doo-doo. Unfortunately, we didn't have anyone available to follow you, so we had to let it go. Until now. Our man at the dog show sees you here, today, and it all falls into place. I'm guessing that's when you received your first assignment. Oleander told you precisely what to do, put you in play, and you've been selling out your country ... secret ... by ... secret ... ever ..."—the chief superintendent relit his pipe and puffed with great satisfaction—"since."

Matthew was speechless, and he prayed Peter was too.

From somewhere at the center of a large, dense cloud, Prye said, "Take them away, Sergeant."

CHAPTER 74

Peter gave up trying to understand the limericks written on the jail-cell wall. He had no idea where Nantucket was, so a good many of them made no sense at all. Another provided no explanation as to why the bloke from Effingham had to be stopped, and another indicated the author's sense of male anatomy lacked all grounding in possibility.

Bored and frustrated, he ambled to Matthew's side and asked, "So how is it I'm a spy when I didn't know I am?"

"You're not," said Matthew, without taking his eyes off the stone wall beyond the bars of their cell.

"That rather rude policeman said I am."

"It's a mistake."

"Oh," said Peter, rocking back and forth from heels to toes. "Too bad, really. I rather like the idea now that I'm used to it."

"They shoot spies, you know. When they catch them."

"Do they? Don't care much for that," said Peter, with a wince. "Better not get caught then, should I?"

"I wouldn't if I were you."

"No wonder Countess Oleander told me to keep quiet about our … you know."

"Very wise."

"Still. I'm surprised she didn't tell me I was a spy then. All this time, I've been thinking I was keeping … you know … doing *it* secret, when all along, it was being a spy I was supposed to keep quiet about. Don't you think that's rather odd?"

"Not really," said Matthew, glancing sidelong to meet his brother's gaze. "Doing it her way worked well enough, didn't it?"

"Yes, I suppose it did when I think about it. I mean: How can you tell people about something when you don't know anything at all about it?"

"You can't."

"Exactly. And I didn't have a clue, did I?"

"Not an inkling."

"Probably why it took so long for the Old Bill to catch on," said Peter, imagining his long evasion of capture was proof of man-of-ill-repute accomplishment.

"No doubt."

"I'll say!" said Peter happily, but his expression changed to doubt. "Oh. And speaking of getting caught, why is it you didn't tell me it's against the law to buy cameras?"

"I didn't think you were serious."

"Oh, right. I suppose I wasn't, really. I just wanted an excuse to chat up Mary Handchester and invite her round to my place."

"How did that go?"

"Quite well, actually. She said she'd come and let me take pictures of her with my new camera. Then she said some things in French, so I sort of lost the thread."

"Mary speaks French?"

"Surprised me too, I'll say!" said Peter emphatically. "On and on she goes about 'lingerie' and 'au naturel' and 'boudoir.' As if I'm supposed to have the foggiest what she's on about."

As diverting as the conversation was, Matthew couldn't keep his mind from drifting back to a near future filled with excruciating interrogations, truncated trials, and firing squads.

"You mention any of this to the police?" he asked with some concern.

"All of it. They didn't half look at me odd!"

Matthew cringed and then decided there's little point in keeping up appearances amid the chaos of catastrophe. "Never mind," he said. "I'm sure it'll all come clear soon enough."

"I hope so. Not knowing what's next is the worst part."

"Really?" said Matthew, with envy of Peter's distance from reality. "I'd rather hoped ignorance is bliss."

"Well, I suppose it could be. If you're prone to that kind of thing, I mean."

CHAPTER 75

The enormity of Lord Dudley Brightwigs's handlebar mustache greatly impressed Matthew and left him wondering how the fellow managed to eat through it. Lieutenant Smythe-Ponsonby-Jones indicated the chair before the Lord's huge desk, and Matthew took it as Smythe-Ponsonby-Jones went to stand by the far wall.

"Brandy, Cratchit?" asked the Lord, in a smug authoritarian tone that Matthew found intimidating despite its amicability.

"Yes, please," he said, confused by the hospitality.

He'd been brought to the War Office with anticipation of the unimaginable. Having heard spies are questioned using methods both medieval and modern, well beyond the imagination of the ordinary person—and he being an ordinary person in matters of espionage—he could not imagine what to expect. Though he did expect it would be rather harsh. So, being offered brandy by his tormentor was something he hadn't expected at all and would never have imagined. Hence his confusion.

"Your case," said Brightwigs, as he handed Matthew a snifter of amber fluid, "is rather more complicated than that with which I'm usually confronted."

"How's that, sir?"

"We don't often see families brought into an agent's network. Most are either without close relatives or choose to keep their dear ones at a distance from the danger. You, however, have displayed tremendous audacity, both in your selection of operatives and in your choice of methods. Given all that"—he lifted his glass in salute—"you are quite possibly the most dangerous man alive in England today."

Matthew could not be certain whether he was being admired or threatened. He took a gulp of brandy that brought tears to his eyes.

"Yes sir. I mean no sir."

"No need to waste words weaseling your way out of it, Cratchit," said Brightwigs with smiling eyes and, presumably, smiling lips. Then he extended those lips out from hiding to reach his glass and take a sip. Matthew noticed a dark purple stain beneath the whiskers and realized the mustache hid a hideous birthmark.

The Lord went on. "We've questioned your brother at some length, and it's quite clear he's as cunning an undercover man as any we've ever met. And believe me, we've met quite a few."

"Oh, I believe you, sir. Whatever you say, I'll believe."

"Don't overdo it, old boy. We do know which way is up, you know."

"Yes sir."

"Yes. Well, as I was saying: your brother, Peter, could convince the most conniving and devious of professional interrogators he's a complete and utter blithering idiot. I've never seen an agent capable of sustaining his cover anywhere near as well as he. Quite, quite amazing. Really! You've trained him remarkably well."

"No sir. It comes naturally to him."

"Come, come, my dear fellow. We've seen the scars on the back of his head and his backside. We've experimented enough with mind-altering techniques, ourselves, to recognize the signs of systematic manipulation of behavioral response when we see them. And he's told us of how you would take turns being tied up and made to go without food or drink until you were nearly mad with desperation. We've been using that method to train agents since William the Conqueror."

"You mean the chap who told us to say 'loo' instead of 'toilet'?"

"Same chap. Different matter entirely," said Brightwigs with an offhand wave. "Oh, by the by: who's this Tiny Tim fellow for whom you have to mind your thoughts? Code name for your master, is it?"

"No sir. He's our brother. Or I should say was our brother. He's

392 DAVID R. COOMBS

been dead, now, some twelve years, but we still feel very close to him. We tell each other we have to keep our spirits up for his sake, as he's still with us in spirit."

"Brilliant!" said Brightwigs. "Absolutely extraordinary! Don't you think so, Smythe-Ponsonby-Jones?"

"Quite so. Most extraordinary, sir!" said the perplexed but agreeable lieutenant.

"I am in awe, Cratchit," said Brightwigs. "We've had chaps come back from the dreariest places with stories of naked little savages doing the most remarkable things in the belief they get their strength from their dead ancestors. Until now, I've written it all off as superstitious mumbo-jumbo. But you! You've cut straight to the heart of the matter, identified the quintessential truth underlying all human existence, and extracted the one key, essential element to sustaining an impervious morale and a galvanized will in the face of all adversity—id est: anchor your courage in the immortal being of those who have gone before us."

"I didn't think it was that obvious," said Matthew.

"Indeed, it is not, Cratchit! Indeed, it is not. By Jove, you couldn't half teach those nitwits and ninnies at Cambridge a thing or two. Pity this all has to remain top-secret, or we'd show them. Give me a failing grade, will they?" said Brightwigs, trailing off in thought only to return moments later along a different angle of attack. "As regards your training of your brother, however, it's clear he inherited a raw native talent. We've interviewed your parents and found they are certainly as well gifted. Or nearly so, at least."

"Really?"

"Quite. There were a few times we thought we'd broken one or the other of them, but they kept coming back to their story with greater commitment than a bishop to a choirboy. And I must say my hat's off to you for coming up with that one. Having your mother give a banker a damn good thrashing to get herself sentenced to transport was a stroke of pure genius. No one works something like that into a plan—no one at all. But it's exactly that kind of attention to detail that makes all the difference. Time and time again, we see cover stories that are just a bit too perfect to be true, which always leads to their calamitous unraveling. You, on the other hand, inject an element of criminality into the tale, just large enough to make the whole thing entirely undoubtable. If it hadn't been for your brother being in the wrong place at the wrong time, talking to the wrong girl about the wrong things at the precise moment the police arrived on the scene, their story would never have been questioned twice."

"Thank you. I think."

"Don't mention it. I always give credit where credit's due, and I'm the first to stand in awe of brilliance when I see it."

But all this praise wasn't lessening Matthew's concern for the relative brevity of his anticipated future.

"So, we're all to be shot, then?" he asked. "Mother and Father, too, as well as Peter and me?"

"What? Who said anything about shooting anybody? Why in the dickens would you say that?"

"Chief Superintendent Prye told us spies are shot."

"Did he now?" said Brightwigs, considering the notion. "Well, I suppose there is a certain amount of truth to that. We do shoot ordinary spies—your standard, run-of-the-mill riffraff caught lurking about ladies' lavatories. That kind of thing. But we don't shoot men of real talent. Where would be the sport in that?"

"So Chief Superintendent …?" said Matthew, but Brightwigs waved him off.

"Chief Superintendent Prye has the luxury of living in a world devoid of moral ambiguity. Everything for him is either correct and within the parameters of legislation or incorrect and just not cricket. Simplicity itself. He simply has to ask, 'Has the law been broken?' and if the answer is yes, he makes an arrest, and if the answer is no, he lets the fellow off with a warning—or perhaps a good hiding, if it's warranted. Be that as it may, it's all quite, quite simple, and quite, quite straightforward, with very little thinking required at all. In my world, however—the world of international one-upmanship—the lines are much blurrier. Much, much blurrier indeed. Scarcely lines at all, in fact. More like shaded areas meant to represent shadows. Oh, that is good, by Jove! I must write that down."

Brightwigs took up his pen and spent several minutes committing his words to paper before looking up again with an expression of deep concentration upon his face, which was exploded with a start when he saw Matthew looking at him.

"Oh, pardon me," he said as he put his pen back in its holder. "Notes for my memoirs. I do tend to get lost. Miles away there for a minute. Where was I? Oh yes, of course. So, the answer is, yes, my dear Cratchit, you have crossed the line. And, having crossed it, Prye would think to have you shot—that being the morally unambiguous thing to do, as I'm sure you would agree."

"Oh, yes sir."

"Quite. But the line isn't drawn in his world, you see? It's drawn in mine. So, you haven't crossed over from legal to illegal so much as from legal to 'How can I make use of you?' If you catch my drift."

In that moment, Matthew knew he was in the presence of a fellow consummate pragmatist, completely without any allegiance to artificial strictures dogmatically imposed by pedantic ideologues, though he could not possibly say so in so many words to one who held his fate dangling by a thread.

"I do, sir," he said instead. "You want me to work for you."

"That's better!" said Brightwigs. "No more beating about the bush. Cut to the chase and bag the blighter before he has a chance to bellow. Eh, what?"

Matthew was a little mystified by the metaphor but smiled and nodded and took a somewhat less nervous sip of brandy.

"Jolly good, then," said Brightwigs. "Well, no doubt you've already surmised my intentions, but—so there's no misunderstanding—I'll spell it out in all its gory detail. To begin, we've had to put the ownership of the camera shop in your name. There was a bit of a mix-up regarding the former owner. Smythe-Ponsonby-Jones, here, ticked the wrong box on the form, and the bounder was shot before we caught the error. No matter. He was surplus to requirements, anyway. So! With a few minor adjustments, we'll simply continue on with what you've already been doing. The one major exception being, of course, that you will no longer be reporting to the Germans what you learn from Captain Trippingly, but what *we* give you to pass on. We've already identified who knows what, what is known, what we need, why we need it, when we need it, where it goes, when it goes, with whom it will go, and to whom it will go. Of course, you know all this already, having put it all in place yourself."

Matthew nodded.

Brightwigs paused to chuckle and shake his head in admiration, then continued. "I must say, you have kept your organization as tight and clean as any I've ever seen in operation. We questioned your Captain Trippingly at great length—exceedingly great length, in fact—but he said nothing of value. It's clear he hasn't the scarcest notion of what you're all about. Not a clue."

"Is he all right?" asked Matthew, concerned Lucy would take exception to her husband being made to talk, as it tended to disquiet him.

"Trippingly? Oh, yes! Never better. Not a mark on him that wouldn't pass for a war wound. Of course, when the War Office takes an officer in for three days of questioning, it's bound to raise a few eyebrows, so I've instructed the Lord of the Admiralty our good captain was no end of invaluable assistance to us and recommended he be promoted to commodore. That should satisfy the doubters."

Matthew was certain, on balance, Lucy would be pleased enough with Miles's promotion to overlook a scar or two, so he was thankful for that.

Brightwigs went on. "And as to the rest of your cohorts, not one knows you by name, saving the members of your family and this Mary Handchester from the camera shop. Speaking of her, she really is quite good, isn't she? She had us all convinced she's no more than another of your innocent dupes, until your brother let slip she's fluent in foreign languages. Not the kind of thing we see in shop assistants, I can tell you. But other than that, I would have to say she's another perfect choice for undercover work."

"Hm. Mary can be quite clever at getting what she wants out of a chap," said Matthew, recalling how Peter had once paid her a penny to see her underpants.

Brightwigs reached for a sepia print from among several scattered over his desk, raised it, and studied it closely for some moments before saying, "Can she now? Good show. From the photographs, I pictured … Never mind. But it does give me an idea. Just to be certain: your brother isn't married, is he?"

"No sir."

"Excellent! First rate! I had been entertaining the notion we arrange for him to have a romantic affair with the Countess Oleander—to keep a closer eye on her, as it were. But him being a commoner was giving me reason to doubt she'd be able to carry it off for long. So, instead, we'll have him wedded to Miss Handchester, here, and send the two of them to France, where they can work as a team."

"A team?"

"Quite. Second oldest trick in the book. Send the wife out, pretending she wants to draw pictures in the margins—if you catch my drift—so she can gather information from every unsuspecting gormless fool who loses his wits over a wink from a pretty face. And this Miss Handchester is what my aide, Lieutenant Smythe-Ponsonby-Jones here, would call a right smashing corker. Wouldn't you, Smythe-Ponsonby-Jones?"

Smythe-Ponsonby-Jones walked over next to Brightwigs to study the photograph.

"Indeed so, sir. A right smashing corker, indeed."

"Well done, Smythe-Ponsonby-Jones, well done."

Pleased with himself, the lieutenant returned to his spot before the wall.

Brightwigs continued. "So, seeing she's perfectly attributed for the mission, we pair her up with the razor-sharp covert intelligence agent—that is, your brother—and we've got the quintessential, canonical elite espionage team."

"Yes, I see," said Matthew, but he squinted doubtfully, since he had to ask, "But—if you don't mind my asking—what's the oldest trick in the book, then?"

"Get off your backside and do the spying yourself," muttered Brightwigs matter-of-factly. "Mind you: the marriage would be nothing more than a formality. Ceremony, certificate, all the usual foofaraw and rigmarole. Makes for quite a good cover."

"Too bad," said Matthew, recalling Peter's comment about Mary when they were tying up Lucy. "I imagine Peter would rather it was a bit more binding."

"Oh? Has religious scruples about the sanctity of the thing, does he? No matter. They're free to thrash out the details between themselves. As to your parents, they testified in court against the smugglers before we could head that off and protect their cover. But we'll hide them in plain sight. Send them to France and set them up with some function or other in the embassy. That will provide Peter with a reason for popping in from time to time to receive his instructions. Until now, we've been channeling intelligence through the embassy, but we know our couriers can't be trusted. With your brother and Miss Handchester in place, we can use the smugglers to carry the important material across the Channel from Normandy and have it carted from Cornwall to the camera shop. You, of course—as I said—are now the owner, and we've told all those you recruited through the former owner you're taking command yourself, as the need for your remaining incognito disappeared with your agreeing to work for us. Needless to say, all your cohorts—being a mercenary lot—have agreed to cooperate."

The thought of working hand in glove with a team of turned double agents, whom he'd never met, raised concerns in Matthew. "Yes sir. But how do we know we can trust them?"

"Same reason we can trust you," said the lord, as if it were obvious. "You'll all be paid double what the Germans are paying you, and you'll all be shot if you attempt to cross us."

"I see," said Matthew, as several unseen parts of his anatomy contracted at once.

"With regard to that," asked Brightwigs, "how much are they paying you?"

"Ten thousand guineas a year."

"Good heavens! They must be dead serious about going to war."

"I'm afraid so, sir."

CHAPTER 76

S o it was that Peter and Mary Handchester were wed three weeks later on a rainy day in a quaint and quiet ceremony in Saint Silias's church. It was a small gathering. On the bride's side were Mary's family and her fellow employees from the camera shop, one of whom was Mary's maid-of-honor. On the groom's side was the family Cratchit, who sat at the front, and Lord Dudley Brightwigs and Lieutenant Smythe-Ponsonby-Jones, who stayed to the rear. Miles Trippingly stood up for Peter as his best man, wearing his new commodore's dress uniform, upon which was pinned the shiny new medal he'd received for a secret mission—a mission that had also earned him the tiny saber scar on his left cheek—which, far from marring his appearance, only seemed to enhance the rugged masculine attractiveness of his already impossible good looks.

The ceremony was nearly fairy-tale perfect for everyone, despite the minor quibbles of some individuals. Lucy was irked Mary was sharing glances with Miles when she said, "I do," in a rather breathy, dreamy tone. The priest was irked that Peter said, "Crikey! Yes, please," when he came to "To have and to hold," and Brightwigs and Smythe-Ponsonby-Jones were irked the roof above them was leaking badly owing to its lead covering having been stolen some months before and still being in the process of being replaced.

Unlike a usual wedding, in which all the guests are unwaveringly attentive to the joys of the happy couple to the exclusion of all self-serving interests, at a wedding in which spy marries spy, nearly everyone is so absorbed in seeking opportunities with the other guests that almost no attention is paid to the bride and groom at all. And while usual weddings bring out the noblest of virtues in everyone, so no one need doubt anything anyone says, at the weddings of spies, everyone knows everyone else is wrapped in layer upon layer of subterfuge, so no one can believe anything anyone says, but all are quite happy to accept that as part of the game.

After the maid-of-honor had spent several minutes studying Commodore Trippingly's medal up close—not to mention the chest upon which it was pinned—she looked up and asked what he'd done to earn it.

"I m ... m ... make m ... m ... maps," said Miles proudly.

"How brave," said the maid-of-honor, knowing in her heart of hearts he was only honoring a pledge of secrecy, masking his true and highly dangerous work.

"Not nearly so much as you might think," said Lucy, still fighting her way through the female component of the guest list—which surrounded Miles in its entirety—to claim her husband's arm away from her mother.

"No need to get possessive, my love," said Mrs. Cratchit, giving Lucy's outreached hand a smack. "It ain't becoming in a wife; it ain't."

As much as Miles enjoyed feminine attention, he sensed an escalating feline quality in the surrounding conversation, which made him rather wish he could abandon the bevy and join Matthew and the other men.

"That brother-in-law of yours—he is a cool one, n'est-ce pas?" said Jacques Oeuf, the manager of the camera shop and Matthew's leading double agent. "I can see why you recruit him."

"The less you know about him, the better," whispered Matthew.

"Certainement, mon patron."

Brightwigs looked about so as to be certain no one was listening and, leaning toward Oeuf, asked, "So, Oeuf, all go well reestablishing ties with Normandy?"

"But of course. Your Parliament is in recess, soon, n'est-ce pas? My contact needs the naughty postcards to sell to the MPs on holiday."

"Bloody Liberals," said Brightwigs, shocked at yet another national disgrace. Then he looked again to Oeuf and asked, "Were there many questions?"

"*Mais non.* I do *seulement* what you tell me to do. I tell the smugglers the German spy, Menschderschiffeimgeheimenzählt, have arrange for their escape and the stealing back of their boat from Scotland Yard. Everyone is happy as *les porcs dans la merde.* As you say in English, they do not look into the mouth of the horse of gift, n'est-ce pas?"

"Good show! You're a jolly good egg, Oeuf," said Brightwigs. He then turned to Matthew. "And what about you, Cratchit? Any trouble breaking the beggars out of prison?"

"No sir. When the warden found out they were French, he put them to work in the kitchen, making crêpes Suzette and crème brûlée. I put a leash on a rat and let him lead me through the sewer, knowing he'd head straight for the food. Then it was simply a matter of opening the grate in the kitchen floor and guiding our chaps out to freedom."

"What a mind you have, Cratchit! Using rats to map out an escape route! Positively brilliant, eh, what, Smythe-Ponsonby-Jones?"

"Yes sir. Positively brilliant, sir."

"Quite," said the Lord. "And what about their boat, Cratchit? How did you manage that?"

"Well, to be honest, I didn't steal back the one they had. I got them a better one. I found one that wasn't being used much, took a few lads with me one night, and painted it in different colors. Then I had a friend of mine report he'd had his boat stolen, along with the description. The police had no trouble finding it, as it was right out in the open. They congratulated themselves on a job well done and handed it over to us."

"That was a bit cheeky, I must say. Who's the proper owner?"

"The Honorable Sir Justice Ruff-Birching."

"Oh, him," said Brightwigs with a dismissive flick of the wrist. "Daresay he won't miss it, doddering old fool."

"That's what I thought," said Matthew, with a momentary enjoyment of a dish best served cold. "So, we're ready when you are, sir."

"Excellent, gentlemen! Capital! Sterling performance all round, eh, what, Smythe-Ponsonby-Jones?"

"Yes sir. Sterling performance all round, sir."

"Steady on there, Smythe-Ponsonby-Jones. Don't overdo it."

"No sir. Sorry, sir."

Brightwigs patted Matthew on the shoulder and said, "Well, give my regards to the bride and groom and tell them to be at the British Embassy in Paris in a fortnight. That should give them plenty of time to thrash out a thrilling honeymoon. Joys of youth, eh, what, Smythe-Ponsonby-Jones?"

"Quite so, sir," said Smythe-Ponsonby-Jones, with his eyes on Mary and his mind a million miles away.

CHAPTER 77

Following the French Revolution and the Reign of Terror—in which thousands upon thousands of aristocrats were sent to the guillotine along with an assortment of intellectuals and other undesirables—Paris gained something of a reputation for erotic romance. To this, Mary Cratchit (née Handchester) felt herself soaring within her element. Armed with both her salary and her expense allowance from the War Office and the fifty pounds Matthew had given her as a wedding present, she shopped her way from one end of the City of Lights to the other and back again, purchasing all manner of intimate apparel, evening apparel, and apparel suited for moods between intimate and evening.

Exhausted from her marathon gluttony of acquisition, clothed only in her light blue satin dressing gown, she leaned on the balcony railing of the honeymoon suite, looked out over the Paris skyline, and sipped the last of the champagne.

Peter came up behind her, wrapped his arms about her waist, and tried to kiss her neck but got lost in the masses of Mary's brunette hair.

"Not now, love," said Mary, squirming to free herself. "I'm too tired."

"Really?" said the disappointed Peter, releasing her. "I rather hoped—as we've been married four days, now—we might get around to doing *it*."

"What's *it*?"

"You know … *it*."

"No, I don't know. What's *it?*"

"What married people do."

"What? Quarrel?"

"No. After they quarrel."

"You want to go to the pub and get blotto?"

"No."

"You want me to go stay with my sister for a bit?"

"No. No. I want us—both of us. Together-like—to go into the bedroom, take our clothes off, and do *it.*"

"Oh! *That!*"

"Yes, *that!*" said Peter, with a sense of getting somewhere at last.

"Not right now."

"Oh, why not?"

"I'm not in the mood, am I?"

"What mood is that?"

"The mood for *it.*"

"There's a mood for *it?*"

"Of course, silly."

"Really? I rather thought chaps just need to do *it* to stop from going bonkers and girls do *it* when … when … Well, I haven't quite fathomed that bit out yet."

"We do *it* when we're in the mood."

"When's that, then?"

"I'll tell you if it happens."

Peter being Peter, he would have preferred a promise with something more definitive in the way of a date and time.

"This mood you need to be in," he said, tentatively. "Are you in it often?"

"Often enough."

"Two, three times a day, perhaps?"

"Some days."

"Which days?"

"Depends."

"On what?"

"Lots of things."

"Like what?"

"It's not always this or that. Sometimes it's something else. And—other times—it's not that at all."

"It varies a bit, then."

"That's it. See? You do understand."

Being told he understood something always pleased Peter enormously, so he smiled and beamed for several moments before it struck him his quest for a definitive arrangement for the doing of *it* was still far from a resolution. He sank and sighed and turned to walk dejectedly away.

Mary could not help but feel sorry for the poor fellow. Suddenly she realized she had married him for purely selfish reasons—a salary from the War Office greater than she had ever imagined herself receiving, a life of travel and adventure in all the high points of Europe, and to not be shot for treason and espionage. Guilt descended upon her as she saw she had never considered how her longtime companion might be affected by the arrangement.

She turned from the railing, set her champagne flute on it, and said, "Wait a minute."

"Yes?" said Peter, spinning smartly on his heel.

Mary smiled affectionately. "I do like you, Peter. I've liked you since we were little. Even when you fell off the ladder trying to peek through my window, I thought there was something nice and sweet and funny about you."

"Really? Your mother called me a horrible little man, and your father put the boot in."

"That's just their way. I rather feel like we was always meant to be together. Like us being caught spying—or whatever it was we got nicked for—and being forced to get married and all. I think it was supposed to happen that way. Like it's God's will or something."

"Exactly what I thought! Sort of."

"So," said Mary brightly, "seeing as we been friends for so long, and we was meant to be together always, it feels to me like we been married ever so long, already. Years and years and years, it seems. Don't it feel like that for you?"

"Yes, it does," said Peter solidly.

"Which is why I've gone off it, see? That's what happens when people is married for years and years and years. They goes off it, for each other—they do—and they starts doing it with others when they has a mind to."

"Really?"

"Don't you want to do it with other girls?"

"Perhaps," said Peter, mindful of the times he'd met with unpleasant reactions when saying yes to this question.

"That's what I thought," said Mary, soothingly. "It's the usual sort of thing. After being married years and years and years, you're supposed to feel that way."

Peter narrowed his eyes in preparation for the trick twist. "So you're all right with me wanting to do *it* with other girls, then?"

"Of course I am," said Mary, and she stepped up to Peter to place her hands on his shoulders. "It's expected, innit? Come to think of it, it's part of our job. Now that I'm a spy, I have to do *it* with other spies. Except you, of course. So I'll be having all the *it* I want. Now, if you want *it* …"

"I do."

"Yeah, I sort of gathered that. Well, you can have *it* with other people, then."

"You mean other girls."

"Of course, other girls, you …" said Mary, but she stopped short to say a silent prayer and continued. "We're spies now, and that's what spies do, innit? That's how Lord Dudley knows they'll be lots of foreign spies wanting to do *it* with me."

"All right then!" said Peter with an enthusiastic leer. But his eyes and shoulders drooped, and he said, "But I was rather hoping to do *it* with you."

"Hmm. Well, perhaps on our birthdays and our anniversary, then.

My mother told us girls once there's a sort of a rule what says married people have to do *it* then."

"Crikey! Our anniversary's not for another year, and my birthday's months away. When's yours?"

Mary's eyes lit up with sudden inspiration. "Oh, I forgot to tell you. It was the same day as our wedding. We'll be killing two birds with one stone!"

As exciting as this serendipitous efficiency sounded—as indeed it did, coming from Mary's sensuous lips—Peter couldn't quite reconcile the feeling he was coming up seven shillings short of a guinea.

CHAPTER 78

S pending a day lashed to a chair and craving crêpes and crème brûlée was enough to disincline Lucy from French cuisine for life, so she was more than happy to go hungry while her husband, her mother, and her father gorged themselves on the excellent food left over from Peter and Mary's wedding.

Jacques Oeuf and the two French photographers from the camera shop—dreading an ordeal of bangers and mash, toad-in-the-hole, or bubble and squeak that would barbarize their delicate palates at an English wedding—volunteered, as their wedding gift to the happy couple, to see to hiring a restaurant for the celebratory meal. This task was made enormously easier as there was only one establishment the disciples of Daguerre ever deigned to frequent, that being the Maison de Foie Haché, long a favorite of expatriate French aristocrats who preferred England to the guillotine.

"You don't know what you're missing, Lucy," said Mrs. Cratchit. "This cocky van ain't half lovely, is it Miles?"

"L … L … Lovely."

"When your father and me gets to Paris, I'm having this every day."

"I had quite enough already, thank you," said Lucy, irritably. "Matthew had me eating nothing but while he worked his last fiddle."

"That's no way to speak of your brother, my dear," said Bob. "He doesn't work fiddles. He's a caterpillarist."

"N … N … Not ca … ca … ca …" said Miles, but he gave up with "Oh, b … b … bother!" and returned his full attention to his coq au vin.

"So he may be," said Lucy. "But he still works fiddles. I know I can't very well complain, seeing how he's given us all we have and all, but I know a fiddle when I see one, and what he does are fiddles. And he never told me he was a spy, neither. I don't appreciate that at all, as it was quite unpleasant being arrested and such, and not knowing why. They asked me some very rude questions, they did, and went on and on and on about me rubbing mustard on Peter's bare bottom."

Miles looked up and blinked with disbelief before recalling this was not the first of his wife's revelations that had given him pause to consider the kind of family into which he had entered, seeking matrimonial bliss.

"You rubbed mustard on Peter's bare bottom?" said Bob.

"Just to give him a bit of comfort after his surgery," said Lucy offhandedly, but she then grew angry and continued. "But they said I did it to turn him into a spy. I mean … Really! I've got no idea what spies *do* do, but I don't imagine they go about rubbing mustard on each other's bare bottoms, do you?"

"I don't know," said Mrs. Cratchit. "You're a military man, Miles. Do spies go about rubbing mustard on each other's bare bottoms?"

"D … D … Doubt it," said Miles, but he was entertaining an idea or two of his own regarding Lucy and the interesting possibilities condiments represented.

Mrs. Cratchit wiped her mouth with her hand and said, "Well, it all come as a rather nasty shock to us likewise, I'm sure. I didn't bring me boys up to be German spies, I promise you. No. They went and done that all on their own, without my permission. But I suppose it can't be helped, seeing's as me and your father had to go to Cornwall and leave you all to go from bad to worse on your own. Likely as not, it was only to be 'spected."

"Don't be too hard on them, my dear," said Bob. "We all go astray from time to time, and now they've seen the error of their ways and become respectable English spies."

"I'm not at all so sure they're all that respectable," said Lucy. "Matthew owns the camera shop now, with that nasty little Jacques

Oeuf, making naughty postcards. And Peter's gone off and married that awful Mary Handchester."

"I th … th … think she's ra … ra … rather n … n … nice," said Miles, but the glare he got from Lucy withered his soul within him, along with all idle speculations over the enjoyment of condiment employment for the foreseeable future.

CHAPTER 79

The reader will be forgiven if one detail in this odd chain of events—which all fell so strangely into place and in which all fingers pointed to Matthew as the master spy—has escaped the reader's attention. That detail being that Matthew—not actually having been a master spy before being arrested for being one—had never sold military secrets to the Germans and was now in the position of having to sell them to them, as if he always had, without raising their suspicions there might be something strange in this.

So it was he arrived at Prussia House with an attaché case full of falsified secret documents supplied to him by the War Office through Lieutenant Smythe-Ponsonby-Jones. Of course, Lord Dudley was completely unaware of Matthew's visit to the German embassy. The Lord Master of British Spies believed Matthew would simply take the documents from Lucy's pie shop, where Smythe-Ponsonby-Jones had delivered them, to the camera shop to be forwarded along with the naughty postcards to Normandy, where they would be received by the waiting German agent, on the presumption this method of sending secret files to France was already in place.

But, of course, this method was not in place—at least not in the sense of Matthew delivering documents to Jacques Oeuf for delivery to Normandy. What was in place was the method in which Untersekretärin Menschderschiffeimgeheimenzählt delivered to the camera shop parcels of secrets that, in turn, were included in the shipments of naughty postcards across the Channel. So, in order for

Matthew to keep things going the way Lord Dudley thought they went—without letting Lord Dudley find out they had not gone that way before—it was necessary for Matthew to meet in secret with Untersekretärin Menschderschiffeimgeheimenzählt with an offer to sell secrets to the German Empire.

"Untersekretärin Menschderschiffeimgeheimenzählt, please," said the dark-wigged and black-mustachioed Matthew to the clerk at the front desk in Prussia House.

"Are you having an appointment?" asked the clerk suspiciously.

"No. Tell him we share an interest in photography. I am the new owner of the camera shop down the street."

"Ah!" said the clerk with joyful excitement. "The one that sells the pictures of the naked ladies! I was wondering why you are in disguise. One moment, please."

Untersekretärin Menschderschiffeimgeheimenzählt was quite cordial when he invited Matthew into his office, but he immediately became gruff upon the closure of the door behind them. "I don't care who you are, I'm not paying you one pfennig more than was arranged. I will say that the pictures are *gefälscht*. No one will believe them. Lots of people know I have a birthmark like a camel on my buttocks, so you would have no trouble making the forgeries."

"I don't know anything about that," said Matthew, imagining his position would be better if he did. "What I do know is you've been using the camera shop to send top-secret information to the German Empire."

"I have not!" said the Untersekretärin, but he then calmed himself and admitted, "Only bottom-secret … Middle-secret sometimes. Not often. Hardly ever. Just the bottom-secret, mostly."

"Exactly as I thought!" said Matthew, leaping to take the upper hand. "Well … I have here something you should see."

With that, Matthew opened the attaché case and slid out the file, which he opened before Menschderschiffeimgeheimenzählt and spread out the contents on his desk. The Untersekretärin pursed not just his lips but his entire face as he gazed into Matthew's eyes. Then he scanned the documents, inserted his monocle in his left eye, and began perusing them.

"Where did you get these?"

"I own a company that sells things to the Royal Navy. That provides me with opportunities."

"What kinds of things?"

"Never mind what kinds of things. All you need to know is I know people who know what you want to know, and I know how to get what you want to know out of them without their knowing it."

"This is quite excellent. This really is the top-secret. Not that bottom-secret Schund I get from … You can get more?"

"Once a month," said Matthew, drumming his fingers on the desk as if he were in charge and growing impatient.

"This is quite excellent," said the German functionary. "They will make me *Sekretärin* for this." But then his eyes opened wider, releasing his monocle to bounce on the desk. "Or I think even *Übersekretärin*, perhaps. Yes, I think so. Übersekretärin Menschderschiffeimgeheimenzählt. Has a nice ring to it, don't you think?"

"It does. But I don't want to have to come here again."

"Nein, das ist richtig. We don't want the people having the wrong pictures in mind. Especially when the wrong pictures are the true pictures. So, what do you intend?"

"You deliver your parcels to the camera shop, exactly as you've always done. I will show you what we have, and when you have paid me, all of it will be sent to your man in Normandy."

"Ah, that is most clever! Always best to keep things simple, yes? Unless, of course, you are Bavarian, in which case you make the good money on the service contracts."

"Exactly," said Matthew, despite the allusion being lost upon him.

"So, what do you want?"

"Money."

"Of course, money. How much?"

"Twenty thousand guineas a year."

"Bah! Madness!" said the German, who then made a fist, shook it at Matthew, opened the fist, and said, "Fifteen thousand or you can push your secrets where *die Sonne nicht leuchten.*"

Having expected a counteroffer closer to five thousand, Matthew was speechless for some moments. Menschderschiffeimgeheimenzählt grew nervous. He flipped over a few pages, studied them, and, looking again to Matthew asked, "Just like this? Every month?"

"Just like that. Every month."

"All right. Seventeen-thousand ... pounds, not guineas."

"Guineas."

"Done," said Menschderschiffeimgeheimenzählt, and he extended his hand to shake.

Matthew made to rise, but Menschderschiffeimgeheimenzählt held up two fingers to have him wait. "So, what happened to the former owner of the camera shop?"

"He's no longer with us, I'm afraid. He was hit by some bits of flying metal while standing in front of a wall."

"Ah. That is life. Everything the same day after day, and then *bang!* The freak accident. Tell me: did you find any pictures among his things of a man looking something like me in the company of some ladies. And other things?"

"I don't believe so."

"Ah. Well," said the German with several tectonic shifts in his Teutonic expression. "If you do find them, I don't want them anymore. You can just throw them away ... After you chop them up. Yes. Just chop them up into small, little, tiny pieces and throw them away ... After you burn them."

"All right," said Matthew, attempting another rise to his feet.

"Yes. When the former owner showed them to me—because the man in the pictures looked something like me—and I was thinking it would be amusing to have some photographs of a man looking something like me in the company of some ladies and other things, I told him I might buy them from him, but now I don't think it is so amusing after all, and I wouldn't want my wife and all the little

Menschderschiffeimgeheimenzählts seeing them by mistake, and thinking that a man who looks something like me does the naughty things."

"I see. What about the man in the pictures? Doesn't he want them?"

Menschderschiffeimgeheimenzählt exploded a nervous laugh. "No, no. *Nein!* He is a very silly fellow."

"So I'll just throw them away, then?"

"Yes. Throw them away. After you chop them up into little, tiny pieces and burn them. Then you can just throw them away … Into the river, perhaps. Yes, that would be *zehr gut.*"

"All right."

"Oh, *wunderbar!* I mean, if you want."

"Of course. Well, bring the money to the camera shop and you can have these," said Matthew, scooping up the documents into his case.

Then he returned to the camera shop, knowing all the while that the photographs the Untersekretärin so clearly wanted destroyed were already in the hands of either the War Office or Scotland Yard, and there was no point in looking for them. But—Matthew being Matthew—he could see the idea itself was infinitely more valuable than any particular set of pictures. He could see in it the full potential for advantage that owning a camera shop provided to him. Money was not even a consideration for him; what he wanted now was power—power and a way to avoid arriving in front of a firing squad when his usefulness to Lord Dudley finally expired.

CHAPTER 80

Bob Cratchit was relieved to find his work at the British Embassy to France was easily within the limits of his bookkeeping capabilities despite the lofty title of senior records officer. He wasn't a high-muck-amuck, of course—only a middle-muck-amuck at best—but still well enough positioned he could arrive late, go home early, and take three hours for lunch every day. His job was to keep the expense accounts for the embassy staff, summarize the information into monthly reports, present them to the ambassador for signing, and forward them to England, where they were filed away for future reference should a future ever arrive when they would need to be referenced.

At first, the only challenging aspect of his work was getting the staff to submit their receipts to him, since one and all treated him as if he were being trifling or picayune or otherwise infected with some self-important sense of bothersomeness. That ended when Mrs. Cratchit informed him she could supply him with any receipt he needed within moments of him needing it. He had no idea why the staff would turn their receipts into her instead of him—whose job it was to receive them, but he was never one to look into the mouth of the horse of gift (as the French would say) and accepted them without question.

Mrs. Cratchit also found her work easier than anticipated. She had not so much acquired actual skills in printing counterfeit tax labels while working for the smugglers as simply memorized the steps required in operating the equipment. Still, that was enough to qualify her to assist in printing the documents the embassy issued. Officially, the task was limited to passports and visas, but unofficially, all manner of official-looking things were needed to support the activities of those unofficially working for Her Majesty in Europe, and for those officially working for her in France when they did things unofficially that needed to appear official.

The ambassador himself was one who often did unofficial things that required the veneer and polish of officialdom.

"I took the chargé d'affaires from Luxembourg to dinner last night, and I seem to have lost the receipt," he would say, for example.

"And where did you take His Chargé d'affaireship?" Mrs. Cratchit would ask, in the case of the example given.

The ambassador would name an establishment, Mrs. Cratchit would select the appropriate stationary and fill out the appropriate amounts, and no one would be any the wiser that the ambassador and the Luxembourgian chargé d'affaires had been somewhere other than the establishment named, doing something other than having dinner. And thus, the pristine decorum of polite diplomacy was preserved.

But the veneering and polishing of ambassadorial activity was merely a secondary activity for Mrs. Cratchit. Her supervisor was Lord Dudley's man in Paris. His job was to conduct the comings and goings and toings and froings of Britain's network of espionage agents in France, which included supplying them with all they needed to come and go, to and fro.

Peter and Mary came to visit his parents often. Seeing as it was a requirement of their job to meet with Mrs. Cratchit's superior, we can scarcely credit them with noble sentiments of familial responsibility, but regardless, they all enjoyed one another's company when they got together.

Lord Dudley had carefully crafted Peter's and Mary's false identities before the undercover Cratchits left England. Peter was said to be the inept, wastrel brother of a wealthy business magnate, born of mid-ranking members of the diplomatic core, given to excess, licentiousness, idleness, and buffoonery, and quite content to live out his purposeless and aimless life, going from entertainment to entertainment, spending his lavish allowance. Mary was painted as a sophisticated artists' model who had married Peter in a fit of passion, having fallen under the spell of the roguish bon vivant, only to regret her actions in the fullness of time. But, having grown far too accustomed to a life of luxury to give it up, she remained with him while secretly seeking companionship in gentlemen of refined taste and intellect.

As with all good false identities, the success of these fabricated roles hinged upon the abilities of Peter and Mary to adapt their lives convincingly and unwaveringly to them. This they did with uncanny ease, but in ways that were quite unprecedented in the world of espionage.

Mary was disappointed at first when she was disabused of her mistaken belief she would be befriending unsuspecting spies as her principal duty to queen and empire. She had imagined all foreign male spies were chosen for their dashing, exotic good looks; their youthful, manly physiques; their devil-may-care courage; and their innate talents in all matters romantic, as evidenced in the romantic novels through which she'd come to this belief. Hence, her view of duty being its own reward changed when she was told her assignments—as they were termed—were to be selected from the lists of aristocrats, diplomats, and uncivil civil servants serving the governments of Europe. In time, she noticed that a number of aging military officers who had survived war after war by remaining religiously in the rear of the fighting were being added to the mix in increasing numbers.

But she made the best of it.

She became known as an *invité de célébrité* in all the great homes, all the noble houses, even a few palaces, all across the continent. Often, she would arrive at parties with Peter, but just as often, not. None questioned her independent nature. Most praised her accomplishments—though no one could say what they were. And all—with the exception of a few suspicious wives—admired her charm and beauty. She came to revel in being an *objet d'intérêt*, a fascination, a provocative flame in a world of wealthy moths.

"Most enchanting," said the aging cousin of the Hapsburg family with military-spending responsibilities, and he clicked his heels together as he bowed to kiss Mary's hand. "Allow me to show you the breathtaking view of the Danube from the balcony of my bedchamber. A river with the most charming, sensuous curves."

"If you say so," said Mary, allowing the descendant of the Holy Roman Empire to put his arm around her waist to lend her support for the climb up the marble stairs. "Count Rostopchin showed it me from his balloon, and I didn't see nothing special about it."

"Count Rostopchin has a balloon?" asked the aristocrat, in fear of being eclipsed before his moon had risen.

"Who doesn't, these days?" said Mary with airy nonchalance. "I do enjoy a bit of floating about in them, I must say. It's all quite exciting, innit? I must confess, I go a bit weak in the knees when a man takes me up in a balloon, if you know what I mean."

"Alas. My allowance does not afford me such amusements."

"Oh, the count's not well off neither. He told his generals balloons are good for seeing things far off, so they bought a few for the Russian army. Now he uses them as he likes, doesn't he?"

The following morning, after Mary brushed her teeth a third time and satisfied herself the taste of Hapsburg was well-masked with mint, she opened her cipher book and encoded the message: "Austro-Hungarian Empire soon to buy fifty hydrogen balloons for purpose of artillery ranging."

Peter, on the other hand, was not disillusioned at all—other than the disillusionment he'd suffered when Mary informed him they would not be doing *it* with the frequency he'd expected. Once Mary had explained to him being a spy meant he would attract no end of girls wanting to do *it* with him, and she had no objection to him doing *it* with whomever he pleased, whenever he pleased, and as often as he pleased, it pleased him enormously to put his mind to doing exactly that.

Like Mary, Peter became an *invité de célébrité*, though for very different reasons. The idea of a man born into the lower middle class having ridiculously lavish resources through no efforts of his own stood in such sharp contrast to everything held to be incontestably true in Europe that those he met could not help but find him a subject of near-scientific curiosity. That alone made him the center of countless conversations, but it was his celestial charm that made him a star of society. And having the beautiful Mary on his arm—when it suited her purposes to be there—enhanced his mystique and, oddly, his allure.

"It must be *très, très magnifique* having all that money to spend on a whim as you wish," would say a pretty partygoer.

"Oh, that?" would say Peter, matter-of-factly. "No, that's just a story they made up so no one finds out what I really do."

"What do you really do?"

"I'm a spy."

At this point, the pretty partygoer would giggle with delight.

"No, seriously."

Here the giggles would erupt into laughter.

"I'm being dead serious here. I send secret thingies to England, and I do *it* all the time."

"What is *it*?"

"You know," Peter would say, leaning in secretively. "What spies do."

"I don't know what spies do."

"Same as what married people do."

"Quarrel?"

"No," he would say, quite didactically. "They go to the bedroom, take off all their clothes, and then they do … *it*."

Here, the pretty partygoer's eyes would widen as she blushed wildly. "Oh, *that*?"

"Quite," Matthew would say quite offhandedly and with a bored but confident smirk. "It's all part of the job. Queen and empire and all that blather."

And quite contrary to all expectations of reason, as often as not, the pretty partygoer would then contrive to get Peter alone somewhere for the purpose of doing *it*, as would many of the other pretty partygoers who had been party to this conversation or been close enough to overhear the audaciously indecorous remarks of the witty British wit.

Peter's reputation as an outlandish iconoclast with no respect at all for constrictive social norms and a profound taste for irreverent humor brought him into the society of the literary elite of Europe, who quickly identified him as an intellect of staggering proportion with a sharp, satirical imagination. Indeed, he did have an odd ability to select just enough of the elements of any question asked of him to formulate a question of his own in return that would have everyone roaring with laughter, slapping him on the back, and declaring he was easily the cleverest Englishman alive.

"Edgar Degas has said, recently, 'Art is not what you see, but what you make others see,'" one aspiring intellect put forward to Peter. "What is your opinion of this, *mon amie*?"

Peter looked aghast and dumbfounded—to the amusement of all watching—and asked, "Is this like when my wife takes me with her to the opera? I'm not at all keen on seeing that!"

So much so was Peter popularized as a celebrity wit, after one lengthy discussion with a group of philosophers, in which Peter repeatedly insisted the correct English pronunciation of "pagan" is "penguin," that his reputation for clever malapropisms reached the ears of Anatole France, who was inspired to write, years later, his novel *Penguin Island*, in which a nearsighted monk, in search of pagans to Christianize, comes across an island of penguins and baptizes the birds, much to the embarrassment of God.

And along with Peter's reputation for cleverness, the story of a torrid affair with a mysterious countess gained currency and was cited as the tacit reason for his exile to the continent. This, in itself, was easy enough to believe, since there were at the time enough rakish Englishmen in exile for similar tacit reasons to populate a small duchy.

"Well, to tell you the truth," Peter would say when asked, "I've given up worrying about her. I don't care how many little counts and countesses she's got running about—they could be countless for all I care—she can't make me marry her, as I'm already married, so getting married again would be offside, which is against the rules, and so it wouldn't count."

Herein we can see an interesting aspect of high-society attitude prevalent at the time. Had Peter been a count admitting to siring countless little counts and countesses by a countess, or a commoner admitting to siring countless little commoners by a common girl, only to run away and repudiate all responsibility, he would have been viewed as an egregiously cowardly cad and wholly rebuffed by the social elite. But being a commoner admitting to siring countless little counts and countesses by a countess, he was seen as something of a mythic hero by the same social elite, for having wheedled his way between aristocratic sheets in serial fashion, which was a feat considered worthy of legend.

Meanwhile, all blame for the alleged misbehavior was leveled squarely on the countess, whoever she might be, since she, being a female member of the aristocracy, had a sacred responsibility to keep commoners out from that which was seen as the rightful place of the male members of the aristocracy. Of course, had Peter been a count admitting to siring countless little commoners by a common girl, eyebrows wouldn't have even been raised at all, as such behavior was only to be expected.

So Peter and Mary traveled about Europe in the guise of a hedonistically inclined, loosely linked married couple with no particular place to go and no particular purpose in going there.

No one questioned it when Mary disappeared as mysteriously as she had appeared from nearly every place she went, leaving only broken wineglasses, broken promises, and broken hearts to show she had been there. And no one questioned it when Peter always headed south to Cognac and then north to Normandy after visiting his parents before setting off to meet with Mary at wherever they had agreed to meet while meeting with the family Cratchit.

Once a month, two kegs would arrive at the camera shop in Saint

James. One was full of cognac in need of aging, which became the property of Matthew, who aged it in the cellar of his stately mansion. The other was full of documents, which became the property of Lord Dudley, who had them analyzed in the cellar of the War Office.

Thus, the military secrets of late nineteenth-century Europe made their way into the hands of the British and the groundwork was laid for the Great War soon to follow. Everyone played their parts so well history never came to record the exploits of the quintessential, canonical elite espionage team consisting of a girl willing to show her underpants for a penny and the only man alive who regretted having paid a penny for the privilege.

CHAPTER 81

In the six weeks between Matthew's arrest for espionage and the first shipment of falsified top-secret documents to Normandy, he had had to neglect his other businesses in varying degrees. But with the parental Cratchits settled in Paris, Peter and Mary posing as perennial tourists in Europe, and Miles off overseeing naval stores facilities all about Britain, things could return—more or less—to what Matthew had come to see as normal.

"I've received a letter from the director of the Ebenezer Scrooge Memorial Foundation," he said solemnly to the board of directors of Kneebreak Holdings. "They held Thaddeus Squidge's mortgage and got all his belongings when he didn't make the payments."

"Hardly surprising," said Moore. "The man was slipshod with finances to begin with, and being hanged wouldn't have improved his sense of responsibility."

"No, not likely," said Matthew. "Anyway, along with his other belongings, the Foundation also got the nonvoting shares in this company. They're saying if we don't give them a promise about when we'll start paying a dividend again, they'll be forced to sell the stock for whatever they can get for it."

"Let them," said Brutus Kneebreak, who was still wallowing in a spiteful, bad mood inspired by his brother-in-law's estate being grabbed up by creditors instead of being passed down to relatives.

"It's not that simple," said Moore. "When word gets out we've suspended dividends, it'll undermine public confidence. At best, it would make doing business more difficult; at worst, it would invite the unwanted scrutiny—by rather unforgiving scrutineers—of some or all of our less wholesome holdings."

"I've got nothing to hide," said Belcher angrily.

"Perhaps not," said Moore. "But not all that happens under the umbrella of our shared interests would appear blemish-free in the full light of day, and we all drink from the same well, so we're all dyed in the same vat."

Belcher took a moment to see through the veils of the references but nodded and added, "What you're saying is we're all tarred with the same brush."

"In a manner of speaking."

Belcher was not in a position to complain. He'd often sensed several junior members of the board appeared to him ill-fitted for business but had decided the profits they reported showed otherwise, so the flattened noses, cauliflower ears, and speech patterns limited to incomplete sentences composed of monosyllables and grunts could not be used as reliable indicators of low financial acumen. "You cannot judge a book by its cover," he had told himself repeatedly, but now—having made his bed among dogs and lain in it, only to wake up with fleas—he was forced to consider that if the words "crime thriller" are written in bold on that cover, then one cannot expect to find an enlightened treatise on moral philosophy in the pages within.

"So, what do you suggest?" he asked.

"Clearly, we must start paying a dividend again," said Moore.

"It doesn't have to be as big as before," said Matthew. "Profits are coming back slowly. If we take a ten percent cut in salaries, we can pay out enough to keep the foundation happy."

"And we'd still be ahead by a pretty margin," murmured Moore.

"I suppose," said Belcher. "I've had to put all I've got for the past few months into the brewery, but we're back to where we were. I say we vote yea to ten percent."

The Ebenezer Scrooge Memorial Foundation received its first dividend from Kneebreak Holdings Company on November 1, 1884.

On November 2, Matthew purchased Cringeworthy's Brewery at auction. Two days later, he bought Titus Crampe's Malt Tonic, and the following day he entered into discussions with Melchior Belcher to transfer all malting operations to Crampe's, allowing for the expansion of brewing capacity at both Belcher's and Cringeworthy's.

Together, from there, the two men set out to secure interests in British breweries, malthouses, and hops farms all over the United Kingdom before sending agents to Canada, where the newly completed railroad was carrying unprecedented quantities of grain from the prairies to breweries in Toronto.

And on and on from there.

By Christmas of 1889, Matthew had laid the complex groundwork for the establishment of the British Royal and Imperial Brewing Enterprises Directive with Melchior Belcher as president and Wordsworth Moore as permanent secretary. The directive acquired the power to set standards for the industry everywhere in the empire such that not a drop of beer was brewed for sale that did not fall under the scrutiny of someone in Matthew's employ. Matthew arranged it, through various political connections he had made and solidified along the way, acting in conjunction with trained experts carrying BRIBED certifications, that industrial regulatory agencies be established throughout the empire to ensure quality and consistency. High ratings were much sought after, as they greatly increased sales. And large export contracts, awarded by the military to supply British bases in the colonies, went to those rated highest.

This, however, was not the end of Matthew's innovations. He used the brewing enterprises directive as a blueprint for other industry regulatory bodies. Granaries, flour mills, and grain farming were the first to come under his universal scrutiny, followed by the vermin control industry, the carriage-for-hire and dray-haulage industry, and the photography industry. Later, all industries related to shipbuilding, navigational equipment, and munitions manufacture were similarly brought in line with regulatory standards of quality control.

Through all this, Matthew had come to a second profound

realization regarding wealth. His first profound realization had come years earlier, when he passed from the wanting of wealth for what it could buy to the wanting of wealth for what it could do. The second profound realization came shortly after his purchase of his fiftieth firm, when he suddenly knew he no longer needed wealth for what it could do, for he could do anything he wanted to do, with or without wealth, almost as the mood struck him.

It is one of the great ironies of economics that the ones who can best afford to buy whatever they want often get what they want given to them for free, while the lowest-paid employees must pay full price for everything they purchase. The highest-ranking executives eat breakfast, lunch, and supper at the most expensive restaurants most days of the week, either as the guests of other highest-ranking executives—in which case, as guests, they are not required to pay— or as hosts to other highest-ranking executives—in which case (entertainment being a business expense) they are not required to pay from their own pockets.

And so it is with all things. The wealthiest men receive gifts upon gifts upon gifts from the other wealthy men and give gifts upon gifts upon gifts in return, but nothing is paid for by the givers; all costs are covered by the companies they own or represent.

So, while a poor man cannot do without the money he does not often have, a rich man's money—by the fact of his having it in quantities far exceeding anyone's needs—is useless to him, in that he has no need of it at all.

Indeed, this would be a ludicrous state of affairs if it represented the sum total of how the world worked. It does not. Having huge sums in savings not only allows the wealthy man to live entirely for free but also allows him to spend other people's money in the acquisition of yet other means of making even more money so he might live even freer still—"freer still" being defined as the ability to get more and better things without spending any of his own money than he could previously get without spending any of his own money.

The wealthy businessman buys or creates companies or expands

428   DAVID R. COOMBS

his existing companies with money from banks or from shareholders without ever extracting a farthing from his own pocket. As he approaches the pinnacle of his success, his life becomes devoted to ensuring none of his own money ever gets spent on anything at all—an occupation so greatly demanding of attention that one is compelled to say a man is not truly wealthy until his money is a greater liability to him than it is an asset, though very, very few ever come to realize this.

Matthew, however, did come to see it as part of his second profound realization. He was already one of the wealthiest men in England and was positioned to buy not only companies but also whole industries with ease. But he saw in that instant that owning great tracts of the landscape of commerce bears with it all the agglomerated minutiae that grow within the cracks and crevices of that landscape. He didn't need that. And he didn't need more income. So he didn't need to own more of the landscape of commerce for the purposes of increasing his income or for increasing his frustration.

So he stopped.

That's not to say he stopped running his own financial empire; he did not. It's not to say he stopped receiving income from his own companies, as well as all the regulatory agencies he held within his control; he did not. And it's not to say he stopped controlling industries and institutions and politicians and journalists and leaders of all sorts through whatever means necessary; he certainly did not stop doing that. What he did do was stop acquiring businesses for the sake of owning them.

Within weeks of Matthew coming to his second profound realization, the change in him became obvious to others. Wordsworth Moore was the first to notice the sudden relaxing away from the urgency of acquisition. It concerned him that the Roman candle had launched its last fantastic flaming flare and was soon to fizzle out completely.

Melchior Belcher noticed it next. He'd assumed Matthew was simply taking a short rest after winning a major victory, but the meteoric energy of days gone by did not return as it always had before. So Belcher, too, began worrying what would or would not follow.

Slowly, all the others in Matthew's inner circle came to see the more relaxed, more content, more mellow Matthew.

Lucy and Mrs. Retch sensed they had a freer hand in running Cratchit Corn and Granary Products and all its subsidiary granaries, flour mills, pie shops, and bakeries, and rose to meet the challenge.

Prudence and Priscilla Cherrytart noticed the substantial drop in questions regarding the dray and carriage businesses, and Mr. Cherrytart noticed a similar drop in the requests to tidy up what was better left unseen.

Similarly, all the little businesses held by Kneebreak Holdings felt the loosening of tacit control, as did the vermin control offices, the regulatory agencies, and the host of other interests Matthew held in whole or in part. It soon became clear there were voids in the management left by the less intrusive Cratchit.

But before Wordsworth Moore could bring the deficit to Matthew's attention, Matthew embarked on a mission to promote an army of capable people to positions of authority to fill the gaps left by his need to back away. The change was amazing. The companies that suffered minor setbacks recovered within months, and every single division was returning record profit within two years. Once again, Matthew appeared to all as having a once-in-a-generation gift for making businesses run better.

The Cratchit comet burned brighter than ever in the firmament.

But the ancients did not call comets disasters without reason.

CHAPTER 82

In the years leading up to the turn of the century, Tiny Tim's emotional reach grew to encompass the whole of Great Britain, and Matthew's influence over markets and attitudes with it. Not only could he drive demand for any one product drastically up or drastically down throughout England, Scotland, and Wales, but within hours of his deciding to do so, he could also change the way voting went in the Houses of Parliament, change the opinions written in the newspapers—even the reporting of events. He could change the fortunes of someone he favored for the better—or someone he disfavored for the worse—or anything else that served his purposes to change.

But while Tiny Tim's power to become one with everyone provided Matthew with absolute power, absolute power corrupts absolutely. That is not to say Matthew used his power only for evil, not in the least—or at least not often. While he did, from time to time, as everyone does, surrender to temptation and do something rather hasty and nasty—sometimes with regret, sometimes without—for the most part, he made life better for Britain. He grew to see himself in the role of benevolent dictator and got altruistic satisfaction upon hearing people were generally pleased with the way he covertly managed the upward spiral of progress.

Unfortunately, the very best dystopias are the result of a tad too much enthusiasm on the part of the powerful idealists who have taken it upon themselves to put the finishing touches on this or that utopia. They always overdo what they decide is the defining ideal of their adopted utopia in ways that escalate exponentially and end up delivering society into the darkest shadows of the monuments to enlightenment.

"This cognac is positively ambrosial," said Wordsworth Moore, swirling his snifter before his crossed eyes, analyzing its tawny fluidity.

"Twenty-one years in the wood," said Matthew. "It pays to be patient."

"Easy enough to be patient when you have sufficient to not have to wait. Eh, what?"

"T ... t ... true," said Miles Trippingly said with an ironic smirk before taking an appreciative sip.

"What's your impression of Europe these days, Admiral?" asked Moore.

"N ... n ... not good," said Miles.

"No, I didn't imagine so. Pity we can't all be British and think like intelligent people."

"Why? What's happening?" asked Matthew.

"Pretty much the usual sort of thing that's plagued the continent since the Romans got lazy and let things go to seed—complete lack of trust on all fronts. No nation can trust any of its neighbors, and none of them will hear common sense from us. The only thing for it is to wait for them to start misbehaving, give them all a thorough good hiding, and send them to bed without supper."

"Here, h ... h ... here," said Miles, and he raised his glass in salute to sound logic well spoken.

Matthew listened with interest. He knew it was important to keep up with global affairs, but he relied entirely on Wordsworth Moore to provide précis of them for him from time to time.

"Consider the history of Europe until now," said Moore. "As a discipline, it's nothing more than a mathematical study in permutations and combinations of allies and enemies going about the business of mutual annihilation. Going back to the Middle Ages, the years of European progress—if you can call it that—have been continually punctuated by war. A allies with B and C to fight X, Y, and Z until that gets boring, at which point A allies with Y and Z to fight B, C, and X, and so on and so on, such that now—from the perspective of this late date—one can point to times when each of everyone has been allied to each of everyone else and equally to times when each of everyone has been at odds with each of everyone else. In the bad times, no one dared trust anyone, but one cannot fight everyone at once, so someone had to be trusted. In the rare good times, when everyone was too exhausted to fight, one might think everyone could be trusted. But of course, no one dared to do so, for to do so was demonstrably historically unwise."

"It's w ... w ... worse now," said Miles.

"Indeed," said Moore. "Of course, God looks after his own, so He saw fit to put the English Channel between us and them, which made hostile advances on the sceptered isle difficult and expensive. More often than not, this gave us the option of sitting one out if we weren't in the mood to dance—so to speak. Add to that the Royal Navy, and not only did we enjoy a greater say in when we might want to dance and with whom, but also what music would be played when we did— so to speak. And all this has made Great Britain the most sought-after partner in the event of any energetic galliard or mazurka—again, so to speak."

"I see," said Matthew, resisting the temptation to say, "so to speak."

But Matthew did see where all this was leading as he put the puzzle pieces together in his brain. The secret files he kept on top-hatted influential gentlemen had swelled alarmingly of late as an ever-escalating flow of ambassadorial traffic to and from the Good Old City provided him with an ever-escalating flow of compromising information made possible by the concomitant increase in carriage traffic of embassy staff within the Good Old City, brought about by the immeasurable rise in the performance of the second oldest trick in the book—according to the later edition of the book supplied to Matthew by Lord Dudley—as the wives of foreign diplomats took to taking lengthy carriage rides in the parks with said top-hatted influential gentlemen. Clearly, the ambassadors were there seeking Great Britain's partnership in an expected energetic galliard or mazurka, and the reason behind this expectation was mistrust—mistrust he'd been instrumental in creating.

Years of surreptitious surveillance of top-hatted influential gentlemen had served him well. The Cratchit Carriage Company—based largely on the reputation for discretion passed down from its days when it was the Thaddeus Squidge Carriage Company—had secured all the business with all the embassies for all the rides to and from and within the city. All intimate conversations taking place inside these carriages were stealthily audited by the few drivers—carefully selected by Matthew for these assignments—and recorded for him to decide upon the appropriate action to take.

Besides the transcripts of clandestine carriage conversations, he kept copious accounts of every bit of information that could be attached to a name, including photographs of surreptitious encounters, surreptitiously acquired by Jacques Oeuf, with the assistance of adventurous friends of Prudence and Priscilla, who were seeking to augment their incomes earned by giving directions to gentlemen who'd lost their way in unfamiliar neighborhoods.

For the further gathering of compromising information, Matthew had his army of boys and young men in hiding from the law, who were both practiced at going about unnoticed and highly motivated to do so. Time spent furtively following top-hatted influential gentlemen could earn a fellow admission to a room in the former mansion of Thaddeus Squidge, so there was no shortage of skullduggerous youths seeking these assignments.

For the most part, this vast collection of information remained idle. Once or twice a year, however, Matthew would avail himself of the influence of a top-hatted influential gentleman when details needed to be tidied up within the big picture painted with Tiny Tim's help. To this, the clandestinely gathered information proved immensely influential in securing the desired influence. And to this purpose, Mr. Cherrytart proved to have a natural talent for stating the persuasive facts to the top-hatted influential gentlemen in precisely the right persuasive way to avoid protracted argument or hint of legal action.

Much more often, however, evidence of top-hatted influential gentlemen being indiscrete with secret information merited forwarding to Lord Dudley Brightwigs at the War Office. This served to preserve Matthew's image as an espionage agent of exceptional merit. Brightwigs would then orchestrate the delivery of details to those naive or treacherous gentlemen who corroborated the false information he was already forwarding to the German Empire through Matthew's camera shop and smuggling enterprise.

But the impact of these years of sowing mistrust in Europe became clear to Matthew in a moment after hearing Wordsworth Moore's dire prediction backed up by Miles Trippingly's expert endorsement.

CHAPTER 83

"Blast!" said Lord Dudley Brightwigs, reading the summary of a summary of multiple reports.

"Difficulties, sir?" asked Major Smythe-Ponsonby-Jones, and he stood to pour tea into two cups.

"It would seem I've underestimated the stupidity of the Germans yet again."

"Indeed, sir? What have they done this time to exceed your expectations?"

"Same thing they did last time. You'll recall we went to great bother to have them believe we're engaged in massive development of several fictitious munitions concepts in undisclosed locations all over Britain."

"The most recent great bother, sir, or one of the previous great bothers?" asked the major, spooning sugar into his tea.

"The most recent, of course. I really thought we had them this time. No one but a total blithering idiot would spend that kind of money building experimental armaments. Not even the Liberals would waste the queen's treasure on complete rubbish with such a profligate disregard for consequences."

"What have the Germans done in response? Or is that a silly question?" asked Smythe-Ponsonby-Jones, adding cream and stirring.

"Only as silly as the answer to the question in question. They've begun their own massive development of the same fictitious munitions concepts, along with development of effective defenses against same in undisclosed locations all over Germany."

"Doesn't that mean they'll be wasting the kaiser's treasure on complete rubbish?" asked Smythe-Ponsonby-Jones prior to taking an appreciative sip of his hot and satisfying Darjeeling.

"They're only rubbish while they're fictitious. Once Kaiser Bill gets the concepts to work, these concepts will prove a deuced bloody inconvenience for the generals."

"But will they get the concepts to work? From what I recall, none of them made much sense."

"One can always trust a German to make sense of a senseless concept, Smythe-Ponsonby-Jones. Read your Hegel and Kant if you don't believe me."

"Then what are we to do?"

"Only one thing to do. Advise the PM what the Germans are up to and get Parliament to fund massive development of our own multiple fictitious munitions concepts."

"Make the fictional factual, is it, sir?"

"Precisely, Smythe-Ponsonby-Jones, precisely. And well put, I might add. I must write that down."

Lord Dudley then picked up his pen and lost himself in the writing of his memoirs. Smythe-Ponsonby-Jones sat patiently while finishing his tea, then rose quietly and left to draft the War Office report to the prime minister before Brightwigs forgot their conversation and meandered off to do something other than the only thing to do.

What worried the major most, however, was the notion that this exponential escalation of armaments building would not stop until bits of flying metal became an atmospheric feature much like fog. But the years had taught him Matthew had an uncanny ability to engineer outcomes different from the feared and expected. And while Germany was not to be deterred by Great Britain—along with her empire and her allies—perhaps the kaiser would have second thoughts about traveling this road if the Americans could be convinced to sign on with the British.

Plots aren't plots without layers, so in plotting how to get Matthew across the Atlantic to parley neutral America out of neutrality and into first gear in making alliances involved first persuading Lord Dudley having Uncle Sam's hand on John Bull's shoulder would give Deutscher Michel reason to think twice about getting into a dustup. Assuming the major could get that accomplished, he'd then have to convince Brightwigs that Matthew could be trusted when out of range of the firing squad and was the only man for the job. And if these two steps could be taken (which was unlikely), the third layer comprised the vast mix of political, commercial, academic, and industrial considerations that had to be blended just so (easy enough if you know what you're doing) to make a British–American alliance appealing to the political, commercial, academic, and industrial types needed to make this ultimate deterrence to war work.

"God bless us, every one!" said Smythe-Ponsonby-Jones as he sat down to pen and paper, but he took a moment to wonder why that sentence sounded so familiar.

CHAPTER 84

"Why do you drink that stuff?" asked Lucy, as she signaled her waitress to clear the emptied plates away. "You don't half make a face after a sip. Can't like it all that much."

"Stomach bitters," said Matthew, as he returned the finely tooled gold flask to his inside jacket pocket. "Dyspepsia has become an integral part of my dining experience, I'm afraid, and a tipple helps with the digestion."

"You're spending too much time with that Wordsworth Moore. You're starting to talk all lofty like him, you are."

"A man in my position must sound like he would have benefitted from a first-class education even if he hasn't had one."

"If you say so. But you know what's behind your bad digestion, don't you? You work too hard and worry too much. Look at you! You're wasting away, you are. You're as pale as a sheet, and your teeth are the color of tea. Mrs. Retch even whispered to me at your birthday party you'd readier pass for sixty-five than fifty."

Matthew was hurt to hear he wasn't hiding his declining health as well as he'd believed.

Lucy leaned closer to her brother and put a hand on his wrist. "Listen to me, my old love. You're plenty rich enough now, and Miles told me the navy's the biggest it's ever been. The country's never been safer, and it's all 'cuz of you. You've been a bloody good spy, you have, and done your duty above and beyond. But enough's enough. It's time to retire and move back in with us. The new house in Greenwich is lovely and peaceful, and a few months with our Tim will put you to rights. Do it now, before it's too late."

The first effects of the laudanum dimmed Matthew's awareness and dulled his ability to formulate a response.

"I'll put some thought to it," he said, rising. "But I must go. I will consider it, though."

On the ride back to his townhouse, Matthew fell asleep in his carriage—an occurrence common enough for his driver to expect it. The driver, having been hired for his unimpeachable discretion—like everyone with close personal access to Matthew—knew to keep driving until his master woke up rather than risk having him seen in public in a stupor in the early afternoon.

You will recall Matthew had started taking laudanum when he was conducting Tiny Tim to put the good citizens of the Good Old City into a state of fear over a growing German naval threat. He'd meant it to be a temporary measure to allow him rest from being always at the center of dread concern. But when this goal had been achieved, Matthew found he could no longer sleep without his nightly dose, and as the effects could be quite pleasing, he saw no reason to stop. From there, his usage grew out of control and into the realm of embarrassment.

Others became aware of the slowing of Matthew's pace before he did.

The first casualty of his diminishing health was his loss of interest in diversions. Prudence and Priscilla Cherrytart and some of the girls from the camera shop had enjoyed diverting Matthew as much as he had enjoyed being diverted, but more and more often, he would say he was too busy for diversion in that moment. Eventually, the girls found they had to turn their diverting to others of their acquaintance, if they were to get any diverting done at all.

Then the outward signs of accelerated aging took hold. The once naturally athletic and powerful build started sagging into middle age and then withering away beneath loosening skin. His gait slowed.

His voice weakened. He became plagued with a perennial cough and runny nose.

But he, like those around him, imagined the decline was the toll hard work took of a man. Though few knew he ever took laudanum, and none knew the full extent of it, everyone could see the long hours he spent in work. He, however, believed he was as sharp as ever—at least once the initial effects of a taste had worn off.

To this, Wordsworth Moore proved to be Matthew's most valuable ally. Moore noticed details being missed, work left undone, and a general loss of Matthew's sense of urgency. He quietly guided Matthew toward delegating more and more of his workload and secretly instructed the executives of Matthew's many companies to watch their master for lapses, fill in the gaps, and bridge the oversights. He could see Matthew fading, but out of respect for all Matthew had made possible, Moore elected to let his friend preserve the illusion he was still rising to his zenith.

And thus, Matthew was oblivious to being on the second half of his ballistic trajectory.

CHAPTER 85

Through all this, Tiny Tim was growing wiser in ways quite unfamiliar to those of us for whom words and reason are essential parts of wisdom. We know wisdom cannot come from study and consideration alone but rather comes primarily from experience, which is greatly amplified by study and consideration. And though that experience will usually have associated with it a selection of memories of events that constituted that experience, wisdom will still present itself in a different form of awareness than recalled images in the mind; it will appear as an instinct or gut feeling that tempers action in ways cold logic cannot and hot emotion will not.

Our hero, however, was different from the rest of humanity in that this instinct flourished within him, not as a result of his own experiences, but from the collective experiences of everyone who came within his wide reach of emotive energy. And since Lucy was his closest and most consistent companion throughout, she shared in Tiny Tim's maturing wisdom, both as a major contributor to its growth and as a major recipient of its bounty.

After the retirement of Mrs. Retch, Lucy became the behind-the-scenes ruler of Cratchit Corn and Granary Products. Legally, Matthew was still president of the company, but he had long since given up real command. Times being what they were, women could not overtly control large businesses, but Lucy had long been established as a purveyor of Matthew's will and continued to rule as such, even well after her will had superseded her brother's in the ruling of the massive conglomerate.

And Lucy ruled wisely.

With the passing of time and the further decline in Matthew's capacity, Lucy took behind-the-scenes command of all the Cratchit companies, with the notable help of Wordsworth Moore, Melchior Belcher, and others who had reason to believe there was something quite special about the sister of the man who had governed with such uncanny feeling for unfolding events. All who were close to the center of command could see in Lucy that same prescience that had enabled Matthew to soar to greatness, and although she was far less audacious than her rapacious brother, all could see her judgment would preserve the commercial empire in its fullness even if its days of insatiate conquest were over.

And so Lucy was allowed to rule wisely.

"You're a wise woman, Lucy Cratchit," said Wordsworth Moore as he signed documents that magically made her wishes come true. "Quite the opposite of your brother."

"Why d'you say that?" asked Lucy, slightly insulted while still suspecting Moore's statement was true. "What could Matthew have done better than he did?"

"Nothing. Nothing at all. The man is a once-in-a-century genius by all measures. But wisdom plays no part in genius—not for him or for anyone else. You see, my dear lady, wisdom boiled down to its heavy residuum is the instinctive skill of loss avoidance. If one has something and wishes to keep it, then one should act wisely, but if one has nothing and wishes to lose that, then one should view wisdom as an impediment and act rashly. And in addition to that, if you always do what you always did, you'll always get what you always got—assuming, of course, the conditions for doing and getting always remain the same. Which they do not. All in all, loss never entered Matthew's swashbuckling mind, so he never had need of wisdom."

"Being wise isn't just about money."

"Very true. But my point remains valid. If a person acts wisely in the execution of physical activities, that person will achieve their goals without the loss of sensory functions, anatomical components, or his or her life. If a gentleman is wise in the conducting of his romantic affairs, he will achieve his goals without loss of financial status, anatomical components, or his love. And if you are wise in the navigating of your estate planning, you will achieve your goals without loss of civil liberties, anatomical components, or your wealth. And since one cannot get ahead when one is constantly falling behind, the instinctive skill of loss avoidance is a skill worth acquiring."

"I see," said Lucy, nodding, but she then asked, "Why would you lose body parts from bad estate planning?"

"You never met Mr. Squidge, did you?"

"Oh!" said Lucy with sudden understanding why Peter had feared Matthew's former partner so much in the early years.

"Regarding Matthew, however," said Moore, "Fortune favors the bold, and that which does not kill us makes us stronger, so—knowing faint heart never won fair lady; one should always venture a small fish to catch a large one; and, as Virgil famously said, all bad fortune is to be conquered by endurance—he based his credo on audacity and unwaveringly acted accordingly. Completely without wisdom."

So it was that Lucy's wisdom served to preserve the status quo for many years, but the inevitable changing of ambient conditions provided times when rashness would have been the better servant. Because of Lucy's wisdom, however, the call for rashness went unheeded, and that unheeding proved to be the failing into which the vast Cratchit fortune eventually fell.

Nevertheless, despite Matthew's decision to concentrate on exercising influence above acquisition, the Cratchit fortune was truly immense when Lucy took the reins from her brother. She took Wordsworth Moore's words to heart, tacitly committed herself to the preservation of that fortune, and ruled Matthew's financial empire wisely—as has been said. Indeed, she ruled with all the wisdom Tiny Tim could condense from all the wise people of Great Britain brought together in the making of life in all its facets, as wisely as their culture, their tradition, and their collective experience could allow. She ruled with the wisdom of the ages, and in doing so—through the conduit of Tiny Tim—she inspired all of Great Britain to become wiser and wiser and wiser and more and more and more cautious in the preservation of custom, of tradition, of empire.

Which proved to be its undoing.

CHAPTER 86

In the spring of 1904, with the Boer War comfortably in the past (and all its acts of brutal nastiness made properly historically heroic) and a new king comfortably on the throne (and all his acts of princely naughtiness made properly historically cherubic), England began taking its exalted position in the world for granted and took to looking upon—of all places—America with something like envy.

The British Empire was at its peak, so there was still no reason to think being born of any other nation than England could have anything near the benefit in the eyes of God and the world as being born to the land of Shakespeare, Newton, and Alfred the Great. But, just as the proverbial grass perennially appears greener on the far side of the proverbial fence, America began appearing more appealing from the far side of the ironically monikered pond.

Some put it to the invention of the airplane, since that lit up nearly everyone's imagination. Even those prone to stating, as if they were entirely original in doing so, "If God had intended man to fly, he would have given him wings," felt stirred to delight when news of the first flight reached English shores.

Some put it to the availability of inexpensive automobiles, though this made no sense at all since those who owned the moderately expensive versions did nothing but complain about them and lamented they could not afford the ridiculously expensive ones. Based on this, no one put any stock in the notion that cheap ones could be anything more than evidence of poor judgment.

In reality, however, this fad for Americanophile sentiment grew in Britain as the British were growing weary of being wise under the relentless, pervasive power of Tiny Tim. And since there was no place on the planet less endowed of wisdom at the time than the United States of America, all things American were seen as highly preferable. It was as if Americans were immune to learning from experience, devoid of common sense, and entirely addicted to risking all for the flimsiest of gains. So to the plodding, stodgy Brits, America was as refreshing a diversion from reality as a balloon flotilla deployed for a dragon hunt.

Still, despite the rising warmth for recklessness bubbling beneath the surface of the British Isles in general, Lord Dudley Brightwigs was stalwartly adhering to deeply engrained habits of sticking to the very well tried and very proven true. But he saw—with the subtle guidance of Colonel Smythe-Ponsonby-Jones—opportunities in America others did not.

"I say, old chum," he said to Matthew at their first meeting in years, "you do look rather rum. Have you been poorly?"

"I'm told I work too hard. But it's hard to see, as I hardly do much of anything anymore—hard or otherwise. It's rather more the endless softness of it all that I'm finding a tad unpleasant."

"I see," said Brightwigs. "Well, I may have precisely what the doctor ordered. As you well know—if you've been following politics—"

"I haven't of late. Can't seem to stay awake while reading the papers these days."

"No matter. What I was going to say is this: we've signed treaties with half of Europe, and the German Empire has signed treaties with the other half. All this brings us to something of an impasse. We've been tossing our coins into the ante for three decades, and the Germans still won't come to their senses and admit they haven't a hope in Hades of keeping up. Of course, we could keep committing more and more treasure to more and more armaments, but I've decided there's a far simpler way."

"And what's that?"

"We sign a treaty with the Americans. Costs us nothing more than a few drops of Her Majesty's ink—I mean His Majesty's ink. Dash it all, I keep forgetting the old girl's snuffed it," said the Lord, and he checked over his shoulder to see whether the portrait of King Edward was in place. Then he returned his attention to Matthew. "Where was I? Oh, yes! We sign with the Americans and tip the scales massively in our favor. That will bring Kaiser Bill to his senses and put an end to this endless chasing of everyone's respective tail."

"I can see that," said Matthew wearily, but then the consequences to himself came into mind in the form of the firing squad he had always assumed would be the path his eventual dismissal from national service would take. Despite years of attempting to gather some compromising bit of evidence of naughty behavior on Brightwigs's part that could be used to convince the Lord to let Matthew simply slip away from espionage unnoticed, he had consistently remained dissatisfied since Lord Dudley proved to be the rarest of the rare in being a man born to the aristocracy without any capacity for scandal whatsoever.

"Does this mean you won't be needing me anymore?" asked Matthew nervously.

"No, not at all. Or, at the very least, I should say, I need you for one more task, and then you can retire with Her Majesty's—Blast!—His Majesty's heartfelt thanks. My thinking runs along these lines. You should be the one to go to America and lay the groundwork for the treaty."

"Me, sir? Why me?"

"Don't be modest, old chum. You've got a truly uncanny knack for making things happen precisely to the way you want them. Some men may have greatness thrust upon them while others just get in its way, but you, sir, have the talent for seizing greatness without consideration for your class, your credentials, or any moral justification in doing so. That's precisely what the Americans admire most in a man. I don't pretend to understand how one can build a society upon standards like that, but they seem to have pulled it off. What I do know, for a certainty, is you're our best man for dealing with the buckaroos and the robber barons. They'll spot you for one of their own the moment you step off the boat."

"I see," said Matthew, thinking his days of bucking roos were well in the past.

"Damn fine cognac!" said Brightwigs, sipping from his snifter. "Thank you for this."

"My pleasure."

"Of course, it goes without saying you can't let them know we're looking for a military alliance. Say what you will about them, they're not mad enough to commit armed forces to a cause for which they haven't got a financial stake—that much, at least, we do share in common with them. What you must do is this: let them see there are opportunities to be had in dealing with you. Offer up some possibilities for mutual profit, sign a few lucrative contracts, and then they'll pay their politicians to write the treaties to ensure their interests remain secure."

Lord Dudley spoke as if all this were the simplest of things and then added, offhandedly, "Any money you make is yours to keep."

"And then I'm to retire?"

"Quite. Quite so. This will be your magnum opus in your service to queen and empire—Damn and blast!—king and empire. Does take some getting used to, doesn't it? Regardless. I've arranged for you to receive the Order of Saint Silias before you leave, so you'll be Sir Matthew to the Americans. They pretend to detest aristocracy, but they don't pretend very hard. They all want their daughters to marry a duke or an earl. Who can say? You may even find yourself a randy bit of fluff to wed and keep you amused. It will work to your favor."

"Thank you, Lord Dudley. Thank you very much."

"Not at all, my good man. You've earned it. We'll contact you when the Palace is ready to receive you."

A knighthood had never been something Matthew considered for himself, but now he was on the verge of receiving one, the thought appealed to him greatly. Above and beyond all the tiny perquisites that came with the honor, Matthew had to believe it signified genuine forgiveness for the treason he had supposedly committed years before and the foregoing of the firing squad he'd come to expect would mark the end of his usefulness to Lord Dudley. To this, he couldn't be certain, but it seemed to him the shooting of a man with a knighthood was universally viewed as just not cricket, and a universal view of anything is as near to a guarantee of certainty as anything life can offer.

As he rode home in his carriage, he considered his position in its fullness and decided he would retire entirely when he returned from America—not only from the War Office but from everything, for he had everything a man could want who had long ago given up wanting companionship of any sort. The only thing that had been missing had been peace of mind, and—with his knighthood assuring he might have years without a fearsome prospect dangling above him—peace of mind was finally his.

He took out his flask of laudanum, but instead of a swig, he hauled in a deep breath and threw the odious thing out the window. Then he looked out onto the streets of the Good Old City and murmured, "God bless us, every one!" to the bustle around him.

CHAPTER 87

Lucy was petulant. "I can't see why you have to take our Tim with you," she said.

"It's important I get this right," said Matthew, looking healthier and feeling sharper than he had in ages. "Without him, I can't be sure the Americans will want to work with me. With him, it'll be easy, and I can come home with all the spy business over and nothing more to worry about, ever again."

"I don't want him getting lonely and such, what with you leaving him by himself while you go off to do whatever it is you do."

"I won't leave him alone for a minute. I'll buy a big house when I get there and have big parties, so everyone I have to meet will come to me. There'll be people around him all the time, enjoying themselves. It'll be fun for him. And then we'll come home—as soon as I know the treaty's in the works."

"Well, all right then," said Lucy. "It's too bad Miles isn't about. He could take you over with the navy and keep you both safe."

"We'll be fine. Where is Miles these days, anyway?"

"He's off mapping the French Riviera. It's funny. He never thought he'd get to make another map, ever, after they made him a captain, but now that he's a full admiral, he's off to the Mediterranean every winter making maps of this and that. I feel sorry for him, sometimes, having to be away so long in all those hot foreign places. I mean, he has a hard enough time of it speaking English. How ever does he get by in French or Greek situations? But he bears up well enough. You'll never hear him complain."

"Stout fellow."

"No, he's still quite fit and trim in all the right places. Though he's grayed a bit about the temples. Oh! By the way! He sent me a letter saying he met our Peter over there."

"How's he doing?"

"Not so well. He's hiding from some Prussian count who wants to duel with him for making countless little counts and countesses with the Countess Oleander years ago."

Matthew snorted and then chuckled. "I had a feeling, at the time, he'd live to regret it. Oh, well. Perhaps when I'm done dealing with the Americans, they'll let Mary and him come home. And Mother and Father, too."

"It would be nice to have us all together again, like we were before. Even if we are rich now."

CHAPTER 88

Wordsworth **Moore met** up with Sir Matthew on the foredeck of the SS *Transylvania* while the knightly Cratchit leaned on the railing to wave his top hat to Lucy, who was waving to him from the dock.

"So, what's the great attraction for America?" asked Moore.

"I needed to do something different. I was beginning to feel like a two-dimensional character in some drawn-out, farcical novel. It was all getting rather too stale, so I thought I'd take one last kick at the donkey before calling it a day."

"You never were one to do anything by half-measures. Still. We've left everything running smoothly here. They won't miss us for a moment, I'm sure. And I must say, I shan't miss being about Belcher for a bit. His nose is properly out of joint with you getting your knighthood and him having to settle with just being the third wealthiest man in England."

"Poor fellow."

"Indeed. But I must say, I am looking forward to seeing New York. Hard to imagine a place that's entirely new after living in the Good Old City all my life."

"Hm. Yes. Do they have lawyers in America?"

"By all accounts, the country was created by lawyers."

"My word! Hard to imagine how that could work."

"It didn't," said Moore with a chuckle. "From what little I've managed to read on the matter, there was an initial flurry of idealistic optimism that died out almost immediately, followed by a quiet takeover by the land speculators, the stockbrokers, and the piratical industrialists. The brigands took the reins and have them still, so there's sufficient savagery installed into the system to keep the rabid-democracy types from bringing everything to a complete standstill."

"Oh, yes?"

"Quite. Damn sight more foresight than we displayed when we created Parliament, I must say. Now we're forced to go to the length of pretending our brigands are incapable of breaking the law while holding them up as examples of honesty and virtue for the lower classes to follow. The Americans, on the other hand, allow their brigands to dictate what laws will be written in the first place, so all need for pretense is rendered vacuous. I have to hand it to them: it's all rather clean and efficient, and I must admit to having a grudging admiration for them."

"Why grudging?"

Moore sighed and said, "Oh, I don't know. Perhaps it comes down to nothing more than jealousy, if I'm honest with myself. They're still frying up the sausage in anticipation of a feast, while we've eaten our meal and are now gorging ourselves on the overly rich and sickly sweet pudding. All we have to look forward to is the port and cigars and hope the gout and dyspepsia don't keep us from having a good night's sleep."

"You fancy a move, then?"

"Don't talk rubbish! I haven't gone completely soft. I've grown far too accustomed to living in a finished society with people in a fine state of polish. The Americans haven't yet received their first coat of lacquer—assuming they ever will."

"I'm not sure I understand."

"Not much to understand, really. Simply that they place no value at all on etiquette and decorum, and they thoroughly eschew tradition and ceremony. Perhaps we are a tad artificial, but there is still a lot to be said for etiquette and decorum, and for tradition and ceremony. These little niceties make the whole pantomime entirely more reliable. Take

454 David R. Coombs

yourself, for instance. When I first met you, you were a well-enough-spoken young fellow, polite enough as well, and clearly as bright as a newly minted sovereign, but it was as obvious as perfume on a tart you were born to the lower class. But now that you've acquired yourself a nice gentlemanly patina, you're entirely more agreeable in every way. There's nothing about you that would have me the least bit embarrassed being seen in your company."

"Thank you, I'm sure."

"Don't mention it. The Americans, on the other hand, have espoused themselves of this ludicrous notion that everyone is inherently equal in value without realizing that when common denominators are sought, the lowest common denominator will invariably be the one that rises to the top. When you extoll the virtues of the ordinary above all else, you automatically imply there is something exceptional about the ordinary, which is, of course, a non sequitur. So, by insisting every fopdoodle who can successfully tie his shoelaces is someone of some importance, you render yourself a society in which importance itself is without definitive measurement, which leads to no one at all having any importance at all. In short: if everyone must be someone, then no one can be anyone."

Matthew took a moment to take this in before asking, "So what has that to do with having good manners and parading about in old-fashioned uniforms?"

"Only that they provide a standard of excellence to which one can aspire—an arbitrary standard, to be sure, but a standard nonetheless. And having accepted a standard to which one can aspire, one can realize that aspiration and feel honestly superior to those who have not. That provides the backbone for a civilization, for you can't have a civilization without some sort of hierarchy in which all individuals fit somewhere on the scale of inferior to superior, but there must be some mechanism in place to allow for those born inferior to aspire to greatness. Otherwise, what's the point?"

A splash of whitewash landed on the railing between them.

"Damned seagulls," said Moore, inspecting his sleeve for

contamination. "Give them the vote and we'll have a Liberal government until doomsday."

"I think I see your point," said Sir Matthew while scanning the sky for more avian attackers. "About civilization, I mean, not the seagulls. The Americans want everyone to be someone, so they don't put any value on how a person behaves, as that would mean the one who behaves better is better than the one who behaves worse, and thinking someone is better than someone else goes against their nature."

"Exactly."

"So you're saying they're not civilized."

"No, they're not. Not really, anyway," said Moore airily. He raised his eyebrows while turning to face his friend and continued. "But you can't run any society—civilized or otherwise—without some form of hierarchical structure, so they've been forced to adopt what could well be the worst possible solution. While we have a social hierarchy and an economic hierarchy, they—in their misguided desire to be without any form of social hierarchy—have been inadvertently forced to accept their economic hierarchy as their social hierarchy. The result is, they still have a social hierarchy, despite their mad notion that they could be without one, but the one they have is based upon how much money a man can make rather than upon how well he behaves. By their estimation, a man like you might well be their de facto king. Now"—he patted Matthew's forearm—"I have the greatest respect for you, old boy, for what you've accomplished in life, but I'm not about to bow down to you as my sovereign, knowing you once caught rats for a living."

"No. I suppose not," said Sir Matthew. "If I found out King Edward had had to do some of the things I've had to do to get where I am, it would take the polish off my knighthood."

"Precisely! You can respect your superiors for never having had to do what you've had to do, while justifiably expecting respect from your inferiors for not having to do, any longer, what you had to do once, but what they have to do now instead because you've risen above it and they haven't."

Sir Matthew nodded. He hadn't expected his knighthood would change the way he looked upon the workings of things about him, but he was beginning to see the grand machinery of the universe in a much different light. He had set out on life's journey to make himself wealthy solely for the purpose of being free of want. Then, for some while, he'd wanted wealth for wealth's sake, and then he'd changed again to want wealth for the power it brought with it. But having accomplished all that far beyond the dreams of most men, it meant far less to him than he would have imagined. What he had never imagined was how much he would come to value the respect of others. That the former catcher of rats could now introduce himself as Sir Matthew Cratchit signified a life more greatly worthy of pride than anything he would have cared to predict in his youth.

He smiled with a wealth of satisfaction and said, absent-mindedly, "God bless us, every one!"

"I beg your pardon?" said Moore, startling Sir Matthew from his reverie.

"Sorry. Just something my brother, Tim, used to say before he died."

"Let's hope it portends better for you."

Sir Matthew let out a quiet snort and said, "Yes, let's."

CHAPTER 89

On their way back from the funeral service, Brigadier Smythe-Ponsonby-Jones looked absently out the side window of Lord Dudley Brightwigs's brougham while mentally drifting back over the years since he had first met the late Sir Matthew Cratchit. Though Smythe-Ponsonby-Jones had never stopped seeing Matthew for the scoundrel he was, he had, nevertheless, quickly learned to like the man, then grew to like him thoroughly, and he was now genuinely saddened at his demise and suffered a twinge of guilt for having guided Lord Dudley toward the idea of sending Matthew on a mission to America.

"Chin up, Smythe-Ponsonby-Jones," said Brightwigs.

"Sorry, sir. I can't stop thinking there must have been another way."

"That goes without saying, old fruit—there are always other ways. But this way was the best of a bad lot, in the service of a service that is replete with bad lots, leaving one with only selections of bad, worse, and worst. Just be thankful I have the power to select the best of the bad and am not forced—like several I can mention but won't, since the poor sods are more to be pitied than derided—with having to choose the worst of the worst simply to satisfy the will of the masses."

"Yes sir. I suppose so, sir. Had it been left to the people, Cratchit and his whole family would have been shot as spies twenty-five years ago."

"Quite so, Smythe-Ponsonby-Jones, quite so. I shan't pretend my motivations toward the bounder were in any way noble, but you must admit he did damn well by me. Over the years, between one thing and another, he's received well over half a million pounds from us, even more from the businesses we helped him acquire, and he got his knighthood. And—let's be realistic about it—after years of living in luxury, he had a quick and painless death with memories of Queen Victoria saying, 'Arise, Sir Matthew,' still fresh in his mind. What more could an Englishman want, I ask you?"

"King Edward, sir."

"What?"

"King Edward knighted Cratchit. Victoria's been dead three years now."

"Oh, right. Don't know why that keeps slipping my mind," said Brightwigs. He scrunched his face in thought. "I was at the funeral, wasn't I?"

"We both were, sir."

"Be that as it may," said the Lord with a fluttering, dismissive wave, "as thoroughgoing bounders go, Cratchit did well by all measures: wealth, respect, honors. But the silly sod was well past his usefulness to us. Well, well past it. And I couldn't have him walking about knowing what he knew, knowing full well that knowing what he knew included a lot of what you and I and a lot of others like us know and what cannot ever be known by those who are not like us."

"*Those* being those not in the know?"

"Indubitably. He was clearly becoming unreliable. Memory failing him, you know. The brightest candle burns down quickest, I suppose. Sad, I admit, but I dared not trust him any longer. Can't have that kind of laxity in this line of work. Have to be razor sharp and spot on down to the last detail. No room for a failing memory in our bailiwick."

"Yes sir. Quite so, sir."

"I mean, let's be honest about it: his own partners—damn it all, even his own sister, by heavens!—were finding ways to move him aside before he wreaked havoc upon his various enterprises. We certainly couldn't trust him, knowing that."

"I know," said the brigadier, sullenly. "I have no illusions about the man. And I dare say his service to his country meant very little to him. But his service was valuable, nonetheless."

"Invaluable! And will be even more so. Those files we retrieved from his offices will be of immeasurable utility in expediting cooperation from Parliament. Not to mention half the clergy in the Good Old City when a patriotic sermon from the pulpit is in order."

"Yes sir," said Smythe-Ponsonby-Jones awkwardly. "And thank you for your discretion regarding those photographs of …"

"Don't mention it, old fruit. They're quite safe where they are."

"Very reassuring, sir," said Smythe-Ponsonby-Jones with a wince.

"Quite. Then there's the matter of Cratchit's assassination. When Scotland Yard discovers the bombing of his ship was carried out by Irish nationalists, the newspapers will have a field day. Imagine the headlines." He held up both hands like a pair of brackets. "Man Awarded Order of Saint Silias for Founding Ebenezer Scrooge What's It Foundation Killed by Terrorists. Think of the possibilities. We won't have the least of problems getting Parliament to fund military action that will put an end to this home rule nonsense once and for all. And that being accomplished, it will distance the Americans from us, since they're all rather soft when it comes to the Irish and won't take kindly to us putting the sodding blighters in their place."

"Excuse me, sir …" said the brigadier in a moment of shock, but he then realized his master was alluding to aspects of the subterfuge of which he had been previously unaware since he had no need to know, and only knew now because Lord Dudley was of a mind to let him know, despite there being no need for it.

"What's that, Smythe-Ponsonby-Jones?"

"Nothing, sir. I remain in awe of your ongoing ability to get your proverbial ducks in the proverbial row and slay them with the proverbial single stone."

"Mixing your metaphors again, old fruit, but point well taken. Though, to be honest, I can't take full credit for imagining how we should implicate the Irish in the bombing. I was going over Cratchit's history and discovered he'd once had dealings with Rankin, Fowle,

O'Durr, and Gazpayne: Solicitors and Barristers at Law. A little research turned up the fact that O'Durr was an Irishman sentenced to drawing and quartering for treason after blowing up his own business offices along with his partners and the rest of his pestilential mob. He'd managed it by having barrels of gunpowder delivered to the building under the guise of libations for the staff. Initially, I found it hard to swallow he could be so careless as to leave so obvious a trail of clues, but once I had the sense of how sloppily these home rule blackguards go about their business, it was simple enough to send out a few lads posing as Irishmen to acquire the necessaries and create the corroborative evidence and damning documents. An anonymous tip to the Yard, and there you have it."

"Very clever, sir. But you say this O'Durr was drawn and quartered? I don't recall a drawing and quartering—"

"Commuted to death by firing squad," muttered Lord Dudley, disdainfully. "Something to do with the executioner being out with the agues that week or some such nonsense. The lazy sods didn't want to muck about with it any longer than they had to, so they took the easy way out."

"I take it you disapprove?"

"Well, of course I disapprove. It's that kind of slipshod tomfoolery that's undermining the penal system in this country. It's the thin end of the wedge that will lead us into moral decay. Thin end of the wedge, Smythe-Ponsonby-Jones," said Lord Dudley with a raised finger, "thin end of the wedge. Discipline is enforced top-down, but it's espoused bottom-up. You can't run a civilized society when the criminal class has lost its sense of self-discipline."

"I'm afraid I don't follow, sir."

"Good God, man! Didn't they teach you anything at Cambridge?"

"I was at RMC, sir. It was you who went to Cambridge."

"Oh? Yes, of course," said Brightwigs, with some confusion. "Well, can't be helped. Be that as it may, to put it in a nutshell, it looks something like this. At the top, we have the monarch, and beneath her the dukes, marquises, earls, viscounts, what have you, and all that.

Then comes the various honorees, followed by the landed gentry and merchants and the labor class beneath that. And, at the foundation of it all is the criminal class: the lowest of the low."

"Excuse me for interrupting, but I would have thought the criminal class is a vertical distinction, seeing as there are those who break the law at every level of society."

Brightwigs stared in bewilderment for some moments before letting out a little chuckle at his companion's naivete. "My dear fellow, you're laboring under a delusion, the result of an incomplete understanding. By your definition, we would all be criminals! No. The criminal class comprises not those who simply break the law, but those who must be punished for breaking the law. See the difference?"

"Not entirely, sir. How is the distinction made?"

"Simple enough, old fruit. If the bounder is breaking the law out of bone-bloody idleness—too lazy to work at feeding his family or to go through the courts to settle his differences with his neighbors or what have you—then he needs to be taught there is virtue in putting his back into life's enterprises. On the other hand, if he's putting in a decent effort to make the system work for him and is breaking the law merely to overcome the obstacles he encounters, then he needs to be recognized as the pillar of society he is and be given a free pass to get on with whatever it is with which he's mucking about."

"I think I see."

"I should jolly well hope so. It's plain enough." Brightwigs tilted his head. "Well. For those of us with a bit of education behind us, that is. Those who haven't had the benefit find it enormously difficult to differentiate between the two. And so, the onus of responsibility to keep things looking correct by our definition of correct falls squarely on our shoulders—you and I and the rest of the privileged classes. We must keep the veneer of absolute virtue from getting scratched, or the cheap and insubstantial, worm-eaten, half-rotted lumber underneath might be exposed for all to see."

Smythe-Ponsonby-Jones appeared to be surprised at the vitriol in his master's voice. "I take it you have no illusions as to the solidity of our cultural values?"

"None whatsoever, my dear fellow," said Brightwigs, attempting a smile. "The entirety of our way of life rests on the illusion of purity of spirit. Empire … Aristocracy … the Church … All electroplated base metal. We may have to teach our soldiers to brass it out, but we don't have to teach our officers to gold it out. They've learned to do that—we've *all* learned to do it—from the time we set foot out of the crib. Pretending the gold plate is more than superficial is so well ingrained in us it nearly qualifies as instinct. What lies beneath, though, doesn't change, and if it were ever properly exposed, Britain would be done for. And that's why when a thoroughgoing scoundrel like Cratchit commits murder or robbery or arranges for some poor sod to lose some anatomical component, the police allow the crime to go unsolved and announce they're looking at all the usual suspects."

"The usual suspects being those who always get punished when caught—the members of the criminal class."

"Absolutely, old fruit!" said Brightwigs. "Now you're catching on. The Cratchits of this world will continue to build businesses that appear to all the world as legitimate, sponsor foundations that appear to all the world as beneficent, and go about whatever else it is they go about while the illusion of a society upheld by unshakable pillars of virtue is sustained. And say what you will about the army and the navy, but it's that illusion of unalloyed moral strength that makes this country truly unassailable."

Smythe-Ponsonby-Jones paused a moment to take all this in.

"I can see all this, sir, but what I still don't understand is how the self-discipline of the criminal class is the foundation of society."

Brightwigs thought back on all he'd said—no small task, considering the amount of it. Suddenly the candle of his consciousness flickered and grew brighter.

"Ah, yes," he said. "As I said: the criminal class is the lowest of the low of society, which makes it the bedrock upon which society is built. If it becomes unstable, for any reason, the whole of the edifice of civilization is at risk of collapse. So, to keep them intact and behaving as God intended, we rain down fear upon them. Fear is the glue that holds the fabric of society together. The nobility is afraid of the queen. The landed gentry and merchants are afraid of the nobility. The labor classes are afraid of the landed gentry and the merchants. But the criminals are not afraid of the labor classes, nor the merchants, nor even the aristocracy. They feed upon their superiors like leeches upon spaniels. We solved this problem by instituting the penal system. Sanctioned by the monarch, empowered by the nobility, run by lawyers selected from the landed gentry and enforced by labor-class thugs in uniform—it has the weight to press down upon the lowest of the low and keep them from rising up, overextending their intentions, and engulfing us all in chaos. And the form the weight takes is fear—abject terror of being caught and punished."

Smythe-Ponsonby-Jones was amazed. "Brilliant, sir. Absolutely brilliant. I must confess to never having understood why we need criminals at all, but it's really quite obvious, isn't it?"

"It is, indeed, Smythe-Ponsonby-Jones, it is indeed."

The two rode on in silence for some while, admiring what there was to admire outside the carriage, before the brigadier turned to Lord Dudley and asked, "Just out of curiosity, sir: why is it we want to distance ourselves from the Americans? I thought we wanted them on our side?"

"Not all of us, Smythe-Ponsonby-Jones," said Lord Dudley sternly. "Granted, there are some who are childishly enamored of their gunfight-at-high-noon approach to world affairs, but those of us with some sophistication see it for what it is: a storybook fiction masquerading as an ethical premise. It only cuts muster in a juvenile society with only decades of experience to draw upon. We, on the other hand—having centuries of history behind us to provide us with a mature understanding—can see that might-for-right is the only true foundation for moral global hegemony."

"Like King Arthur, sir?"

"Absolutely, Smythe-Ponsonby-Jones. Absolutely."

BOOK 3

CHAPTER 90

The explosion that tore apart the SS *Transylvania* did so with vicious efficiency. Not only were Sir Matthew Cratchit, Wordsworth Moore, the rest of the passengers, and the entire crew shredded to seagull food in a flash, but the whole of the upper deck and most of the lower ones were shattered to slivers in the same fateful instant.

Which was extremely bad for everyone on board. That is, with the single exception of our hero, Tiny Tim, who—encased in a solid oak shipping crate and protected by masses of wool batting and stowed in a distal portion of the ship's hold behind masses of luggage—simply floated away from the scene of the wreckage along with the rest of the cargo buoyant enough to float and far enough from the center of the explosion to survive the blast intact.

This is not to say the circumstances for Tim were entirely good. Far from it. Within minutes of the catastrophe, he sensed having been left alone. And not just alone in the sense of being somewhat distant from the nearest person—no—he felt completely alone; infinitely alone; utterly, totally, and without any doubt alone in the universe.

It had been many, many years since he had been so very alone. Not since he first noticed there was nothing but his own feelings left to him in the way of life's experiences had he felt this so very alone. That period of aloneness had lasted mere days and had come to an end with the realization he was in the company of the morgue staff. This, however, was a much more profound aloneness, for his previous aloneness had ended with an ongoing awareness of people around him that had grown more and more and more powerful as his emotive reach expanded farther and farther and farther, such that losing that enormous connection to humanity in the instant of the explosion tore at him like the ripping away of the totality of his existence, leaving only the tiniest portion of his soul.

He had become concerned when the SS *Transylvania* steamed a short distance out to sea and he lost contact with the vast population of Great Britain—even though there were still some three hundred people close by and proximity intensified their presence. But the explosion was the blowing out of the last candle. Tiny Tim was in the darkest of the dark and destined to remain there for a long, long time.

Water had the strange effect of dulling his emotive reach to only a mile or two beyond shore. This accounted for his having reached a limit within the confines of Great Britain when he was still a resident of the Good Old City, and it explains why he never felt the influence of the Irish or the French—despite both those nations being more emotionally radiant than the English, Scots, or Welsh—and why he was unable to influence their behavior. This dampening effect of the sea had never been a problem in the past, but it now severely limited him in his search for life around him.

Occasionally he would sense the presence of fish, though these poor creatures lacked for subtlety of feeling and could not adequately feed his need for companionship. What's more, he had some vague recollections of eating fish and chips and enjoying them ravenously before entering his vegetative state. This he found a little disquieting, and without rational capacity from which to draw rationalizing thoughts, he decided he preferred loneliness to the company of erstwhile dinners and was glad when they moved on.

Seagulls were worse still. They would often land upon Tiny Tim's crate as he bobbed up and down on the ocean waves, and they might have proved decent enough companions had their kind been blessed with a more congenial history. Unfortunately, the birds brought with them a reminder of days gone by when the ancestors of this current generation had taken to tormenting him in spoiling his childhood visits to the seaside with his uncle Ebenezer. Though he had no visual memory of these events, the emotional scarring was still quite livid. He could not forgive the sons and daughters for the sins of their fathers and mothers and radiated such vitriolic animosity toward them when they alit, they quickly sensed they were unwelcome and immediately left in search of more affable accommodations.

Whales proved to be a lugubrious lot. In varying degrees, they were cursed with exceedingly long memories and had accumulated over time more than enough reasons to mistrust humankind. However, when they found Tiny Tim floating atop their domain, they did not immediately identify him as a representative of the reprehensible infestation that had become a blight upon their world.

They picked up on his emotive presence and were moved to profound curiosity. They discovered his emotional resonance with whatever it was they were feeling in the moment, decided this was an intriguing phenomenon, and took to traveling with him for long stretches as he drifted with the mighty ocean currents.

This pleased Tim greatly at first. He knew they were creatures of a far different sort from any he'd known before, but they were creatures nonetheless, and despite their unflagging nostalgia for the time preceding the advents of boats and sharks—the before time, according to their religion, when the oceans were a true and unspoiled paradise—Tim could feel ponderously comfortable in the ebb and flow of their compassionate, undulant temperament.

Time was largely irrelevant to the whales. They had their sense of a perfect time in the distant past, but since then, they simply drifted in an ever-present now that varied very little from moment to moment to moment. Moments felt like eons, and eons felt like moments. This tended to make Tiny Tim feel he wasn't getting anywhere at all. While this feeling can be upsetting for most people, it didn't bother him terribly much. He had had a fulfilling life thus far, in which all that was of value to him—people he loved and who loved him—had always come to him, so the need to go places to get something had never really arisen in his consciousness. He wasn't yet sure he loved the whales and didn't get the feeling they loved him, but they did create for him an aura of aliveness that alleviated his aloneness.

This lasted several months, though a month in whale time can be an instant or an eternity, depending on the whale and the month and what the whale is doing during that month.

Unless you've actually been a whale, this will be a difficult concept to grasp. To facilitate understanding, compare the passage of time experienced while taking a bath in ice water to the time spent chatting with a potential lover and magnify that difference to leviathan proportions, and you will arrive at a close approximation of the parameters of the referenced variations.

Tiny Tim was content enough throughout. His old skills of connecting had to be refined, however, since the consciousness of whales is in some ways different to the consciousness of humans. Over time, he gained the ability to sense specifics in their emotional communications, much the same as he had learned to do with people. This, unfortunately, led to his final rift with the cetacean population.

Drifting south, past Africa, he sensed a mother sulfur-bottom telling her child a story. It was an old tale of good versus evil, in which the champion was a great all-white giant who had taken upon himself the heroic task of ridding the world of that most despicable of humans, the whale hunter. The white whale had sunk ship after ship until he came upon his archnemesis—a one-legged whale-hunter mad enough to hunt the white whale himself. The great white whale charged at the madman's ship, stove it in, and took it to the bottom. But the champion had been harpooned many times and was tied by many lines that were too many to break free from. The great white whale went down with his enemy and was drowned along with his vanquished foe.

The story terrified the juvenile whale, as all such tales are meant to do. It also terrified Tiny Tim, which led the other whales to think, rather sentimentally, he might be merely a child of some sort, after all. But then the horrifying truth came out when they discerned that

Tim's terror was felt for the slain villain and not for the hero at all; if he wasn't human himself, he was a sympathizer and no friend to whale-kind. Within seconds of their discovery, they parted ways with the wave-borne Cratchit and left him to find himself, again, alone.

Dolphins and porpoises proved to be fairer companions, though of a far flightier kind. While whales could spend days entertaining a single thought or single feeling, their smaller cousins could streak through the entire spectrum of consciousness in a flash and return to their starting point before Tiny Tim could sense their beginning.

He found them to be a lot of fun, but alas, they followed the fish, and the fish, not wanting to be eaten by them, kept swimming quickly away; so the dolphins and porpoises could never stay long, since their next meal was always somewhere where they were not. And so to have their next meal, they had to be somewhere else.

The great global currents were his only constant companions but were not companions he could sense in any real way. They took Tim where they may, and much more often than not, he was solitary in the vastness of ocean and time.

CHAPTER 91

Months stretched into years. Tiny Tim floated and floated. At times, he would wash up on an uninhabited island or on a deserted coastline and spend some long while there before a storm would wash him out to sea and set him adrift again.

All the while he floated on the sea or lingered on some unseen shore, he searched for someone—anyone with whom to share his sense of being—anyone at all. The drive to connect with another living soul grew more and more massive within him as his desperation grew. And, in his desperation, the delicate senses for discerning life about him grew finer and finer in their touch.

All animate things that came near entered his attention. All fish, all birds, all insects came to him in passing but touched him only lightly. Too lightly to satisfy. Just enough to tantalize.

He floated from the Atlantic Ocean into the Indian Ocean and circumnavigated it several times. His years spent drifting in these waters saw a tremendous refinement of his feeling. He learned to sense not only single conscious beings but the collective awareness of various species. In time, he could appreciate, in an intuitive way, the processes of life—all life—around him.

And, in the time after that, he came to sense the Almighty.

This discovery had a titanic impact on our hero, as is true of all who come to this mystical juncture. For a while, Tiny Tim had no further need for human contact—contact with the Almighty was more than enough to remedy his aloneness. This initial flush of contentment did not last, however. In time, Tim's natural instinct for mortal companionship swelled again within him, and though the knowledge of the presence of the Almighty was comforting, he yearned for another person with whom he could share existence.

Still, he was not about to abandon his acquaintanceship with the Almighty. Company is company, after all, and there is a lot to be said for the saying 'If you can't be with the ones you love; love the ones you're with.' So, despite his preference for the company of someone on a more equal, fleshly footing, he struggled to find ways to strengthen the connection.

Now, the feelings of the Almighty are infinitely more refined than the feelings of corporeal beings. It took Tiny Tim years to make sense of even the coarsest of them. But then he started to break through.

This breakthrough was made possible by a fascinating adaptation unique to our hero and a brilliant verification of necessity being the mother of invention. To understand how this adaptation came about, you must first remember Tiny Tim had lost all language ability and all ability to create mental pictures. He lived in darkness and silence. All that had been left to him was his emotions, which he had learned to project. Later, he learned to feel the emotions of others. Later still, he somehow developed the skill of inadvertently sending sounds and images along with his feelings, though in this, he was only a conduit; the sounds and images never registered in his own consciousness. In short, he was without language and means of illustration in any sense familiar to you or me.

To overcome this crippling deficit, Tiny Tim was forced to reinvent language. This he did with unrivaled brilliance, as delineated in the following paragraphs.

To begin with, language is a curious phenomenon when you think about it. Spoken language is entirely based on meaning carried in the manipulation of discrete mouth noises. Sign language carries meaning in the manipulation of discrete gestures. Written language relies on memorizing significant discrete squiggles (to which long-established cultural habit has ascribed connection to discrete mouth noises) and then manipulating the positions of those significant discrete squiggles, one against others, to symbolize the flow of spoken language. As noted above, Tiny Tim had lost all ability to utter mouth noises, to make gestures, and to memorize significant squiggles and chain them together into significant meaning.

But he still had his emotions.

In his earliest days of emotive awareness, he'd learned to juxtapose feelings in strange and unfamiliar series for the purpose of amusing himself and those around him. This talent had waned within him after he was resettled with his family, but now, in the presence of the Almighty, he resurrected this practice and practiced it over and over until it became something resembling language. As difficult as this is to imagine, I will attempt to explain the mechanics—within the limits of my own understanding, of course.

For Anglophones, the word "dog" can be communicated by uttering the discrete sound associated with the letter D (a voiced dental plosive), followed immediately by one of the several discrete sounds possible for the letter O (in this case, a near-open back rounded vowel), and ended with the discrete sound for G (a voiced uvular plosive). That much is simple enough. What Tiny Tim learned, quite serendipitously, was that by stringing together discrete feelings in precise ways—just as speakers of English string together discrete sounds for D, O, and G in that precise order to mean "dog," he could, in effect, substitute emotions for letters and effect communication. Just as an example, "d-o-g," for him, may have been "love-excitement-satisfaction" felt in quite rapid succession.

And I have to call this discovery serendipitous because if he had attempted it with anyone other than the Almighty, it would have gone nowhere at all, but the Almighty—as it turned out—was the only other being capable of communicating in this fashion, and being infinitely patient and overly willing to meet anyone halfway, the Almighty was happy to make the effort to find out what our hero was all about. So in this, Tiny Tim was more than typically fortunate in these quite singular circumstances.

This process took considerable time to refine, but this book is already stretching beyond the limits I set for it on the offset, and there is still more to tell, so if you will forgive the foregoing of the tedious stumbling steps toward full fluency, I'll skip to Tiny Tim's first full conversation in decades.

"Are you God?" asked Tim.

"Oh, some call me that," said the Almighty, offhandedly. "It's a topic for a lengthy discussion of relatively little consequence."

"Don't you care what people think about you?"

"Not very much, I must confess. There was a time … But they never seemed to get it quite right, so I've given up worrying about it. I'm much happier simply letting them sort it out among themselves and thinking whatever they please."

"That's interesting," said Tiny Tim. "I seem to have some sense there's satisfaction to be got from getting everyone to think what I think. I remember something … though I'm not sure … something to do with my brothers and sister … but I'm not sure.'

"No matter," said the Almighty. "When you've been at this as long as I have, you learn not to get attached to temporary things. It tends to make them permanent, which defeats the whole object."

"What is it that you do?" asked Tiny Tim.

"Hmm … That's a very profound question. To be honest, I'm not entirely certain anymore. In the past, I was in the habit of redefining my role quite frequently; adapting to circumstances as required. But, somehow, that always tended to confuse matters rather more than expected. I'd make little adjustments, here and there, to try to get things back onto some sort of worthwhile course. However, whatever I did would end up being viewed negatively, so I simply decided to back away from the day-to-day and leave the running of things to the things that wanted running."

"Does that work?"

"Not very well, no."

"Then why don't you do something?"

"Well, that's the difficult bit, isn't it? You see, when I came to the decision to allow things to find their own course, I committed to remaining uninvolved until things get really out of hand. Tempted as I am from time to time to interfere, I can't quite get away from the feeling things will improve on their own once a few more lessons have been learned. One thing I do know for certain: if I keep making adjustments, they'll never get a sense of how to do it properly. So, regardless of what I feel about the situation in the moment, I keep coming back to the wait-and-see stance and keep an eye on things from a safe distance."

"But you won't let things get really bad, will you?" asked Tiny Tim optimistically.

"That depends on your definition of 'really bad,' I suppose. It is a relative concept, after all. What's really bad for you might not be so bad for someone else, and perhaps even rather good to someone yet again. But if you don't mind, there's a fellow in Tibet who's been trying to get a hold of me for some while now, and I do have to go. It's been more than pleasant making your acquaintance and most enjoyable feeling with you."

And with that, the sense of the presence of the Almighty vanished from Tiny Tim's awareness.

CHAPTER 92

As you might well imagine, this grand mystical experience was less satisfying for our hero than our cultural conditioning of expectations of the Almighty would have us anticipate. We have it on faith—those of us who have faith, that is—that connection with the Almighty comes with an overwhelming sense that we, having made the connection, have the right to get everything we want when we want it, because we are now the favorite and all the rest simply got it wrong, making us better than them, so we deserve treats, treats, and more treats from here on in since that is what the Almighty does for those in favor. Being confronted with the realization one will have to keep on doing what one has kept on doing in order to keep on getting what one kept on getting—and without infinitely less work—is most disappointing for most.

And in this, Tiny Tim was one of the most.

"I should have asked for help," he felt, feeling greatly irritated with himself over not thinking of this during the conversation. But then dejection replaced irritation as he felt, "Doesn't matter. He would have just said no, anyway."

The following day, he drifted into the Straits of Malacca, where he was spotted by pirates. They had no idea what he was, but a large oaken crate had to contain something, and when they sailed nearer it, they felt a most pleasant sense of togetherness—which they tacitly interpreted as comradery for each other but which still made for a positive association with the floating crate, nonetheless—so they took him in tow and pulled him toward their hideout east of Java.

Tiny Tim was elated to be again in the company of humans. True, there was something slightly off-putting about these fellows, as all who have had the pleasure of sharing the company of pirates for any length of time will tell you, but Tim recognized in this a feeling not unlike feelings he would get from Matthew, on occasion—a sense that the end always justifies the means and a little nastiness is a necessary thing. He could accommodate this easily enough, since accommodation of feelings was one thing he did with extreme facility.

A full day and night passed in the company of the pirates as they sailed for home. They were greatly pleased with having found Tim and taken possession of him, and Tim was greatly pleased at having been found and been taken possession of. It might be amusing to speculate what the pirates would have done with him once they'd broken open the crate to find our hero masquerading as a solid gold statue, but alas, Fate had yet another plan for Tiny Tim, and the opening of the crate was not to fall to the pirates.

The island the pirates called home was volcanic in nature—one of the offspring of Krakatoa. Though this mighty mountain had erupted to catastrophic effect more than once, it tended to remain quiet long enough between eruptions to convince people it was safe to assume it was done erupting for all time. To this, the fact that the original volcano had blown itself into oblivion thirty years earlier seemed to confirm that the worst was indeed over. So it was that the pirates felt quite secure in building their hideout within sight of what had been one of the world's most destructive natural disasters.

Fortunately (I think we're safe to assume), the volcanic forces of the region chose the moment Tiny Tim's crate was untied from the pirate ship to let loose a hiccup of seismic proportion—not enough to do much damage but enough to swamp the pirates' vessel and drive our hero yet again out to sea and out of reach of his captors.

Completely unaware his adventure with the pirates was not entirely without risk to him, he felt horrible grief at being separated from them in such a violent fashion. He began to wonder whether he would ever feel anything but loneliness and disappointment for the rest of his life.

He drifted and drifted. He drifted north into the South China Sea.

Out of desperation, he sent feelings to connect with the Almighty.

"I'm terribly lonely," he said.

"I'm not surprised," said the Almighty. "Floating about all by yourself. What put you in mind to do it in the first place?"

"I'm not sure. I was quite happy being with my sister all the time. But then it stopped. And I don't know why."

"Typical. Your kind is always landing itself in situations for which you have only the vaguest idea of how you got there and no notion whatever of what to do about it. But at least you're not blaming everything and everyone—including me—for your predicament … You're not blaming me, are you?"

"No. I'm not blaming anyone. I really don't have any idea at all how I got here. In fact, I don't know anything at all about anything at all."

"Excellent!"

"Excellent …? Why excellent?"

"It's infinitely better to know nothing at all than to know, with absolute certainty, everything that is completely false while believing it to be completely true. Since that sums up nearly the entirety of your kind, then in knowing nothing at all, you are immensely more knowledgeable than they. Infinitely so, in my estimation. And the infinite is something I do know something about, so you can trust me on this. I must say, that one like you exists at all proves there's hope for your species yet."

Tiny Tim took time to take this in before responding. "I'm having a hard time feeling good about it."

"No doubt. Your species was designed to look for the good in everything, but unfortunately, you went off on a tangent, trying to find good by casting off the bad. That you haven't realized yet that the two are inextricably linked is the primary reason I have trouble feeling more sanguine about you."

"About me?" asked Tiny Tim, a tiny bit hurt.

"Not you, personally—humans in general."

"Sorry. I forget I'm not everyone."

"Quite easily done. And to the point at hand, that can be a good thing or a bad thing or a thing of no consequence whatever depending on how you choose to view it."

Tiny Tim went back in time to when he lived with Lucy and felt the presence of everyone in Britain. He compared that to his current condition of extreme isolation.

"I almost feel as though I understand," he said at last. "Though I would still like to be back among people."

"That is natural enough. To that, I can say you're not far from being so again. Another sixty days, give or take the effects of a good onshore breeze."

"Couldn't you give me a push? Get me there a little quicker?"

"That would be breaking my own rule, and despite the pervasive belief I do that all the time, I don't do it at all. You're on your own, in this, I'm afraid. Oh, I am sorry. That probably came across as a bit callous, under the circumstances."

"That's all right," said Tiny Tim, being the passive sort he was.

"Well, I should get going. But before I do, I talked it over with the powers that be, and we've decided it will be all right for you to call me God, if you like."

"The powers that be? I thought you were the powers that be."

"Not entirely. I'm only the local authority, in fact. It's a vast universe out there. Far too big for one entity alone to govern."

"God bless us, every one!" said Tiny Tim ironically, as he considered, in his amazement, the implications of all this.

The Almighty was not accustomed to being addressed directly with other than literal meanings and took this to be a request.

"That much I will do," he said, and he blessed everyone in the world. "Well, feel you later."

Had the world been in a more settled state at the time of this blessing, it would have been universally accepted with deep gratitude; but with far too much going on in the world to allow for anyone to enjoy a quiet moment, the effects went largely unnoticed.

But be that as it may, our hero was once more alone upon the sea.

Sixty days later, he washed up on a beach in Japan.

CHAPTER 93

The tentative prediction of the Almighty—that the effects of a good onshore breeze might prove beneficial to our hero—proved to be true, much as tentative predictions of the Almighty often prove to be. Tiny Tim was floating northward past the mouth of a southern bay when the wind picked up almost imperceptibly, though enough to push him into the bay itself, where he circled about until another gust took him into a tiny cove during high tide, where he came to rest on the gentle slope of the sandy beach.

As the sun rose over the mountains in the east, the children of the fishing village nestled in the cove came out to do their early-morning chores in preparation for breakfast. Had Tiny Tim's crate been much smaller, it would likely have gone unnoticed until later in the day, but being large enough to catch even the most unobservant eye, it quickly caught the attention of several who had come down to gather driftwood for the fires.

The bravest of the children ventured forth to investigate, and the bravest of the brave, one Koshinuke Yarō, venturing farther than even the second-bravest of the brave would dare, ventured to climb up upon the enormous crate to see whether he could see what it might be all about. To this, his investigation proved fruitless in any cognitive sense, for the huge wooden box appeared just as huge, just as wooden, and just as boxlike when viewed from above as it had been when viewed from all sides. What was much more greatly rewarding, though, was the sudden, overwhelming sense of joy that flooded upward into Koshinuke and outward to all his comrades.

The more timid of the troupe did what timid children everywhere do when faced with a need for bravery: they ran and got their parents. Soon word of a giant wooden box washed up on the beach in the night reached everyone in the village, and everyone, saving a few of the elderly who were less inclined toward excitement over novelty, as well as the select few who distrusted novelty, were crowding to the site of the discovery. One Aho Baka, being a wise man who always came prepared into every situation, had the foresight to bring a mallet and a pry bar with him and so was ready to pry open the enormous crate the moment he arrived upon the scene. And that he did.

Aho strode straight up to the hut-sized box, studied its structure for long enough to identify the best method of its disassembly, and began hammering the pry bar between two planks at one end. The crowd pushed in closer and closer, driven by rising impatience of curiosity. Never had the people been in such great need to know what secrets lay within a box. Never had a box of this magnitude washed up on their beach, but that alone was not the magnifier of their need to know. Without knowing he was the object of an investigation, Tiny Tim had sensed the people's painful spirit of inquiry, embraced the need fully, and become infused with it until it lit up his own spirit like a furnace.

With the help of three others, Aho pulled the front panel of the crate free from its last binding nails to expose a wall of batting. The batting fell away of its own weight to reveal what appeared to be a life-sized golden and bejeweled statue of a smiling, peaceful, corpulent, reclining man, with eyes closed while engaged in quiet meditation. All present were gripped in paralyzing awe at the wonder of the sight.

"It is a Buddha," said one fellow in hushed amazement.

"A golden Buddha!" said another. "The gods have sent us a golden Buddha!"

The overwhelming awe was transformed to overwhelming reverence, as all those present knew they were in the presence of something holy. Almost instantly, that sense of reverential mystery began spreading beyond those near at hand to those who had not yet made their way to see the wonder that had washed up on the beach. Of these, the local leader of prayer and ceremony, Hentai Sukebe by name, was one. Being of the belief new things represented disruption in the grand order of things, and disruption of the grand order of things was something a holy man must avoid at all costs—since preservation of tranquility rested on the undisturbed steady continuance of the grand order of things in never-ending continuity—Hentai chose to remain aloof until the collective will demanded he pass wise judgment upon whatever it was that was threatening the preservation of tranquility by its mere presence.

By the time Hentai could be fetched and brought back to the site of Tiny Tim's landing, the crate had been completely dismantled, the wood claimed by the village carpenter, the batting claimed by the village futon maker, and our hero left glistening in the morning sun. A wonder for all to see.

The right to be the first to touch the golden statue was reserved for Hentai, for though he was not a true priest, he was the closest thing the village had to one and was considered such when he wasn't out fishing with the others. Well before that first touch, though, Hentai could feel the extraordinary presence that awaited him. The sense of holy mystery awash in pure, sublime serenity was being magnified by Tiny Tim and diffused out into the world. The crowd held its collective breath as Hentai approached the sparkling Buddha. He reached out to the round shoulder. His fingers tingled with anticipation. And then the touch. And surprise.

"The Buddha is covered in wax!"

"Wax?" said Aho. "But he is made of gold."

"Perhaps," said Hentai. "Or perhaps brass, which tarnishes. It matters not. He is made with great love. I can feel that."

And all present agreed, for they could feel it too.

"What does it mean, Hentai Sukebe?" asked one lady. "Why have the gods sent him to us? We are only a poor fishing village."

"Precisely!" said the fisherman-priest, thrusting a confident finger skyward. "What good would come of giving him to a wealthy temple. None. But I feel it in my liver that we are to do some great thing and this Buddha is given to us for that great thing."

"What great thing?" asked many together.

"That I cannot say, as yet. But I do know the gods want us to be Buddhists. Why else would they send us a Buddha?"

Most nodded in respect for this, though one, Utagaibukai Hito, had to ask, "But we are Shintoist. We have always been Shintoist. Our ancestors were all Shintoists. Why would the Shinto gods command we become Buddhist?"

"It is not for us to question the will of the gods," said Hentai. "Only to obey."

"So the gods will it that we no longer believe in them?" said Utagaibukai, closing one eye in doubt.

"Precisely," said Hentai, with no doubt at all.

"But how are we to obey the will of those in which we do not believe?"

Usually, the villagers didn't doubt the word of Hentai, but the two ends of this rope could not be brought together and knotted. For the first time in living memory, the simple people had to question the religious wisdom of their part-time priest. This sense of dissatisfied searching for truth took them all deeper and deeper into disbelief.

"I can tell you are all full of doubt," said Hentai, himself suddenly and mysteriously riddled with a thirst for certainty of something. "This is very good, for the Buddha said we must doubt what we believe for us to come nearer truth. That we are all now doubting, then, is proof we are all now Buddhists. The will of the gods has been fulfilled!"

The unassailability of this logic was ineluctable. One and all, the villagers once again accepted Hentai's word as sacrosanct. That the gods had transformed them into Buddhists was as clear and obvious as daylight and rain. That this meant the people were no longer to believe in these same gods was a mystery for another day. And with this much collectively decided, doubt gave way to rejoicing.

"We must move the Buddha to the shrine!" called out Hentai.

From among the strongest of the young men came eight volunteers who hefted Tiny Tim's divan up upon their shoulders to begin the slow process of moving him off the beach and into the village.

The initial novelty of finding a huge crate and the later novelty of finding a golden Buddha inside the crate were diminishing over time, as all novelty tends to do when the differentness of it fades imperceptibly into usualness. Though excitement still ruled in the minds of the adults, the children—being children—had accepted the presence of Tiny Tim as commonplace with far greater rapidity and were now turning their attention to the lateness of their breakfast.

The phrase "I'm hungry," expressed in that squeaking, importunate tone only a child can render, was heard repeated everywhere throughout the slowly advancing crowd.

"You want fish for breakfast?" asked one young mother, which might have seemed a silly question in light of fish being served for breakfast every day, but to which the response was, "Yes! Yes! Fish for breakfast."

Within moments, the chant was taken up by all the youngsters. "Yes! Yes! Fish for breakfast. Yes! Yes! Fish for breakfast."

Soon the adults were recognizing their own hunger, and the want of fish became nearly maddening. No one could recall ever having had such a powerful craving for what was, for them, so everyday a meal to be almost punitive in its unvaried repetition. Still, they craved fish, and a great love for fish and wanting of fish and dire need for fish was radiated out into the world.

"Look!" shouted one man. "Fish are washing up on the beach! Thousands of them!"

All looked. It was true. The waves were glistening silver with masses of fish, and the lower reaches of the beach were covered with the shimmering, squirming, flopping bodies of hordes and hordes of fish, lured landward by an unrefusable pull of pure love for their kind.

"Fetch baskets!"

"Gather them up before the tide comes back in!"

"Hurry; hurry, everyone!"

Tiny Tim was set down again on the sand, freeing his eight bearers for the harvest. The gathering went on for hours, and by noon, the village had taken into its stores much more than any usual day's take—without the sailing of a single boat or casting of a single net.

Still, it was fatiguing work. A wish for this bounty to come to an end started to take hold of the villagers, and as miraculously as the great flow of piscine abundance had started, it ended. The fish still at sea stopped feeling the magnetic pull of the powerful love and, slightly saddened by the fickleness of their unknown lover, gave up their quest and went back to their usual fooling about.

Food of all sorts was prepared in celebration of this sudden rise in the village wealth and the unscheduled half-holiday that accompanied it.

"It is the Buddha who brought the fish to us," said one man while Tiny Tim was being transported the rest of the way to the shrine.

"The Buddha is only a statue," said Hentai Sukebe sternly, who was always on the lookout for his people slipping into the primitive ways of superstition. "It is the gods who gave us the fish to reward us for becoming Buddhist."

"But we no longer believe in the gods," said Utagaibukai Hito. "Why do you insist they have willed it?"

"It does not matter if we do not believe in them," said Hentai. "They still believe in us. But no more talk of this. Now that we are Buddhist, I feel it in my kidneys it is time I must stop being a fisherman and become a priest for all time and not only for prayers."

"You cannot be a priest without a temple, and our village is too small to merit one," said Utagaibukai—who you have already determined, no doubt, was one of the perennially argumentative sort.

"Too small for a Shinto temple, as the emperor has decreed. But a Buddhist temple is another matter. There is no law governing that. We have a Buddha now. We must have a temple to house him."

"The shrine will do well enough for that," said Utagaibukai, with a pragmatic scowl.

"Only for now," said Hentai. "It must be made larger. There must be rooms added where I will live and where we will keep the books."

"Books?" asked Aho Baka, in dumbfounded amazement, since the idea of the village owning a book struck him as a ridiculous extravagance.

"Of course, books," said Hentai. "I understand confusing things better than anyone here, but clearly, I must understand them better still. All religion is confusing, but Buddhism is most confusing. We cannot be proper Buddhists without one who understands confusion. Since no one else wants to do this—"

"How do you know no one else wants to be priest?" said Utagaibukai.

"Very well," growled Hentai. He then shouted defyingly, "Does anyone else wish to be priest?"

The villagers all glanced at each other, but none dared to speak.

"Then it is settled," said Hentai after a reasonable passage of affirmational silence. "I must take the responsibility myself, as I said I would."

"But can you even read?" asked Utagaibukai.

"Of course ... Well enough ... I am told one gets better with the doing of it."

"Much like anything else," said Aho, and he nodded, which got everyone nodding.

"Precisely!" said Hentai "So! I will go to market this afternoon to sell the fish given to us by the gods this morning. With the money, we will build the temple. This is the will of the gods who sent us the Buddha and the fish."

To this, the villagers settled into something like agreement. Individually, they still sensed tiny gaps in Hentai's position—gaps that allowed this small doubt or that small doubt to shine through, but collectively, they considered, in general, the collective understanding of his position, in which a gap seen by one would not be seen by another, and so the collective understanding shared in common was collectively seen as seamless. And in this, they could sense that this understanding shared in common was, indeed, solid enough to merit acceptance by all, as is the common-sense experience common to all groups committed to a common undertaking.

And despite the entire discussion having been conducted between Hentai and Utagaibukai, with only minor contributions from Aho, all present—including Utagaibukai, whom one could argue lost the argument—felt an overwhelming satisfaction of having triumphed in achieving their goal. This anomalous feeling did not go unnoticed by any, but all concluded within themselves that this must be a Buddhist feeling and that it felt unexplainable only because they were so new to the religion.

CHAPTER 94

That afternoon, **Hentai** and Aho, along with a collection of youths looking to be among the foundational contributors to the grand enterprise, took the eight cartloads of fish to the city to be sold. While there, Hentai commanded they visit a Buddhist temple to get a sense of design required to build a reasonable facsimile. Aho was permitted to pace out distances and make notes while Hentai spoke with a novice who provided him with two books written for the instruction of the very young in the ways of the religion. The novice, thrilled to be called upon to display his knowledge, was quick to point out words that would be unfamiliar to the outsider and instructed Hentai in the proper pronunciations.

And, before leaving the city, Hentai bought enough black cloth to have fashioned for him his priestly robe, and a razor to shave his head. He knew full well the priests of the city would not recognize him as one of their own, since he had not gone through any of the proper training, but he had been chosen by the gods, and that should be good enough for even the most pedantic observer of formalities.

Upon return to the village, those who had gone to the city were bewildered to find that every fishing boat was still beached and every villager was diligently engaged in idling about.

"What does this mean?" said Hentai.

"It seems to us," said Utagaibukai, "we don't need to go out in boats anymore when the Buddha will bring fish to us. We have only to ask—or I should say *you* have only to ask, since you are now priest."

"I told you this morning," roared Hentai, "the Buddha is only a statue and cannot bring fish!"

"That is not how it seems to us," said Utagaibukai, with a crafty sneer. "Is it, my friends?"

"No," said the villagers in unison.

"But that is how it is! There is nothing more to say about it. Go and fish while there is still light," said Hentai, and he turned his back to walk away in the direction of the shrine, where Tiny Tim had been installed under its protective canopy.

Utagaibukai followed him and was, in turn, followed by the rest of the villagers. Hentai was so certain of himself and of the ineluctable power of his commands, now that he was fully a priest, that it did not occur to him his command could be ignored by anyone, let alone by all, and so he never thought to look back to ensure obedience was in evidence. So it was he was startled nearly into apoplexy when he reached Tiny Tim's side and Utagaibukai said, "Just ask the Buddha to bring us more fish."

"The gods do not send fish for the asking," said Hentai, half in fear from being startled nearly half to death and half in anger from having his priestly assertions challenged. "They send fish when it is their wish to send fish."

"We think you know you are not really a priest," said Utagaibukai. "And that is why you will not ask. A real priest would ask the Buddha, and the Buddha would do as the real priest asks."

"The Buddha is a statue. It is the gods—"

"The gods in whom we no longer believe?" asked Utagaibukai, leadingly.

"Precisely!"

"If we do not believe in them, it must be because they are not real. That is the only answer that makes any sense at all. And yet you say these gods, which you say are not real, bring fish when they wish to bring fish and not for the asking. That makes no sense at all."

"That is the paradox," said Hentai, authoritatively raising a finger toward heaven and proud to be able to use a word he had learned only that afternoon.

Utagaibukai was nonplussed. "What is a paradox?"

"A paradox is two things that are both true because the gods say they are both true, although both cannot be true because humans say they cannot both be true since for one to be true, the other must be false."

"That makes no sense at all," said a shaken Utagaibukai—far less confident and far more angry than the last time he had uttered the sentence.

"Not to you. You are not a priest," said Hentai, having taken the higher philosophical ground by force of superior intellect.

"If you are a priest, prove it!" said Utagaibukai. "Ask the Buddha for the fish!"

"Ask him yourself!" said Hentai in response.

Until this point, Tiny Tim had not sensed what to do. Some of the feelings he felt were angry, while others he felt were purely prideful and arrogant. Many of the feelings he felt were uncertain, while all he felt was confusion, which had everyone confused. In this moment, though, both Hentai and Utagaibukai were effusing anger and hatred for one another, so this, then, told Tiny Tim what was wanted. He turned into an inferno of anger and hatred, radiating the intense heat of his emotion out to the villagers and all the island of Honshu beyond.

The villagers, being under the direct, unalloyed, undiluted influence of Tiny Tim at its most malevolent, turned upon one another in revenge for every infinitesimal infraction ever committed, one upon another. And every infinitesimal infraction was conjured up in the memories and imaginations of all. One and all—men, women, and children; elderly and young; able and infirm—took to beating, scratching, choking, berating, and belittling one another in ways that had never been seen in the peaceful little village throughout all of time until then.

The battle raged on toward evening.

Fortunately for all, they lived in a fishing village and not a village of farmers, cabinetmakers, or stoneworkers. Had they been other than what they were, their tools of the trade might well have been more readily at hand—those tools of the trade being sharp, pointy, or blunt and hard—the kinds of things that can easily serve as weapons when weapons are not to be had. But as they were what that they were—denizens of a fishing village—their tools of the trade were kept some distance from the scene of the battle, and so it was that injuries were limited to scrapes, scratches, and bruises, and the only clear victor to emerge from the brouhaha was fatigue, to which all combatants were forced to submit.

The square of the village, dyed orange by the setting sun, was littered with the panting bodies of the people. They were too tired to fight. They were too tired to hate their neighbors. They were too tired to feel angry anymore. But when anger and hatred surrender to exhaustion, they do not evaporate from the spirit; they change to feelings of a more inwardly directed hostility, which, though equally unpleasant, require less energy to sustain. So it was that the people recovered from their physical depletion only to find themselves consumed with grief, guilt, and despair—grief, guilt, and despair amplified by our hero, who could not know better than to sail, full-sail, with whatever wind was blowing.

The village took to wailing and the gnashing of teeth in grief, which had carried on well into the night when, one by one, the people fell asleep in accordance with the unyielding demands of the flesh.

Morning found them all feeling greatly refreshed, much like one might feel after a marathon viewing of tragic plays that inspire one to all the feelings one would wish to avoid in real life but which one wishes to invoke when viewing works of tragedy for the purpose of feeling catharsis afterward—assuming one accepts Aristotle's proposed reason for wanting to watch tragedy, which, since it more than adequately explains why the villagers felt refreshed after a day of torment and anguish, we will accept as fact, since doing so allows us to move the plot along without bogging down in tedious comparisons of the relative merits of alternate theories of literary criticism.

So hugely contented were they with themselves, the villagers could have stayed where they were, lying in the open in the village square for ever and ever, had not the emptiness within them—brought on by missing supper the previous day—put them all in mind of food and the necessity of getting up and going about the business of getting it.

In precisely the same way it had been Lucy—the youngest of the Cratchits—who was the one to identify Tiny Tim as the source of collective emotion, so, too, it was the youngest children of the fishing village who first sensed that this contentment to the world was radiating from our hero. They had kept to the periphery when the violence had erupted the day before, but the morning after, they were drawn to the little shrine where Tiny Tim resided and gathered about him to enjoy the wonderful sense of well-being.

In the strangeness of it all, the children were not missed until food had been prepared in every hut, and they were not there to partake of it. Adult heads popped out doors and windows to look this way and that for children who were not about. The entirety of humanity that could be seen anywhere by any adult was the heads of other adults extended into the exterior for the same purpose.

"Have you seen Ichi?"

"No. Have you seen Ni or San?"

"No. But Kuchigitanai On'na says Go is missing too."

So it was that a child hunt was launched by the worried mothers, who, numbering twenty-three, had some difficulty in delegating who should look where since the tiny village barely offered twenty-three distinct places to look, so the children were found before the last of the mothers had received assignments for searching. As disappointing as that may have been for those left unappointed, the relief felt by all quickly extinguished all concerns for who would contribute what to the community project.

The thirty-six children of the village under the age of eleven were seated on the stone floor of the shrine, gazing passively and tranquilly at Tiny Tim, who was joyfully keeping them joyfully passive and tranquil.

"Aren't you hungry for breakfast?" asked the mother who had found them.

"Yes," said her son dreamily, "but I like it here."

Had the mother not felt warmed by the joy of it all, she would have gotten angry. The other mothers began arriving shortly, and the questioning continued one child or two at a time with much the same question being asked and much the same answer forthcoming. It was not long before all twenty-three mothers were standing behind the thirty-six children seated on the floor before our hero, feeling the feelings he unconsciously radiated out to them.

This state of dreamy paralysis of the will to move came to an end only when Kuchigitanai On'na, the sternest of the village mothers, given to impatience at the best of times, became impatient with the inactivity despite the pleasantness of it and said to her son, "Go, come."

"I want to stay with the Buddha," said Go.

"You bring shame on your family when you disobey your mother."

This statement of fact might have been lost on others of the children present, but Kuchigitanai Go—being the overly well-disciplined son of Kuchigitanai On'na—responded immediately to his mother's admonition, and shame welled up from deep within his soul.

"I am sorry, honored mother," he cried out as he rose to leave but instead burst into tears and, wailing miserably, stood where he was, unable to walk, blinded as he was with eyes shut tight in a face dominated by a mouth opened to the fullness of its limits.

Soon all the children were riddled with guilt, and soon after, so were all the mothers of the children.

Apology upon apology was tendered.

"I am sorry, honored mother."

"I am sorry, honored daughter."

"I am sorry, honored son."

"I am sorry, honored neighbor."

"I am sorry, honored friend."

All with polite bows of appropriate respect.

The precise nature of the misdemeanors was unclear, though vague recollections of past infractions surfaced in the minds of all since feeling guilt for a crime cannot be felt without a crime, so some crime must have been committed for the feeling of guilt to have a place in a world governed by logic.

After the third or fourth round of contrition, the crowd began to break apart as mothers took the hands of their children to lead them home to breakfasts grown cold in waiting.

CHAPTER 95

Upon their arrival home, the women found their husbands in a terrible state of regret for all manner of offenses to which each man confessed his own list—long, longer, or extremely long; major or minor or incidental. Each man had acquired—through years of failure in virtue, according to the strength of his character to draw him away from temptation; to the strength of his fear of discovery to push him away from temptation; or to the power of the temptation to overwhelm both his character and his trepidation—a heavy burden of guilt.

Needless to say, these burdens of guilt had been light enough before Tiny Tim led the men into a spirit of self-examination. But as any accountant will tell you, small change can add up to a small fortune when properly watched.

At first, the fountain of forgiveness that flows continuously in every loving heart—in varying degrees—provided the women with the will to soothe their men away from their despair. But as time wore on and the confessions showed no sign of arriving at any kind of timely conclusion, the fountains began to run dry, and noble sentiments grew ignoble when feelings of forgiveness succumbed to feelings of outrage and revenge.

So it was that the men of the village took to sleeping in their boats at night and eating about fires built upon the beach after returning from fishing every day.

"I thought it would be easier being Buddhist," said Aho Baka.

"When the Buddha brought us all the fish, I thought he wanted us to be rich and happy."

"The Buddha did not bring the fish," said Hentai yet again. "He is merely a statue and wants nothing and does nothing more than remind us we are Buddhist."

But the men were weary of Hentai's well-rehearsed responses, and their lack of patience showed on their faces, which told him he had to be more priestly and wise if he were to sustain their support. So he said, "But the Buddha does want us to be rich and happy. First, however—and I feel this in my spleen, so I know it to be true—we must rid ourselves of our sinful past and our sinful ways. That is why he guides us into all this trouble: that we can see our error and mend our ways."

"The Buddha does?" asked Utagaibukai Hito, leadingly.

Hentai was quick to see the trap. "Only in a way of speaking. It is the gods that do all this. But they do it in secret since they wish for us to not believe in them anymore."

"I ask again: how can this be?"

"I have thought much on it," said Hentai, and those nearby perked up their ears since everyone was curious to know the answer to the paradox of the intercessory provision of fish that had been circling without resolution in the minds of all since Hentai had first proposed it. "The gods are our spirit parents, and they have provided for us since our beginning. But they want us to be grown up now. They want for us to look after ourselves, to stop asking for the things we want. So they sent us the Buddha and told us to be Buddhists. The fish were a gift to start us on our way."

This Hentai said with profound self-assurance. The men who were near enough to listen thought about it and nodded to each other in concurrence. A feeling of pride took hold and spread to those too distant to have heard Hentai speak. It was the same feeling of pride a man feels when he leaves his parents' home to go off to make his own life in the full knowledge he has all that is needed in the way of skills to do so. All felt this.

Even Utagaibukai felt it.

And Hentai felt it, too.

After some while of glowing with great pride, the confidence of the men began to rise, and the bravest among them began murmuring that they had slept and eaten under the stars long enough; they had enjoyed the company of men long enough, that they had gone without the pleasures of women long enough, that their period of atonement had gone on long enough, and that it was about time they galvanized their collective will and put their collective foot down to reestablish their individual dominion over their individual households.

Now, pride and confidence are wonderful things to own, to be sure, but they do bring with them certain drawbacks—one being the exaggerated perception of one's own correctness in matters of opinion, and another being the unwillingness to entertain the possibility that others might not share that same opinion. These two weaknesses led to further complications, then, as the men of the village roused themselves to rise up and march off as imperiously as they could— the effect of imperiousness being rather diminished while marching barefoot on loose sand—toward their homes. This they accomplished without loss of pride or confidence.

Upon arrival at their front doors, however, the illustrious owners of pride and confidence were, quite to their surprise, rather rudely and abruptly robbed of their emotional possessions. Contrary to the men's expectation, the village women were far less ready to account the time required for the achievement of forgiveness as having passed. And to make matters worse, the suggestion made by many men—that being they were absolute rulers of their homes, and their male assessment of acceptable behavior was the only one that truly mattered—only incensed their wives to new heights of indignation.

Hentai, alone, was spared an overtly stunning defeat on the marriage front. That is not to say he was triumphant. He was not. But unlike the other men of the village, he was not sent scurrying back to the beach with his dignity in tatters. He was, instead, allowed to remain in his hut—with his dignity blasted to dust.

Hentai had married the prettiest and most intelligent girl in the village. This had led to him being selected as leader-of-prayers since no one could see one scintilla of a reason why the most sought-after bride for miles around would choose him over others deemed more manly, more clever, and more personable than he—unless, of course, he was mysteriously favored by the gods. This divine preference, being the only clear answer to the question, made him the obvious choice to lead the community in the petitioning of celestial favors, since clearly and obviously, the favorite always has an easier task of winning favors than those less favored.

And since we are uniquely positioned to discount entirely the role the gods played in the lovely girl's decision to marry Hentai, we can look upon her earthly motivations in greater detail than was permitted to the villagers.

Hentai's wife, Kin Saikutsu-Sha, was actually a most pragmatic sort of person and, being so, had had practical considerations to satisfy in the choice of a husband, over and above the considerations provided to her by the gods. She had decided the manlier men of the village were too difficult to control and the cleverer men of the village asked too many questions. And since she had little intention of ever spending much time in conversation with her husband under any circumstances, there was little advantage in having one with a fetching personality. On top of all that, Hentai was reliable, predictable, and little inclined to spend money on himself. To Kin Saikutsu-Sha, Hentai was a match made in heaven—just as the villagers had said.

All that had changed, however, when Hentai announced his intention to retire from fishing and become the village's full-time priest. The proceeds from fishing were not rich, but they were comfortable in Kin Saikutsu-Sha's eyes since her sense of plenty had been shaped within the parameters of village experience and since most of the spending of the household income fell to her with no interference from her husband. The proceeds of the priesthood, though, constituted an uncertain and questionable quantity.

She had heard Buddhist priests survive by begging and asked

Hentai whether this was true. He had to think about this, for his decision to devote himself to religion had been driven by the current of enthusiasm for a life without labor and not by any rational assessment of earthly necessities. Then, just as Kin Saikutsu-Sha was beginning to suspect his silence portended the worst, Hentai managed to state, with some certainty, the villagers would all contribute to the upkeep of the temple and its priest. This she would have doubted with all her being, knowing her neighbors as she did, but for the miracle of the fish washing up on shore that had accompanied the arrival of the Buddha. If Hentai could continue to keep them convinced of his central importance to the Buddha's well-being, the villagers might well part with enough of their income to keep her in silks and sake.

Kin Saikutsu-Sha's willingness to suspend disbelief in her husband's ability to provide from the proceeds of priesthood came to an end with the serial strangeness that descended upon the village—the insane rage that had enveloped everyone in a daylong brawl, the children going missing, the mass confessions of the men (including Hentai himself) that had led to their summary exile from their homes—which told her that whatever it was Hentai was doing to keep the Buddha pleased, he wasn't doing it at all well, and that continuing to be attached to him would likely lead to disaster by association.

So it was when Hentai arrived at his cottage to reassert his patriarchal right to dominion over his household, he met with no resistance at all—there being no one there to resist his assertions. This made him the only man in the village to achieve the goal of sleeping under his own roof that night. Unfortunately, the absence of his wife tended to dampen the enjoyment of this victory, such as it was, for the nature of victory tends to hinge on the necessity of there being a vanquished for the enjoyment of it to have any substance.

Not only did the absence of a vanquished party diminish Hentai's enjoyment of his moral victory, but the absence of furniture, food, and eating utensils diminished his enjoyment of all life's basic pleasures. And to add to all this, he discovered the following morning that Kin

Saikutsu-Sha had left on the first day of the exiling of the menfolk, which meant he had slept in his boat for five nights for no reason at all.

This made him feel like a fool.

But what made him feel worst of all came in one horrifying discovery. Along with all his furnishings and minor possessions, Kin Saikutsu-Sha had taken his ox and his oxcart (no doubt to carry away the meager haul), and, worst of the worst, she had taken all the money Hentai had gotten from the sale of the miraculously provided fish—money entrusted to him by the villagers for the building of the temple.

Being a Buddhist was not working out for him anywhere near as well as he'd imagined.

CHAPTER 96

T he next morning, Hentai did not come out of his cottage to
bless the men setting out to fish. They assumed from his absence
during the night that he alone had succeeded in the collective putting
down of the collective foot and was in the process of making up for five
nights of missed intimate affection with the lovely Kin Saikutsu-Sha.

"Say what you will about Hentai," said Aho Baka, "he is the
favored one."

"Humph," grunted Utagaibukai Hito, who had his doubts.

Hentai was in terror of confronting the other villagers with the
news that the money for the temple was gone and his wife had taken it.
He knew not what to do. Should he walk away and seek some other life
in another place where no one knew him? The villagers would think
he stole their money and would hunt him down, chop him into little
pieces, and use him for bait. Should he tell the truth and trust them to
be understanding? They would say he was not fit to be their priest; that
all the calamities were his fault. And they would chop him into little
pieces and use him for bait. It was difficult to decide which was better.

Kin Saikutsu-Sha had not taken every single thing from the house.
She had left the two books on Buddhism, the razor, and the black cloth
destined to be Hentai's priestly robe, along with scissors, a needle, and
enough thread to accomplish the manufacture of components and
the final assembly of the garment. Unable to decide what to do from
within the limits of his own imagination, Hentai desperately read the
two texts for an answer to his dilemma.

Without discounting the possibility that somewhere in all the books written within the Buddhist tradition there is something that specifically addresses the concerns of a man whose wife has run off with everything he owns, including the collective treasure of the community, Hentai was disappointed to find the two books in his possession were not so availed. There were, however, enough references to enlightenment to convince Hentai the solution to his problem might lie in that, for without knowing what it was, there was some suggestion it came with feelings of bliss, which was precisely what he was not feeling at all but very much wanted to.

To this, he decided the best course of action would be to see the Buddha. Although he knew the Buddha was merely a statue and could not do anything but remind him he was a Buddhist, he sensed that in talking to the Buddha, the gods, in whom he no longer believed, would hear him and respond to his petitions through the Buddha, thus preserving for themselves the illusion of their not being real.

When he arrived at the shrine where Tiny Tim reposed, Hentai found the children of the village seated before the statue in a state of serenity.

"What are you all doing here?" he asked.

"We come here every day to be with the joyful Buddha," said Ichi, who was the oldest of the boys who were too young to go out fishing.

"Do you want some cake?" asked Ni, the little girl who always carried snacks and who always offered them out.

"Yes, please," said Hentai, suddenly aware he had not eaten that morning.

Hentai took the tiny rice cake wrapped in rice paper. Ni smiled up at him, greatly warmed with the spirit of giving, and was warmed in return by his grateful smile. Then others felt the warmth of gratitude. And more and more and more, the children grew in their gratitude, though for what they did not know.

They looked to one another, nodding coyly and shyly murmuring, "Thank you."

This spirit of giving and gratitude spread throughout the village, inspiring the women, the elderly, the infirm—all who were not out fishing for the day. And it inspired those who were nearing the village on the main road that connected the tiny communities along the coast to the city. The villagers and the travelers sensed there was something wonderful happening somewhere and were drawn toward this wonderfulness like butterflies to nectar-filled flowers.

The villagers were quick to realize that the source of the wonderfulness was the shrine as they climbed up the path toward it. The travelers, though, could not know what drew them down the path from the main road and so were the most surprised to find Tiny Tim in his peaceful repose, surrounded by children and simple village people.

"What is this place?" asked one.

"Our shrine for the Buddha," said Hentai, and he was about to introduce himself as the priest but sensed his soiled fisherman's garb was not corroborative evidence of the claim, so, aware he was standing amid a crowd of seated children, he said instead, "I am the teacher here."

"What are you teaching, Hentai?" asked Kuchigitanai On'na, who was natively suspicious of anyone teaching anything to her son, Go.

"I am teaching about the goodness of giving," said Hentai hesitantly, since nothing else came to mind.

"You must be an excellent teacher," said another traveler. "Even from the road, I could feel the joy of your lesson."

To this, the other travelers agreed. The people of the village were not so easily convinced of this since they had known Hentai for years and had never had reason to consider him anything more than average in anything at all, and knew him to be decidedly inferior in this and that.

But they could not argue that something had greatly raised the spirits of the community, and if that something had been the result of Hentai teaching the children about generosity, then, just perhaps, he had tripped over or stumbled against or fallen into a native talent heretofore unseen and unsuspected.

"If it does not offend you, honored teacher," said a traveler who stood downwind of Hentai, "I would like to make you an offering of ten sen, in gratitude for your good work, that you might have a change of clothes."

Hentai was taken aback but soon gathered his scattered wits and was about to accept when the thought struck him that the women of the village were watching—especially Kuchigitanai On'na (whose acidic stare he could feel in that moment)—and they might take his enthusiasm for receiving as conflictual to his teaching of the virtues of giving.

"I want nothing for myself," he said, "though I would accept anything for the building of our temple."

"But you already have enough money for the temple," said Kuchigitanai On'na. "You got that from the sale of our fish. Remember?"

"Did I say temple? I meant school. The Buddha wishes us to build a school … Attached to the temple. Yes, that's it. We are to build a school attached to the temple so our children will learn their lessons."

Kuchigitanai On'na was about to speak again, but a different stranger spoke out ahead of her.

"A noble ambition," said the traveler as he stepped forward. "I will give twenty yen toward the project. And, when the school is done, I will move my family to this area, and I will conduct my businesses from here."

The well-dressed man then stepped his way through the seated children. He was tall and thickset, with demanding large eyes framed by thick eyebrows like those of wild demons seen in many a pen-and-ink drawing. He bowed to Hentai and introduced himself. "I am Yokubari Buta, a land and business owner. I was planning to send my children to the city for schooling, but this is much better. I will buy property here and build a new estate. All who wish to come and work for me will be welcome."

Everyone was greatly impressed. All were still basking in the bliss of giving, for Tiny Tim had not yet grown bored with emitting that glorious feeling, but atop of that the travelers were thanking their good fortune in having been in the right place at the right time—for once in their lives—to be first in line to work for a wealthy and generous man on a brand-new estate in a pleasing place made all the more pleasing by a talented teacher with a beautiful Buddha. And the villagers were thanking their good fortune in having the beautiful Buddha that had granted unto the mediocre Hentai the talent for teaching and had brought into their presence a wealthy and generous man who was going to build a rich estate that would enormously improve the treasure and honor of the village. And the children were thanking their good fortune in having acquired a teacher who could teach them wonderful lessons without boring them to desperation with a lot of dry and meaningless words.

Yokubari extracted his purse and made his donation to Hentai. The other travelers came forward, too, and gave generously—partly for the joy of giving but partly as an investment in their future, since the building of the school was a condition to be met for all else to transpire.

Yokubari promised to return in three months to see the progress being made. He led the way as the travelers returned to the main road to continue to their various destinations.

When the strangers were all gone, the village women asked what they could do toward the building of the school.

"The Buddha believes each family should give two fish of every hundred caught to him," said Hentai, and all agreed this was a small price to pay.

And Hentai was thankful the gods had seen fit to stop punishing him for his sins and favor him again.

"It is hard not to believe in you when you are being so kind to me," he said within his thoughts. "But I will try."

CHAPTER 97

E nough of the spirit of generosity from the day had spilled over into the evening for the women of the village to go down to the beach and greet their husbands, upon their return from their day at sea, with words of forgiveness for the sins confessed the week before. When asked what had happened to bring about this sudden and universal change of heart, the women told their menfolk the events of the day and of the great good fortune the village would soon see as a result of the rising of Hentai to teacher as well as priest.

"So, it is plain," said one husband with the certainty of the learned, "Kin Saikutsu-Sha has favored Hentai with great affections, cleared his mind of constrictions, and now he has become a wise and noble teacher. There is a lesson there for all wives to learn."

"If she has," said the husband's wife, with little inclination for being taught, "she has done so in his dreams. Kin Saikutsu-Sha moved to the city the night the Buddha made the men confess their offenses."

"Ah!" said another husband in another house, but in much the same conversation. "The gods do not hold with Buddhist priests being married, and they compelled Kin Saikutsu-Sha to seek a new husband elsewhere."

"That must be it," said this husband's wife, recognizing the tone of a conclusion set in stone in her husband's mind.

Early the following morning, the men spoke among themselves as they prepared their boats for a day's fishing.

"Did you hear Hentai sent Kin Saikutsu-Sha away because he cannot concentrate on his priestly duties with her around?"

"Is that what the women say?"

"No. But why else would he send away the one woman no one but an idiot would send away?"

Later that morning, the women spoke among themselves as they took their daily break from their chores.

"The idiot men think Hentai sent Kin Saikutsu-Sha away because he cannot concentrate on his priestly duties with her around."

"Your husband told you that?"

"No. But I know the way they think."

"Yes. On the night the Buddha made them all confess, mine told me he often pictured Kin Saikutsu-Sha naked in his mind."

"Mine too."

"Mine too."

"Mine too."

So the villagers arrived at something like a universal consensus regarding Kin Saikutsu-Sha. Through no fault of her own, she had been a disruptive influence on everyone and had had to be sent away for the village to begin on its tranquil spiritual path toward whatever purpose it was to fulfill. The more sophisticated persons of the population—those who believed all truth comes wrapped in paradox, as Hentai was now often heard to say—believed the gods, in whom they no longer believed, had sent her away. The simpler people believed that the Buddha had sent her away, because that was simpler to believe. And whether it was the gods or the Buddha, the men averred that the divine had acted through Hentai in respect for the natural order of things, while the women agreed among themselves that Kin Saikutsu-Sha had received the spiritual guidance directly, as that was the natural order of things.

Only Utagaibukai held the opinion that Kin Saikutsu-Sha had, quite simply of her own volition, wearied of Hentai since he was, by all accounts, a quite boring person when he wasn't at the center of miracles and catastrophes, and the thought of him being about the house all day, every day, now that he was a priest, could well have been more than the vivacious woman would be willing to accommodate. But Utagaibukai was well known for his cynicism, so no one took his negative notions seriously.

In the weeks that followed, the spirit of generosity that had brought the menfolk back to familial comfort lingered within the villagers. They made promises to one another inside the confines of their homes to do what they could to help Hentai build his temple and his school, as well as to give him time to learn to be a proper priest.

Hentai was pleased to discover he no longer needed to do any of the things he had grown tolerantly accustomed to doing. Kin Saikutsu-Sha had never been one to cook or sew or clean or much of anything about the house other wives simply accepted as their lot. To her mind, what could be made could more easily be bought, what could be repaired could more easily be replaced, and what might seem to be a wifely duty to most could more easily be seen as a husbandly duty if one had the will to see past the accepted norms of society. Furthermore, there were any number of local children willing to wash and scrub for a few sen if Hentai didn't have time to do it himself. And he was a quite tolerable cook—especially when most of the meals they ate were eaten raw.

On the first morning after the evening of the great and divine forgiveness, Hentai was awakened by three women who arrived at his cottage to bring him breakfast. Since each had thought she was the only one gifted with the idea of making the priest his meal, a short squabble ensued as to which would be the lucky giver.

"No need to argue, honored ladies," said Hentai. "I fasted all day yesterday, and so I can eat all three. I feel it in my stomach that the Buddha has seen this and chosen you all to provide for me in my need."

Knowing their breakfasts were deemed superior by the Buddha pleased the women enormously, and they sat to watch Hentai eat with great satisfaction—both his and theirs.

Similarly, Hentai was provided with lunch and supper—and rice wine and treats and entertainment. And one offered to take his black cloth to make him his robes, and another shaved his head for him. Others took to tending his meager garden, and everyone volunteered to help with the building of the temple and the school.

Everyone, that is, except Utagaibukai Hito, who, despite the general belief that Hentai had mastered the skill of getting the Buddha to bring blessings upon the people, still had his reservations about the self-proclaimed priest. Indeed, had Utagaibukai not been born into a simple fishing village, destined to become a simple fisherman, he might have been a thinker of thoughts that lead to the realization of reality in the manner of those gifted with the gifts of higher learning, instead of being limited to the doubting of all things that did not make immediate sense in the light of his experiences of life.

Utagaibukai knew Hentai well enough to know there was nothing particularly special about the fellow—unless the extreme lack of qualities deemed special, by any and all, qualifies one as special owing to the rarity of people so completely devoid of any characteristic, trait, or talent remotely special. And it was Utagaibukai's complete unwillingness to accept that the Buddha had chosen Hentai to be his mortal representative that allowed him to see the possibility other factors were afoot.

"A rope is made of many strands," said Utagaibukai to himself after casting his net out from his boat. "But what strand is threaded through of all Hentai's miracles? First, the children were chanting, 'Fish for breakfast,' and a great bounty washed up from the sea. What came next? Everyone confessed their secret shames, and we men slept on the beach for a week. Not as good a miracle as the first, but a mystery even so. Where did it begin? That is the root of all mysteries. The children had brought dishonor on their families and were crying from shame. The children? Yes, that's it! And when the wealthy traveler arrived to endow the village with his honorable and profitable presence, it was while the children were listening to Hentai speak of the joy of giving. So. It is the children who the Buddha hears."

Utagaibukai hauled in his net, which was disappointingly devoid of fish, but he was elated at having solved the mystery. "I have you, Hentai Sukebe! When the women find out they've been waiting hand and foot on a fraud, they'll chop you into bait!" He basked in the profound satisfaction that comes only with the complete discrediting of the completely discreditable.

The gentle rising and falling of the sea beneath him relaxed him and lulled him into further thought. And the ongoing emptiness of his net gave him little cause for distraction.

"Hmm," he thought. "I have lived among simpletons long enough to know that once an idea has taken up residence in the mind of one, it becomes a difficult tenant to evict. If I speak of what I have reasoned, it will be me who gets chopped into bait. And we cannot make the children village priest, even if they are the ones from whom the Buddha seeks the pure way. Bah! The gods give me brains just to mock me."

But the continued gentle rising and falling of the sea beneath him relaxed him and lulled him into further thought—again. And the ongoing emptiness of his net gave him little cause for distraction—still. So a conclusion was not long in rising.

"Hentai doesn't know it's the children. And he hasn't the brains to be a fraud. So he could not have planned to attract the generous givers to the shrine by teaching a lesson on the joys of giving. No. That was pure luck. But if I teach the children lessons, they will get for me what I want from the Buddha."

And as if the gods were given to giving signs and wanted to tell Utagaibukai he was on to something, his net was full for the first time that day. Or perhaps it was only coincidence. It doesn't really matter.

What does matter is that by the time Utagaibukai had emptied his net into his boat, he'd devised a plan for his advancement. He would put himself forward as a teacher of arithmetic (his talent for doing sums was locally renowned) and reading and writing (his small library of medieval romances was looked upon locally as pretentious) and use his influence on the children to get the Buddha to do his bidding.

When Utagaibukai cast his net once more out to sea, he did so with elation.

"What does it matter if Hentai is the priest? Let the simpletons bathe him in honor he doesn't deserve. Let them waste their time and goods on pampering him and providing for him. I will get the Buddha's blessings without anyone knowing how or why. They will simply think I am favored for reasons too mysterious to imagine, for that is how simpletons think."

So, after Utagaibukai finished loading his day's catch onto a cart and saw it off on its way to the city, he paid Hentai a visit.

Utagaibukai bowed as he said, "I most humbly apologize for being too long absent from your presence, honored priest."

Hentai said, "The Buddha teaches us not to notice such things," which had become his stock answer for everything that escaped his attention.

"Very wise, to be sure. But I believe it is the Buddha who has summoned me to your honored self. As you may know, I have suffered much doubt over the need for a temple and a school."

"Life contains inevitable, unavoidable suffering," said Hentai, proud to show he had mastered page one of his first book on Buddhism.

"Yes. But while I was out fishing today, my doubts evaporated from my soul as if blown upon by a divine wind. And in their place, I heard a voice. And the voice said, 'The great benefactor, Yokubari Buta, will not be happy if the school does not employ the best teachers. And while the honorable Hentai Sukebe is best for teaching Buddhism, you are best for teaching reading, writing, and arithmetic.' And when the voice said 'you,' it meant me, Utagaibukai Hito. So, I come to you now, honored priest, to say I give up fishing to work full-time building the school, and when it is done, I will work full-time as teacher of reading, writing, and arithmetic."

Hentai was hesitant. He'd grown to enjoy the respect his dual role as priest and teacher had brought him and didn't much like the idea of trimming off a piece of that respect for another—especially one who'd challenged his every word and phrase since the uttering of words and phrases had become one of Hentai's characteristics.

But then he recalled Yokubari Buta's demonic eyes and realized the great benefactor would have expectations regarding the education of his children, just as Utagaibukai had said. The teaching of Buddhism presented no risk, since all Buddhist teachings are paradoxical—no one expects them to be understood. Indeed, if the children went home confused and puzzled every day, that would be proof of Hentai's paradoxical success.

Literacy and numeracy were another matter. A man as wealthy as Yokubari Buta would want his children as capable with sums and the written word as anyone in Japan, while Hentai was only adequate at best. Failure would mean loss of the great benefactor's sponsorship and closure of the school. And the temple. And worst of all, Yokubari Buta would move his rich estate somewhere else and dismiss everyone who had taken jobs as servants and staff. Hentai would be chopped into bait unless there was someone else to blame.

"Clearly the Buddha has seen that the temple and the school are too much for one man alone," he said. "And he has chosen the one most clever in words and numbers to assist. Please honor my humble home with your presence that we may share tea. But first let us go to that tree that we may piss on it together to seal our agreement."

"I would be honored to piss with you," said Utagaibukai with a bow.

And so it was that Utagaibukai took the first step toward leading Japan into great turmoil, as history will show.

CHAPTER 98

Through all this, Tiny Tim was, quite literally, happy beyond description—that being an honest statement, since the experience of having one's entire being appreciated as pure emotion, completely unalloyed by physical influences both exterior and interior, is so far beyond that of normal sentient beings it cannot be adequately described in the feeble likes of prose.

That being said, being finally in the company of people after decades of aloneness was, for our hero, the defining pleasure of all pleasures. But having the daily company of children sharing in the simple joy of existence was a higher state of happiness than any statue of Buddha can commonly expect.

It was for this reason Tiny Tim had not made any effort to emote with the Almighty since his landing on the beach, and while this might be evidence of gross and unconscionable negligence on the part of any other statue of Buddha, I should remind the reader our hero was not a true statue of Buddha but merely an unconscious man who appeared to be so, through a case of mistaken identity that was not a result of his own invention. In short, he was masquerading as a statue absent any plan of what else to do under the circumstances. Added to this was the fact he couldn't have any real notion of everything going on around him, since he was aware solely of the feelings surrounding those events and had no way of knowing the content of the events themselves.

One night, while the whole village slept, our hero reconnected with his old friend.

"I like it here," emoted Tiny Tim to the Almighty.

"I'm not at all surprised," said the Almighty. "Though I suppose that is a bit redundant since, being omniscient, I'm never surprised at all about anything at all, so I'm not at all sure why I said that. Still. That said … happy to feel you're happy."

"Thank you. One thing bothers me, though: I get the feeling the people think I'm some sort of god."

"Really? How extraordinary! That's not to say we haven't seen other fellows mistaken for gods. Or fellows mistaking themselves for gods—that sort of thing happens all the time. Usually, though, those who get mistaken for gods are somewhat more ambulatory than you—not to mention more openly opinionated."

"I don't follow."

"No matter. What is it that leads you to believe you're being mistaken for one of us?"

"It's just a feeling."

"That goes without saying. Can you quote it?"

With that, Tiny Tim attempted to replicate a great want for something while wrapping that wanting in an aura of reverence and sanctity in exactly the same way he felt the presence of various persons.

"Oh, I see," said the Almighty. "Yes, we do get that a lot."

"It feels a bit like when Mother used to make me go to church and ask to have my hip made better."

"Ah. Sorry I couldn't have been of more help at the time, but rules are rules, and we do have to make room for free will and all that ballyhoo. If I give in for one, I can hardly say no to the next; then, before you know it, I'm back to muddling about in the minutiae, day in and day out, as if I haven't better things to do with my time."

"Like what?" asked Tiny Tim out of simple curiosity and without any hint of a challenge.

"Well," said the Almighty, pausing to think for a moment. "Nothing really. Though I should point out the whole thing was intended from the start to be more along the lines of an investment than an occupation. We put in the initial work to get things rolling—assembled all the odds and sods for the singularity and then lit the fuse. *Bang.* All good. Funny. It seemed like an eternity getting everything in place, but it's all done now, so perhaps it wasn't. Doesn't matter. The point is, we didn't plan on having to provide more than tertiary maintenance—simply sit back and watch it grow. As far as that goes, the universe has done better than we imagined. Growth-wise, that is."

"My brother Matthew felt that way sometimes."

"Yes, well—back to the original point—you feel you're being petitioned for favors of the more miraculous flavor?"

"That's it. And I believe they feel I'm having some effect. I keep getting this sense of enormous want, which is always followed by enormous gratitude—and not much else. Just want, then gratitude. Want, gratitude, want, gratitude. Over and over and over."

"Interesting. Still, I wouldn't put much worry into it. They tend to believe as they want to believe regardless of what's put before them and regardless of my opinion. Furthermore, they invent all manner of nonsense, then imagine the ideas are mine and go off in pursuit of the most ludicrous aspirations in an effort to please me. It does get a bit much from time to time, though I must confess it's far more entertaining than having them come and go on command the way some of my more autocratic associates like to have it. In fact, it gets to be quite hilarious at times. Off you go, fumbling about from disaster to disaster in total chaos and justifying all your idiotic missteps on God's will instead of making the slightest effort to reason the whole thing through and take responsibility for yourselves."

"Hmm. I never pictured you finding that much enjoyment in people's misfortune."

"Really? I take it you haven't read much of the Old Testament, then."

"Not much, no. To tell the truth, I never enjoyed listening to all that 'Thou shalt not' lark very much when Mother had Martha read it aloud to us. Nor going to church, for the matter of that."

"Oh, I'm in complete agreement with you there. All that kneeling and standing up and sitting down, over and over, ad nauseum. More like elementary calisthenics done at a glacial pace than anything spiritual or reaffirming. No. I avoid that farcical ballyhoo as often as possible. And since I am the Almighty, 'as often as possible' means 'always.' I haven't been inside a church since churches were made of camel hide flung over wicker frameworks. Oh, and by the way, I was joking about the Old Testament. That's just another example of them putting words in my mouth."

"Really?"

"Oh, quite. I've been the victim of propagandist journalism since we taught you lot to read and write. I mean they don't even bother to quote out of context; they merely fabricate whatever gobbledygook will clear the hurdle of plausibility in a world of blinking, grinning nether-wits. Every religion constructs whatever mystifying tale supports its claim to set the rules, and there you have it: printed, bound, and bought by all."

"So you're not religious, then?"

"No, I wouldn't go so far as to say that. It's difficult to not believe in the Almighty when you are the Almighty. That Descartes fellow of yours had something to say about that. Rather good, too, as I recall. Dressed it up in Latin and everything. Cogito Ergo Sum."

"What I mean is, you're not C of E," said Tiny Tim.

"Only when necessary. I have to wear a lot of hats these days, what with all these cults and sects and covens and such popping up here, there, and everywhere. There's little time for more than a cursory glance this way or that, then on to the next. In the early days, I could be more focused. When there were far fewer of you and far more of us."

"There were more of you?"

"Oh my, yes. We had a staff of thousands running things hereabouts for a while."

"What happened to them?"

"Reassigned. It's an expanding universe, you know. New territory being added every second. It won't be long before I'll have to move on and leave you lot to look after yourselves."

"But you're not doing anything, anyway, as it is."

"Well," said the Almighty. "True enough, I suppose. Now that we've got everything operating automatically, there's no more need for fiddling or fine tuning. When we first set up operations, I was in charge of sunsets. That kept me going, I can say without exaggeration."

"Why? There's only one a day."

"Here there is. But as soon as that one's done, there's another one looming up just a little farther west and then a little farther still. I had to circle the world once a day, every day, to keep up. If it hadn't been for my sister conjuring up the occasional storm, I'd never have had a moment's rest."

"So how does it work now?"

"One of the higher-ups figured out how to create colors by bending light through air, and the whole thing was set to run independently. It's all rather scientific, actually. Quite interesting if you're prone to that kind of thing. Of course, I was made redundant. Mucked about for a couple of millennia, looking for something to do; got into a bit of trouble with a goddess here and there—fatal attraction to wildflowers, I'm afraid. All rather disappointing and discouraging, to be honest. I was about ready to chuck the whole lot in when the decision came down that we'd got the place functioning more or less all right and there was no further need for full-time supervision. I got promoted to general manager, and the rest of the pantheon lit out for the new territories, leaving me to keep an eye on things."

"How awful!"

"No, not really. I rather prefer working alone."

"But you don't do anything."

"Is that the only tune you've got to play?" said the Almighty. "Not like I don't lend a sympathetic ear when one is called for. You have to give me that. I mean, I'm feeling along with you quite nicely, right now. You can't tell me that's not something."

"No, of course not. Sorry. I didn't mean to come across as unappreciative."

"Oh, never mind," said the Almighty. "Perhaps I'm being a bit sensitive over the issue. It's just that when I was only a subordinate, I could hardly keep up with the demands, but now that I'm in charge of the whole show, I'm hamstrung by regulations."

"Didn't you write the regulations?"

"In a manner of speaking, yes, but we've already gone over all that. And it really is quite necessary, I assure you. Even after a few thousand years of nonintervention, you lot are only just getting a handle on how the system works. It's apparently hard enough for you to get a grasp on things as it is, without me circumnavigating standard operating procedure every time someone finds it all a bit too much to navigate. You know, I really had higher hopes for your ability to make advancements, but it's painfully obvious the variables provided strain the limits of your comprehension, despite me keeping matters as simple as possible by keeping my fingers out of the works."

Tiny Tim was taken aback.

"Sorry," said the Almighty. "Sorry. I shouldn't take my disappointment out on you personally when you're clearly doing your best."

"Oh, that's all right," said Tiny Tim. "But why is it so important we understand how the system works?"

"Well, you'll need that when I'm gone. Unless, of course, you're willing to give up all the tools and toys and go back to monkeying about in the forests with the lemurs and such."

"Well, I wouldn't mind. But I can't speak for the others."

"No, of course not. And I wasn't really being serious. Come what may, you're all destined to reap the rewards of your folly. I'll grant you one miracle to ward off some all-consuming catastrophe, but after that, it's fly free or plummet."

"That's fair, I guess."

"Whether it is or not, it's what you've got. Nevertheless, keep all this between us … Oh, sorry. That was thoughtless. You don't have much choice in the matter, do you?"

"Not really, no. But I'm fine with it. Everything will turn out all right. At least it feels so to me."

Through all this, the villagers slept the best sleep of their lives as the dialogue between Tiny Tim and the Almighty was conducted in highly rapidly shifting emotions—as has been described earlier—and the resulting blur radiating from our hero had much the same effect on those around him as the chanting of "Om" has on a meditating monk.

CHAPTER 99

Hentai and Utagaibukai had independently concluded the children were the essential link connecting the village and its wants to the Buddha and his beneficence. But neither Hentai nor Utagaibukai knew the other had arrived at this conclusion, and both desired to keep the other ignorant of what he thought the other didn't know.

Hentai still believed the not-believed-in gods were behind the miracles, but the coincidence of the children being near to the Buddha and being first to feel the feelings the others felt was not a coincidence at all, but part of the intricate and elegant plan laid out by the not-believed-in gods. However, his position was far too delicate for him to reveal this disturbing conclusion, for to do so would be admitting he was not the choice of the not-believed-in gods for the village's spiritual leader—the children were. Perhaps worse still, it could lead to the discovery his wife had stolen the money destined for temple construction. And worst of all, he would have to go back to being a fisherman, wrapped in a mantle of shame that would never wear thin or drop away.

Utagaibukai, on the other hand, still believed the Buddha was a magical statue that would provide whatever was sincerely desired of it, though he, too, sensed the desiring had to come from the children. But, while Hentai did not tell of his secret conclusion out of fear doing so would compromise his future, Utagaibukai kept his secret conclusion to himself out of a sense that doing so put him in the superior position.

Had their roles been reversed, Utagaibukai would have been suspicious of this sudden change of heart from dubious obstructionism to enthusiastic facilitationism, but Hentai was thrilled to have the lone decrier of his priestly right to rule acquiesce to him in the unexpected and most welcome manner in which Utagaibukai had approached him.

In the months that followed, Utagaibukai appeared every day at the shrine where Hentai conducted the early-morning Ritual of Generous Giving and Grateful Receiving with the children who saw it as something of a game in which they would playact being grown up to perform the ceremonious exchange of sweet treats accompanied by the bowing and uttering of polite phrases used by adults when conducting business.

Following the ritual, Utagaibukai would teach a few lessons, then read to the children from one of his books. Quickly enough, he realized the last emotion conveyed in the story being told would become the dominant mood of the village for the rest of the day, so unlike most storytellers, Utagaibukai never finished on a cliffhanger but kept reading until the hero of the story—and therefore our hero— reached a positive life-affirming point in the plot.

Also, following the morning ritual on many days, strangers would arrive, diverted from their travels on the high road by the overwhelming desire to give. When they saw how joyous the children were in learning their lessons, they were moved to make donations to the building of the school. Both Hentai and Utagaibukai accepted the donations with smiles, blessings, and low bows of respect.

Soon, Hentai was able to repair the gaping hole left in the temple funds made by his wife's rapid egress to rosier arrangements.

And no one was the wiser.

And Utagaibukai was able to live without the income from fishing when all assumed he was living off savings—of which he had none.

And no one was the wiser.

"I am most humble and grateful," said Kuchigitanai On'na, mother of Go. "Our honorable priest and honorable schoolteacher have taught my son well, despite the doubts I once had. Go is most polite now when he used to give me so much trouble."

"Yes," said the mother of Ichi. "Ichi counts fish as well as his father. Even better when they get past ten."

"Ni and San invent the most enchanting stories," said the proud mother of the two.

"But the honored Yokubari Buta," said Kuchigitanai On'na, "will return soon and expect to see a school. Not a single foundation stone has been laid yet, nor is a single framing plank being sawed. I wonder if the temple and the school will ever cast shadows down the hillside."

Paradoxically, fortunately for Hentai and Utagaibukai, this ongoing collection of donations came to an end when the children grew weary of being grateful—as children are prone to do. In reality, neither Hentai nor Utagaibukai had need of further funding, but the habit of accepting large sums of money on a regular basis for nothing more than being present to receive is a much more difficult habit to break than those of us not so habituated might imagine.

Since Hentai was the priest, it fell upon him to make the wise announcement: "The Buddha has decreed all signs are propitious for construction to commence."

And neither Hentai nor Utagaibukai showed one whit of their despair over the fabled death of the fabled goose that laid the fabled golden egg.

The two buildings rose rapidly once work was begun. Despite the danger of being tripped over by carpenters or dropped upon by roofers, the children were permitted to remain in a tight group around Tiny Tim while the temple rose all around him. Hentai and Utagaibukai took turns telling them entertaining stories which kept them and the workers and the whole of the village in a state of blissful entertainment quite unlike the state one normally inhabits when engaged in one's mundane routine.

The priest and his assistant were universally praised for their ability to orchestrate a project, though both became more and more certain with time that the mounting evidence proved the children were either the true chosen ones of the gods or the true chosen ones of the Buddha.

The villages ascribed the wonderful feeling that enveloped them day in and day out to the progress they saw in the construction and the sense this was only the beginning of great things to come. And while the villagers agreed the Buddha had changed Hentai and Utagaibukai for the better and put the unlikely pair together to create a divine force, no one suspected the telling of tales to children could be more than an innocent entertainment.

But that is the power of fiction.

CHAPTER 100

The temple and the school were completed so quickly it amazed even the builders who had done all the work—perhaps even more so since they had had much experience seeing buildings being built and had acquired some sense of how long the building of buildings took under normal circumstances of building.

"This temple and this school are a miracle," said Aho Baka, who had set out the floor plans based on observations of similar structures in the city. "They are not normal. Normally, building a building too quickly means steps that must be taken are not taken in order to save time, so the building is faulty and falls down. Or, also normally, building a building too well means details must be observed in great detail and too much time is spent, so the building is superior and stands forever but is wasteful in its cost."

Hentai had focused on the gorgeous details and the intricacy of the decorative elements. So he sensed Aho was wrong and was about to say, "No, they cost less than expected," but Utagaibukai spoke first. "You mean they are faulty and will fall down?"

"Not at all," said Aho. "They are built to stand forever. I am amazed so few men could work so fast and so well. Truly a miracle!"

By this point, Hentai realized saying what he'd been about to say would reveal there was money left over from the project, and the villagers would expect a refund. And so he said instead, "And the Buddha is good with numbers, because it all was completed right on budget."

Utagaibukai being Utagaibukai, he doubted this statement but decided he would have his opportunities in time and so let Hentai keep the loose change without a challenge.

But while Aho's assessment of the realities of civil engineering was not without merit, he barely grasped the degree to which Tiny Tim—a.k.a. the Buddha—influenced the workers. Without realizing it, they had worked harder, faster, and with greater care than workers would deem possible. They had grown less weary while working and taken fewer breaks for meals or rest. They arrived at work earlier than they habitually did and went home later. And they had done all this without noticing they were doing any of this while they were doing any of it.

The great irony in all this was that—after the building of the temple and the school was completed—the supervisors of the workers went back to believing the best work is done by those afraid of being punished for tardiness, laziness, or carelessness, while the workers themselves went back to believing the best work is done by those most highly paid for promptness, diligence, and exactitude, while, all the while, the reality is that the best work is always done by those who would happily do the work for nothing and without threats of any sort, as they find the work itself more entertaining than what is typically recognized as entertainment. And so the satisfaction of doing something as close to perfect as possible, in the cause of entertaining oneself, is the greatest reward for one's efforts. But while all of them experienced this for themselves during the construction of the temple and the school, they all forgot it almost immediately upon the project's completion.

Everyone forgot what it was like to breeze through labor as if it were recreation, while only Utagaibukai remembered how pleasant the time of the construction had been, because he had been careful to choose stories for the children that told of the joy of hard work. For him, the telling of the tales was as much experiment as practical application of a mystical technique, for while further proof for his theory was something he always found gratifying, atop that he sought to measure the limits of the Buddha's reach and influence.

"The ceremony was most different," said Yokubari Buta, "But I am no priest and have never witnessed the blessing of a new temple and school before."

"The Buddha teaches us," said Hentai, with meaningless mystical gestures, "what is different is inevitable, for always the same makes change impossible."

"If you will come this way, honored guest," said Utagaibukai before Yokubari could question Hentai further, "the children have prepared entertainments. Some have written haikus in honor of their school, while others have composed songs."

The wealthy businessman had not grown wealthy wasting time and was hesitant to sit through lengthy amateur attempts at art. But then his business sense told him he should assess the success of the teachers at teaching things beyond generosity and gratitude. The possibility rose in his mind he might have been hasty in promising to bring his children to this rustic setting.

At first, Yokubari was impressed with the subtlety and sophistication of the poetry, both spoken and sung. But then doubts welled up within him as to whether the children were the true authors or merely memorizers of the works of more mature writers. He considered that perhaps Utagaibukai had written the haikus and songs to give the false impression his pupils had been well taught in the skills of composition.

The more Yokubari listened, the more he was convinced he was being duped. And though he had no moral aversion to counterfeiting, plagiarism, or general misrepresentations of this for that, he did take exception to being taken for a fool. The last of the poets to recite was Omoshiroi Uta, a girl of eight with eyes that wandered here, there, and everywhere regardless of what was happening.

Yokubari waited for her to bow, then said, "Come here, little one."

Omoshiroi put a finger in her mouth and approached. She stopped before the imperious man and, after a moment empty of further instructions, allowed her eyes to wander from his gaze to more interesting sights upon the ceiling. She caught sight of a large green spider lowering itself upon Yokubari, then Yokubari saw it too. He reached out a hand to provide the arachnid a perch.

"Create for me," he said, "a poem about this spider."

Omoshiroi took her finger from her mouth and asked, "A haiku?"

"Any kind of poem. But be quick."

The finger reinserted itself, and the eyes blinked back to the ceiling.

Silence. Silence. Silence.

Yokubari was about to lay accusations of fraud at the feet of Utagaibukai and Hentai when Omoshiroi held her wet finger to the sky and said, "Spiders are such filthy things/They feast on little flies/They wrap them up in dragon's beard/And suck upon their eyes."

The children burst into tittering, which proved more infectious than juicy rumors. Yokubari's surprise was great. His earlier suspicious inclinations persisted a moment and led him to sense he was being mocked, but then he repeated the poem in his mind, saw the humor in it, and joined in the laughter with a mighty roar.

"Most clever," he said, his doubts dispelled.

Omoshiroi bowed once more, put her finger back in her mouth, and looked again at the ceiling.

Yokubari wondered what so fascinated the little girl, so he tilted his head back and looked up to see dark polished crossbeams held in place by intricate filigreed brass brackets. And in the square spaces encompassed by the beams were crimson chrysanthemums painted on a butter-yellow background. Such a ceiling one would see in only the richest homes, yet this one adorned a fishing village school. Suspicions of flagrant waste arose within him, and he rose to inspect the craftsmanship of construction more closely.

Hentai—lacking the wisdom to grant personal space to men who look like demons from pen-and-ink drawings—crowded Yokubari as the school's major patron strolled about assessing the fine carpentry and precision stonework.

"Does the school displease you?" asked Hentai.

"Wasteful," said Yokubari. "Extravagance must be earned. Children should not be taught it comes freely."

"But we did not ask the workmen to do anything more than they usually do. I have never hired anyone to build a school before, so I believed what they did was only usual and even feared they might take advantage of my inexperience in such things and do inferior work."

"Your inexperience in such things is apparent. They tricked you into paying for much more than you need."

Utagaibukai had kept his distance—having the wisdom to grant personal space to men who look like demons from pen-and-ink drawings—but was near enough to hear the gist of the conversation and, fearing Yokubari would withdraw his promise to relocate to the vicinity, ran to get the records of materials purchased, work done, and amounts paid. He returned and offered them to the businessman.

"If we have erred in negotiating the best prices," said Utagaibukai while handing the books to Yokubari with a bow, "we humbly ask your forgiveness."

Yokubari was surprised the priest and the teacher had kept financial records, believing as he did that financial records existed outside the realms of religion and academia. But he opened them to scan the rows and columns in expectation of finding evidence of excessive spending. With each page turned, his eyes opened wider and wider as he found more and more proof the two were geniuses at driving hard bargains.

"I have none in my employ," said Yokubari with a smile, "with such talent for hiring. But the craftsmanship speaks for itself. Those who built this school will build my new home. Please provide me their names."

"A list will be prepared," said Utagaibukai, taking back the books with a bow.

And so Yokubari contracted the craftsmen who had done the work so well on the school and temple, along with the supervisors who had done such an excellent job of watching that work being done. He set them to building his enormous home in the fashion of a medieval samurai fortress—that being the latest architectural fashion.

The local lord was more than happy to sell Yokubari the farmland upon which the estate would be built. The displaced peasants who had worked the land were all hired to tend Yokubari's gardens. Then Yokubari started planning what manner of business would best suit him in his new location.

And when the villagers went into the city to sell their fish and told the city dwellers of the great estate that was being built, it inspired enterprising young men to make the short journey to the little cove and imagine the benefits the future would bring to those with the foresight to establish themselves in the cozy environs of vast new opportunity.

To all this, both Hentai and Utagaibukai were independently and privately pleased.

CHAPTER 101

Hentai had come to see the promise of prosperity as a sign that the gods were favoring the village for having adopted Buddhism and was quick to remind anyone and everyone of this on every occasion in which the mention of it could be deemed remotely relevant—and about half of those in which it could not.

Utagaibukai, conversely, never mentioned at all to anyone at all that he believed the magical Buddha was operating quite independently of the gods, and while he believed Hentai believed the beneficence of the Buddha could be petitioned directly—which, of course, Hentai implied but did not truly believe—Utagaibukai believed he alone believed the Buddha provided in accordance with the whims and caprices of the children. And he alone, as the children's tacit leader in all things whimsical and capricious, was the wielder of the ultimate power that was actually bringing good fortune to the village.

Included in the new temple was a small library of Buddhist books—the initial two, plus a few more acquired from various donors. Hentai committed himself to reading them all and learning their contents.

"'The first noble truth is: Life is Suffering,'" he read aloud from one text.

"Hmm?" he pondered. "I wish I had known that before agreeing to be the priest."

Without reading further, Hentai put a lot of consideration into this apparent contradiction. So far, since the arrival of the Buddha on the beach, fortunes had risen—apart from a few minor complications, hindrances, and irritating obstructions that were all quite dismissible and all fading rapidly from memory.

He even saw the virtue in much of what had been seen as evil at the time of its occurrence. Hentai had been quite distraught when he learned Kin Saikutsu-Sha had left him, for example, but now saw the blessing that had been wrapped in that calamity.

Many thought it tragic he'd lost the companionship of his beautiful wife, but Hentai—now able to judge from some distance in time—could see that the companionship of a beautiful wife can truly be appreciated without discomfort by a husband only if he can avail himself of the intimacies her beauty inspires him to appreciate. And to not avail himself of those intimacies perennially—which he cannot help but be inspired to appreciate perennially—can only lead to discomfort bordering on maddening torment. But, to avail himself of those intimacies, his wife must first be available for the sharing of them. And, to this, Kin Saikutsu-Sha was perennially uninspired and, therefore, perennially unavailable.

In short, Hentai was much more comfortable and content living alone than he would have imagined possible in the days before the arrival of the Buddha.

Likewise, all the trying events that had happened in the early days of the village's conversion to Buddhism could be interpreted as necessary preparation for circumstances more profoundly preferable to those preceding the conversion.

The great battle that had pitted neighbor against neighbor, friend against friend, and sibling against sibling had been horrible to experience but had cleared away all the niggling little complaints each had against the other, as each could feel within his or her heart that whatever had been bothering him or her about the others had been brought out into the open and justly settled.

The evening of the great confessions that had seen the menfolk banished from their homes had been nasty to live through but had removed all doubt from the minds of all that all could move forward in all honesty.

Following this line of reasoning, Hentai concluded that life is suffering only in the sense that through suffering, life achieves great joy. And this renewed his enthusiasm for the priesthood.

Of course, Utagaibukai was not bogged down by the need to learn Buddhism, since he taught only reading, writing, and arithmetic. With his mind not cluttered with philosophical questions about why it was good to be a Buddhist, he could ponder full-time upon what benefit being a Buddhist would be to him and what he needed to do to derive the fullness of that benefit.

To that, he had already seen some evidence. Teaching was easier than fishing—especially since the children who learned quickly radiated tremendous pleasure from learning, which was in turn amplified by Tiny Tim to make those trailing in their learning keener to keep going into the as yet unconquered territories of numbers and letters. And teaching was better paid, thanks to the patronage of Yokubari Buta, who could see his children would receive the best education possible. And, on top of all that, Utagaibukai received frequent gifts from grateful parents.

But once Utagaibukai became content with his present, he put his mind to creating a better future for himself and his family. Satisfied as he was to be a teacher for the time being, he imagined being idly wealthy in years to come—and not so many years that he would no longer be young enough to appreciate genuinely the fullness of the joy of being genuinely wealthy and genuinely idle.

Unfortunately for both Hentai and Utagaibukai, fate once again rose up to obfuscate their plans and their progress.

The workers and supervisors who had built the temple and the school fell behind schedule on the construction of the great manor home, and elements of that construction were not meeting the expectations of quality of the estate owner. Yokubari was furious and demanded of Hentai that whatever he had done to get the builders building with superior speed and skill before, he must do again, or he, Yokubari, would move his estate to somewhere else and see to the destruction of the village and the destitution of the villagers and the dishonoring of Hentai and Utagaibukai as charlatans and makers of false promises.

Needless to say, Hentai was horrified. Utagaibukai was merely frightened, at first, but soon his fear twisted itself into resentment, which then tied itself into a knot of pure rage. And though the feelings of both men were disquieting to bear within themselves, when they spilled over to Tiny Tim, they burst outward in all directions like an all-consuming conflagration.

For three days, madness ruled. Wave upon wave of emotion poured forth to embroil the population for miles and miles and miles around. Anger and hatred rode atop the waves, while terror filled the depths of them.

Hentai hid himself away, quite unable to formulate what to do beyond suffer through the moment to moment to moment of torment.

Utagaibukai, though, had just enough reason left in reserve to conclude that the only way out of the storm was to wade his way to its center along with the children and calm it at its source. This proved impossible since the parents had taken to keeping the little ones indoors out of fear for their safety while the village was steeped in this madness. Not one of the mothers would surrender her child up to Utagaibukai, and most of the fathers chased him away with threats or even blows.

In pure desperation, Utagaibukai went alone to Tiny Tim, believing all the while his efforts would go ignored and unrewarded without the children present to provide intermediary interaction with the Buddha.

But the desperate are driven to hope for the impossible.

CHAPTER 102

Tiny Tim was beginning to feel like the concertmaster in a second-rate symphony orchestra being led by a mediocre conductor conducting a banal version of a tedious concerto composed by an uninspired, though conceited, music student attempting to mimic Wagner by overemphasizing the dramatic elements of composition. This is not to suggest our hero hadn't felt this way before—as we all do, from time to time in this or similar fashion—but his patience for this kind of thing was growing thinner as he grew older. Much as it does with all of us.

He was just starting to commence a communication with the Almighty when Utagaibukai's presence made itself known to him through an overwhelming wanting for something.

"There they are again," said Tiny Tim.

"You'll get used to it," said the Almighty.

"If you say so. It's just … Hmm. I don't want to appear unappreciative, but I can't get really comfortable with any of it. When I feel exactly how they want to feel, they feel like they want more and more and more until, suddenly, they don't want that at all."

"Nature of the bête noire, I'm afraid," said the Almighty offhandedly, but he changed to a more excited mood when a thought struck him. "It is rather interesting, though, how much their behavior has come to resemble the behavior we designed into the inanimate objects."

"I didn't know inanimate objects behaved any way at all."

"Well, of course they do. Your present problem reminds me of it, so allow me to use it as a for instance. When we put the universe together, one of the principles we put into play was the idea that some force or other will have to do some pushing or pulling to get an object moving, and once it's moving, some pushing or pulling will be necessary to get it to stop."

"That's obvious."

"Only because we made it that way and you've never known anything to operate any differently. Personally, I thought it lacked for sophistication, but I was overruled."

"How could …?"

"Don't bother yourself about issues that will never come up. Just be happy the arrangement works well enough to keep things going for the next few trillion years or so. But—to your observation of human behavior—we had no intention of applying the concepts of inanimate objects to human modes of activity beyond their needing to move objects about. As to the rest of it, we left well enough alone to let them figure out what to do of their own accord. Now, had they been as rational as they claim to be, they'd simply do what needs to be done and have done with it, yet they resist doing anything without being absolutely forced to do so by something or other or someone or other. But once they're moving, they don't want to stop—even when it makes eminent sense to put a halt to the idiocy. Furthermore, when we designed the universe, we made it so the denser an object is, the more pushing or pulling will be required to get it moving or stopping; and much along the same lines, humans have become exactly the same. The denser they are, the more resistant they are to move when needed to move, or stop once they're going. Quite fascinating really."

Utagaibukai injected a particularly sharp stab of desire into the emotional field.

"They never stop," said Tiny Tim.

"No, they don't. That's why I've come to prefer the atheists. They fumble about in the dark with the worst of them, but at least they've accepted they're on their own in finding their way out. They may say the stupidest things from time to time, but they never pester me with stupid questions."

"I never suspected you were so impatient."

"Oh, I have infinite patience for those making a decent effort to make the best of it. It's those who expect me to make fundamental changes to reality to accommodate them alone with the most minor of details that inspire me to puke—figuratively speaking, of course; I don't actually do that."

"I'm sorry."

"Don't be. It's not your fault. I only wish they'd accept that it is what it is and that's all there is to it. Art is never finished; it's abandoned, as someone or other once said ... Or will say ... da Vinci, was it ...? Sometimes it all gets lost in the blur," said the Almighty, meanderingly. "Regardless, I'm done tinkering."

Utagaibukai needled them again.

"Perhaps I should let you go," said Tiny Tim.

"No, it's quite all right. I'm used to ignoring them."

"But I'm not. It's odd. When I was alone for all that time, I only wanted to be with people, but now I'd like a little quiet now and then."

"Then have it. Believe me: whatever it is they think they want, they likely won't in the long run, so a few days of peace and quiet won't hurt them in the slightest."

"You really think ...?"

"Just do it. You'll be much more helpful to them when you're satisfied within yourself."

So Tiny Tim drifted back to times when all was well and all was calm and all was peaceful within the tranquility that enfolded pure and perfect satisfaction.

The Almighty slipped silently away.

And Utagaibukai emitted a short burst of greedy glee.

CHAPTER 103

U tagaibukai walked home much less a man than a brilliant star of self-satisfied serenity. His desperate supplications to the Buddha—against all expectations—had been answered beyond his most optimistic hopes. He, the village, and all the surrounding areas were bathed in pure peace after days of terror and loathing.

What was more, Utagaibukai now knew the children were not the only ones who could influence the Buddha. He, too, had the power to manifest the divine grace of the magical statue. And—best of all, for his purposes—he was the only one who knew he could do so.

He still sensed that the Buddha favored the children. That was not so strange, as there were many who would give a coin or a candy to a child while eschewing generosity to others. But if he were sincere enough and earnest enough and diligent enough, Utagaibukai could persuade the golden Buddha to perform acts of kindness for him too.

Of course, this was a secret of monumental magnitude. Knowing the children held unwitting sway over the Buddha was precious enough knowledge to keep to oneself, but knowing that anyone with sufficient will to last out lengthy sessions of pleading and groveling, with knees and nose and hands to the floor, will eventually get his or her way was a piece of intelligence more valuable than all one's worldly possessions combined. At all costs, Utagaibukai had to keep his discovery to himself lest the temple be permanently crammed to bursting with kowtowing supplicants wanting greater wealth, better health, and an increased capacity for getting their way in dealing with their neighbors and spouses.

To all this, Utagaibukai could see in the light of pure reason that it was his civic duty to keep quiet about his newly found knowledge lest the community should descend into a chaos of grossly self-indulgent torpidity and greed. And in the light of pure emotion, he could see that if he did things correctly, he could live a life as free of trouble as a life can be when everything one wants or needs is provided free for the asking.

But, for a little while, he could enjoy the radiant peace he had brought upon the village.

CHAPTER 104

The following day, the children returned to the school with their parents, who were content it was now safe since the strange time of horrific happenings had ended as abruptly and mysteriously as it had started. Utagaibukai confidently received them with shallow bows and greetings of "Honored student," to which they bowed more deeply and said, "Honored teacher," though they giggled at this unusual formality.

Hentai came out of hiding too and headed straightway from his private rooms into the temple proper to give thanks for the cessation of the terror that had kept him behind closed doors, under blankets, and in a state of trembling dread. Just having knelt to begin his prostrations, he heard the crack of a fan being closed in the air behind him. He rose and turned to see Yokubari Buta entering through the main door.

Hentai stood and bowed low—as low as his anatomical restraints would allow, in fact—and greeted the haughty owner of much land and great wealth.

"It is a most pleasant day," said Yokubari.

"It is," said Hentai. "I feel it in both of my big toes that it is, indeed, a pleasant day."

"It is indeed. It is so pleasant a day, in fact, I nearly decided not to come to see you. But I am a man who does not decide one thing one day and then decide another thing another day. I decide one thing, and I do that thing. Unless, of course, I learn of something I did not know before which makes me decide what I decided on one day was incorrect in some way, and then I will decide another thing on another day, but only then. And never will I decide another thing on another day when there is no sound reason to doubt what I decided on one day only because it is another day. To do so would be indecisive, and I am not indecisive—not on this day, nor any other."

"Clearly so," said Hentai, even though he had not yet arrived at a sound understanding of Yokubari's meaning.

"I decided yesterday to come and see you, and here I am."

"I am most honored."

"Yes. But I am not a man to see another man without a reason. If there is no reason to see a man, I do not waste my time in seeing him. The reason I came to see you is to tell you I am not pleased with what has happened these past several days. I expected you to correct the errant ways of the workers and shame them into fixing what they have done wrong and work with greater care in the future. Instead, you have inspired them to fight among themselves and damage that portion of my house that has been finished. What am I to think of a priest who asks the gods for one thing and gets the opposite?"

Hentai was about to answer, but Yokubari continued. "I must think that priest is of little use to anyone, and I should have his head chopped off and seek a replacement."

"That won't be necessary, honorable Yokubari Buta," said the paling and quivering Hentai as he bowed. "The Buddha tells us evil must be rooted up before good is planted. That is all that has happened, and now we have a pleasant day to plant the good."

Yokubari was dubious. But he had to imagine there might be some sense in what was said, and it certainly was a pleasant day, which seemed to be the proof of Hentai's words.

"Very well," he said, and he cracked open his fan. "My home will be completed in three months to my satisfaction, or I will send my man for your head. And you will have it ready for him, or it will not go well for you."

Hentai remained still, bowing low with his eyes to the floor, too terrified to respond, too terrified to agree to the terms or to plead for greater leniency. When the silence grew too burdensome to bear, he looked up to find Yokubari had left.

Fortunately for Hentai, he had had a reason before Yokubari's arrival to reason his way through the reasons why the Buddha caused turmoil in the community, so he had a reason ready to provide Yokubari for the days of irrational terror, rage, and wanton destruction. Had it not been for that, he would have been completely dumbfounded and likely awaiting the imminent loss of his head—a circumstance which he would have found most unfortunate. And so he thanked his good fortune for having had that reason to reason.

Also fortunately, as soon as he was aware of Yokubari's departure, he was inspired to deal with the situation immediately, and since the only way he knew of dealing with it was to get the children around the Buddha and inspire them to think joyful thoughts of hard labor, dedication to detail, and the honor of completing one's work on time and properly done, he left Tiny Tim and the temple to make his way to the school. And this was fortunate because Tiny Tim was just beginning to get bored with being calm and pleasant and was only then starting to sense Hentai's trepidation over being beheaded when Hentai left the immediate vicinity of our hero, and so our hero lost interest in unwittingly provoking a potentially devastating series of beheadings before he could get started.

The children were reciting their arithmetic lesson in unison when Hentai arrived through the entrance at the back of the class.

"Pi is equal to three point one four one five nine two six five three five …" chanted the children.

Utagaibukai caught sight of the priest and was instantly concerned over the look of panic on Hentai's face.

"Keep going till you run out of numbers," said the teacher. "I will be back soon."

Utagaibukai walked through the cluster of novice mathematicians to meet with Hentai and enquire about the nature of the problem. After hearing the blubbering account of Yokubari's visit to the temple and Hentai's date with destiny three months hence, Utagaibukai was most alarmed but—in the secrecy of his thoughts—imagined that allowing his alarm or Hentai's horror to reach the Buddha was the making of a catastrophe of tsunamic proportions.

"You cannot dishonor the Buddha with your presence in such a state," said Utagaibukai. "Go to the rock in the cove and climb upon it and meditate. Remain there until the tide has come in and gone out. Then you will be your honored self again."

Hentai did as he was told. He did not believe it would work, but he had to do something, and sitting on a rock for several hours was something. His initial intention had been to have Utagaibukai take the children into the temple and pray for the needed miracle, but he had realized while he was recounting Yokubari's visit that he could not suggest that without revealing he knew the children were the true intermediary with the Buddha and he was merely an ordinary man masquerading in black robes and a hairless pate.

Meanwhile, Utagaibukai put his mind to a solution. He tried to recall what was happening when the builders were building the temple and the school—what it was that made them work as well as they had worked.

The children had long since reached the distant limit on their recitative path of pi's infinite string of decimals. When the cleverest of them arrived at "three two eight two three," an empty, expectant silence followed for some long while, which became increasingly oppressive and suddenly sounded paradoxically loud in the ears of their teacher.

"Why have you stopped?" asked Utagaibukai.

"I have not learned past one hundred five decimal places," said Ni, the little girl who had led the chorus since the passing into the previously unexplored territory beyond the one-hundredth place.

"I would have to look it up," said the teacher flatly, but he immediately recalled it had been the sense of being entertained that had sustained the community and the builders through the time of temple construction.

"But the time has come to learn of something else," he said as he imagined the best way to recreate the sense of wonderment without raising suspicions about what he was about. "Let us all go into the temple and have honorable Hentai Sukebe tell us stories of the Buddha."

Utagaibukai then filed the children out of the school and into the temple and set about looking for Hentai even though he knew the search was futile.

He returned with a feigned expression of disappointment and announced the priest was nowhere to be found.

"But perhaps you would like to hear me tell a story …?" said Utagaibukai leadingly.

The children responded with gleeful concurrence to the proposal.

"Of course, I do not know any stories about the Buddha."

Some disagreement followed, since half the children wanted to hear stories about heinous crimes and severe punishments, and the other half wanted the tales of romantic love resulting in unabridged contentment. Utagaibukai grew worried the discord would erupt into something worse and set off the opposite effect than the one he wanted.

He held his hands out to signal silence in his audience and said, "Long ago there was a peaceful little cove—much like ours—where there lived many pretty crabs …" He continued to relate the adventures of a boy crab and a girl crab who worked hard and played well and were attacked by terrorizing seagulls until they made friends with a protecting monkey who gladly eviscerated the nasty birds with a sharp oyster shell so the boy crab and the girl crab were able to grow up and get married and live in pure and perfect peace until the end of time.

The story was immensely satisfying, as it provided flavors of all types to tastes across all spectra from cruel to kind, from pragmatic to idealistic, and from harsh to sentimental such that the children felt reassured they were living in a universe in which good always triumphed over evil in ways both horrendous and magnificent.

But to Utagaibukai's delight, Tiny Tim glowed with the quiet thrill of being entertained just as he had in the days of temple construction. With luck, the workers would be inspired to great heights of creativity in their labors, finish Yokubari Buta's manor home, and thus ensure the continued anatomical integrity of Hentai—unsevered cervical vertebrae and all.

CHAPTER 105

I n all likelihood, you have surmised Utagaibukai had no real concern for Hentai, per se, and would not have shed one iota of a tear over the beheading of the priest had it not been that his own future was founded entirely on the completion of Yokubari's home and the wealthy man's continued patronage.

He might have preferred to address the Buddha personally, as he had when he'd requested the miracle of serenity which ended the hostilities, but he reasoned that for there to be a feeling of being entertained, there must be one who is doing the entertaining for the entertainment of others, and although it might be possible to achieve a sense of entertainment by attempting to entertain oneself, it seemed much simpler and more efficient for him to be the entertainer and the children to be the entertained.

By the time Hentai returned from his fitful meditations while seated on the cold rock in the cove, a vast area surrounding the village was being bathed in the warm satisfaction of hearing a good story despite there being no story to hear for any but the children in the school. In the days that followed, this warm aura of contentment spread over the entire island of Honshu with the subsequent increase in productivity that took hold and would drive Japan to become an industrial giant.

So it was that Yokubari Buta's manor home was completed on time, and the lord of the estate was greatly delighted. Quite uncharacteristically, he gave Hentai a bag of gold to show his appreciation. Hentai accepted gratefully, without knowing for certain whether he deserved it or not. Utagaibukai was quite certain that if anyone deserved it, it was him, but he equally knew he could say nothing to that effect.

After that, the village prospered. It soon grew into a town and then into a city. Yokubari's businesses flourished. His processing factory paid more for the fishermen's fish than the fish market miles away. This additional income provided for incremental improvements, and the modest cottages and huts surrounding the cove became prettier and prettier and more and more comfortable.

And Yokubari had docks built on one side of the sleepy, quiet cove for transport ships to bring in goods from near and far and take away the products of his factories to markets around the world. Yokubari prospered. And the people prospered, too. And Hentai became a much-respected priest as his reputation for sustaining the favor of the Buddha grew in breadth and certainty. And Utagaibukai became wealthier and wealthier by means no one could fathom but everyone accepted as proper since he brought great honor to the school and to the community.

For this to happen, Utagaibukai had had to adapt as times changed.

"I have meant to ask," said Hentai to Utagaibukai as they strolled through the flower gardens. "What is pi? I hear the children reciting, 'pi is equal to three point one four ...' and so on. What does it mean?"

"Simply a measure of mathematical intelligence," said Utagaibukai. "The more places to which the mathematician knows pi by heart, the better the mathematician he is."

"Ah! I envy you this precision. Buddhism offers no such measures. I read and I read, and I ponder and meditate, and I still don't know if I know anything at all."

"And yet the community is tranquil and prosperous," said Utagaibukai, who wanted Hentai in a giving mood. "You must get more right than you do wrong."

"Yes, that is true. I should be more certain of myself. If the Buddha did not tell us to doubt and to suffer, I would not suffer any doubts at all. Forgive me for burdening you with my burdens."

"No burden at all," said Utagaibukai with a bow of his head. "But while we are on the subject of the children and their mastery of mathematics, I must tell you, the school is now large with many pupils. The time has come to hire another teacher, and while I have taught them all I can in the ways and workings of numbers, their mysteries and elegances, their uses and abuses, a gifted algebraist and geometer could take them further on the path of scholarship."

"And you would continue to teach reading and writing?"

"Precisely, honored headmaster. The time I now spend in teaching arithmetic, I would spend learning more of the crafts of authorship. This I would pass on to my pupils that they would bring even greater honor to our humble selves."

So it was that Utagaibukai continued to tell stories and studied the art of writing, which he taught with great passion. The cynical among us might say his passion was spawned by his knowledge that the telling of stories provided for the spirit of entertainment that had proven itself so profitable—and they may be right—but regardless of his initial motive, he became famous for his passion, and the city that grew up around him became famous as a center of literary genius.

Now, despite his vast learning, Utagaibukai's love of literature never provided him with a genuine gift for writing. He knew what to do and how to do it, but he always despaired that his work lacked for something. There was never within it, he sensed, that spark of spirit that makes the reader want to read.

As disappointing as this might have been for him, he nevertheless did acquire an overwhelming appetite for reading. He amassed a huge library of works, both ancient and modern, and he read aloud to the children from these works every day. And of these many and varied stories, it soon emerged the tales of the samurai warriors were by far his favorite and the favorite of his classes.

CHAPTER 106

The real samurai were to Japan what the knights in armor were to Britain. And the samurai of popular fiction were, then, for the Japanese, much akin to what King Arthur and the Knights of the Round Table were for the British. In much the same way, while chivalry was still seen as virtuous—though idealistic and generally impracticable—by the members of the British aristocracy, the code of Bushido, the way of the samurai, was still espoused—though more in spirit than in practice—by the more romantically inclined of the sophisticated members of Japanese culture.

The reading of samurai adventures at Utagaibukai's school inspired the young boys to emulate the warriors of old in their quest to display their masculine worthiness and inspired the young girls to admire the young boys who best emulated the warriors of old, in their quest for puppy love attachments.

The boys daydreamed of triumphant battles to the death in which they would suffer many honorable wounds but would end with the decisive bisecting of their foes, either top to bottom or side to side.

The girls daydreamed of elaborate flower-festooned weddings in which they would magically be rescued from their lives of duty and obedience to their lowly fishing-village parents and delivered into lives of duty and obedience to their noble warrior husbands.

And the fervor and sense of Bushido—the heart and soul of the samurai—spread throughout all Honshu.

"Japan has strayed onto the random path of the round-eyed idiot," said one aristocrat, admiring his reflection in the mirror-finish of his sword blade. "But I sense a return to the refined ways of honor and the belly slicing of those who fail."

"It is true, honored lord," said a second aristocrat. "For years, the youth have grown rude and unobservant of etiquette, yet I have noticed of late they become more and more rigid in their insistence upon the observation of finer and finer details in the observance of ceremonious good manners."

"Standards are universally improving," said a third, who was a high-ranking officer in the Imperial Japanese Navy. "The noble ways of our ancestors provide the nation with ethics and social structure. The way forward is to keep repeating the past until the skills of making futures are properly learned."

"Practice makes perfect," said the first, and with all his might, he swung his sword to pass a hair's breadth from the throats of his comrades, who stoically refrained from flinching.

CHAPTER 107

Tiny Tim and the Almighty spent many a pleasant night feeling their way through the feelings our hero was conveying to the people of Japan.

"It is all rather exciting," said Tiny Tim, "but some of them seem to dislike it. Not many. But some."

"That is only to be expected," said the Almighty. "When we first sat down to design humankind, we imagined a fairly uniform set of operating instructions, but considering one of us, alone, would eventually be stuck watching over you all for some considerable stretch of time, it was decided the introduction of a few indiscriminate bits of tomfoolery would add a little spice to the sauce. I had my doubts at first, but then I didn't know I'd be the one minding the pot. Now that I am, I can say quite honestly things could not have turned out better. You've been most fascinating—not you personally, of course. Humankind in general."

"Yes, I did sense that."

"I mean, you're a personable enough conversationalist, but you don't actually do very much, do you now?"

"Yes, I'm aware," said Tiny Tim, growing irritated with what he perceived to be an unfair criticism of his lack of effort. "But I'm curious. I've been transmitting the same feelings for what seems like forever. What are they doing with them all?"

"That depends on whose opinion you value most, I suppose. From my perspective, they seem to be doing much the same thing humans have done since they first decided a few should do the telling what to do and the rest should do the doing of what they're told. From the viewpoint of those who are doing the telling and the doing, they appear to be quite pleased, for the most part—with the usual exceptions, needless to say. But for those watching the telling and the doing from afar, there seems to be a certain uncertainty rising, though I can't be certain why, or even if that's what it is."

"Who are the usual exceptions?"

"Artists, mainly. And, of course, the critics."

"Why 'of course'?"

"Simply goes without saying. Their assumed role is to see what the artists see, whether they see it or not, and then tell the others what that is so those who can't see it can then see it too, regardless of whether it's there or not. So, if the artists see something out of place no one else sees, then the critics will see it out of place too, or at least see that the artists see it as being out of place, and will tell the rest what it is the artists are seeing, so those who cannot see there's something out of place will see there is and then see to it."

"I see."

"Mind you, there's always a bit of a debate about it, since the artists don't always agree what it is the critics say everyone is supposed to be seeing in what it is the artists do, but the critics argue the artists aren't the reliable judges of what it is they see since they're too close to what it is they're seeing to see it clearly."

"Is that true?"

"Possibly. It's all rather subjective and doesn't lend itself well to objective judgments. In the end, they all see what they want to see, whether they listen to the artists, the critics, or no one at all."

"I think I understand. The artists see things other people don't— either because the other people can't see them or because they aren't really there—and then the critics see what the artists see, or at least see what the artists think they see even though it isn't there, and they're the ones everyone listens to—or not. So if there's something wrong nobody's seeing, then the artists will see it first, and the critics will see it too, and then they'll tell the rest, and whatever's wrong will get fixed. Unless there's nothing wrong at all and the artists only think there is, and the critics think they see it too, in which case everyone goes about trying to fix what isn't really wrong. Or not."

"Quintessentially?" said the Almighty. "Yes. The critics would give you an argument, but then that's one of the things they do."

"Why do you feel that?"

"Well, they tend to take credit for what isn't wholly theirs—not out of dishonesty, mind you. They do believe they're all brilliantly original and coming up with everything all on their own. But I've watched them for centuries, and events always follow the identical pattern. The brightest of the artists create something different, something new, and the critics roundly denounce it as worthless because they can't see what it is the brightest artists are about until the brightest of the critics finally sees what the brightest artists are attempting to do, and then they put it into words, and since the putting of things into words has been the foundation of human activity since words were invented, the one who does the putting into words is the one who gets all the recognition for being the first to think of it."

"But it's really the artists who get there first."

"Indeed. The brightest ones, anyway. The critics crystalize the ideas the artists concoct, but then take credit for concocting the concoctions. Then the less-than-brightest artists get criticized by the critics for being outmoded in their methods and not keeping up with what the critics claim is now, always has been, and always will be the correct kinds of things for the world to see."

"Interesting," said Tiny Tim, and he mused for some moments before he recalled what was really bothering him. "But you were saying the people I have around me are feeling feelings that are good to feel? That didn't come out right. What I mean is, Is everything that's going on good?"

"That's difficult to say. What humans do with what they feel varies from one to another and from time to time. What's good is often put to bad purposes, and what's bad often spawns the greatest good," said the Almighty noncommittally. He then added, "Between you and me, there isn't really any such thing as good or bad. The concepts are the products of limited perceptions."

"Really?"

"Yes, but don't worry over it. From where you sit, they still have their uses. It is rather like using letters to represent unknown numbers in algebra. Or perhaps not. I never was strong on metaphor. Much prefer symbolism. Be that as it may, why the sudden concern?"

"I'm not sure. Maybe it's because the last time I was sharing wonderful feelings with everyone like this, it suddenly came to an end, and I was alone for a long time. Sometimes I feel like that might happen again."

"Not to worry. You're in for a bit of a shift, but you'll still have lots of company."

"Just so long as nothing bad happens."

"Once more—bad, good—not actually relevant to anything. Just enjoy it while it lasts."

CHAPTER 108

The shift in Tiny Tim's future, of which the Almighty foretold, came in the form of a visit to the temple by three Buddhist monks who journeyed west to meet Hentai. Rumors of a priest who embodied such a perfect mystical state that events akin to miracles seemed to arise spontaneously around him started coming too thick and fast in the stream of news to be ignored any longer, so investigation was in order.

The trio of holy men had their doubts about the tales that had been circulating, but not about the priest at the center of the tales. Superstitious nonsense was often attributed to the utterances of the more accomplished of their number, but the attribution of nonsensical utterances to an utterer does not necessarily render the utterer nonsensical, since the perception of being sensible or nonsensical is concomitant upon the utterer of utterances either making sense or not to those perceiving the utterances. Thus, the perception of meaning within utterances is not entirely the responsibility of the utterer, since the utterer of utterances cannot be held responsible for ensuring the perceiver of utterances is adequately endowed with sufficient understanding to perceive the meaning of the utterances uttered by the utterer to ensure the perceiver's perception is sensible. For this reason, the monks knew what it meant to have their quite sensible utterances improperly perceived by those who had not taken the trouble of preparing themselves for proper perception, and then to have those sensible utterances improperly reiterated in reflection of this improper perception thus rendering them nonsensical.

That changed when they arrived at Hentai's temple, for they quickly discovered that the tales being told were quite true despite being nonsensical and that Hentai was nonsensical despite the willingness of the local people to believe he had a far firmer grasp on truth than was given to ordinary mortals.

But although the monks were immediately taken aback by Hentai's manner, they were not as quickly ready to suspect the legitimacy of his priestly status. Their first thought was that he must be one of those so magnificently accomplished in the envisioning of reality from an elevated awareness that his insights were subtle beyond even their lofty reckoning, and to hear him speak would impart upon them, within moments, wisdom that would otherwise require years of meditation to acquire.

"What is the sound of one hand clapping?" asked one monk.

"A slap?" said Hentai, and the three laughed at the joke that had not been told.

Further discussion revealed, however, that nearly everything Hentai said was quite laughable and, beyond that, quite increasingly indecipherable. At first, as has been noted, the three shared some sense that Hentai's indecipherability was due to a refined subtlety of thought combined with that nearly divine expression of the humor the most enlightened among us experience upon achieving elevated levels of profound enlightenment, and this led them to ask more and more questions that quite taxed the supposed priest's wisdom.

The three sought to see—within the simple statements so confidently given—the distillation of the complexities of the universe. And they fought to draw the distal points of paradox together within the words of apparent wisdom.

At first they caught glimpses of reality beyond the reality of illusion in the irreconcilable utterings of illusory sagacity, but the complexity of existence refused to be distilled, and the distal points of paradox refused to be drawn together, and the glimpses of reality stubbornly refused to expand into any fullness of vision of what lay behind the veil of illusion that is the realm of duality.

At length, it became clear that the reason the three could make no sense of what Hentai said was that what he said legitimately made no sense at all. Far from being well beyond the understanding of the greatly gifted, he was, in fact, well behind the understanding of the sagacity-impoverished.

"Where did you serve your novitiate?" asked the first to surrender to his doubts.

"I did not serve any novitiate," said Hentai, quite certain those to whom he spoke had been sufficiently impressed with his autodidactic accomplishments to realize that formal preparation for the priesthood was a complete waste of time in his case.

"How, then, did you become a priest?" asked the second and third together.

"The gods commanded it when they provided us with the Buddha."

"What gods?"

"The Shinto gods, of course. What other gods are there?" said Hentai. He then grinned, leaned forward conspiratorially, and added, "But do not worry. We no longer believe in them."

The three stared agape at Hentai for several seconds before turning to one another in complete bewilderment. None of the three was able to formulate a phrase. Likewise, Hentai, whose intellect had been taxed well into debt by the lengthy questioning, was mentally exhausted and at a loss as to what to say.

The silence exploded, startling the holy men when a young lady meekly announced that tea was ready.

Hentai led the monks into his own chambers and into the room where he ate his meals. The monks were amazed and unsettled by the number of beautiful women who were busying themselves about the place while the four men sat upon cushions around a low table.

"Who are these people?" asked one of the visiting priests.

"They are my mistresses," said Hentai, as if no answer were actually needed.

"How many are they?" asked a second, quite aghast.

"There are twenty-three in all right now. But the Buddha keeps bringing them to me, so I cannot say how many there are to be. I feel it in my elbows, though, that too many more will be a strain."

"You say the Buddha brings them to you?" asked the third in disbelief.

"Oh, yes. Of course, they do not know that is why they come when they come. They come to ask me to pray to the Buddha for some little thing or other. Then they smile at me, and I feel it in my lungs they want to be my mistress."

"You feel it in your lungs?"

"Oh, yes. I find I cannot breathe when I look upon her loveliness, and I know then the Buddha is telling me I must take her to me. So I say, 'Never mind that little thing you think you want; the Buddha wishes you come and live with me.' And then she feels this too, and so she does."

"As simply as that?"

"Yes. Why does this surprise you? Does not your Buddha provide for you in the same way?"

Before any of the trio could think how to reply, the tea arrived and was drunk in silence while eight of the ethereally pretty ladies sat in a circle around the men who sat around the table. At last, the tea was finished, and with many a bow, the ladies cleared the table and glided out as quietly and gracefully as wispy clouds scudding across a sunny sky.

"You say you have twenty-three mistresses?" asked one monk.

"Yes. I am abundantly provided for," said Hentai, confident his elevated worthiness was the reason behind the abundance of the provision.

"I think we have heard enough," said a second monk.

"You are no priest," said the first.

"You are a trickster, a charlatan, and a jackanapes," said the third.

"You will leave this temple immediately," said the first.

"We will send a new priest, a proper priest," said the second.

"And we will send men to take the golden statue from here," said the third, who had not forgotten the sense of profound peace he had felt in Tiny Tim's presence.

Hentai could not have been more shocked. Until that moment, he had taken the expressions of awe upon the faces of the trio of holy men to mean they were quite given to profound admiration of him. He had noted that their sedate, monastic way was at great variance from the usual effulgence of expression of praise to which he had grown accustomed, but nevertheless, he had had no reason to doubt that their admiration for his priestly being was as pure and genuine as the more demonstrative affections of the hordes comprising his everyday audience who came to him for divine intervention and always left with some sort of satisfaction.

Without knowing what to say, Hentai leaped to his feet and called to his ladies to accompany him out and away from the temple. Fueled by fear, shame, and confusion, Hentai had no trouble hurrying himself away from the monks who had so viciously denounced him. His bevy of beautiful ladies, however, dressed, as they were, to be as decorative as possible, were not shod for speed and were soon given to pleading for their master to slow down. Before they began their descent down the steps that led into the village, Hentai heard their pleas and returned to them.

"Where are we going?" asked Ferachio, his favorite.

This stopped Hentai where he stood, for he had not put a scintilla of thought to the question of where? beyond the concept of not here.

"You are right," he said with conviction, which made Ferachio feel quite proud. "We must go and talk with Utagaibukai. He will know what to do."

Hentai then passed his way back through his bevy of beauties and led the way to the school, followed by the clopping clatter of forty-six wooden shoes across the flagstones of the wide courtyard. Again the lovely ladies fell behind in their attempt to keep up with their master, but they knew where he was going and so made no requests for him to slow down.

Utagaibukai was watching over the children of his class while they quietly engaged their imaginations in the writing of entertaining tales to tell. He glimpsed the disgraced priest enter at the back of the room with the accentuated look of disgrace on his face that told the teacher plainly all was not well.

Utagaibukai arrived at Hentai's front at much the same moment as Hentai's ladies arrived at his back.

"Monks have come and say I must stop being the priest," whispered Hentai in near panic.

Utagaibukai looked over Hentai's shoulder at the swarm of sweet and fetching faces. "You have money. You have ladies. Retire," he said without patience, and turned to return to his class.

Had Hentai been moving when he heard this, it would have stopped him where he was, but since he was already stopped, it merely froze him there in a state of amazed enlightenment. It was so obvious. All he needed to do was announce his retirement, and no hint of shame or dishonor need spread into the world at large. No more would he spend his days listening to the whining wants of those come to petition the Buddha; no more would he have to read the dull documents of religious philosophy that made no sense and hurt his brain; no more would he have to conduct the tedious and confusing ceremonies to purify the temple—he could simply give himself over to pleasure after pleasure after pleasure, punctuated by yet other pleasures. It was too beautiful a solution to have come from a teacher; it must have been the Buddha who had decided the time was right for this, and only used Utagaibukai to put the intention into words.

"Of course," said Hentai. "I feel it in places I cannot mention out loud, so it must be absolutely right. I will buy a big home under the mountain, where we will live a life of quiet luxury."

This met with great approbation from the bevy of lovely ladies, though this state of contentment ended rather abruptly when Anaru, the youngest of the lot, asked, "Will the Buddha still provide for us?"

"Not anymore," said Hentai with a sad smile. "The Buddha is being taken away."

"What?" roared Utagaibukai, exercising his right to panic as he spun on his heel.

"The monks are having the Buddha taken a—" said Hentai, but he was interrupted by Utagaibukai moving sharply toward him with a most frightening expression on his face.

This exclamation of shock startled not only Hentai but also his bevy of beautiful ladies. While Hentai remained frozen in fear and indecisiveness, they sensed their loyalty to him being strained and quietly clip-clopped away in retreat to a place of less potentially fumatory sentiment.

It was not that the beautiful ladies were without affection for Hentai as a companion and as a romantic partner—the influence of Tiny Tim had provided them with an attraction to him equal to his attraction to each one of them—but they all began to sense that outside the mystical aura of the Buddha, Hentai would be without his indefinable allure. And it had only been that indefinable allure that had enabled them to overlook the extensive following of feminine company into which they had had to immerse themselves in order to avail themselves of his company, and without that indefinable allure, he would be just another man already sufficiently ensconced in connubial conditions to render him unavailable for consideration as a potential partner.

The twenty-three lovely ladies, then, left Hentai to face Utagaibukai alone while they returned to the temple to decide their futures. Each of them believed she was the only one secretly planning on leaving until it became abundantly obvious one and all were of the selfsame mind. What was more, Ferachio had had the thought Hentai would not begrudge her a little money to resettle, to which Anaru added her opinion that she had done far more than any wife would have done to please Hentai and deserved a lifelong pension for her services, and after a brief discussion, the twenty-one remaining ladies arrived at the agreement that there was more virtue in Anaru's position than in Ferachio's, and Ferachio, with very little reluctance, then made it unanimous.

Meanwhile, in the middle of the schoolroom, Utagaibukai thundered and roared at Hentai, describing him in the most unflattering terms while accusing him of single-handedly ruining the tiny city that had grown up in the influence of abundance embodied in the Buddha.

CHAPTER 109

Hentai sat upon the rock in the cove while the tide came in and waited there until the tide went out. Those who had known him long had seen him do this often enough to know he did this only when problems were large and needed the deep thought of a disciplined meditator. What they did not know was that he did not do this for the purpose of thinking deeply, but rather for the purpose of avoiding all possibility of learning his problems might be getting worse while he was still insufficiently prepared to handle them in their unexacerbated, fledgling state.

And Hentai was aware, from being a much-experienced victim of problems, that problems are bound by mystical laws of mathematical proportionality. That is to say, the likelihood of a problem solving itself while one waits and does nothing is inversely proportional to the significance and scope of the problem—or, in other words, the worse a problem is, the less likely it will go away or diminish or become more manageable with the passage of time unless some reasoned effort to solve it is brought to bear.

But Hentai's feelings were so badly hurt, and his confidence so badly shaken from the stern and brutal lecture Utagaibukai had given him, that he was not able to prepare himself for the handling of the problem he had had upon mounting the rock, let alone the problem that might be awaiting him upon his return.

So, after sitting on his cold and pointy rock for twelve hours, Hentai was terrified to go home and run the risk of discovering that the removal of the Buddha had been completed; that the news of its removal had spread throughout the city; that his honor and status had been thereby excoriated; and that he was now a figure of shame and derision, and there was nothing left for him but to retire to a mansion some distance hence with nothing but his wonderful memories, his wealth, and his twenty-three beautiful mistresses to show for his years of dedication to the well-being of the community.

So it was after the tide had long ago gone out and the sand about the base of the rock had long ago dried out in the warm evening breeze, when the eyelash-crescent moon finally decided to set between the two long, fingerlike peninsulas that formed the mouth of the cove, that Hentai finally decided to give into his hunger and thirst and brave the grave dishonor awaiting him.

He walked across the deserted beach to the path leading up to the temple, feeling certain he was being derisively watched by villagers hiding in the dark. Even the sound of the crickets seemed mocking and accusatory in his ears. But on he walked with stoic readiness to face the worst Fate had in store for him. He would enjoy—as best he could—one last supper in the temple, drink his fill of sake, and indulge his need for intimacy with as many of his mistresses as he could before exhaustion collapsed him into sleep. Then he would rise early, before the citizenry of the city was about the business of active citizenship, and bravely take his mistresses away from this place in search of a new home where he could live out the rest of his life in quiet and anonymous luxury.

It was something of a relief to him there was no one to meet along the way—no one pointing at him and blaming him for the loss of the Buddha. It was a great relief to find the Buddha still in place in the temple. He wondered whether, perhaps, the monks had changed their minds, but he then remembered they'd said they would send someone to take the statue. And it was a small relief to find that the monks were nowhere to be found; he had no wish to talk to them any further.

But the temple was as quiet as the word "quiet" can mean in the fullness of its meaning. It was so quiet that the sound of a spider humming to herself while weaving her web would have been quite audible if spiders were inclined to such absent-minded diversions.

The relief Hentai had enjoyed began ebbing into doubt as he continued through to his quarters behind the temple proper. There was not a lamp lit in the place, and the darkness echoed with the squeak of his sandals on the stone floors.

"Hello?" he said tentatively to the silent blackness around him, but an answer came there none.

He felt his way to where he knew a lamp was kept and fumbled about for matches. Finally he had light to see, but what he saw emptied his heart of hope, for his home was empty of life and all but the scantest evidence life had ever adorned the place. He went from room to room in search of his lovely ladies but found not one of them nor any of their clothing nor anything small enough to be transported without the help of muscular moving men. And Japanese tastes being what they were—favoring light furnishings—that meant that virtually nothing in the way of furniture remained.

Memories of Kin Saikutsu-Sha's desertion of him years before came back to him as if the intervening time had been an illusory flash. His stomach rumbled viciously, yanking his thoughts back to immediate concerns. He plodded his way to the kitchen and blessed his luck when he found his lovely ladies had left him plenty to eat. He then prepared a meal as best he could, having been so long out of practice. Instead of eating in the dining room, which was replete with happy memories of meals shared with his lovely ladies, he took his food out into the temple proper and sat before the Buddha to eat in grief and loneliness.

And as Japan slept, dreams of loss of loved ones plagued everyone's slumber.

CHAPTER 110

Hentai awoke stiff and cold on the floor of the temple next to Tiny Tim. It took him some seconds to clear the sleep sufficiently from his brain to recall why it was he was there instead of in bed with a mistress or two. On the trail of that memory came the recollection of his plan to evacuate himself from the city before the population was at large in the streets and pathways. That would be much more easily accomplished without his horde of mistresses in tow, but that thought proved to be of little consolation to him when his rational mind presented it for approval to his emotional self.

He sighed heavily over his losses. It was difficult to say whether he regretted the loss of his ladies or the loss of his honor more, but he eventually concluded he had hoped his ladies would ease him through the worst of his shame over his loss of honor. Had he kept his honor and lost the ladies, his honor would have done little to ease the pain of that loss, so the loss of the ladies had to be ranked as a greater loss than the loss of his honor. But, having lost both his honor and his ladies, the thought required to reach that conclusion was the folding of disappointment upon disappointment like the making of an origami monster.

He rose and faced the Buddha.

"Kin Saikutsu-Sha left me because I was poor," he said to his one friend in all the world. "Why did my mistresses leave me now that I am rich?"

Of course, Tiny Tim could not hear this question and so could not provide an answer, but no answer was required, as—in the exact moment of the final question mark being invisibly written into the universe—Hentai realized his mistresses had no need of him to provide them with his wealth. Terror clenched his soul, launching him into a run to his bedroom in search of his strongbox. And he was not long in looking for it, for it was right where he'd always kept it; but instead of being closed and full, it was open and empty. Shock filled the brief gap between terror and rage as he strained the limits of language in a quest for appropriate invectives to bounce off the four walls. With the worst of the expletives having been offered twice into the echoing enclosure, he began punching the air hard and rapidly to dispel the searing, scorching, unbearable anger burning huge holes in his soul.

At last, gasping with exhaustion, he slouched about the room, gathering his clothes into a bundle in preparation for his departure into anonymous aloneness and poverty. He was still filled with grief and anger, still tasting want of revenge, and still afraid of what was to come when he tied the knot that secured all his worldly possessions he was not wearing into one scarlet orb. He hoisted the bundle over his shoulder and took one last look around.

And he left—never to be seen again.

But the feelings of loss and betrayal, the feelings of anger, fear, and resentment, did not leave with him, since he had been long enough in the vicinity of our hero to get Tiny Tim resonating with these horrific emotions. Soon the little city was awash in accusations and insults and plots for revenge and large-scale plans for the destruction of those who had done or were believed to have done or were planning on doing or were believed to be planning on doing heinous wrong to those making the plans.

Yokubari Buta, from his vast manor home built in the medieval style, looked out upon the turmoil that surrounded him. He was, perhaps, the most suited to living within chaos since he had an instinct for creating it among his rivals as a means of weakening their hold on what they held to facilitate his taking hold of whatever he deemed worthy of being held.

His tastes for medieval architecture, medieval history, and medieval literature—indeed for all things medieval that had been sufficiently flavored by romanticists for palatable consumption by twentieth-century audiences—had marked him as a reactionary eccentric in the days before the revival of samurai values in Japan. But after the revival, they marked him as a born leader of men, a decider of fortunes, and a visionary of glorious days to come. He was nicknamed Daimyo (meaning "feudal lord") by those in the surrounding areas, though he secretly called himself Shogun (meaning "warlord"), which much more accurately described his inner self.

"The time has come," said Yokubari, "to spill blood, eviscerate foes, and decapitate impediments as in the glorious days of our great and noble ancestors!"

Those about him—his various aides whose job it was to come and go with reports and instructions from and to his many managers—bowed with approval at this pronouncement. Each was angered and resentful for no apparent reason, and each took pride in knowing their leader had grasped the situation ahead of everyone else and was prepared to take action against whatever it was that had angered them and made them resentful.

But after some while, while Yokubari strutted amid the horde of aides, who were all frozen at a deferential angle, one brave soul asked, "Whose blood, which foes, and what impediments shall we spill, eviscerate, and decapitate respectively, honored master?"

"That will be decided," said Yokubari, "as circumstances arise. I have chosen limitation for too long under the rule of pacified bureaucrats. We have grown constricted like the indolent one who foregoes answering the call of his loins. Now anger and resentment have us in their grip, but our ancestors show us the jiu jitsu necessary to break free. Expansion is the way forward. Expansion."

The horde of bowing aides agreed, partly because what Yokubari said sounded irrefutable, partly because their backs were aching from remaining bowed so long, and partly because they were paid well to agree.

But Japan was not a lawless land, and Yokubari knew he had to be careful in the spilling of blood, the evisceration of foes, and the decapitation of impediments lest the minions of the emperor take exception to his behavior to such a degree that he would have to pay for the privilege of acting according to his instincts. Still, the doing of noble deeds, in his estimation, suffered a diminishment of honor if one could not be known to be the doer of the deeds. What was required was for everyone to know Yokubari was behind the spilled blood, the eviscerations, and the decapitations without being able to prove any of it. It was a challenge worthy of the greatest shoguns of history, and one Yokubari could embrace with relish and execute with ruthless efficiency.

In the months that followed, men of power and authority met with gruesome ends as Yokubari's competition dwindled to nil and laws and regulations restricting Yokubari's businesses were rescinded or rewritten in accordance with his dictates. All this made Yokubari mythically happy, despite his being angry and resentful for no apparent reason.

His success in getting exactly what he wanted was not without a setback or two, however, as anyone who has achieved success will tell you is inevitable. Over his years of acquaintanceship with Hentai and Utagaibukai, he had concluded that the priest and the teacher were the keepers of a secret, and that secret was that their power of persuasion lay not in themselves but in the strange Buddha that occupied the place of honor in their temple. Yokubari wasn't certain of this and had no way of knowing how Hentai and Utagaibukai were able to use this power, but nor was he concerned about it; that he had the two at his disposal was enough for him in much the same way as he had cooks to cook for him, drivers to drive for him, and swordsmen to spill blood, eviscerate, and decapitate for him as needs arose.

When the news of Hentai's disappearance reached Yokubari, it disturbed him, and he dispatched a lieutenant to ensure Utagaibukai was still in place. Secure in the knowledge the teacher was going nowhere, he went back to his plans for hostile acquisition and thought nothing more of the valuable Buddha, since he was fairly certain the Buddha was without the capacity to leave his post in the temple.

But in this, he was wrong, and being wrong for a samurai—even a self-styled though not real samurai—is dishonorable. And when a samurai is dishonored, he will attempt to diminish the loss of honor as much as possible by an act designed to save face if the possibility of doing so is available to him. This face-saving act nearly always involves another person whom the samurai sees—or wishes to see—as being ultimately responsible for events leading to his loss of honor, and usually comes in the form of something rather more severe than a simple loss of honor for the one deemed responsible for the loss of the samurai's honor. So, when the loss of the Buddha from the temple caused Yokubari to feel he had made a gross error in believing the Buddha was going nowhere—and was much dishonored by it—he blamed Utagaibukai.

One of Yokubari's well-paid bowing minions bowed and said, "Many monks have arrived at the temple, honorable master."

Yokubari looked at the minion with some disdain for wasting his time. "Why should this concern me? Monks sit in solemn silence for interminable spans of time. An inactive kind of man by any measure, so their actions do not merit monitoring unless one is seeking a state of profound boredom."

And Yokubari said this with such certainty that the well-paid bowing minions elected not to elaborate on the news for fear of becoming tedious. If they had, however, Yokubari would have learned of the Buddha's commandeering and marshaling away at the time of the commandeering and marshaling away and not days later, when it was inarguably too late to stop.

Utagaibukai had been expecting the monks and had gathered together a small army of fishermen armed with the scarier implements of fishing for the purpose of scaring the purloiners of statuary away. What Utagaibukai had not taken into consideration—because he had no knowledge of it—was that several of the monks had been trained in various Oriental fighting disciplines and all were chosen for the assignment because of their prodigious strength, since it was estimated a solid gold statue the size of Tiny Tim would be enormously heavy. Utagaibukai's team of defenders proved no match at all for the monks determined to carry off the Buddha.

So it was that our hero went to Nagasaki and became the centerpiece of the great temple there.

And so it was that Utagaibukai was called before Yokubari to explain the loss of the Buddha.

"You knew they were coming and did not think to tell me?" said the one called Daimyo.

"I thought it was a simple matter we could handle alone."

Yokubari did not answer. In an instant too quick for Utagaibukai to react, the one who secretly wished he were called "Shogun" deftly drew his sword and sliced the teacher's head in two from the crown to the neck and thus preemptively eliminated the possibility of anyone mentioning aloud he had blundered through lack of foresight. Yokubari then, having acted out this aforementioned act of saving face, could feel a little better about being dishonored, since on balance, he had fared somewhat better than the one whose cerebral organs were decorating his floor.

CHAPTER 111

The relocation of Tiny Tim to Nagasaki did not in any way diminish his mood of anger and resentment. Despite his being in the presence of several genuine Buddhist monks—who are universally renowned for their ability to remain calm in even the worst circumstances—his belligerence lingered on.

The monks who had come to claim him had been caught up in his fury without realizing it and accredited their foul temper to having been attacked by Utagaibukai and his gang of implements-wielding fishermen. Individually, they felt a certain embarrassment for having overreacted and for continuing to feel violently unsettled in the distant wake of the battle, but one by one, each decided it was evidence of personal negligence on some spiritual level in their quest for detachment. Whatever that negligence was, they could not yet know, because prior to the battle for the possession of Tiny Tim, they had been unaware of harboring feelings of attachment for anything, but it was clear they still had such feelings for something since they were suffering, and they knew the cause of suffering is attachment.

As these thoughts and feelings matured with time, the monks became grateful for having discovered this proof of ongoing attachment to something because they were now aware of what they were previously unaware of and therefore had something from which to detach themselves in their ongoing quest for detachment. In short, they were ecstatically overjoyed to be viciously enraged.

The hostility Tiny Tim had been radiating since the day Hentai disappeared had swelled beyond the little city where he'd lived since arriving in Japan and had spread to many neighboring communities. But now that he was a resident in Nagasaki—a city of five times the population—the effect of infectious ill will escalated in its virulence.

Within days of Tiny Tim's arrival in his new home, the whole of Japan was in a state of rabid disgruntlement over real and imagined losses. Those who had suffered genuine loss felt that loss more keenly, but what was far worse was that those who had lost nothing were convinced they had been victimized in ways they could not put into words. And—as any opportunist will tell you (any honest one, at least)—therein lie the seeds of discontent upon which opportunists feed.

It took no time at all for the politics of discontentment to dominate the political landscape. Politicians preaching all stripes of discontentment put words to the feelings felt by those who were certain they had been robbed, swindled, or abused in ways they could not say. And since the whole country was living through the revitalization of the samurai mystique, the words that rose to the peak of the collective sentiment were those of a military nature. Soon everyone was finding examples of how Japan had been put upon by other nations that sought to stunt the rate of progress toward modernization, industrialization, and economic domination. And the people listened with swelling lust for revenge to those politicians and high-ranking soldiers who advocated immediate action.

The country was swept over and flooded by a tsunami of bellicosity.

CHAPTER 112

"I'm sorry I'm in such an unpleasant mood," said Tiny Tim. "I can't seem to shake it."

"No matter," said the Almighty. "It's best to let these things flow through."

"I suppose. But this constant irritation is getting to be quite … irritating, I guess."

"I can see that happening. I sense there's something else going on, though. What else are you feeling?"

"Strange, really."

"What's strange?"

"What I'm feeling."

"What's strange about it?"

"That's what it is. Strange. I feel strange."

"Oh. What's it like, then?"

"Something like a mixture of heart-bursting, groundless pride; unquestioning faith in something vague; and addictive attachment to shared flattery, punctuated by bursts of vicious disdain toward someone or something indeterminate."

"Oh, that? That's nationalism. Haven't you run into it before?"

"Sort of … I guess … No. Not like this."

"No, I suppose not. Your family wasn't much for it, what with one thing and another. And Britain was crossing the apex when you were living there."

"What do you mean by that?"

"Just that the British Empire was at its peak. We don't see nationalism much when things have climaxed. During those times, it only gets trotted out on special occasions, only to be put away again along with the formal attire. On the way up, a nation's pride is much more prevalent and flavored with ridiculous optimism—much like what you're feeling now. On the way down, it emerges again—though it's turned bitterly pessimistic since everyone has given up rallying to achieve the best in favor of rallying to avoid the worst. But while they're at the top, nationalism gets eclipsed by uncertainty of what to make of it all and what everyone is to do with their success. You'd think people could simply feel grateful for arriving at a goal, but people being people, they look for reasons to feel dissatisfied. You're your own worst enemy, you know."

"Me?" said Tiny Tim, sensing he was being chastised for something.

"Not you, personally. Sorry. Being omniscient, omnipotent, and eternal tends to bring out too much of the generalist in me. But, in regard to feelings of nationalism in England, you left before things went into decline, so you missed out on the phase of desperation despite the role you played in bringing it into being."

"Are you feeling in generalities again when you say that?"

"Not at all," said the Almighty. "I mean you specifically. Don't you remember that long stretch spent in fear of ships?"

"Vaguely, I guess. I remember being afraid of something, but …"

"That was your brother's way of convincing the government to increase the size of the navy. He got you worrying the Royal navy was too small and too old, and that led to everyone being afraid of the Germans, which, in turn, led the Germans to be afraid of the British, which led to a running competition between all the countries of Europe to have the biggest military, which led to the forming of alliances for mutual protection, which all ended in the Great War, as the politicians like to call it."

"The Great War?"

"Yes. Though it's soon to be retitled World War One."

"Why is that?"

"Well, they called it the Great War because it was unquestionably the largest orgy of mutual extermination within which mankind has ever immersed itself, but there's soon to be another to which the Great War will pale in comparison. No one will want to call that one "the Greater War," since that would imply the Greatest War is yet to come, and with everyone's appetite for annihilation sufficiently sated for the foreseeable future, they'll opt for "World War Two" as a title and change the name of "the Great War" to "World War One" so it fits more logically into the series."

"I see," said Tiny Tim, feeling rather overwhelmed until the realization struck him. "And I caused World War One?"

"I'm afraid so. An unwitting error on your part, no doubt, but still … all you."

"Damn! Oh, sorry."

"I've heard worse."

"But what will cause World War Two?"

"World War One," said the Almighty as if the answer were obvious.

"No. World War Two."

"Yes. World War Two. Oh, I sense your confusion. What I mean to say is World War One is the cause of World War Two. Things haven't been properly settled, so they'll have to have another go-around for the purpose of getting it all put to rights. In a sense, it's more like one protracted set-to with a lengthy bathroom break in the middle rather than two separate dustups. Of course, that's just Europe we're talking about. Here in Japan, the bloodlust is still freshly kindled, so it still has that intoxicating elation about it."

"You make it sound like a good thing," said Tiny Tim dubiously.

"I'm neither here nor there in that regard, as I've said before. But you must have noticed the dizzying romanticism of glory in overwhelming struggle sentiment, since you're at the center of it all."

"I am?"

"You didn't know? All those feelings about swordsmanship and honor and the thrill of chopping people into little bits? Surely that can't have escaped your attention."

"Not entirely," said Tiny Tim hesitantly. "Actually, it feels rather exciting."

"Well, of course it is. That's how it always begins. And what about this bad mood you've been in lately? You must have felt that was getting people worked up."

"I have," said Tiny Tim as he connected the points the Almighty had already made with the one he was making then. Our hero was then gripped in shock as he said, "Does this mean I'm causing these people around me to go to war?"

"Yes. But—once again—no one's blaming you for anything. It's obvious to anyone you didn't do it intentionally. And by 'anyone,' I mean me, who is, after all, the only one paying attention."

"I have to stop it before …"

"Too late, I'm afraid. You've flung the stone that's put the stars to flight, and the moving hand, having writ, moves on, and no hand or wit can erase a line of it."

"What?"

"Omar Khayyam," said the Almighty airily. "Eleventh-century Persian poet. I've always rather liked him. Rubaiyatic quatrains. Most effective."

"But I don't want any more war," said Tiny Tim, ignoring the Almighty's diverted train of thought. "Especially not ones I make happen."

"Don't take it too personally. It's not like you're imbued with bad intentions—you know: not steeped in avarice and misanthropy like some I could mention. Compared to most, you're quite a decent sort of fellow, actually. Pity about the coma, no doubt. But you have done rather well despite it. There aren't many who would rise above a setback like that, I can assure you. I'd feel quite good about myself if I were you."

"But I never wanted to cause a war."

"Oh, I have no doubt of that whatsoever. Perish the thought. Had you not suffered the unfortunate incident in the operating theater, I'm quite certain fomenting global cataclysm would have been the last thing you would have set out to do. Likely as not, the thought would never have entered your mind. But being a witless pawn in the machinations of cruel Fate is a sizable portion of what it is to be human, so you can take some comfort in that. Despite what I said earlier—and all the salient facts of the situation—you needn't feel as though you're being singled out specifically for blame. It's obvious to anyone, you simply followed along mindlessly like everyone else, taking in all the falderal you were fed without question and passing it along with some degree of amplification to suit your own emotional needs. So, in that regard, you're entirely like all the rest."

"You mean we're all making bad things happen without knowing it?"

"That's it exactly! Bit of a design flaw if you ask me, but I didn't get a say in the matter. I can't recall precisely what it was for—something to do with needing a check on free will … Not exactly sure … To be honest, I wasn't really paying attention when it came up. And—as I've said before—bad or good, it's all the same in the end, so don't get yourself all knotted up over it."

"But you won't let things get completely out of hand, will you?"

"No. I'm keeping one last miracle in reserve, just in case. After that … Well, who knows?"

"What do you mean, 'just in case'? I thought you knew everything."

"Only what's already in motion. I prefer it that way, actually. From my point of view, chaos is quite underrated, and far too much of what goes on is completely predictable based on prior behavior. Fortunately, there are enough random elements in the mix to keep it interesting. If it were all laid out like some repetitive, formulaic fiction in which all the characters are slaves to plot, I'd have died of boredom ages ago. I'm speaking figuratively, of course. I don't actually die."

"So I've heard," said Tiny Tim, uncertain there was much comfort to be found in the Almighty's reassurance. "So you say there's nothing more to do but lie back and feel what happens?"

"That's what I'd recommend. But you suit yourself. Far be it from me to tell people what to do."

"Well, pardon me for saying so, but I think I'll try to stop this World War Two before it happens. I have to try, at least."

"If you feel that strongly about it, I certainly won't fault you for giving it a go. But I'll have to leave it there for now. I'm meeting up with a little goddess from an alternate universe. She's got this fascinating notion of controlling everything based on the outcome of rolling dice. I know, I know. It strikes me as a little crazy too, but she's a lot more fun than the local talent, so feel you later."

All this left our hero in a perplexed state. He was deeply wounded to learn he had catalyzed the suffering of so many and was gravely disappointed in his friend, the Almighty, for not having pointed out to him the error of his ways before he'd triggered this cascade of catastrophes. And as much as he wanted to stave off further mayhem, he sensed the Almighty was quite correct in opining it was too late to make a difference.

"It is better to have tried and failed than to have done nothing and lived to regret it," said Tiny Tim finally.

And with a specific goal to occupy his time, he shifted with determination out of his funk.

CHAPTER 113

I t is one of the great ironies of the human condition that the worst destruction is often committed not by those who set out to destroy but by those who set out to build but are ill-equipped to build, and so build based solely on a baseless confidence in the illusion of their ability and their absolute conviction in the rightness of their cause. The road to hell is paved with good intentions, as the saying goes, and one could even imagine the paving itself is full of cracks and potholes since the pavers pave without competence.

So it was with our hero, whose tragic flaw lay in his belief that unadulterated love and infinite compassion can fix all wrongs in all people in all circumstances when his understanding of love and compassion was limited to his own experience. Of course, he was not alone in having this particular tragic flaw. It is the tragic flaw of nearly all humanitarian heroes who have yet to be disillusioned by fatal collision with those who understand virtue by a different set of definitions.

Tiny Tim set himself to feeling love for all humanity with all his being. This was most difficult, at first, since the whole of Japan was still immersed in the flood of bellicose nationalism polluted with the flotsam and jetsam of resentment, anger, and hatred toward foreigners. Fortunately, Tiny Tim's residence in the Buddhist temple facilitated his task of shifting the population toward a more loving and compassionate frame of reference owing to the influence of the monks who had commandeered him. They were growing impatient to feel the sense of infinite peace to which they had dedicated their existence and were, therefore, ready to accept great love back into their hearts.

But I use the term "fortunately" with reference to Tiny Tim's perspective only, for while he felt he was making enormous progress in the direction of restoring Japan to a state of gentle pacifism, he was actually making matters worse without knowing it.

Precisely as the Almighty had indicated, any attempt to turn the tide of events away from the inevitability of war was laden with the seeds of its own frustration. The forces of history were already in motion, with the people hungering for hostilities upon their neighboring nations. The one impediment to military action in the hearts of the Japanese, however, had been as follows: Their appetite for aggression was not limited to those perceived as barbarian nations across the seas but included all those who could not be described as self. In other words, Japan was steeped for a brief while in discord, and though there was universal agreement on what needed to be done, there was universal disagreement on how to proceed.

That all ended when Tiny Tim won the monks over to the way of light, and the sense of unlimited love began spreading throughout the population. Families became families again; communities regained their sense of community, and all rediscovered their love for the emperor. Politicians, military men, and leaders of industry who had been squabbling for some months suddenly put aside their differences and agreed to work together toward the common good.

But, as history would show, that sense of common good did not extend across the waters surrounding the islands.

CHAPTER 114

"**Everything feels peaceful** and serene again," said Tiny Tim.

"You do have a talent for it, I must say," said the Almighty. "I've watched entire generations pass from birth to oblivion without producing a single one who has your leadership ability."

"Leadership?"

"Clearly!"

"I've never imagined myself to be a leader."

"Of course not. Only the worst leaders think they're born to lead and lead by telling others exactly what to do. The great ones lead by pointing a finger in the right direction and staying out of sight while the lesser lights take charge. But the best of the best lead without knowing they're leading at all. That's why history is replete with characters who were believed, by their contemporaries, to have caused all the memorable events while historians, looking back over the span of years, can argue that all the memorable events would have happened regardless because the time had come for them to happen."

"I'm not sure I follow."

"It is a bit of a paradox, I know, but I'll give it a go. The worst leaders not only want to lead but also want to be famous for leading. The great leaders are more likely to shun the limelight or divert attention to those who do the heavy lifting, but they often get credit nevertheless, because all the evidence leads back to them. But the best leaders of all never get any recognition, because they never overtly suggest anything for anyone to quote. Without any bits of information to prove they're leading, no one can imagine they are."

"But how do they lead if they're not telling anyone what to do?"

"In part, by example, but mostly in much the same as what you do: by creating an atmosphere conducive to action."

"Oh," said Tiny Tim with a touch of pride. "So you really feel I'm a great leader?"

"One of the best."

"So I can stop wars from happening?"

"No, of course not. I told you that before."

"But if I'm one of the best leaders ..."

"You are. No doubt of that. Perhaps even the best of the best," said the Almighty in light of other leaders he'd known. "It's too soon to know for certain, and difficult to sense, but when it's all over—in a million years or so—I'm sure you'll be on the short list."

"Why can't I stop the wars, then?"

"That's beyond anyone's ability, I'm afraid."

"But you said I caused all this."

"You did. Not entirely single-handedly, as I may have intimated earlier, but certainly enough to put you in the running for best of the best."

"Causing the two worst wars in history makes me the best of the best?"

"Most definitely. We don't judge based on good or bad ..."

"Not based on good or bad?" said Tiny Tim in disbelief.

"I don't want to keep harping on about it, but from where I sit, they're irrelevant concepts."

"How can they be ...?"

"Here. Do you remember what coins are?"

"I have a feeling for it."

"Well, imagine heads are good and tails are bad. You want to make the world a better place, so you eliminate all the coins with tails. What are you left with?"

"Nothing."

"Precisely."

"I still don't …" said Tiny Tim, half-defeated. "So what do you judge on, then?"

"On how big the events are that are put into motion, of course. And in that regard, you're right up there."

"But … I'm … Damn!" said Tiny Tim before collapsing into despair. Then, out of utter frustration, he said, "Oh … God bless us, every one!"

Their unique mode of conversation, however, lacked meaning-bearing intonation, so Tiny Tim's sarcastic intent was lost on the Almighty. Taking the request literally, he said, "If that's what makes you happy," and all humanity was blessed once more.

But, yet again, the world was too caught up in the minutiae of day-to-day existence to notice the effulgence of divine well-wishing raining down upon it.

CHAPTER 115

There is no need to trot out the events of the next fifteen years beyond saying that Tiny Tim continued, with the fullness of his being, to expend the whole of his energies in the vain effort to rein in the grand forces driving full tilt toward massive destruction.

Tirelessly, he loved and loved and loved. He felt the insanely optimistic nationalism of the people around him wane into that phase of dislocated complacency described by the Almighty when the limits of conquest were reached and hopes for a cessation of conflict were balanced with anxiety over the possible extent of a counteroffensive. Some short while later—precisely as the Almighty had described—there followed a resurgence of nationalistic fervor, but it was now growing rabidly pessimistic as everyone prepared for the final confrontation growing nearer and nearer, when the honor of the nation would be decided in a moment for all eternity.

Tiny Tim loved with all his might, but even his titanic will was not enough to stem the terror and despair that were looming larger and larger. He did his best, but suddenly one day he felt the colossal impact of an entire nation stunned into disbelief.

"I'm afraid," he said.

"That goes without saying," said the Almighty. "If I were you, I'm certain I'd be terrified under these circumstances."

"If you were me? Aren't you frightened, then?"

"No, not really. To me, this is simply another wave of human folly crashing on the beaches of destiny."

"Do you ever get frightened?"

"Only for entertainment purposes. I don't feel the need otherwise. But I'm not averse to helping you through your current crisis—assuming, of course, you'd find a little conversation comforting."

"I would," said Tiny Tim, and he gathered his feelings. "This sudden shock a short while ago. What does it mean?"

"That the end is at hand."

"Of everything?"

"No, not everything."

"Is it time for that miracle?"

"Funny you should mention that …"

"Funny? Funny, how?"

"Only in that it's an amusing coincidence is all. I was considering that very thing when I felt you feeling for me."

"So, what do you think?"

"It's tempting," said the Almighty. "But not right yet."

"Why not?"

"Hmm. Good question. I suppose I sense that if lessons aren't learned here—and they won't be if I don't let the mistakes be made—then the next time around will be worse. And where will you lot be then with all your miracles used up?"

"I still don't understand why you can only do one miracle."

"It's not a matter of *can*. I can do as many as I want. I am the Almighty, after all. I used to scatter them about like blowing dandelion seeds to the wind. It was quite fun, actually. Rather like the joy one gets from feeding the cat despite the ingratitude built into feline design. But then I realized indulging the habit was defeating the whole purpose of creating a species capable of thought and reason."

"Yes, yes," said Tiny Tim with a growing sense of desperation. "That much is clear. What I don't understand is why you refuse to do another one if this one isn't enough?"

"Oh, it's simply a decision I've come to, and I make a point of not breaking my own rules. Rather dulls the point of divine edict. Chipped in stone. That kind of thing."

"Well, that's just—"

"Intransigent? Yes, I've been told that before. In fact, that cute little goddess from the parallel universe I've been seeing says inflexibility is a sign of moral insecurity, and rigid adherence to arbitrary standards of behavior is indicative of arrested development in someone my age."

"I thought you were perfect."

"Oh, I am," said the Almighty, but he then added with less enthusiasm, "Well … It's all relative, isn't it?"

"So why won't you give us a miracle now and wait to see if another is needed later?"

"It's a matter of integrity, I suppose. I simply feel I won't be able to live with myself knowing I've been unfaithful to my core principles. And—being immortal—living with myself is something I really want to be able to do."

"Oh, for …" said Tiny Tim in withering, hot frustration. But completely unable to put his feelings into a coherent sequence, he simply said, "God bless us ev—"

"What was that?" asked the Almighty after some moments of silence, but no answer returned. "Ah. What a pity. I was really enjoying our little get-togethers. He was a decent enough fellow and a far sight more engaging than most of his kind."

The Almighty heaved the cosmic equivalent of a sigh, which had radio-astronomers scratching their heads for decades.

"I am going to miss him. But I do believe he was in the process of begging another blessing. Never let it be said I denied a dying man his last request."

And so it was the Almighty blessed all humankind again—literally everyone—and in his great respect for our hero and in a profound desire to do his best for him this one last time, he blessed with all his might, and being the Almighty, that made for a mighty blessing indeed. As always, however, humanity was too preoccupied with the events of the day to pay attention to divine offerings, and so despite the awesome magnitude of the blessing, the sense of being blessed has gone largely unnoticed even these many, many years later.

ABOUT THE AUTHOR

David Roy Coombs writes across the spectrum of speculative fiction from surrealism to magic realism to historic fantasy, alternating between works of farcical comedy and psychological drama. Drawing from his polymath set of interests and checkered career experiences, David crafts stories of fantastical imagination about unique characters faced with odd and curious challenges.

Milton Keynes UK
Ingram Content Group UK Ltd.
UKHW010910050724
444921UK00010BA/130/J